GETTING EVEN

Edward Behr

NEW ENGLISH LIBRARY/TIMES MIRROR

First published in Great Britain in 1980 by Hamish Hamilton Ltd

The lines from *Collected Poems* by John Betjeman are reproduced by courtesy of the author and John Murray (Publishers) Ltd

First NEL Paperback Edition August 1981

NEL Books are published by
New English Library Limited, Barnard's Inn, Holborn,
London EC1N 2JR.

Printed and bound in Great Britain by
©ollins, Glasgow

0 450 05218 4

Foreword

A Chinese diplomat called Liao Peh-Shuh, with known intelligence connections, defected from the Embassy of the Chinese Peoples Republic in The Hague in 1970, later in 1973 returning 'voluntarily' to China.

Similarly, a Chinese mission official requested political asylum while passing through Orly Airport in May 1970 but was handed back to the Chinese authorities against his will a few days later, after being told that the French Government could not, after all, grant him leave to stay.

Beyond these two events, none of the characters or institutions in this book has existed or exists to my knowledge in real life, and any similarity, as with persons living or dead, is purely coincidental.

My thanks are due to Jean Pasqualini for putting his immense fund of Chinese knowledge at my disposal, to Pierre Lellouche, of the 'Institut Français des Relations Internationales,' and to a host of friends, of many nationalities and backgrounds, for helping me in other ways. I know they wish to remain anonymous.

Chapter One

THIS PARTICULAR London suburb was full of cloned streets and Monopoly houses. It was conceivable that a tired City clerk might, after work, sit down to dinner, watch TV, go to bed with his wife and find out much, much later that he was in the wrong home. It was a drab, grey neighbourhood without charm of any kind. Only the industrious Asian community provided much-needed touches of colour. Plump Asian ladies in pastel sarees led docile, kohl-eyed children by the hand, quivering with fat as they walked, and leaving behind them a sandalwood spoor. There were large numbers of late-night food stores, also run by Indians, and many Bangladeshi restaurants masquerading as Punjabi.

The Chinese Embassy hostel was drab in a different way. The staff quarters, surrounded by a high wall topped with broken glass and barbed wire, consisted of a five-storey concrete box, all windows frosted over like so many office latrines.

Few people had been inside, and those who had reported an austerity reminiscent of an impoverished preparatory school, complete with unbreakable institutional furniture, and rows of two-tiered beds. Gadgetry was not absent: a closed-circuit TV system guarded the only entrance and was wired up in such a way as to hint at other cameras, in dormitories and communal rooms perhaps. The door itself was not really a door, but a slab of mobile concrete on a steel frame, which slid sideways at the touch of a switch. It frequently jammed. An allotment garden stood where once the builders had planned a lawn, and parked inside the compound was a grey Volkswagen minibus, a picture of Mao next to the rear-view mirror, ready to run its herd into central London just before the 8.30 a.m. rush hour.

In the evenings and at weekends, the sound of ping-pong could be heard beyond the wall, sharp shrill Chinese cries denoting excitement and the pleasure of winning. Twice a week, in groups, the herd shopped at the local supermarket.

It all started because one of the check-out counters was manned by a Chinese girl from Malaysia. Anh had been in London since 1972, long enough to acquire a worldly, big-city contempt for these suspicious provincials. She also had a boyfriend called Albert who she suspected was in the police. The manager was always on the look-out for Chinese girl cashiers. They were faster, more reliable than English girls, he used to say. Had their wits about them. Can't avoid it, money's in their blood, thousands of years of those abacus calculations, stands to reason.

Anh couldn't help it: every time the Embassy shoppers came by, she looked and listened. Sometimes they spoke among themselves, though what they said, and what she overheard, was guarded, banal, and totally devoid of interest.

There was this one girl, though. Later, Anh said: 'I spotted her because she was different. A real beauty. Her Mao jacket was taken in a shade more at the waist. But even if she had been wearing a paper bag you would have noticed her.'

Anh was short and, when she got excited or annoyed, bright red patches appeared on her round cheeks, making her look, Albert said, like one of those wooden Russian dolls – the Soviet Union's only successful export, if you discounted vodka, caviar and the KGB. In due course, Anh told Albert about the sullen Chinese beauty.

'She stood in my queue at my counter. Because we were both unmistakably Chinese, I smiled at her, and as I returned her change, I said, in Mandarin: good luck. She gave me a nasty look, didn't say anything, picked up her bag and walked out. I hated her. She was so – hard.' She made another appearance in the store a few days later, and again found herself at Anh's check-out counter. Her purchases this time were token ones: a packet of kleenex, the cheapest brand of soap. Anh toted up the amount briskly and impersonally, not even looking at her. She didn't want to be snubbed again. But the girl looked at Anh intently, almost longingly, as if to say: please, don't look away. It wasn't my fault last time. I was being watched. She had a cloth purse, old and frayed, and it was only after she had paid and gone that Anh realised she had left it behind, and that none of the other members of her party had noticed. A few minutes later,

8

she rushed in alone, grabbed her purse, and as she took it she slipped a scrap of paper into Anh's hand. On it, in Chinese characters, was written: please help me.

Anh gradually, inconsequentially, told Albert. In bed together, she went over the whole story. Naked, she went to the dresser and picked up the note, quickly got back to bed, cuddling up to his warmth. Albert's hand lingered on her bottom vertebra. Its prominence always surprised and delighted him. Must have been a tail there, at one stage, my little monkey, he had said when they made love for the first time. Anh hadn't known whether to laugh or be offended. She had adjusted, since, to his curious brand of humour.

She had learnt to kid him back.

'Is that what you do when you're not picking up poor Chinese girls from Singapore to find out if their papers are in order and they're not concealing brown sugar in their bras? Feeling my bottom?' She spoke with the clear enunciation of a convent-taught Chinese girl, fee-ling my bot-tome, the lls only occasionally derailing into rrs, and just listening to her he had an erection. He gently turned her over on her back, sliding one hand from belly to breasts. 'Not much room there for brown sugar, is there, love?'

Their first night together, Anh had put her hands across her chest, and said, coyly; 'I have the smallest breasts in the world.'

'That's what turns me on.'

Ahn hadn't, at the time, fully understood. Later she lost all shyness, and told her shocked Chinese girlfriends in the supermarket that the reason Albert was crazy about her was because, in bed, he could make believe that he was making love to a child. 'It's his Lolita syndrome,' Anh giggled. She pronounced it: rorita sindlome. And to Albert, she had said, much later: 'Is that what you were doing with the paratroopers in Malaysia during the insurgency? Going to bed with twelve-year-old Chinese girls? You're worse than the Chinese warlords. My father would kill you.'

'You'd be surprised,' Albert had said. 'Even some of the Ambassadors of your puritan Peoples Republic of China come equipped with teenage mistresses pretending to be secretaries, provided by their Ministry of Works.'

'How do you know?'

'I just know.'

Albert's vagueness infuriated her. He was explicit about his sexual fantasies, but discreet, to the point of idiocy, about his work. After all these months, she didn't know where he worked, or even what he did. At first she took him for a dealer in stolen cars, for he was never driving the same model. They were always shabby and inconspicuous, but all came fitted with fire extinguishers and walkie-talkies.

'What are you, a minicab driver or something?' she asked once. Later, Anh believed he must be in the anti-narcotics squad. She couldn't believe he was learning Chinese just for her. In the middle of the night, the phone would ring, and he would answer in a kind of guarded code. Another girlfriend? But the voice at the other end was always unmistakably male.

Now Albert picked up the note, folded it and put it under an ashtray. An old bargain-hunter's trick is to pretend an interest in other things, and then come back casually to the object really desired, seeking it out casually and with apparent indifference. Albert's interest in Anh's body was not faked. But, after prolonged and strenuous love, he whispered: 'Think you could get me a temporary job in the supermarket?' and Anh realized for the first time that he wasn't exclusively interested in drugs.

Offended, she stiffened, rolling away from him. Was this what he had been after all along? Bastard. Foreign devil. Gwalio. She stroked his chest, tenderly at first, ending up with a sharp squeeze and a jab with her tough little nails. 'So that's what you want,' she said. 'Otherwise, I'll be put on the first plane to Singapore? Anh Chan's papers not in order, immigration official decides. Is that it?'

'I wouldn't want to do anything against her will. Only respond to the note. Find out what she wants. Help me, she says. How?'

'You help her if you want. I could lose my job. She could be testing us. It was so *odd*, what she did. It's the only time I've ever seen one of them alone. She might have wanted to trap me.'

'So you don't want to help?'

'I don't want any trouble.'

'Maybe *she*'s in trouble herself?'

Silence. Albert moved, kissing her ear.

'Suspicious people, these Chinese. Always looking for an ulterior motive. You Chinese distrust everybody, don't you, outside your own family?'

Anh hit him just below the groin. For someone so small, she was surprisingly strong. He doubled up, only half in jest.

'Seriously, love. Can't you help me find out a bit more about her? Slip her a note back? Let me in there with a camera under my coat? Have me move some crates around? I'll be good.'

Anh said: 'You know there's nothing I wouldn't do for you, Albert. Let me kiss it and make it well.' And that, in a way, is how the whole sorry business began.

Blame it on literacy, or the proliferation of paperbacks: the vocabulary of the secret service is now something of a cliché. No more mystery about the true meaning of 'mothers', 'lamplighters', 'moles', or 'cousins'. Even the address of MI6 and the name of its current chief are known to anyone who regularly reads so-called 'insider' magazines.

As with all proliferating bureaucracies, space is at a premium in MI6's Lambeth headquarters, as it is, also, in MI5's grim Curzon Street building known as the Bastille. Successive prime ministers have been generous with both services – while cutting back expenditure on almost everything else – but even with the best will in the world it was impossible for them to sanction a new foolproof building where both MI5 and MI6 would come together to combine operations and pool research on specific cases.

Such a system would be unthinkable in the USA, where the rigid CIA-FBI distinction prevails, as Nixon discovered to his cost when he attempted to sanction CIA operations on American soil. But in Britain the lines are blurred and the division of labour more formal than real, though by force of habit MI6 deals mostly with foreign parts and MI5 with the domestic scene. Where does security end and intelligence-gathering begin? Fouché asked this question in his day and came to the conclusion that the two functions were really one – twin sides of a single coin.

So, with a combination of pragmatic expediency and

British muddle that marks official policy, this truism found expression in a hybrid London offshoot of both combined services, and, so far, no journalist's indiscretion has revealed the existence of the Kensington 'safe house' known, in the trade, as 'the hospital'.

It has been said, usually by those who have avoided a spell of duty there, that this 'safe house' is safe only for misfits. Indeed there's some truth to the legend that those unlucky enough to be selected for service there are the flotsam and jetsam of both security and espionage, older men on their way down, young men failing to make it at the top, for a variety of reasons: British institutions are never forgiving never forgetful, curiously competitive in various insidious ways. A single glaring failure, a suspected indiscretion, can stick for the rest of one's working life.

The building's only distinguishing mark is a private car entrance, leading to a basement garage, accessible only by one of those perforated laminated cards that are an increasing feature of urban living. The cards bear no inscription except for the date. They are changed at irregular intervals. Their possession is a minor status symbol, for which affiliated government officials are always bickering, never with success.

Again, unlike the popular conception of such clandestine establishments, there is no 'front', no 'Acme Copying Services' or 'Transglobe Investment Inc.' brass plate on the door. The only concession to subtlety is the existence of a row of push button bells, corresponding to imaginary apartment dwellings, retained when the house was bought in the mid-fifties, and serving no purpose whatsoever. The almost illegible names are a fairly apt illustration of the warped humour of the then house administrator:

6th floor: N. R. Vannah
5th floor: Valerie Sittart
4th floor: Ahsan Bogri
3rd floor: Mr and Mrs Archy Franks
2nd floor: H. Hoover-Kettering
1st floor: Mrs Clyde Tolson
Ground floor: housekeeper

Albert was Mrs Clyde Tolson. That is to say, he shared an office on the first floor with six other people, and a section which monitored some phone tappers in another part of the building.

Of the several thousand diplomats in London, all of them enjoying diplomatic immunity, some actually are diplomats: they write long, stylish position papers on sterling, the need for an incomes policy and the move towards the left of the British Labour Party, all of which are dealt with, more concisely but also with greater speed, by any number of experienced Fleet Street reporters and foreign correspondents. They call regularly on Foreign Office officials, entertain each other lavishly but decorously, and a tiny minority even pays its parking fines.

Others simply use London, and are used by it: over-ambitious Latin American generals sent away to a safe ambassadorial slot by uneasy dictators usually do a little marginal plotting, but mostly just bide their time; friends, relatives, tribal supporters and business agents of some African Heads of State, with convenient diplomatic accreditation, account for London's thriving escort services; those Arabs who only deal with the best girls are seen more often at the Clermont or in Harrods than at the Foreign Office or in the visitors gallery of the House of Commons, while the lesser diplomats in most Middle Eastern embassies seem to spend their time booking sick Arab families in and out of hotels and clinics for expensive, private medical treatment.

All this causes little concern, and helps to bolster the British economy, with Jaguars for the doctors, and sleek living for the makers of outrageously expensive glass and metal furniture sold only in the vicinity of Sloane Street. In recent call-girl trials, many a diplomat shuddered at the thought that the courts would reveal all. To their considerable surprise and relief their existence was never even mentioned.

Albert, street-wise, unabashedly suburban, was a brash injection into the 'hospital' mix. He had neither an MI5 or MI6 background, but had been seconded from Scotland Yard. At first, the services had requested a liaison figure. Subsequently, he had made himself indispensable, and risen high in his new hierarchy. Repeated requests from Scotland Yard to return him to more conventional duties had been met with appeals to prolong his stay.

What he didn't know about the sex lives of London-based diplomats was not worth knowing. Part of his value lay in his low-level contacts, policemen on the beat, taxi-drivers, small shopkeepers. His special concern was running herd on a small group of diplomats, mostly from eastern Europe, and a few Arab countries, who were known to be recruiting not only spies but thugs, whose role, it seemed, was as much the destabilization of society as the penetration of its governmental Establishment.

It was at one of the daily conferences that the subject of Anh emerged. 'She's a bird I know,' Albert said, with none of the reticence of the British upper casses compelled to reveal details of their sex life. 'Smashing little thing. Works at Safeways.'

Most of those present tittered. Mayne, the superannuated deputy director of the 'hospital', was appalled. 'You mean you've entered into this – er – relationship with a Malaysian immigrant without our knowledge?'

'Singapore, actually, guv.'

'Well, let's get on with it.'

Albert told them the story, the passing of the note, Anh's willingness to help.

'She obviously wants to scupper.'

'Vamoose.' This from Maurice Wicks, an MI6 reject, whom the Poles had photographed in a compromising position with an eighteen-year-old sailor in Warsaw, thereby temporarily ending a previously brilliant field career.

'If we're talking about defection,' said Mayne, 'what makes you so sure we want her? We're turning them back at Lo Wu by the hundreds as it is.'

Mayne had served in Hong Kong before going to the Lebanon. Legend had it that his Arabic was limited to the cry of 'Boy, wahad whisky'. His colleagues, behind his back, called him 'barapeg' Mayne. Barapeg was the Sahib's word for doubles.

'That's just the point. We ought to find out,' Albert said. 'Might turn out she's someone of value, someone exceptionally well-connected.'

'She could also be a plant '

Later, Albert and Mayne went over the whole business again.

'Okay, she slipped her a note,' Mayne said. 'Why didn't she wait for an answer? And why didn't she write it in English in the first place? Your – er – friend could have been Filipino.'

'She couldn't, you know. You might not know the difference, but they do.'

Mayne's obtuseness was partly deliberate, partly induced. He was the litmus test, the lowest common denominator, whereby the rest of the section determined whether Cabinet Ministers might grasp what was being proposed. If Mayne understood and approved, the dumbest minister would.

'Old fellow, old buddy, what do you really know about the way these people live? How many years were you in Hong Kong? Three? Four?' Albert had lost his cockney banter. His voice was hard.

'There wasn't any embassy personnel in Hong Kong, naturally, but did you ever find out how their own people in Hong Kong lived? The Bank of China staff, for instance? I'll tell you: cubbyholes shared by three other people. No privacy. Not a minute to yourself. Even in Hong Kong. It's worse in Paris, and here. They have a place in Chevilly Larue, over there, same as this, worse perhaps.'

'Now wait a minute . . .'

'You wait. What do you know about what things are like in there? It's not like you, drinks at 6.30 with other poofters and a tame politician or two. You went to a prep school, didn't you? Well, it's like that, with less time to call your own and probably a little less mutual masturbation. This girl, I can tell you, doesn't have a minute to herself – and she's not expected to write in English when she's at home. So she's smart – damn smart. "Please help me" at the start of a blank piece of paper. Could be a letter home: please help me to be a good communist. Please help me by sending me volume three of Chairman Mao's works. The point is that she's under continuous supervision from the Bureau of Political Defence. Heard of them? Our MI5. Very nasty, though. Makes Savak look like the Beatles. She doesn't even know who all the undercover representatives from the Bureau of Political Defence are. All she knows is they're there. All the time. Watching and making reports. She's scared, see. Scribbling notes to outsiders isn't what solidly motivated

Chinese diplomats usually do in their spare time. So she makes it look like doodling, or writing home, or whatever. And maybe she wants to test out Anh – see whether she can communicate with her.' A pause.

'Tell you what,' Mayne said, lighting his twentieth cigarette of the day, 'I'll take it up with our masters, or rather you will. I'll be fair: my recommendation will be based on the kind of information we're likely to get out of her. Close the door, will you, there's a good chap, as you go out?' And Albert, unsurprised, thought: the art of avoiding hard and fast decisions. Barapeg's only claim to fame.

'A Chinese in a supermarket, you say. Really! And what am I supposed to do with *that*?'

There were no loose papers on his desk. Everything was so neat and orderly that the entire room could have been a stage set for a junior minister's Whitehall office, by the most unimaginative designer in the business. The dark red leather chesterfield was unadulterated Office of Works. The matching dark-red leather desk set was Heal's, a present from the Minister's wife, a formidable German lady known behind the Minister's back as Ilse Koch. The ritual family photographs were in small, expensive Asprey frames. The Minister's own large uneven teeth, and the domineering nose of Frau Koch, were mirrored in the unflattering portraits of his progeny. The Minister's wife was also framed, and her photograph was three times the size of the others. Jesus, Albert thought, if I had a family like that, I'd keep those pictures locked up.

Albert had come to the Minister's office by a deliberately round-about route. From the 'hospital', in the unexpectedly early spring heat, he had walked all the way to Whitehall, where a Life Guards trooper stood on ceremonial duty near a mounting pile of horse manure which was being trampled into the pavement by tourist hordes. Albert had watched the trooper, beneath his absurd helmet, squint lecherously at an American girl in halter and pink satin shorts and nothing else, who was almost near enough to the edge of his drawn sword to suffer serious injury. The trooper looked as if he wanted to nick her a little, maybe cutting a shoulder strap.

The tourists had been packed around the Life Guardsman in loose, unmanageable scrums: jostling French, with Harrods shopping bags, vacant, back-packing Scandinavians, adenoidal Dutch, a bird-like Tamil family. A short distance away, a predator observed their antics: from an illegal but tolerated mobile street-corner store (postcards of the Queen, London Underground T-shirts, Piccadilly streetsigns, all the paraphernalia of a London pilgrimage) the red-faced ex-convict beamed. Rob the fuckers blind; his mark-ups were higher even than those of his colleagues around Piccadilly Circus, and he was also skilled at short-changing foreigners baffled by a foreign currency. The police left him alone. They knew he wasn't Irish. To show his gratitude, he saluted the Minister every time he happened to stroll by on foot, which wasn't often. 'Hullo, you old rogue,' Albert had said to him, out of the corner of his mouth, without stopping. 'Robbing 'em blind, still, are you, squire?'

Now the Minister looked at his watch, not covertly, but with open nonchalance. Who am I having lunch with? He yawned. Must get rid of this dreadful man.

'Well, what's the opinion of the Department? Don't tell me: you want her to go back to China and work for us, is that it? Plant a bug inside the Forbidden City offices. A blind drop outside the Hall of the People. God knows, you people are mad enough.'

Petulant little sod. Can't wait for the next elections. Couldn't be worse than this lot. Keep temper. Humour him, Mayne had said.

'Actually, sir, the thought had crossed our mind. Ha ha. But all we want to do right now is find out a bit more about her. Can you authorise that?'

'It depends.'

'You see, sir, we won't know for sure whether she's of interest until we do make further contact. We could always drop her if she proves completely uninteresting.'

The Minister didn't say anything, but his spoilt, overfed, Old Etonian's face registered a slight *moue*.

Another pause. Then: 'Any precedents for this sort of thing?'

Albert had done his homework. There were precedents and precedents. Some even ministers couldn't be told about.

'Very few, sir. A junior Military Attaché, some years back.

17

Walked out in Africa. The Yanks got him, of course. Opened a chain of restaurants in California, done very well, apparently, and keeps a pistol under his pillow still, even though he has a new face. The story never leaked. He was quite valuable, I'm told, especially about personal and ideological differences within the top military establishment – stuff like that.'

Then there was the Hague affair. Better not mention that. 'Is that all?'

'I think so, sir. Very few and far between, you see. There may have been others. Our list isn't complete. But what it adds up to, she's a very rare bird indeed.'

'Pretty, too, I hear. Think she has a boyfriend outside?'

'Extremely unlikely.' But get his approval first. 'We don't know, sir. At this stage, all we'd like is the authorization to explore all the possibilities.'

'Anything else we could use her for? A trade-in? Someone tucked away that we want back? Don't be coy. I've got to know these things.'

'No one of interest, sir, on our side. Don't know about the Yanks. Couple of English residents, long-time Maoists, fell foul of the Cultural Revolution boys, haven't been heard of since, but nobody's made any noises about *them* yet.'

'They *would* tell you, presumably?'

Not necessarily, you patronising shit-face. 'I think they would, in this case.'

'In this case.'

The Minister fingered his diary, found to his dismay that he was lunching with his wife, scowled in mock-thought. 'I'll let you know by the end of the week,' he said. 'But to tell the truth, so far the only reason I'm giving it a try is that, for once, we may do something that'll make the Russians happy.'

It was the habit of Party Secretary Ma, Comrade Ma, as the rest of the Embassy called him, to hold informal group meetings of certain selected members of the staff on Monday mornings. This, of course, was quite separate from the big six-monthly sessions just before May 1 and October 1, which everybody attended, and during which all Embassy work ground to a halt for days at a time.

Those involved were told the previous Sunday to stay behind after the rest of the staff had left by bus for the Embassy in Portland Place. It would come back for them later.

Comrade Ma preferred to hold these sessions in a small dining-room reserved for the senior members of the community next to the canteen, inside the hostel itself, rather than in one of the Embassy conference rooms where he was liable to sudden interruptions from the Ambassador. There was another reason: Comrade Ma had his own quarters inside the hostel, and it was easier for him, after the public sessions, to ask individual members of the staff up to his room for a 'little chat'.

He only summoned staffers who were members of the Foreign Ministry to the Monday morning meetings. The Bureau of Political Defence, whose members also lived in the hostel, had indulged in a long, muted power-struggle in a successful effort to conduct their own meetings. Their titular head within the Embassy, who happened to be the Ambassador's personal driver, though back in Peking he had the rank of colonel, had made it clear to Comrade Ma he was holding separate sessions for his own people on the grounds that the special nature of their duties and the 'higher consciousness' they had of their role as watchdogs required more discretion. Comrade Ma had finally appealed to the Ambassador – and lost. His Excellency needed to remain on good terms with his driver.

The struggle reflected the competing claims of the Foreign Ministry and the Bureau's parent Ministry, that of Internal Security. Staff meetings were only one aspect of the conflict: the Bureau had requested, and obtained, that all copies of the Embassy's messages and cables be sent, also, to the Bureau of Political Defence Headquarters in Peking, a rococo building which had once been the residence of the Apostolic Delegate, in the days when there had been one. The Bureau also exacted its own 'loyalty tests' from all the members of the Embassy staff, usually organising such tests shortly after Comrade Ma's sessions, thereby neatly upstaging him.

As the youngest official in the hostel, Comrade May, who had slipped the note to Anh, the supermarket cashier, presented a special problem. She was the Embassy's cypher officer, having graduated from the school of languages after leaving Peking University, and done so well that she was the only one of her class to be selected for Foreign Ministry training: the rest had been assigned jobs either as interpreters or translators in various departments or with Luxingshe, the Chinese tourist and travel bureau. May had then completed her cypher course at the Internal Security Ministry, and in the process had been vetted by the Bureau of Political Defence, though she retained her Foreign Ministry affiliation – and her official rank was that of Third Secretary. As a result, shortly after her arrival in London, she found herself required to attend both sets of meetings, Comrade Ma's and the Bureau's own.

Nobody enjoyed Comrade Ma's little meetings. He was a prissy, schoolmasterish man, in his late fifties, with a talent for probing the weak spots in the staff, always quietly and with immense self-satisfaction. His assistant was an ageless lady who only spoke to Comrade Ma, never to the others, and at every Monday morning session she made copious notes of what everybody said, which were carefully filed away in Ma's room.

This meeting began, as usual, with individual comments around the table about events of the past week. In a group, the previous Saturday afternoon, they had been on an excursion first to Hyde Park then to the Tate Gallery, to see a Henry Moore exhibition. This made a suitable starting-point.

'What,' Comrade Ma began, in his soft, precise voice, 'were some of the lessons learnt by the group as a result of our Saturday outing?' Silence at first. Then an apparently safe response, from Tsian, a secretary in her thirties.

'Chairman Mao teaches us to spot the social injustices inherent in the capitalist-imperialist system even when the ruling classes do their best to conceal them. After Saturday's outing, I came away with the conviction that, despite appearances, our society is better in every respect.'

Comrade Ma smiled, a toothy, stony smile. 'Despite appearances? Did you ever have any doubts that this was so, comrade? If so, why did you not speak up earlier? I can't remember you voicing such doubts before, and you have

20

been here – let me see – over a year? Eighteen months to be precise.' It was a statement, not a question. Comrade Ma knew everything about everybody.

You can't win, May thought, while carefully controlling her features to register first surprise, then mild indignation, and finally approval of the Party Secretary. He's got her where he wants her. They've all got us where they want us. And sure enough, after some inarticulate protests, Tsian was being admonished, and ordered to write a full confession, and to come and see Comrade Ma early on Tuesday morning.

'And you, Comrade May, what struck you most about the day before yesterday?'

If you really want to know, what struck me was the carefree mood of the people in the park, the way they were necking, making love, laughing, some with their shirts off, the lack of any kind of regimentation, while here we are, 800 million of us, behaving like hypocritical sheep, and here I am, missing out on everything, simply because I'm trapped in my skin, my job, my country, my ritual phoney confessions. While she thought all this, what May actually said was: 'I feel that Comrade Ma is correct in drawing attention to Comrade Tsian's confused remarks. What struck me most about last Saturday was the standard of degeneracy it revealed about British capitalist society. The lewd behaviour of the people in the park, the distorted, deliberately ill-proportioned examples of so-called "bourgeois" art – so different from our own, which is designed to be understood by the people – all this reinforced me in my love for the motherland and the determination that we must avoid the pitfalls of such a type of society.'

'Good. Was there anything in particular that you wish to emphasise?'

'Yes, there was, Comrade Ma: While we were walking along a street – I think it was the Embankment – there was a traffic accident. A car swerved to avoid hitting a pedestrian, and crashed. We stood and watched: the speed with which the police and and ambulance arrived was impressive, but then it was necessary to look at the make of the car: an expensive Jaguar, I was told. A clear example of class privilege. Also there was a small van bearing the initials

21

RAC, which I am told stands for "Royal Automobile Club". This, I believe, is some form of private police, a mercenary organization at the beck and call of the super-rich, to supplement an inadequate police force – a clear example of class discrimination and arrant privilege.'

I may have overdone it this time, May thought. But no, Comrade Ma was beaming. 'Excellent,' he said. 'But how did you gather all this information?'

Tsian butted in, determined to get her own back. 'Comrade May was talking to all and sundry,' she said, 'in strict contravention of our standing orders not to mingle spontaneously with the local population and make our presence known.'

May was expecting some such kind of criticism. Demurely, she lowered her head. 'Chairman Mao tells us,' she said, 'risk nothing, accomplish nothing. I believed that the calculated risk of initiating a conversation with bystanders was, in this exceptional case, justified. In any case our appearance and our dress were sufficient to identify us in their eyes.'

May was careful at these sessions to wear the baggiest, cheapest tunic, but her pertness, cheerfulness and astonishing beauty were not lost on Comrade Ma. He couldn't think of a pretext to ask her to his room, however, until the session came to an end. 'Comrade May,' he called out, as they were filing out of the room. 'I want to ask you a question.'

May stood still, holding her breath, hoping her expression remained the same. He is aware of the note, was her first thought. But if this were so, why the pretence of approval just now? Don't be scared. Chairman Mao tells us . . . But comrade Ma was talking.

'. . . and perhaps Comrade Tsian needs your help, since your political consciousness is so much higher than her own. You are roommates, are you not? After I have talked to Comrade Tsian tomorrow perhaps you could come to my room, and we will discuss matters.'

May knew what those morning meetings in Comrade Ma's room were likely to entail: beneath a prim exterior, he was said to be a lonely, lecherous old man, taking particular delight in his victim's humiliation, and, hopefully, tears. In the days before the Cultural Revolution, it had been possible for selected students to read the works of Molière, and May remembered the play, *Tartuffe*. Comrade Ma was a perfect example of priestly hypocrisy. The fact that he intended summoning her immediately after his session with Tsian meant that he found Tsian unattractive, and would simply browbeat her into tearful submission. May would then be asked to help spy on Tsian, reporting her movements, her most insignificant comments, even what she said in her sleep. If need be, she would be required to invent them. In return, Comrade Ma, old, soured, lonely Ma, would, indirectly, offer her his protection. It was Embassy gossip that he lusted after her. He might even propose: this would not be the first 'service' marriage, and to refuse the proposal of a Party Secretary would itself be regarded as suspect, especially when May's personal records, she knew, showed that there was no one else in Peking with whom she had an 'understanding'. I'm caught in trap, she thought. If Ma is persistent enough, there'll be no way out. If only his breath wasn't so foul.

The next shopping day, another message changed hands. Albert, overalled and unobtrusive, took some quick shots of May which ended up on Mayne's desk, with a hand-written note: 'May Wong, Third Secretary, believed to handle codes or cyphers. Could be part of the Bureau of Political Defence contingent. Arrived four months ago. Exact status and responsibilities unknown. Fantastic bird, isn't she? Wonder what she looks like in a bikini? No problem finding her a job. She could always model for *Vogue*.'

The Minister's dining-room was rarely used. He complained that Government hospitality catering reminded him of his Cambridge College, uniquely famous for its brown windsor soup and pungent flaked haddock pie. The hazards, he used to say, were too great: one never knew whether a particularly dreadful dish would not be accompanied by a splendid Haut Brion or a tart Portuguese rosé. The Minister preferred what he called the reliable mediocrity of his Club, with its unpretentious claret and ham and pheasant pies.

But ever since he had been caught discussing state secrets there with a senior civil servant while a well-known gossip columnist at the next table memorized their every word, the Minister resigned himself from time to time to lunching in his

23

office, as he put it, simply to avoid a recurrence of the storm that had ensued on that occasion, and the Prime Minister's consequent wrath. In any case, he consoled himself with the thought that Hackenback would find the dining-room, with its Edwardian trappings, 'quaint'.

Hackenback found the whole experience disconcerting: the elderly lady who served at table, a relic of World War Two days, had the irritating cheerfulness of an ARP warden consoling a terminally stricken Blitz victim buried to the neck in rubble. The Minister, when in a good mood, would tell his guests that he expected her to say: 'You'll be all right, duckie,' and administer morphine instead of sherry. On this occasion the 'Ong Tray', as she called it, was a prawn cocktail, the prawns themselves sharp to the teeth because inadequately defrosted, and the wine a Luxembourg Riesling of curious extraction. The Minister examined the label. Doppelgänger? That couldn't be right. Must get some new glasses.

Hackenback said nothing. Small talk by British Cabinet Ministers always made him uneasy. In any case, he didn't drink. The serving lady, losing her mock genteel accent, had positively squeaked with disapproval when he had asked for coca-cola. Her acrid underarm odour proved her to be either an arrant feminist or singularly devoid of friends. Very different from the efficient white-coated blacks in Hackenback's Embassy.

Already the Minister regretted extending the luncheon invitation. He should, of course, have asked the Ambassador, or at any rate the Minister-Counsellor. But, as he pointed out to Hackenback over sherry, making the whole thing sound trivial, but at the same time a little demeaning, 'He would only have turned the whole thing over to you, so all I did was cut out the middleman. Isn't that what you chaps say real competition is always about?'

Again, Hackenback didn't reply, flashing a brief, mirthless, mechanical Nixon grin instead. The Minister, Hackenback recalled, had, over the secure telephone, mentioned he needed to talk to him, 'an old China hand', about 'a rather confidential matter'. Could it, Hackenback wondered, have something to do with another Philby in the woodpile? Or another couple of Oxbridge Brits, maybe, Burgesses and

Macleans, more homophile Marxists in MI6, turning out to be long-time sleepers for the Chinese? Hackenback pondered the thought, and decided not: if the news were really that terrible, he decided as he attacked a piece of overcooked veal, the lunch would have been more elaborate.

'So how can we help you, Minister?'

The Minister sipped his wine, made a spoilt child's face. Typical of Americans to get down to business at the very start of a meal. 'This is strictly confidential,' he said, regretting the cliché as soon as he had uttered it, and realising that Hackenback was in duty bound to relay the substance of their talk back to the Agency as soon as he had left, 'but we have a possible Chinese defector on our hands and we need the advice of people with direct experience in these matters. I'm told you've been personally involved, in the past, and might be able to help.'

Did the Minister know? Hackenback allowed himself a tired smile. Of course. The Hague, 1970. They would have had the records, or at least some of them.

'I don't know that you've really come to the right man, Minister. I was in the Hague all right, and got the fucker out. And it's been – ' Hackenback paused for a few seconds, to cling to some self-respect – 'something of an embarrassment for me ever since.'

'I thought it was a good deal at the time,' he went on. 'So did the Agency. I remember Helms saying: if your hunch is correct, Hack, we've got the overall Intelligence boss for the whole of Western Europe raring to go – and he's all ours.

'You know what it feels like to pull off something like that? Probably not, Minister. We should have known it looked just too damn easy. Liao He Shuh. Minister-Counsellor. Number two at the Chinese Embassy in the Hague. Every goddam third-world informer and undercover agent in every rinkydink leftist movement from here to Reykjavik swearing he was it. And we believed them.'

The Minister had stopped eating. He was making hieroglyphic notes in an Asprey ostrich-skin notebook with gold edges, and this for some reason increased the CIA man's irritation. To hell with self-respect.

'Well, that's why I'm here, Minister, instead of being in Helms' shoes, didn't you know? Let's give the top London job to old Hack-in-the-bush. Liaison work, can't go wrong if he tried, and a pension in eighteen months. Try and forget it ever happened. Can't win 'em all. Back to the drawing-board. It never works out that way, *you* know – ' this with some savagery.

'What you're trying to tell me – ' the Minister sipped some wine again – 'is that Liao He whatsisname wasn't quite the *rara avis* you thought he was?'

'The what? Oh, yes. No. He wasn't. We came to that conclusion, all right, and it'll be a long time before I fuck around with another Chinese defector who turns out to be a plant.'

'How did you find out he wasn't bona . . . on the level, I mean?'

'Pretty soon after we got him out. He wanted to go to America. I want to go to your cuntley, he kept saying. Sounded pretty natural at the time, but he might have had the decency to ask the Dutch, who helped him out.'

The Minister looked up from his gold pencil.

'What exactly was he supposed to be that made him so important in the first place?'

Hackenback sighed, pushed his plate away. 'Just about the most important Chinese Intelligence co-ordinator in the West. Senior official in the Bureau of Political Defence, section two. Information-gathering. Penetration. Sabotage, in some countries. Industrial espionage. The works. Moscow-trained. One of the really juicy guys. Everbody said so. And not just the fringe political groups. He really had spread the word around, and that, of course, was just what he had hoped would happen.'

'You mean you had a Chinese mole on your hands, all this time.'

'Bang on, Minister. They did a really wonderful job.'

'And then?'

'Oh, it wasn't apparent to start with. There had been the circus in the Hague, our friend barricaded in the Embassy, the Chinks trying to ger him out, the Dutch grabbing him, finally, in a cloud of tear-gas and self-congratulation and rights of man. So we get him to Virginia. Our best people. Half our Hong Kong Consulate is there, practising its Chinese. A real gala event, how the BPD section two works, who it reports to, how big the budget, how extensive the European operation, how it functions in the USA, through which Overseas Chinese – we were prepared for a long, long debriefing, a real whammeroo. And it starts off well enough. You take these things chronologically, you know. Born in Szechuan of poor but dishonest parents. Schooling, rebellion, the civil war, revolutionary consciousness. So far so good. Holds nothing back, apparently. First sexual experiences. Highly detailed account of his KGB training – GPU as it was then. The courses. The locations. The Soviet instructors.'

The lady in black with white lace cap and apron, a real upstairs-downstairs figure, Hackenback thought, removed the plates, brought others. They kept silent. Stilton, sir? Again the smell of under-arm BO, then the clunk of a closing door.

'But then we start on some of the interesting bits. And we get nowhere. Finances? I didn't deal with that. Training? That wasn't section two. US penetration? Not my department. Immediate superiors? Everything organised on a need-to-know basis, and no evidence that Mao or Chou ever even read anything from BPD. He didn't even toss us a bone, except where he knew we knew, which wasn't much.

'So we tried another tactic. Hostile witness. Padded room. Truth drugs. Lie detector tests. Permanent observation. Even some subtle sleep deprivation. Inconclusive. We start all over again. We bring in the only other defector we've ever had – the army captain who came over from Burundi in 1963 while Military Attaché there – and that's no good either: our guy never dealt with him, couldn't decide whether or not he was what he said he was. And, after all that, fucker Liao admits that he wasn't all that important in the first place, that his only real function was keeping an eye on the so-called Maoist movements – and he spills a few beans, but it's real crap, insignificant, useless, about the various German, French, Italian and Dutch Maoist movements, their internal differences, their splits, their leaders. And this really gets him into deep shit with us, Minister, because if we know one thing about the BPD-two, it's that they don't give a blue-assed fart about Maoist movements, they stay away from them, you know, don't want to know about the crazies. So then we figure he's a plant. And we let him go.'

'You *what*?'

'I said: we let him go. On your way, boy, nice knowing you, with a first-class, one-way ticket to Geneva, we figure the Chinese will look after him from there onwards, and there's a good PIA flight to Shanghai. Why? Kissinger tells the Chinese, while he's fixing things for Nixon's trip, that's why. Liao's attempted penetration of the CIA, he says, is "an unfriendly act", but we're prepared to ignore it. And the Chinese don't bat an eyelid. They practically acknowledge he's still one of them! So the fucker goes! Doesn't even break down at the thought of hoeing cabbages on a corrective farm for the rest of his life! Never begs to stay, on the grounds they'll have his balls for breakfast. He almost thanks us, as if it hadn't been his idea in the first place, but orders are orders, and he had, as you people say, a bash. Infucking-credible! and Hackenback gets the London assignment.'

The lady again. Coffee. White or black, sir? Lunch is over, and so is the Minister's flight of fancy. No sense in bringing up the case in hand. I'll kill those sodding people over at the hospital, he thinks, all the while maintaining a bland, politician's mask.

Back in his office, a stream of summary phone calls, again on the secure line.

'I want to see that young man, Albert,' the Minister is saying. 'I have a few questions for him. Yes, very urgent. Anything specific? You're too right, there is. You can tell him, before he even gets here, that the supermarket operation is off, and that if anything goes wrong I'll see he's transferred to Belfast as fast as you can say the word China – and it's a pity I can't tell the IRA that's where we're sending him.'

Chapter Two

THE RUE Des Saussaies begins only a few feet from the Elysée Palace and is only about a hundred yards long. With its sombre stone nineteenth-century apartment buildings it looks like a bad Utrillo painting, one of those he dashed off at great speed, dead drunk, in the last, hopeless years of his sad life. Apart from a few privileged Parisians, three cafés, a hotel, an estate agent's and a tiny grocer's shop, the living space in all the odd numbers of the Rue des Saussaies is wholly given to law enforcement. The street is in fact a sprawling annex of the Interior Ministry in the nearby Place Beauvau, and the Ministry and all the buildings on the left-hand side of the Rue des Saussaies actually inter-connect – rabbit warrens, up and down, ill-lit steps, hastily constructed passages linking the Ministry's impressive 'Hôtel particulier' in the Place Beauvau to the slum office annexes of the Rue des Saussaies – all part of the Ministry compound.

Parking in the Rue des Saussaies is impossible, except for a chosen few. Round-the-clock uniformed 'agents', stationed every thirty yards or so, peremptorily keep the traffic flowing, and whistle sharply wherever the uninitiated try to stop, waving them on with the high-handed contemptuous gesture of a tourist brushing off beggars in some tropical dictatorship.

The main police building is at number 11, with two doors side by side: one for pedestrians, leading into a small antechamber with half a dozen elderly police, some in plain clothes, acting as receptionists behind a wooden counter. A door to the right leads to an inner courtyard. The other door, equipped with an obsolete hinged metal bar, enables cars to enter the inner courtyard – but only just. A Cadillac can't make it, and a US Embassy car remained jammed, one afternoon, for several hours until the door was dismantled to let it out again with scraped sides.

With the characteristic sense of secrecy that pervades the French police system, and the French Government as a whole, there is no indication, anywhere in the Paris telephone directory, that number 11 houses the French 'Sûreté Nationale', the headquarters of the national police force. Instead, in the book, there is a cryptic annotation: 'Interior Ministry – information for families of victims of traffic accidents' – which happens to be the smallest of the various departments at number 11. Any caller dialling the number – 2658108 – will indeed, during office hours, stand a fifty per cent chance of finding out whether his loved ones have been mangled in a car crash anywhere on French soil in the past twenty-four hours.

It was in the Rue des Saussaies that Forgeot parked that afternoon – or rather, one of the uniformed policemen on duty did so for him. He was popular with the Sûreté's small fry, not because he did much ritual after-hours drinking with them but because of his romantic reputation: it was a combination of his rather frayed Anglo-French playboy looks, his spy-catcher activities and the fact that he had been the youngest of the French prisoners taken by the Viet Minh at Dien Bien Phu.

Forgeot had an appointment with his boss, the Interior Minister. He would have used the main entrance, the Place Beauvau one, but there had been papers to pick up in his own office safe – papers, Forgeot knew, which would make the Minister wince.

They had to do with the xeroxing propensities of Mlle Marie-Louise Duval, one of the top confidential secretaries at the French Foreign Ministry, the Quai d'Orsay. For the last eighteen years she had been an impeccably loyal, hard-working functionary, handling increasingly sensitive material. And for the last six months, Forgeot knew, she had been turning over every single secret position paper coming her way to a representative of the Algerian Sécurité Militaire. A house rule required that all cases of treasonable behaviour on the part of civil servants be notified, personally, to the Interior Minister himself, and Forgeot and his department now had the kind of evidence which required him to do so.

As always, it was a strangely clinical experience, not unlike breaking the news to someone close that he was seriously ill. Look at it this way, we're doctors, Forgeot had said in an earlier case. We use the equivalent of X-rays, our diagnosis is scientific, not based on hunches. There's no personal animosity involved. To which the Minister had replied that, in hands like Forgeot's, no one ever recovered. He had meant it as a compliment.

The Minister listened to Forgeot in his inner office, the one he used when he didn't want to be disturbed, or wanted to make sure he couldn't be bugged. Forgeot was concise, and spoke without looking at his notes: the initial reports from Forgeot's own people at the Quai, the monitoring of the Quai's own xerox machine, details of her taped phone conversations, transcripts of pillow-talk: her apartment had been bugged so efficiently, Forgeot told the Minister, that whenever she and the agent made love the sound was quadrophonic. The Minister was not amused. Finally, reports of her movements, her modus operandi in transferring the xeroxed documents to her lover – a surprisingly simple combination of dead letterboxes and straightforward key swaps, including luggage lockers at the Invalides Air Terminal across the road from the Quai. It was almost as though she had wanted to be caught.

There were details, photos, tape recordings for the Minister to peruse at his leisure, together with some of the contents of the items she had transmitted. It was up to the Minister to decide how to follow this up. As usual, he had been first appalled, then, despite himself, fascinated. He was experienced enough not to ask Forgeot how some of the evidence had been accumulated. He grudgingly admired the way the traps had been set, and sprung. He also wondered, privately, whether Forgeot didn't enjoy this sort of thing too much . Forgeot had once been with the SDECE, the French Intelligence network, he remembered. It was only after he had unmasked a conspiracy within the SDECE which threatened French security that de Gaulle, with that belly laugh of his, had said: 'If he's so good at catching spies, let's have him do it full time.' It was unprecedented for SDECE personnel to move to the Interior Ministry, but in those days de Gaulle's slightest hint became an order.

'It's the old, familiar story,' Forgeot said, while the Minister flipped through the file. 'It's not only the West Germans who fear for their spinsters' loyalty. There's a secret weapon everywhere against which no amount of security can prevail: we call it love.'

Forgeot knew that he could to some extent influence the Minister's course of action. The alternatives were: pension her off, and hush up the whole case, retire her immediately, or prosecute. Prosecution meant a trial before the State Security Court, a messy business. Let the Minister decide, that's what he's there for.

The Minister was in philosophical mood, and obviously wanted to spend some time with Forgeot. He pressed a button indicating he did not wish to be disturbed. Not that he wanted to talk about the Duval case itself: he was interested, he said, in its overall implications. 'Your organisation,' he said 'is on a constant and natural collision course with the Quai. They'll always accuse you of seeing spies under the bed, and you'll always complain that they're taking an over-conciliatory attitude towards agents masquerading as diplomats. It's only natural.'

It might teach the Quai a lesson, he said, if an occasional, spectacular defection reminded them of the prevalence of spies among the diplomatic community – like the time the British had expelled 120 Soviet diplomats in one fell swoop. And if the DST could involve itself more in turning agents around, getting them to defect, this might have beneficial consequences too. He didn't under-estimate the difficulties. The Minister added that he knew this was a tricky area, with the DST in natural competition with the SDECE.

Forgeot understood the real gist of the Minister's thinking: a spectacular defection would take some of the sting out of the Duval case, if it ever came to light in the press. The Minister had not been in his job long enough to remember some of Forgeot's more spectacular successes: a whole Hungarian network neatly disposed of, its members expelled without fuss or trouble, a South Korean industrial espionage ring nipped in the bud, the Aeroflot affair of four years back. There had been other minor trade-offs that hadn't even come to the Minister's attention: defectors, like valuable antiques, were subject to the equivalent of international auctions, and the buyers were almost invariably American. Forgeot could think of half a dozen individuals on French soil, all under surveillance, all of them possible defector material. Any one of them might cross the line tomorrow. Alternately, they might all, in the last resort, hope to win points with their own side by screaming blackmail and enticement. The perils of involving oneself with defectors were never understood by Interior Ministers, who blandly took credit when things went right, but were quick to criticise when anything went wrong. Forgeot toyed with the idea of giving his Minister a short lecture on the problems involved, to point out that the only really satisfactory defectors were walk-ins, as they were known in the trade. He decided against it.

But the Minister had other things on his mind. First the small talk, then the real message. He was very much the shrewd peasant politician, the devious Normandy farmer from an ultra-conservative rural constituency, who was never quite comfortable with Parisians.

'By the way,' he said. 'People are beginning to talk about you.' Forgeot wasn't altogether surprised. Who was it this time? Chantal? Florence? A husband? He tried to appear unconcerned, and ended up looking slightly sheepish.

'I wouldn't talk like this to anyone else in my Ministry,' he said. 'But, after all, you're supposed to be different, aren't you? Here you are, a graduate of the Ecole Nationale d'Administration, with an eminent part-time teaching post at the Ecole Nationale des Langues Orientales – I'm told, incidentally, that your colloquial Chinese is superb – and an outstanding record as acting head of the DST, a job that usually goes to people considerably older than you. And you're risking throwing it all away, if I may put it crudely, all because you compulsively chase after women – other people's women – in a way that went out of fashion with the Third Republic.'

The Minister tapped a folder on his desk. 'Your dossier,' he said. 'No, I won't let you read it. It might go to your head. And you might do something foolish, because you'll probably spot where the bad parts come from.'

Forgeot thought again. Surely not Chantal. Possibly Florence. But more likely one of the *chers confrères*, jealous of his access to the Cabinet. Can I help it, thought Forgeot, if the rest of my spy-catching colleagues are content with rugby football on Sunday mornings, and watching Kojak on TV in their garden suburbs when they're through with their own work?

'Minister,' said Forgeot, 'you make a lot of enemies in this business. No one knows that more than you. And some of the ways people have of settling scores are very rough indeed.'

'It can be rough on husbands, too,' the Minister said, 'even in an era that doesn't put a premium on marital fidelity. No, I won't ask you what you were doing in Montfort Lamaury over the weekend. I presume you weren't riding horses all day.'

Isabelle. Of course. Young diplomats' wives were off limits to cops. Besides, she had insisted on taking her car. The CD plates told all, and the Gendarmerie now had a computer system of its own. Forgeot could almost see the gawking gendarme punching the numberplate into the system, just for something to do, and putting two and two together. It had been awkward that the husband had, after all, returned early from a Brussels Commission meeting. Usually those sessions went on all night. But Isabelle had known what she was doing. Hell!

Forgeot made his little boy's face, caught in the act.

'Minister,' he said, 'I can't promise you that nothing of the kind will ever happen again. But I do sincerely say that – partly as a result of what happened later that weekend – you can tell the Ambassador in question that I'm through with married women for ever.'

'I'm glad to hear it.'

Back in his own office Forgeot reflected on the talk. Things could have been worse. The Minister could have found out where he had been spending his lunch hour, and with whom.

The phone rang, on Forgeot's second private line, used only for overseas calls.

An English telephone operator was saying: 'Is that Mister Fordjott?' He overheard another English voice say, irritated, 'Not Fordjott, for Christ's sake. Forgeot. The G is pronounced DJ. Like For-Joe.' It was a voice he knew.

The operator said again: 'Mr Forgeot? Just a minute please. Someone on the line for you.'

It was Albert. No small talk, no preliminaries needed. 'Have to see you, old sport. Can't say more right now. I'm calling from a hotel in London. It's got to be today. In Paris. You say where.' And Forgeot, not at all French in his informality, his immediate understanding, replied. 'Hire a car. My place. Don't use the front door. Use Avis at Orly. They'll have something for you. It'll get you in. Remember the garage entrance? Not before nine. don't be a *con* this time, if you can help it.' And Albert, more subdued than usual, said, 'I think I already have been.'

Despite their differences in rank, and the fact that, from time to time, they spied on each other, and always watched each other warily, Albert and Forgeot had a kind of professional closeness. There had been a shared botched caper in Biafra. Since then they had become friends. But Albert had only once visited Forgeot at his Paris apartment before. He collected an envelope from the Avis counter; it contained the little black box with which to open the garage door. Common in American households, it was still a rare status symbol in France, and at first even Forgeot had got a vicarious thrill from stabbing a button on a small box and seeing the garage door to his Neuilly apartment house raise itself in front of his eyes. His friend Roman Polanski went one better: he had a switch incorporated in his Mercedes, but then Polanski was gadget-crazy, like all Poles.

Almost on time, Albert pressed the button on the little black box, parked his hired car, and took the lift to Forgeot's apartment. He had an overnight bag, which he left in the car. With luck, the following day being Saturday, he might not be missed.

Forgeot was alone. A bottle of Bushmills was ready, and Albert knew it was for him. He smiled, with some effort. 'You won't believe this,' he said, in English, as he settled down into a deep leather armchair, 'but we've just turned down what might be the most unusual defector of the decade – and, what's more, I blew it. Blew it to such an extent that I'm either out of the service or off to Belfast within a week, and the defector . . .' He punched the armrest.

Forgeot spoke English too – with a trace of his mother's Irish brogue. He said: 'You're not making much sense, to me.'

Albert told him about Anh, the supermarket, and the message from May, the Chinese Embassy shopper. 'I took pictures of her without her knowing it. We identified her as an extremely worthwhile catch: Embassy cypher officer,

35

trained by the Bureau of National Security, fluent English speaker, officially Third Secretary, but could be in Intelligence herself. And a niece – or great-niece, we're not sure – of Liu Shao Chi into the bargain. A real catch.' He told Forgeot how the Minister had talked to the CIA, and suspected a plant. 'And now we're not only letting her go: we've practically sentenced her to a living death.' Forgeot said nothing.

Albert went on with the story. The last forty-eight hours had been difficult ones. After the Minister's decision to drop the case, no appeal was possible. Nevertheless, Albert had argued that the case in question and the Hague affair of 1970 were not at all similar, and that – on humanitarian grounds alone – the British Government could not prevent Comrade May from requesting political asylum. 'If she wants political asylum, she has to say so,' the Minister had ruled. 'No monkey business. All she needs to do is to walk out of her hostel, and report to the nearest police station.'

'What our Minister didn't understand,' said Albert, 'was that she couldn't just walk out like that. The chances of doing so were always pretty bad. Now they're hopeless. They've got her. All because we had to get ministerial clearance before we do anything like that.'

Forgeot guessed what had happened, and what Albert was going to propose.

'My mistake was that I slightly jumped the gun. I never believed we'd be turned down. So I'd already slipped a note back to May, telling her to contact us as soon as possible. I'd intended to whisk her off to somewhere safe. My mistake. She must have aroused their suspicions, somehow. Maybe too many trips to the supermarket. Anyway, they behaved as though they suspected nothing. She went into Safeway's once more, to say time was running short, and she needed to know where to meet one of our representatives – whether she could just walk out at any time and be sure of being picked up.'

'And the people who had her under surveillance waited for that very moment and grabbed both the note and the girl?'

Albert took a sip of neat Bushmills. His face was pale and his hand shook slightly. He nodded.

'Under our very noses. And there was nothing we could do.

What I wanted to tell her – but never got the chance – was: try and make it on your own. Go to the police. I never had time. There was a scuffle. I was alone. The place was almost empty. The people in the supermarket just stared. Must have thought the Chinese were dealing with a shoplifter, one of their own. They took her out, and back to the hostel. She's there still. Tomorrow they're taking her out of the country. We know that because they have to book seats, don't they? London to Paris, then on to a PIA plane that does the Paris-Shanghai run. They don't want her to have to hang around. That's the only reason they've kept her in London so far. They've booked seats on tomorrow's plane to Orly. One that has almost immediate connections with the plane to Shanghai.'

Forgeot grinned. 'And you want me to step in and put things right? Is that it?'

'It would,' said Albert, 'be a favour. Something I'd remember.'

'What makes you so sure she's not a plant, after all?'

'If you'd seen her struggle and the expression on her face as they frog-marched her out of the supermarket, you wouldn't ask.' A pause. 'The point is, can you do it? There's so little time. Don't you have to get clearance from someone? It's not a personal favour. I'm in the doghouse already. But it would be nice to win one for a change.'

'That's what my friends, colleagues and fellow-officers used to say after Dien Bien Phu. That's what made them try to blow up de Gaulle. That's why we had to put so many of them in jail. It's not a question of winning one for a change, my friend. It's a question of results. You vouch for her? You believe the operation is worthwhile? Obviously you do, or you wouldn't have taken the risk of coming to see me – at your own expense, I assume – and at some risk? To me it's just a job. A rush job. Same-day laundry. Very difficult to get your laundry back the same day, in France, you know. But in your case I'll try and make an exception. Unlike you fellows, it so happens my Minister allows me to use my own discretion, occasionally. Excuse me a minute. Have another drink.'

Forgeot got up, and went into the next room. Albert could hear him on the phone. His tone was casual, with some laughter. He came back into the sitting-room. 'Since you're in this up to your neck already,' he said, 'you might as well give us a hand yourself. What size clothes do you wear? In centimetres. Inches don't mean much to the chap I'm talking to. And if you ever breathe a word of this to anyone – what do they say in the Royal Navy? – I'll have your balls for a necktie.'

Orly at mid-morning. The early passengers, businessmen with briefcases, charter flights to off-season Club Méditerranée ghettoes, had already left. There was the usual small crowd waiting for incoming passengers, watching the arrivals and departures board on the first floor. The bar at the end of the departure hall was crowded. The low bedroom voice of the airport announcer told all and sundry that Pakistan International Airways flight number 203 to Karachi and Shanghai would be slightly delayed.

Uniformed NCOs from the French Interior Ministry's 'Police de l'Air' handle airport passport formalities, with a customs official standing by at a separate counter, to look into the occasional briefcase or handbag. That morning, the glass booth of the passport-handler was occupied by three men. One, seated, was the regular assignee. The man behind him in the dark blue képi, and wearing the uniform of a CRS sergeant, was Forgeot. To his right, looking slightly embarrassed in a too-tight uniform, was Albert. From time to time Forgeot looked at Albert, with raised eyebrows and the hint of a smile. In the booth there was almost no room to move. Out of sight, behind a partition, were a couple more uniformed CRS men. Among those waiting for passengers in the arrivals area were a surprising number of Chinese officials from the Embassy, in grey Mao suits. There were also a few men from Forgeot's own outfit, unobtrusively eyeing the Chinese. Man for man the Chinese outnumbered the DST, but Forgeot's people had one advantage: traditionally the DST draws its strength from bright young cops from the South-West and rugby football is almost as much of a cult in Southern France as it is in Wales. Forgeot's men were all big, and knew how to tackle. Rugby players only this time, Forgeot had said.

The bedroom voice told the assembled gathering that

British Airways flight number 802 from Heathrow had just landed, and would be shortly proceeding through gate 51. The passengers arrived in a fast dribble. First off were the sleek first-class passengers, businessmen all, in Paris for the day, carrying heavy briefcases and looking at their watches. Then came the French shoppers, jauntily wearing their new Burberry macs and Marks and Spencers pullovers, and fooling no one. As Forgeot had anticipated, the Chinese were last.

First came Comrade Ma. Albert recognised him. He looked irritated, and small wonder. Normally, passengers in transit were not required to go through customs, Mr Ma had argued. The ground hostess, however, had been well briefed. 'You must fill in the landing cards,' she said. Mr Ma had reluctantly headed for the exit. He was still arguing. The ground hostess was saying, 'You cannot check in on a PIA flight directly. It is not the same terminal,' over and over again, as she led him in the direction of the exit. One advantage of living in a regimented society, Albert thought, is that you can get them to follow instructions, provided they're given by people who appear to be in authority.

Mr Ma plonked his passport down on the counter. His ticket showed that he was booked on a PIA flight to Shanghai. 'Transit,' he said impatiently. His passport was quickly stamped, but Mr Ma stayed where he was. He didn't want to be separated from the rest of the group, but the policeman waved him on, while the customs official turned to Mr Ma, gesturing him through the line. Mr Ma, still looking behind him, reluctantly followed. The Chinese on the other side of the barrier now clustered round Mr Ma. He spoke to them in a low voice. A Frenchman in a raincoat reluctantly folded away his *France-Soir*. The rest of the group came in a tight pack. All had Chinese diplomatic passports, but the first three to go through the exit line were obvious thugs. Then came three people. Two men, with a girl in the middle. They had their arms around her in smiling, comradely concern. The older of the two men carried two passports – his own and the girl's. 'Elle est malade,' he said in reasonably good French. 'Our comrade had a slight malaise on the plane!' He handed over the passports with one hand. The other retained a firm grip on May's arm. The other man had his arm locked around May's left arm. Both men were in effect propping her up, after frog-marching her off the plane. Her face was devoid of any expression. Her mouth was open and her eyes half-closed. She had no handbag. Her face was chalk-white. A sleep-walker, Forgeot thought. Sleeping pills or pentothal? A strong tranquilliser, most likely, almost certainly injected.

Unexpectedly, the 'Police de l'Air' man sitting at his table took a long time thumbing through May's passport. She almost pitched forward, but the two men held on to her. Forgeot shouted out, in Chinese, in a deliberately high-pitched tone, to make sure she would understand: 'I want to help you.'

May looked at him. They've kept her conscious, Forgeot thought, because they couldn't very well bring a corpse through Orly.

He said quickly: 'Are you travelling of your own free will? Or do you want to stay here? You must answer me. Unless you say something I can't help you.'

The Chinese escorts, furious, tugged at her, but the policeman kept their passports in his hand. He had a fist like a large knuckle of pork. They started shouting, one in Chinese, the other in French. 'You have no right! Let us through. This is an outrage.'

Their raised voices appeared to be waking May up. The Chinese in their grey suits on the other side of the barrier had sensed that something was wrong, and were trying to push past the customs official, to join in the struggle. The customs official stretched out his arms. 'Non, non,' he said. The men in the raincoats, with practised casualness, formed a line and started pushing them back, not brutally, simply using their bodyweight to compel them to stay behind the barrier.

In a semi-coma, barely audible, Forgeot heard her say: 'Please help me!' And then he shouted: 'Allez-y.' At this signal, more uniformed CRS men appeared from nowhere, twisted the arms of the two men holding May, broke their hold on her and rushed the two Chinese through the customs booth to the arrivals area outside. The French civilians quickly broke ranks, helped them through, and immediately stood shoulder to shoulder again. A small crowd had gathered. The whole incident had maybe taken two minutes.

40

As the Chinese escorting May were being propelled past customs, a couple more CRS men grabbed May, and whisked her back where she had come from, out of sight from the waiting Chinese. By now the latter realised their only hope was to get her back by force. Mr Ma, followed by the rest of the pack, ran a few yards to the departures gate, dodging the CRS men there, and ducking under the metal bars. But Forgeot's men were waiting for this to happen. They too scrambled into the custons area (the customs men made no effort to stop them) and – again using minimum force – blocked them as they tried to race after May. 'Entrée interdite,' said one of the plainclothesmen patiently. But Mr Ma, small but wriggling like a snake, managed to get away. He sprinted down the corridor in May's direction, Albert after him in hot pursuit. Mr Ma was dodging other passengers moving past him, new arrivals from another flight, which made tackle impossible. Albert caught him by the collar, and pinned him to the wall. Mr Ma, screaming and raging in Chinese, aimed a kick at Albert's shin, making painful contact, and without further ado, as a reflex to the pain, Albert punched Mr Ma in the face, breaking his nose.

Forgeot skipped out of the booth, and started following the two men who were taking the girl out of the airport building. He had arranged for an ambulance on the tarmac itself, at one of the passenger exit doors along the corridor nearest the passport control area. He too had parked on the tarmac: he drove out fast, following the ambulance part of the way. At Montparnasse, reassured, he turned left as the ambulance went on towards the Hôpital Cochin: people at the gates there, he knew, had already been forewarned. One of his men was waiting at the entrance.

Back at the Orly arrivals floor, there was now pandemonium. The crowds of alighting and departing passengers, waiting relatives and sightseers were treated to a strange and incomprehensible sight: in serried ranks, some twenty Chinese, their Mao buttons visible, furiously and vociferously chanting slogans in Chinese at a group of embarrassed CRS men, protected from Chinese wrath by a line of plainclothes policemen. They appeared to be trying to storm a passport booth, while one of their number, a small, rotund man with spectacles, sat hunched over on the floor, his back to the wall and his head in his hands, a bloodstained handkerchief over his nose.

'What's going on?' someone asked.

'It must be the Cultural Revolution.'

'I thought this sort of thing only happened in Peking.'

While all this was happening, passengers were being channelled through another gateway, and a squad of riot-equipped armed police drew up outside Orly airport. They were never used. After some forty minutes' shouting, a senior figure from the Chinese Embassy in Paris arrived on the scene. He told his men to stop.

He then asked who was the senior French official present. A uniformed CRS sergeant came forward. Pulling out a piece of paper, he read, in clear, angry tones, in French: 'I wish to lodge an official protest. Our Embassy will take this matter up with the highest instances of the French Government. One of our comrades has been kidnapped, and another has been seriously hurt. This naked aggression and hooliganism, doubtless the work of imperialistic provocateurs in the midst of the French Government, is a grave, most unfriendly and vile act which will have extremely serious consequences. I am informing the highest authorities in Peking of this inexcusable breach of conduct.'

Slowly, the crowd dispersed. The Chinese sorted themselves out, leaving in cars and minibuses.

Albert had witnessed the whole scene. With considerable aplomb, he walked out of the airport, his uniform giving him total protection. His overnight bag, and his civilian clothes, were in his hired car in the parking lot. He would drop the uniform off with the CRS headquarters in Orly before flying back to London.

Ten miles away, in a room on an inner courtyard of the Hôpital Cochin the Chinese girl May slept a deep, drugged sleep, while a uniformed policeman, told to keep all visitors away save a doctor whose name he had been given and Forgeot, mounted guard outside her door and wondered how long he'd be stuck there before being relieved. And, some 16,000 miles away, a tall Chinese in his middle fifties heard the news on his private phone in the early morning in his apartment inside the Internal Security Ministry and threw a priceless Ming teacup across the room.

Chapter Three

'IT'S unbelievable.'

'Grotesque.'

The two men were on opposite sides of a Louis XVI table in the Quai d'Orsay, looking through the morning papers. The taller one, Aymeric de Lémeric-Dutoit, was the Foreign Minister's Chief Aide. His colleagues, and the Minister, called him plain Lémeric, though he liked to be known, by his subordinates, as 'Monsieur le Comte'. American Embassy diplomats in the Political Section, behind his back of course, referred to him as Dew Twat.

The shorter, stouter man was Lucien Menhir, head of the Asian Affairs Department at the Quai. British Embassy officials in Paris nicknamed him Stonehenge. It had been one of the Head of Chancery's many bad private jokes.

All the papers had the Chinese story on the front page. Only *France-Soir*, though, had a photograph, taken by a resourceful Dutch tourist who had sold it to the highest bidder on the Rue Réaumur.

'It couldn't have happened at a worse time.'

'These people never seem to realise there are more important matters at stake.'

Menhir, the kind of strident Anglophobe who orders his suits from Savile Row and his shoes from Lobb, knew he could rely on the Chief Aide. They said, within a fraction of a second of each other, but, as it were, from opposite ends of the sentence:

'If only de Gaulle had still been alive . . .'

'. . . none of this would ever have happened '

There was a silence. Each knew what the other was thinking. They were custodians of a particularly sensitive piece of information, a closely guarded secret, even though a brash *Newsweek* reporter had run a story the previous week, admittedly as a 'Periscope' item, ending in a question-mark. Lémeric made a mental note to investigate who had leaked it. Both Lémeric and Menhir were among the handful of senior officials aware that the French President was dying of Waldenstroem's disease, a rare, unremitting form of blood cancer, that he was in constant pain, and that his attention span had been dramatically curtailed by the drugs he took to get through the day, even though he had cut his official functions to the unavoidable minimum.

The fiction up to now, to explain the President's constant cancellations of appointments, public appearances, receptions and foreign trips, was that he had a bad case of 'flu, which he had been unable to shake off. Someone, thought Lémeric, had better come up with a more convincing story soon, or the speculation caused by the *Newsweek* item would spread, and who could predict the outcome?

'The time has come,' said Menhir, 'for a hard look at the antics of that Forgeot. I'm sure he's behind it all.'

'It is up to the President to decide.'

They nodded gravely, two men imbued with a sense of mission, agreeably tempered by their own self-importance and a sense of a shared secret. It was significant that neither had invoked the authority of their master, the Foreign Minister. The little man was infinitely malleable, if unpredictable at times. On this occasion, as in the past, he would do as he was told.

Forgeot too had seen the morning papers. The Interior Minister had been briefed. He could be relied on, Forgeot knew, to keep trouble-makers away, at least for the time being.

He too looked at the display on his desk. 'Astonishing scenes at Orly,' said *Le Figaro*. 'Angry Chinese diplomats,' said *L'Aurore*. And below, in huge characters, both papers ran:

'Chinese girl chooses freedom'.

The *France-Soir* photograph, Forgeot noted with satisfaction, was sufficiently blurred for his own presence to be almost impossible to discern. There was no mistaking Albert, however. Did the 'hospital' take *France-Soir*? I If so, Albert would have a certain amount of explaining to do. Forgeot gathered the papers together and put them in a folder. He was going to start the debriefing himself, and these might make a good opener for his first session with

44

Comrade May, ex-Third Secretary and possible Intelligence catch. He pressed the intercom.

'I'll be gone most of the day,' he told his secretary. 'If the Foreign Ministry calls, tell them to address themselves directly to the Interior Minister. Tell them nothing else. And, if they insist, tell them to get stuffed.'

The Hôpital Cochin is one of the largest, as well as most distinguished, of Paris hospitals. Some of its inner court-yards, looking a little like a series of Cambridge colleges, are of considerable historical and architectural interest. The cloisters give it a religious flavour, and most of the nurses are lay sisters of a Catholic nursing order.

The President's own doctors monitored the course of his disease in a closely guarded laboratory at Cochin, and the DST had access to a couple of rooms there, no questions asked, 'discrétion assurée', as the interns put it, using the jargon of the short-time hotels.

French reporters and photographers have the irritating habit of slipping into hospitals disguised as doctors, complete with white coats and stethoscopes, in order to photograph famous people on their deathbeds or film stars after their carefully contrived unsuccessful suicide attempts, but no one has ever photographed a Cochin patient against the Cochin hospital authorities' will.

Forgeot and a doctor were in the corridor. The two secure DST rooms were on the right. One of them was equipped with a see-through mirror. From the sound-proof corridor, it was possible to see into Comrade May's room. The uniformed cop who was on guard was staring intently through the mirror when Forgeot arrived. He reluctantly stood aside.

Forgeot often wondered who had had the mirror installed in the first place. Probably not the DST but the Germans: like the OECD bulding in Paris, once the pre-war town house of the French branch of the Rothschild family, then a Gestapo headquarters, also full of see-through mirrors.

The police doctor was staring now. He was an oldish man, with the lined face and hard look of someone who has seen too much of the seamy side of broken minds and bodies, and given up the human race as a bad job. It was Forgeot's theory that France was the only country where doctors and surgeons looked like chefs and butchers, and where chefs and butchers had impeccable bedside manners, and looked like doctors.

This doctor seemed to be liking what he saw. For a few seconds, even he looked quite human. 'Lovely, isn't she?' he said. He stepped aside, inviting Forgeot to look.

The high white hospital bed was tidily made. May wasn't in it. At first the room seemed empty. Then Forgeot saw her, or part of her. She was naked, doing press-ups. Invisible when her straight body was close to the floor, but all too visible in the upward position, her long hair hiding most of her face, but not her slim arms, her shoulders, her straight back, her small firm breasts. She was indeed beautiful, with a dancer's cool, muscular grace. What Forgeot could see of her face indicated perfect bliss.

It was a wrench to move away. The doctor looked at Forgeot, knowingly, and Forgeot was aware of a sudden, schoolboy tumescence. What a way to start a debriefing! Assume a detached, cop manner, you fool.

'How long has she been awake?'

'Must be a couple of hours. Yesterday, on arrival, she cried a lot. She refused to take the pills we gave her. She wouldn't eat. Finally she fell asleep, and didn't wake up till nine this morning. They must have given her some stuff.'

Forgeot couldn't resist another peep. She was dressing now, slipping on an absurdly large coarse cotton nightgown, French Social Security issue.

Forgeot waited briefly, to make sure she was dressed, then knocked and entered. May's nightgown billowed around her, an oversized tent. She made him welcome with a slight gesture, indicated that he take the only chair, turned to climb on to the bed, tripped over the gown and almost fell. Forgeot caught her, steadied her. She made no motion to move out of his arms.

'I apologise for the hospital clothing,' Forgeot said in Chinese. 'It's Government issue. One size fits all.'

She looked up at him.

'I know you,' she said, also in Chinese. 'You're the one in the uniform, at the airport, who shouted at me.'

'I wanted to make sure you understood,' said Forgeot. 'If

46

you hadn't replied, you would have made me look pretty silly.'

May climbed on to the bed, and sat huddled up, clasping her knees.

'And if I hadn't said anything?'

'You'd be in Shanghai by now.'

Forgeot produced the papers, spread them on the bed.

'Look,' he said. 'You're famous.'

May frowned. She looked closer. 'Why?' she said, angrily, then again, pleadingly, softly, 'why did you let them take pictures?'

'I didn't. A tourist took it. He sold it to the paper. They gave him a lot of money for it. That's all.'

'You mean you can't stop people from taking your picture?'

'That's how things are, over here. I got the impression you liked the way things are, in our part of the world. Am I mistaken?'

May shook her head. She said, 'I was only thinking: this will make things worse – for them. A bad loss of face for Mr Ma.' She giggled. My God, Forgeot thought, she's really something, this one. Does she know how attractive she is? May was laughing now, her head buried in her arms. She looked up, all anger forgotten.

'I forgot,' she said. 'I saw what happened, over my shoulder, as they were taking me to the ambulance. Not loss of face. Hurt of nose for Mr Ma.'

'Poor Mr Ma.'

'Not poor Mr Ma.' She switched to English, interrogatively, to see whether he understood. Forgeot nodded. She went on: 'Almost every day, I was wanting to do that to his nose. Many people will be happy, in our Embassy in London, when they hear what happened. Many.' She nodded gravely. 'Unless they take him straight back to Peking. Even then, they will hear, eventually.'

There was a knock on the door. A tall black nurse, from Martinique, came in with a lunch tray.

'You must be hungry,' Forgeot said, also in English, embarrassed suddenly by this cool assured spontaneity, so different from his past experience of the immediate post-decision, jet-lag, did-I-do-the-right-thing confusion that is the usual hallmark of a defector's first forty-eight hours in a strange environment.

May looked at him, her dark eyes huge and not at all hostile.

'May I eat?' she said. 'Or must I sing for my supper first?'

Forgeot poured her a glass of Vichy water. She ate delicately, like a cat. She finished the slice of roast veal and the mashed potatoes, tasted the small triangle of Camembert cheese, wrinkled her nose and put it back on the plate.

'So this is your French cheese,' she said. 'I've never had any before.'

'It doesn't look very good,' said Forgeot. 'It's hospital cheese. The British have a kind of cheese they call mousetrap. You must have seen it in the cheese counter of that supermarket.'

'There is a place in Paris I read about once,' said May. 'Perhaps you could take me there one day? Androuet. I once read an article in a magazine which said it had the best cheeses in the world, hundreds of them.'

This getting out of hand, Forgeot said to himself. I should be asking the questions, not her. He said briskly: 'I'm only here to ask you a few questions.'

'I know: you want me to write my life story. Then you'll take me through it over and over again, picking holes in it, looking for omissions, lies, insincere thoughts. Like Mr Ma. Then I'll write a new version. You'll criticise that one too. I'll write some more. Is that it?' There was a hint of laughter in her voice, in her eyes. 'Then, if you're satisfied with the final version, you'll take me to Androuet. It *is* a restaurant as well as a shop, isn't it?'

With hindsight, this was where Forgeot's resolve faltered, and his first unprofessional lapse occurred. What he should have said was: I'm simply interested in the information you are able to provide us. But instead, he looked at the girl, perched on the bed, full of gentle mockery, infinitely desirable, and said: 'My dear, Androuet's full of tourists. I'll take you to a place on the Rue de Granelle the Japanese tour operators haven't discovered yet,' and immediately rationalised his failing thus: after all, I'd only be putting her in a suitable mood. Don't ever get involved with a case. Didn't they teach you that, in your days at the SDECE? Yes, but there are valid exceptions to any rule.

Forgeot said: 'You'll be staying here a few days. Don't worry. You're quite safe. Nobody can contact you here against your will.'

May looked at him. 'But this is a *hospital*. I'm not sick. Look.'

She swung off the bed, and before he could prevent her, she had turned a cartwheel, jumped and grabbed the aluminium rail of the shower-curtain in the corner. She swung dangerously, dexterously, obviously a skilled gymnast, using it like an exercise-bar. Christ, thought Forgeot, that bloody gendarme is probably watching the whole performance. And here he made another mistake. 'Stop it,' he shouted, reverting to Chinese. 'We're not alone here. Don't you understand? They can see you through the mirror. Get back on the bed and start talking.' And he added, still in Chinese, for after all, you never knew who might be listening: 'I'll take you to Androuet. I'll get you out of here. But we'll do things my way.'

While Forgeot was talking to May in the Hôpital Cochin, Lémeric was answering a telephone call from the Chinese Embassy in Paris, informing him that His Excellency the Ambassador wished to call on the Minister of Foreign Affairs at his earliest convenience. No, it was not possible to disclose what His Excellency wished to talk about. Doubtless Monsieur Lémeric already suspected that it might have something to do with a recent deplorable event.

And in the Chinese Embassy itself, incongruously located almost opposite the most famous strip-tease cabaret in the world, the Crazy Horse Saloon in the Avenue Georges V, some of the protagonists of the Orly demonstration were meeting in a partitioned school-room, the cheap furniture and tacky fittings contrasting with the ornate mouldings and high ceilings of the elegant mansion, formerly the Embassy of Chiang Kai-Chek's China.

For once there was little jargon and ideological time-wasting involved. The Head of the Bureau of Political Defence in the Paris Embassy, a surprisingly tall Chinese called Feng, had marshalled his troops to discuss whether, at this late hour, there might still be an outside chance of extricating poor misguided Comrade May from the clutches of the French security services.

The consensus at the meeting was that she was probably holed up in some hospital in the Paris area, but where? Feng's informers so far had produced nothing. This was hardly surprising: the Paris network was notoriously weak. restaurant-owners, a few paid informers, what did they know? The shambles of the French open society should make our task easy, thought Feng, but in situations of this kind they still manage to run a pretty tight ship.

One of the questions discussed was what should be done if she *was* located: the consensus was that it was worth while making a determined effort to get her back, even if this caused diplomatic problems.

Including violence? Most certainly, Feng agreed. The French Government was so eager for good relations to be maintained that they were sure to do no more than protest verbally, and the whole incident would eventually be forgotten.

If they did succeed in getting her back, Feng was certain that his methods would ensure that she retract her request for political asylum. The drugs used for her journey from London had obviously not been properly chosen. Feng had never liked Mr Ma, and he was determined to make him look even more ridiculous.

In practical terms, what could be done? In the first place, try to keep a close watch on those French security agents who might be involved in the case. And on this occasion, Feng told his subordinates, it would be worth using any source, no matter how unreliable – he baulked at the word 'Maoists' – to find out if they could come up with something.

Normally Feng kept them at arm's length. They were an embarrassment, even if they were genuine. After prolonged vetting of those Maoists who had volunteered their services to Chinese Embassy officials, often making crude and laughable overtures, it had been impossible, in the past, to use any of them, even as occasional informers. Either they were hopelessly unreliable, or stark, raving mad, merely using Chinese Marxist-Leninism as a vehicle for their own agressive hostility towards authority in any form. Or else they were so hopelessly naive as to make any relationship impossible. One of Feng's men had the permanent French Maoists' beat: he was asked to bring everything to bear, exceptionally, to try to locate the girl.

Less than a mile away, across the Seine, at the Quai d'Orsay, Lémeric had had a similar kind of conference, but with fewer people, and was busy writing a brief for his Minister.

His draft was, as usual, designed to flatter the little man and so leave him with the impression that the policies outlined in the text were not only the Minister's own, but also designed to enhance his stature with the rest of the Cabinet and to draw attention to his exceptional gifts.

The thrust of Lémeric's paper was that the American pull-out from Vietnam and the signing of the Paris agreements now enabled France to make a fresh bid to exert her influence there. The 'third force' Vietnamese politicians had already told the French Ambassador in Saigon they hoped to turn to Paris to ensure that Hanoi respected its part of the agreements, guaranteeing a plurality of parties and a separate Southern Vietnamese 'specificity'. But France's image as a Western country independent of 'Atlantic' influence would be thoroughly jeopardised if political asylum were granted to a junior Chinese diplomat in transit.

It was unlikely that her debriefing, however skilled, would result in the accumulation of any really worthwhile information. She was not even resident in France or from a country under French influence. On the other hand, the damage done to Franco-Chinese relations would be incalculable. It was therefore essential for the Foreign Minister to bring all possible pressure to bear on the Government to get the Interior Minister to reverse his stand and hand her back to the Chinese. This gesture of good-will would, more than anything else, convince Peking that France pursued an independent foreign policy; it would confirm France's status as the one Western power with privileged friendly relations with the Peoples Republic of China, at a time when it was still dangerously isolated, and would effectively counter the impact of the Nixon trip to Peking. The Minister's personal status vis à vis Mao Tse Tung would be considerably improved, and would almost certainly lead to an invitation to visit China, and to a personal session with Mao himself.

The brief, as such, ended there, but Lémeric appended a personal 'eyes only' note: the only real issue at stake, the note pointed out, was the kind of pressure to be brought on the DST to give up its prey. It was unlikely, the note said, that it would be convinced of the validity of the arguments contained in the brief. They were country bumpkins interested only in the narrowest parameters of security and counter-intelligence. All attempts to reach the DST director on the case by telephone had failed, with referrals made to contact the Interior Minister, who, for some reason, in this case, had decided to back his DST men to the hilt – at any rate for the time being.

The only way of persuading the DST to reverse its decision, then, was through a personal order from the President of the Republic himself. For obvious reasons, the note concluded, it was essential to get the President to issue this order as soon as possible, while there was still time.

This was why the Foreign Minister should try to see the President of the Republic immediately, and if possible get him to issue a personal order to have her handed back to the Chinese. If an audience with the President was not feasible in the time available, the matter would have to be raised at the next Cabinet meeting, the following Wednesday.

Doing so, the note continued, would present advantages as well as drawbacks. It ensured that the Minister might, in the meantime, enlist the support of other Cabinet members likely to feel as he did.

There were two dangers: one was that the DST, behind the Cabinet's back, might do a deal with the United States, and simply hand the defector over to the CIA. Such trade-ins had occurred before, but not in France. This would be truly disastrous, for it would confirm that, in Chinese eyes, France remained an 'Atlantic' US puppet, and would remove any credibility from any later French attempt to play a rôle in Asia.

The other was the possibility of public opinion becoming mobilized, with the press demanding that 'la belle Chinoise' be allowed to stay, invoking rights of political refugees, etc. For this reason, it was essential that all Cabinet Ministers be cautioned, once again, about the need for total secrecy of Cabinet proceedings. The only way of avoiding a public outcry when she was returned to China, the note concluded, was for interest in the case to be allowed to lapse. Then a careful 'leak' from a Government source to a likely journalist might lead to an 'echo' in the French press that she had quietly been allowed to proceed elsewhere. Her true destination was not to be divulged. The President's chief press aide should not be informed of the details of the case, so that he could truthfully say, if asked, that the defection had not been discussed at the Cabinet meeting. But, to guard against a campaign in favour of the defector being mounted by do-gooders, human-righters and other cranks, she should be hustled out of the country as soon and as secretly as possible.

The object of all this unusual activity, meanwhile, was being smuggled out of the Hôpital Cochin in an ambulance, all blinds down. Forgeot was taking her home.

Once inside, he closed the shutters and drew the curtains, made a mental note to call in some scanners to ensure that his apartment was not being bugged, undressed and bathed May and took her to bed.

They moved like sleepwalkers. Forgeot tasted the bitter-sweet, nutty flavour of her skin, a dim reminder of another world. Her shyness was touching. Her cleft was small, almost hairless, and as he covered it with his hand she trembled, convulsively, beads of sweat on her hairline. Then she moved her head from side to side, mouth open, eyes closed, her back arched. She was warm and moist. There was no fumbling. He was hardly aware of entering her. He held her to him and smiled, stroking her cheek, her hair, and she clung to him, sobbing quietly, saying, over and over again: Joe, Joe. For Joe. He kissed her ear, her mouth, and, still inside her held her and turned so that she sat astride him, and she moaned and bent down, kissing him and thrusting her tongue in his ear, saying: It's so good. So deep. I don't want it to stop. Ever. And later, as she nuzzled against him, her head on his shoulder ('am I too heavy?'), she whispered: 'I don't want to talk about the past. Please don't make me.' And Forgeot said: 'You must. It's part of the deal I'm forced to make. Nothing personal. I don't want to force you. It's got to be of your own free will.'

'What is free will?'

It's something invented by the bloody Protestants, Forgeot was on the point of saying, it's all part of the the Judaeo-Christian ethic that's turned us into the hypocrites and puritans we are, making us do the things we least want to do. Instead, he said: 'It's nothing. Sleep. I'll think of a way out,' knowing that something unexpected and irrevocable and almost unbelievable had taken place, that his job, his career, his loyalties now took second place to the quietly breathing, small, smooth-skinned body in his arms. He watched her as she slept.

There is a certain time of year, after Easter but before June, when Saint-Tropez becomes, for a short period, the paradise on earth it once was. The nightclubs are closed, and the tourists, those August Mongol hordes, are only last year's bad memory. There is room to park on the Rue du Général Allard, the panhandlers and the drug addicts are still in Nepal or Afghanistan, and the waitresses at Sennequier on the waterfront are civilised human beings, and not the overworked harridans they later become. The cafés and restaurants still open cater to the locals, not to foreigners, and the open-air market on the Place des Lices is not yet a German and Scandinavian preserve. Georges Bain, the Café des Arts owner, has time to grumble about his latest tax audit, and threaten, as he does every year, to pull up stakes and retire to Corsica.

Years before, Forgeot had bought a tumbledown fisherman's cottage in a neglected part of Saint-Tropez called 'la glaye' which, in local dialect, means 'the rubbish dump'. It had been a rickety four-storey affair with rooms as small as cupboards, badly damaged by neglect and the sea salt from the 'mistral'. But it overlooked the sea and the only expanse of beach within the city limits, and had a spectular view: the harbour on the left, the tower and hill-top cemetery on the right. At the time 'la glaye' well deserved its name: an open sewer had flowed into the sea under Forgeot's very windows, the pebble beach below flecked with excrement. There had been flies everywhere and an overpowering stench of urine.

Forgeot's friend Battini had advised against buying. But, grumbling at the expense, he had rebuilt the house, torn out the partitions on all four floors, added two bathrooms, transformed the unsafe balcony into a modest-sized terrace. The mayor, coincidentally responding to a public outcry against local neglect of 'la glaye', had ordered the beach cleaned up: an underground sewer had been dug. The 'la glaye' houses were now part of the privileged, unchanging Saint-Tropez landscape, as secure against developers as any National Trust houses. It had all been a minor miracle: Forgeot hadn't even had to use his influence for all this to happen. And values at 'la glaye' had risen so spectacularly that Forgeot had sold off the two lower floors, and with the spare cash not only paid off Battini's building fees but bought himself a 33-foot Dufour yacht into the bargain.

It was here that May's debriefing began. Forgeot knew he had already broken all the rules. But since he was the only really fluent Chinese speaker within the DST he held most of the cards – the trump one being the loyalty of his staff. He was assured of their protection, even if, in private, they disapproved. Forgeot's folly, they called the girl. They were right: no woman had ever caused him to behave like this before, not even Linh, lissom, heavenly Linh, who came from a long line of Dalat 'notables', all of whom had eyed him with such disapproval, back in his old Indochina days.

Smuggling May out of Paris had been like running the gauntlet of all the husbands he had ever dealt with. He had been reluctant to leave her alone in his apartment, but had gone on a brief shopping expedition at the local Prisunic: jeans, sneakers, a windbreaker. The rest she would find in Saint-Tropez. They had left at dusk by the service door, May wildly giggling but running trippingly in her new shoes, clutching an airline bag, her only luggage, scrambling together in and out of taxis, laying a complicated fugitives' trail: Neuilly to the Bastille by taxi, them a quick dash down the Métro steps, changing trains no less than three times, emerging at the Gare de Lyon just in time to board the first-class Wagons-Lits sleeping compartment he had reserved under the name of 'Monsieur et Madame Méderic'.

And within moments of the Train Bleu leaving the station, blinds down, out of breath, they had made love: first on the upper bunk, then on the lower, then with May astride him, cradling him, finally falling asleep in each other's arms, the train going thumpety-thump.

Forgeot couldn't believe it: he was amazed by her inventiveness, her unashamed enjoyment of sex. 'I came so many times,' she said in his ear, in their compartment. Was there a Chinese word for orgasm? Indeed there was, said May, and told him. It was as though she were trying to remove the very memory of her former repressive, puritanical environment. He was equally amazed by his own continued physical desire, his constant fascination with her. She was so quick to respond to everything. Her enjoyment included the sunrise near Saint-Raphael, the sheer spectacle of the cypresses and olive-trees of Provence as they flashed by, French everyday life, sights and sounds, the good-natured complicity of the Wagons-Lits attendant who took them for runaway lovers, the garrulous taxi-driver who insisted on treating them to coffee in Sainte-Maxime.

Another thing that amazed Forgeot was her poise and self-confidence. At Choses, the only waterfront store open at this time of year, she had tried on this and that with the chic instinct of the true Parisienne. Forgeot had been dragged to dress shops by girlfriends before: it had always been torture. Not this time. 'She knows what she wants, your friend does,' said the attendant at Choses, with approval. 'Do I know her? Is she an actress?' And Forgeot, who had been in the store many, many times, always with spectacularly attractive girls, knew that even the jaded Tropézienne salesgirl was impressed. He said: 'I don't think so. She's a very well-known model – in Hong Kong.' May, at the time, was in the minuscule changing-room booth, its curtains imperfectly closed, and she said, in Chinese, to Forgeot's delight: 'Forgeot, do you know what it says on the label? Made in China! Would you believe it?' And Forgeot, secure in the privacy of their common bond, said: 'Now you know what Chiang Ching wears when she's at home' – And May said something startlingly obscene, still in Chinese, about her erstwhile leader's wife.

In tight white jeans and dark silk T-shirt, she was entrancing, even disguised by huge Mickey Mouse dark glasses and a headscarf. People turned and stared as they walked back to Forgeot's house.

At noon the sun was strong enough for them to sunbathe

nude on the terrace. She had no shame. Overnight, she had become not only sexually awakened but almost hoydenish. Trying on a bikini, making tea, trying to decypher *Nice-Matin, Elle, Vogue* and *Paris-Match*, she was a constant delight. He took her out on his boat, and after a brief moment of panic – she had never been anywhere near the sea before – she had responded with extraordinary, innate athletic skill to his simple commands. It was on one of those days, quite unseasonal in its perfection, that Forgeot realized that he wanted her – not just for a brief passionate affair, but for good. They sailed to Porquerolles and back, a whole two days and she acquired an all-over tan that gave her an added, perfect gloss. Her questions were never naive, her mind that of a determined, questioning, sophisticated young woman. She asked him astonishingly frank questions about his own life, his work. She had found lipstick, hairpins, perfume in his bathroom, silently collected them in a plastic bag and thrown them out. 'Why aren't you married?' she asked him. 'I was once,' said Forgeot. He expected her to ask the usual question: what was she like? Instead, she put her arms round him from behind, and said: 'She doesn't know what she's missing.' He attempted any number of debriefing sessions, but they seldom got very far: sooner or later, they both broke out in peals of hysterical laughter, ending up on Forgeot's oversize bed. Time was so short. 'I want to learn to sail your boat,' May had said – and after a hard day's sailing, how could he possibly start writing notes on Cypher Officer Wong, former Third Secretary and BPD member? She didn't help, either: she clowned around, superbly mimicking Chinese villains in traditional Peking Opera, or an embarrassed cadre under questioning: me no lemembah. My spillit all confused. There was nothing contrived about her evasions. 'Forgeot,' she said 'I have to catch up on twenty-three years of my life. There'll be lots of times to talk about the past. Say there'll be time? Say it?' And Forgeot, knowing that at best he would have to leave the DST, and at worst might face more serious problems still, said: We'll have time all right. But I suppose you realise we'll be poor?' It was the nearest he could bring himself to say what was really on his mind. And May said: 'I'll work. It says here top *Vogue* models make a thousand dollars a day. Do you think I'm good enough?' And Forgeot, moved but wanting to appear gruff, said: 'I don't like my Chinese concubines to work.'

Another time they began a serious session, and she reached out and put her hand on his crotch. 'As our Chairman puts it so well,' she said, 'big things come from small.' 'He didn't mean it that way,' said Forgeot, but May, holding him tighter, said: 'If he had, think of the lives that would have been saved.'

The one time they did have a more or less uninterrupted session was when she gave him a lengthy account of her early life in the Chinese Young Communists League, and in the Foreign Languages Institute in Peking. 'I had four alternatives,' said May. It was dark. The weather was changing. Forgeot had lit a fire. 'I could join our foreign publishing house. It deals with all our export literature. *China Reconstructs* in thirty-five languages. You must have seen it. It's all under the supervision of the Information Service, but not part of the Foreign Ministry.

'Then there was the possibility of working for the Foreign Trade Companies. You must know about them, too. Negotiating with foreign buyers at the various trade fairs, interpreting, translating sales literature. I could have done this, but someone,' she pulled a demure face, then a caricature vamp's leer, 'said I was unsuitable because I – I didn't look ordinary enough. A teacher said foreign businessmen would be,' she thought for a suitable word, 'perturbed. Also I was told they would try and corrupt me.

'Then there was Luxingshe, the Tourism and Travel Bureau. As you know, Forgeot, being yourself a counter-revolutionary spy, it's riddled with police, informers, people like that. And it's not very sought after among Institute graduates, because the top twenty-five per cent are picked for other jobs, so Luxingshe gets what's left, including the duds. These were the days, remember, when grades still counted for something, before the Cultural Revolution.

'That left the Foreign Ministry. There is still a great deal of Party and family influence in our society. You know that too. My great-uncle pulled a few strings. You remember who he was. It was one of the last things he was able to do before he was struck down by Mao and the Red Guards. My grades were good. So I went to the Institute of Political Law. Then I was told that I could join the Foreign Ministry, but only if I specialized in coding and decoding. It was either that or no hope of a foreign posting.'

The phone rang. It was Leguerrec, Forgeot's assistant.

'Briefings going all right?' Leguerrec's tone implied disapproval.

'We're in the middle of one now.'

'I can guess.'

'Leguerrec,' said Forgeot, 'you can keep your comments to yourself.' The voice at the other end said, quietly: 'They're not very pleased. They want you back in Paris.'

'They know I'm here?'

'I didn't tell them. No one from our section did.'

Forgeot knew Leguerrec well enough to be able to ask him: 'Am I in the shit?'

Leguerrec said: 'I don't know. The Minister is on your side. But the Quai is furious.'

'Tell them,' said Forgeot, 'that I'll be back on Monday.'

May had heard most of the conversation. For the first time since Orly, she looked slightly haggard. Forgeot drew her to him. 'Listen,' he said. 'I've been in different tough spots before. Sometimes in wars. Sometimes in dirty little operations that didn't make any sense. Sometimes through my own sheer stupid self. But just now, I wouldn't change places with anyone.'

And May laughed and laughed, Forgeot knowing that she was reacting out of sheer nervous tension and relief, laughing as a Westerner might cry. 'Whatever happens,' he said, 'I won't allow them to hurt you. In my own way, I've taken the same kind of step you took when you passed that first note.'

'Please help me?' said May. 'Was that it?'

There was a distant thunderous rumble, and the faint zig-zag trace of lightning through the thick evening clouds. Forgeot could hear the first of the heavy raindrops, pitter-patter on his red-tiled roof. 'Storms are usual at this time of year,' said Forgeot, but she shivered just the same, and that night, waking from a dream, she clung to him, sobbing, all her poise and composure gone, repeating, over and over again: please help me, help me, help me.

Chapter Four

THEY RETURNED to Paris by train, and Forgeot, simply out of habit, took the same roundabout way home. May realised her confinement in his apartment was necessary, at least for a while. 'It sounds silly,' she said. 'But I want to be a tourist, with Forgeot as a very, very experienced guide.'

'First,' said Forgeot, 'you must try and remember everything you can about the cypher school – and the various coding procedures. It's my bread and butter. And it's our only chance of proving how valuable a catch you are.' He kissed her. The telephone rang. 'The Minister wishes to see you.'

'Go to work,' said Forgeot. 'And whatever you do, don't answer the phone. Or open the door. Trust me.'

The Minister was seated in his main office overlooking the inner courtyard with his back to a huge window, making it difficult for visitors to focus their gaze on him without being blinded by the light. His two Dobermans rose from under the Louis XV desk, sniffed the visitor briefly, and reclined at his feet again. Everything about his office, including the uncomfortable antique chairs, was designed to make his visitors feel ill at ease.

On this occasion, he was not alone. Forgeot didn't recognize the shabbily dressed man standing next to the Minister. And Forgeot knew all the members of the Minister's cabinet by sight.

'My dear fellow,' the Minister said, 'I must congratulate you on your remarkable operation at Orly. Most efficient. And I gather your catch is –' he looked down at some notes on his desk – 'quite important? Most unusual?'

Forgeot nodded.

'Excuse me.' The Minister leant over to the complicated wooden telephone console, the one linking cabinet ministers to all ministries on a direct line, and said, talking into the phone, 'I don't want to be disturbed. I am expecting a call soon.' He simultaneously pressed a red button on his desk.

More gadgetry, Forgeot thought. They're all the same. Forgeot had never seen him use it before.

His heart jumped. He must get out of here, find her a really secure hiding-place. *I was a fool to leave like that.*

'Oh, I know what you're thinking,' the Minister said, his plump, patrician features twisted in the semblance of a smile. 'You want to apologise for not giving me due warning of the operation.'

Forgeot was about to speak. The Minister waved a pudgy hand.

'No, no, I quite understand. The circumstances were special. You acted alone. The decision was yours. And in your shoes I would have made exactly the same choice, after our little talk. I must say I hardly expected such a quick reaction.

'But, unfortunately for us, the President has decided that there are more important considerations at stake. Such as the consequences of what is being construed as a most unfriendly act by our Chinese friends, at a time when long-term questions of political strategy tend to override any intelligence-gathering or security activities. Lémeric was most persuasive, I gather. So was our Ambassador in Peking. Very irate, he was.'

Forgeot tried to guard against any overt show of emotion. He stared fixedly at the Minister.

The phone rang. The Minister relaxed. For the first time since Forgeot entered the room, his voice was down to normal. 'I'm sorry,' he said, turning to Forgeot, and handing him the telephone, 'I didn't want to be the one to have to tell you this. Exceptionally, the President himself wants to talk to you directly.'

Forgeot took the phone. The shabbily dressed man moved away. Close to, Forgeot could see that he wore a shoulder holster.

'Forgeot.'

It was the strong, low, rasping voice, with just a hint of the Auvergne in it, familiar to millions of French people from countless television addresses.

'Monsieur le Président?'

'Forgeot, I have given instructions for the return of your defector to the Chinese.' The President may be dying,

61

Forgeot thought, but there's no hint of it in his voice.

'Forgeot?'

'Yes, Monsieur le Président.'

'I expect your full co-operation, as a loyal servant of the State. Even if you were to try to contravene my orders, the matter would be taken care of. Do I make myself clear?'

'Absolutely, Monsieur le Président.'

'And I should warn that any indiscretion on your part, any attempt to tip off the press, will lead to your instant dismissal, and other sanctions.'

'Naturally, Monsieur le Président.'

The voice sounded a little tired. But the President wasn't finished.

'And Forgeot?'

'Yes, Monsieur le Président.'

'Don't think this has been an easy decision to take.'

'I'm sure of that, Monsieur le Président. But may I say one word?'

There was a grunted assent.

'You're aware, Monsieur le Président, of the fate that awaits a defector who is handed back to the Peking authorities?'

'Unfortunately, Forgeot, humane considerations can't be allowed to intervene in this particular case. Bigger issues are at stake. As General de Gaulle used to say to me often: sometimes, one has to be hard.'

'Monsieur le Président?'

'Yes?' The voice now had an irritated edge to it.

'Monsieur le Président, how do we stand, in future, with other possible defectors? The word will get around. Don't you think you're providing the other side with undue advantage, at no cost to them?'

'Each case will continue to be decided on its merits. I hope that, thanks to your cooperation, the word will not get out. I have said all I had to say.'

Click. The President was off the line.

The significance of the armed creature next to the Minister now became apparent. He must be either from the Brigade Mondaine, Forgeot thought, or else possibly from the 'Brigade anti-gang' further down the road, at Number 127 Faubourg Saint-Honoré, But he was a little old for that.

'I thought,' the Minister said, 'that you would prefer not to be directly involved in this painful business. It also occurred to me that your identity had better not be disclosed to our Chinese friends, for obvious reasons. However, it was essential – you heard the President – that the transaction take place as soon as possible. There was a great deal of pressure on the President, from Lémeric, Menhir, and of course our ineffable Ambassador in Peking. They have been pestering him continuously.'

He nodded in the direction of the stranger. 'We decided, Monsieur Guillaume and I, that it might be wise to avoid too much contact with the Embassy officials. The assumption accordingly is that she simply changed her mind. A woman's privilege, no? And that she reported of her own free will to her own people. Let's say she had a change of heart. Monsieur Guillaume here has had some earlier experience in these matters, and I entrusted him with this little operation – exceptionally.'

The Minister smiled apologetically. 'After all, you have been rather naughty. And we had no means of knowing how you would react.'

Guillaume, real name Abecassis. Forgeot remembered now. He hadn't been in the regular polcie then. More a kind of pimp. A French colonel on the run during the Algerian war, an OAS leader called – was it Clément? – had been kidnapped in Frankfurt, driven back to France and conveniently 'discovered' by a police patrol in a parked car in a street near the Préfecture. The Guillaume squad had handled that one. A freelance job, Forgeot recalled, decided on against his advice, and exceptionally well paid.

The Interior Ministry computer had its ups and downs, but it could do a pretty good retrieval job. The pattern would be the same.

Guillaume was pulling a walkie-talkie out of his raincoat pocket. There was the usual crackling, then his casual question, almost whispered. 'All going to plan?'

A voice from outside, faint but audible. The speaker seemed out of breath. 'Not quite. Can't explain at the moment. Call you back in five minutes. Over and out.'

The Minister scratched the head of one of his Dobermans. Forgeot, ignoring Guillaume, said: 'I will, of course, submit my resignation in writing, as soon as this – gentleman – is through. I take it he's here to make sure I don't interfere. Charming of you to display such faith in your subordinates.'

The Minister rose, hands in pockets, and his huge bulk, even when concealed by a particularly expert tailor, became even more apparent. He really is a living caricature of himself, Forgeot thought, in an irrelevant aside. He and the President were almost the same size. France likes its leaders to be big men, in every sense of the word. But repeated doses of cortisone had made the President look even more bloated recently.

The Minister said: 'I shall refuse to accept it – at any rate for the time being. I have the very highest regard for your department, and for the way you run it. This is an unfortunate accident, a – what's the word? – *péripétie*. But admit we were justified in handling things our way. There was no certainty that you would co-operate. There was the possibility that your staff might – justifiably – baulk at reversing their recent action. We didn't want either you or them to make fools of yourselves – especially over an obscure defector. Now,' he beamed at both men, 'if you'll wait in the salon? I have some work to do.'

They sat in silence.

Forgeot rose suddenly. 'If it's all right with you,' he said, 'I'll be on my way.'

Guillaume got up too. 'Just a minute,' he said. He played with his walkie-talkie again. The crackle was worse, and he walked around the room, trying different angles. 'Okay? Okay?' No answer. 'Is it over yet? Please answer.'

The same voice came through, a little less rushed this time.

'It wasn't a piece of cake.'

Guillaume said slowly, stressing his words: 'Is she inside yet?'

'We've just made the delivery.'

'Why did it take so long?'

'Inspector Debure got hurt.'

'How?'

'The bitch didn't want to come quietly.'

'I can understand her.'

Forgeot said to Guillaume, a fraction too cordially: 'I'll leave you to report to the Minister. I hope you haven't wrecked my apartment. How on earth did you get in?'

Guillaume looked sly. 'We used Leplantier. Remember him?' Then, embarrassed: 'Tell me, why on earth did you make things so difficult for us, by taking her home? Surely it's against all the rules?'

Forgeot said: 'I wanted to amuse myself a little with her.'

Guillaume laughed: 'You were right to have fun while you could. She won't get very much of that where she's going.'

Forgeot delayed returning to his apartment for a long, long time, dreading what he expected to find there.

Conscious that he might be followed, he drove down the Avenue Georges V. The tourists outnumbered everyone else. A few hard-faced young women sat at the wheels of parked cars, or lolled seductively half-perched on the bonnets of their Renault 20s. They didn't seem to be attracting many takers.

The Chinese Embassy gates were sealed, as usual, and there was no sign of any unusual activity outside. Nor were there many lights on inside. All the windows were, as usual, heavily shuttered.

He could detect no trace of Guillaume's men in the vicinity. It was entirely possible that she was being held in another location. He ran through the various 'safe house' possibilities he knew about, dismissing them one by one. He phoned the Hôpital Cochin, and assured himself that she had not been returned to the special security ward.

He felt like an exposed agent in enemy territory – his own. There were so many wheels within wheels in post-Gaullist France, and some of them were known only to a few people. Guillaume was almost certainly a member of the Mondaine – but he could also be a capo mafioso in the 'Service d'Action Civique' (SAC), the Gaullist bullyboys who would do anything for their masters – provided there was money in it. The secret fund account of the President was of the order of twenty million dollars a year, strictly unaccountable. And the SAC would be able to use any number of places, known only to themselves, and not be found by frontier police, airlines and the like.

On impulse, he drove to Orly. Like an ordinary passenger, he made enquiries about flights to China. Any special planes arrived lately, or expected? The bored ground hostess at the information counter eyed him with loathing and unconcealed suspicion. Just another nut.

He toyed with the idea of driving to the military field at Villacoublay, using his top clearance pass. Not to try to prevent any departure, but simply to know. It hadn't been too easy for the Chinese to get her out of London. Was there no hope that, on the way, some other country might not intervene? There was only Karachi: and he couldn't see the joker in charge there doing anything without some kind of a go-ahead from his masters at the CIA. Anyway, there wasn't time, and the CIA hadn't so far shown much interest in her.

He considered the possibility of putting his whole staff to work to trace her whereabouts. But this, too, would dangerously confirm all Ministerial suspicions. He made a mental note to change his apartment.

Hours later, he returned there. Whoever had broken in had done so with consummate skill. The code buttons on the outside would have sprung the outdoor ground floor entrance, but not the apartment door, which had another complicated set of signals, locks and alarms. Nothing looked as if it had been tampered with. They must have had casts of keys and the whole code for some time, Forgeot thought. What a fool I was. Inside someone had obviously tried to repair the damage. There were faint traces of a struggle, nothing else. A long gash on one of the leather armchairs, a broken window, a couple of smashed ashtrays. She had been a strong, tough, self-willed, determined girl. There were a few drops of blood on the bed, and a few smears of blood on one of the doors. A hopeless mess. May gone, his own credibility affected, and her fate on arrival didn't bear thinking about. Except that he could think of nothing else.

He sat at his desk, a glass of neat whisky by his side. Somehow, try and salvage something. Count one's friends. Have a plan. Hope against hope for some kind of exchange material coming into one's hands. But from where? He recalled Albert's first account of her first appearance: please help me. They had helped, all right. And at the back of his mind, thinking of the Minister, the President, Lémeric, Guillaume, Menhir, the self-satisfied diplomats who had provided the more detailed arrangements, the recurring thought: with swine like these, we don't deserve to win.

The flight plan for the Transall was an unusual one: it wasn't often that a French air force transport plane was asked to fly to Tirana on official business. This was by special authorisation of the President, no questions asked, no flight plan relayed to any civilians, destination officially Milan. No cargo, either: just a stretcher with a body on it and three one-way passengers.

'But don't you concern yourself with that,' the French colonel in charge of GLAM, the 'groupe des liaisons aériennes ministérielles', told the pilot. 'You stay at the airport. You don't even get out of the plane. You don't look. You don't see. You don't refuel. You'll do that in Milan, on the return journey.'

But the pilot, that night, at Villacoublay field, did see what looked like a stretcher being loaded on to the plane, followed by two small figures, possibly Chinese, and a third, much taller. He stored the event away in his mind. He kept his mouth shut. A 10,000-franc bonus, in the shape of a cheque on a Crédit Lyonnais account signed by an illegible squibble, sent by the Presidential aide, who administered the secret fund, helped him stay that way.

The convoy – three Zis limousines and a jeep – didn't bother to stop at the roadblocks on the road from Tirana to Durres. Albania doesn't have a formal curfew, but people go to bed by ten, and since there are almost no private cars the countryside was deserted. Cabbage fields and wooden shacks: Feng could make out little more. Not unlike a rural road in his own native Szechuan at this time of night.

The leading jeep dipped its lights. Forewarned, a soldier scuttled out to pull back the barbed wire fence. The girl was next to him. It was difficult to make out whether she had recovered consciousness or not. She was gagged. Her hands and feet were tied. There was still blood on her face, and traces of vomit on her shirt.

It had been so simple: a phone call to the operator in the Embassy, in French. 'Looking for someone? Come and get her. She's in a black Citroën outside the American Cathedral, up the road.' The car had glided down the side-alley, and the girl been bundled out. The heavy door, wooden on the outside, steel on the inside, had swung open for a few seconds as she was carried in. No one spoke. One of the Frenchmen had handed Feng a letter. It informed the Chinese Ambassador that a French military aircraft, cleared for Tirana, would be waiting to take off from Villacoublay that night. A single car should show up at the main entrance. A map was appended. The letter was to be destroyed.

Feng had raised his counterpart in Tirana on the Embassy radio. It had helped that the BPD chief there was known to him. He had taken on himself not to inform the Ambassador until the girl was safely aboard the plane. To prove that the Chinese were not over-concerned about what had happened at Orly, the Chinese Ambassador had chosen that evening to accept a dinner invitation from a former French Prime Minister and prominent Gaullist politician. Showing the flag, he called it. Just as well: the old buffer would only have complicated matters. To get into the act, and earn points with Peking, he might even have wanted to delay proceedings, insisting on a preliminary interrogation himself. Luckily, as head of BPD in Western Europe, Feng had considerable autonomy.

Feng didn't blame his Tirana counterpart for making a snap decision not to use a commercial airline again. There had been enough trouble at airports already. To get her out by air from Tirana would have been complicated: a flight to Belgrade, a stop-over in Geneva. Two more airports. What if, after all, the French were simply pretending to co-operate, while quietly urging other intelligence services to act in turn? The Yugoslavs were unlikely to do anything to endanger Chinese relations, though they were somewhat unpredictable. But the Swiss, the neutral, legalistic Swiss? And, given the bad state of Soviet-Chinese relations, a train ride from Moscow all the way to China, fourteen days more, was out of the question. The girl couldn't be kept under sedation all that time and still be expected to live.

Not for the first time, Feng regretted China's primitive infrastructure. The earliest Chinese Peoples Republic air link to Europe was still, he knew, at least a year away. In America, if this sort of thing had happened, there would have been a US Air Force C-130 available within minutes.

The old man's obsession with self-reliance was all very well, Feng thought, but we really should get ourselves a real air force soon.

So, by elimination process, the BPD man in Tirana had hit on the Greek freighter solution. Not as crazy as it first appeared. The Greek captain of this ship had made the Tirana-Shanghai run before, and had said that refuelling in Singapore was no problem. He agreed to take four passengers, after a handsome dollar cash payment had been made. He would not talk. Those dollars were not destined for his owners. The cost was barely more than four combined air fares.

The question was: should Feng board the freighter and travel with her all the way?

Not if he wished to look good. The trip would take at least three weeks. The correct solution was to write a full report which would leave by special courier and arrive in Peking before the girl. That way, Feng could stress his own role in her recovery. The fact that the French had handed her back on a plate, as it were, must be minimised. It was a perfect opportunity to come to the attention of the Internal Security Minister.

It could mean lightning promotion: Feng knew that the Minister himself owed his meteoric rise through the Ministry ranks to services rendered to Chou En Lai during the Cultural Revolution: then, this obscure archivist-librarian, a desk man with practically no field experience and nothing remarkable about him except his large size and his vague links with Chairman Mao (they both came from Hunan Province), had put Chou firmly in his debt by transferring on micro-film all of China's sensitive government records, including the personal dossiers of tens of thousands of Communist party bigwigs and summaries of secret meetings, storing them in a vault where they had been safe from the destructive rage of the Red Guards. Surely, in his own way, Feng was also contributing to the security of the mother-land? Who in Peking was to know that the recovery of the girl had occurred solely through French goodwill?

The convoy swung into Durres. Feng had made up his mind. The girl would board the freighter with the escort from Tirana. He would return to Paris and start writing the most important report of his career, with an 'eyes only' appendix to the Internal Security Minister. Taking it out of his pocket, Feng fingered the letter from the French Interior Ministry, signed by the Minister himself, which the French had told him to destroy. This he would keep. It might come in handy later on.

The easy way for Forgeot was to pretend that nothing had happened. That there had been no Orly incident, no week in Saint-Tropez, no session with the Minister, no raid on his apartment. He was helped by the mute consideration of others: as with a spectacular cuckolding, people refrained from alluding to it to his face. This round had gone against him. It happened all the time. No sense in rubbing it in. He was still, officially at least, a department head and from their point of view, perhaps, salvageable.

There remained the grey zones: at first he could think only in terms of individuals. The sinister Guillaume, and his SAC connection; the manner of her hi-jacking, the responsibilities of those most immediately involved: Lémeric, Menhir, the French Ambassador in Peking. No one must suspect the depth of his rage.

The week after his return from Saint-Tropez, he had picked up Malcolm Lowry's *Under the Volcano* in the early dawn hours, to read again, a possible weapon against insomnia. He got as far as Chapter II, 'A corpse shall be transported by express', and was shaken by dry, silent sobs.

The subject came up only once, and indirectly at that: Leguerrec said, with some bitterness, that the DST no longer appeared to have a credible mandate since a Presidential whim could result in such a destructive blow against the service as a whole. And Forgeot, blandly concealing his feelings, had said: not so. There were always imponderables. Theirs was an unsatisfactory calling at best. One shouldn't try and judge everything. The 'big picture' invariably escaped them. Doubtless the President had had good reason to act as he had.

The late President: the man responsible for May's return was no more. Divine justice? In any case, it had been a painful and undignified end. First that disastrous trip to the Crimea to meet Brezhnev. The President had insisted on keeping the appointment in an effort to show the world he was not as ill as was rumoured.

Reporters had accompanied the President in large numbers simply to take a close look at him since they no longer often saw him at close quarters on his home ground. In the same way ghouls had attended every one of Edith Piaf's stage performances shortly before her death, hoping to witness her ultimate collapse on stage.

In the Crimea – Forgeot knew this from his own contacts – the President had spent most of his time squatting on a lavatory seat in his dacha, haemorrhaging through the rectum. Then he had struggled through a short press statement, obviously fighting severe pain. The end had come soon after that, and it had been ghastly.

The President had insisted on spending what turned out to be his last weekend in the country, in his house west of Paris, about an hour's drive away. On Monday, when the pain had become unendurable, he had begged to return to Paris to die in his familiar apartment there, and begun crying like a child. His aides, subservient to his every whim, but incompetent in this as in other matters, had made no real contingency plans: back in Paris, there were grotesque scenes as they tried to squeeze him into the lift, then, when he protested with screams of pain, they had carried him upstairs on a stretcher, bumping him at every turn, nearly dropping him at least once. An aide had been sent to buy morphine, only to discover that, in that part of Paris, all pharmacies were closed on Mondays.

And, just as the whole of France seemed to go into shock at the news of the President's death (to ordinary people, unaware of the extent of his illness, it had been totally unexpected), so Forgeot began emerging from his own, almost catatonic state, made worse by the need for its total concealment.

He would not resign. He would – on the contrary – behave with exemplary cynicism. He would exploit his many contacts to the hilt. He would use his modicum of power, his specialized knowledge, for a single purpose. Others behaved that way for greed, advancement. He would do so not just to get even, though this was a part of his rage, but to get her back.

It would mean a savage betrayal of the principles he had once taken for granted. He had fought dirty in the past for abstract concepts: grandeur, independence, an imperfect but on the whole acceptable political system, in its time a tricolor flag halfway round the world. Now he no longer cared. He had crossed a line, or rather, they had crossed it for him. It was only justice that they should get hurt. There was no limit to the number of people who might get hurt.

Imperceptibly, dimly perceiving his game plan, and its enormity, he felt, along with the numbness, the guilt at her betrayal, a small but growing sense of elation: it could be done. He didn't quite know how. Individuals *could* influence history. The odds were against him: you poor booby, he thought, you're taking on the whole world. With the resolve came a kind of peace. For the first time since she had gone, he slept soundly that night.

Chapter Five

THE PRESIDENT was dead, and all the ministries, including Forgeot's own, were in a state of suspended animation. The Presidential campaign took up all the Cabinet's time. Forgeot's case, suddenly, had become past history – a minor entry in his dossier, certainly no longer a major scandal.

Some of the ministers belatedly realised, as the campaign gathered momentum, that their future might not be all that bright, under a new President. This was particularly true of the Foreign Minister, who dreaded a court case involving Mlle Duval, which might bring the Quai, and perforce the little man himself, into disrepute. His only real power base, he realised, had been his own personal bond with the dead President.

Once openly hostile, the Foreign Minister turned his considerable charm on Forgeot. 'Minister,' Forgeot told the little man, 'I'll do whatever I can.'

Mlle Duval might as well be squeezed for whatever she was worth. Forgeot had a long session with her. She was not under arrest, or even charged, though she had surrendered her passport. She was composed enough when Forgeot assured her that he could not guarantee that there would be no trial, even though it might take place in camera: some of the evidence was sexually explicit enough to invoke that rule under French law.

'And under certain circumstances,' Forgeot told her, 'a trial might prove unnecessary. For that, I need your special co-operation.'

He glanced at his notes. 'You have been at the Quai now for – what is it – eighteen years? I want you to sit down and write a full report on everything that ever came your way. What I really want –' for Mlle Duval had become flustered, fingering her battered Chanel bag – 'is a complete catalogue of all the dirty little secrets you must have accumulated since you began working at the Quai. Nothing's too insignificant. I want it all. Obviously, no one must know you are doing this. If anything gets out, I'll no longer be able to protect you – and I'll of course deny this meeting ever took place.'

'How soon do you want it?'

'The sooner the better.'

'Is it a deal? Will I get off scot-free?'

'That will depend on your report.'

They made no attempt to shake hands. She said: 'It's a pleasure doing business with you, Monsieur Forgeot.' A tough old girl. And a bright one. He got the impression she well knew what he was after.

And, when he did get the report, Forgeot almost became his old self again – to such an extent that his secretary thought he must have a new mistress. 'I saw him on the Boulevard Haussmann twice this week,' she told his office. 'He didn't see me. He had said he was working at home and didn't want to be disturbed.'

Forgeot had disappeared, she said, into one of those huge nineteenth-century stone buildings, all plush red carpets and hallway mirrors, which do their best to protect the anonymity of their occupants by providing no information in the lobby, and no visible concierges. She had had a look. It was right next door to Lazarian Frères, the well-known antique dealers. 'Whoever she is,' she said, 'she's doing all right.'

Lazarian Frères is the best-known, most expensive Oriental antique shop in Paris, more museum than store. Its window displays scarcely vary from year to year: a Korean war chest, a huge 'Six Dynasties' celadon jar and a horseman of the Northern Wei period, next to some Japanese furniture so scrubbed, pale and delicate that it looks as if it is made of paper. One of the brothers lives above the shop, in an apartment far richer even, in its contents, than the downstairs showroom. Upstairs is where most of the major deals are done.

Lémeric's Rue de Varenne apartment was also filled with Oriental art, of the kind an intelligent collector accumulates over years of service in Pnom Penh, Djakarta and India. In India most diplomats collect things if only for something to do. Moghul ivory paintings of dubious authenticity, even nineteenth-century Indian Army campaign medals, hoarded from generation to generation in Sikh villages and then sold for dowries to middlemen in Delhi: some of them are worth hundreds of pounds each, as the middlemen now know, thanks to their much-thumbed Spink's catalogues.

Lémeric was no exception. Forgeot had seen his collection: it was pleasing but contained nothing of real value. Some wooden carvings from broken-up Hindu temple chariots from Kerala, judiciously lit by small spotlights; a few good naive Indonesian paintings. But if Mlle Duval was to be believed, Lémeric had, over two years, removed from India, under the cover of the diplomatic bag, a huge assortment of far more valuable items. She had been in charge of the diplomatic bag traffic at the time, and had a good memory, even if she had no written records.

Putting together an estimate of Lémeric's Asian purchases had been the equivalent of a crash course in Oriental art history. There had been unglazed ceramics from the Indus Valley, 3000 to 1500 BC. And not only ceramics: seals, copper tools, at least one stone torso from the same period, damaged but invaluable.

There had also been small fragments of bas-reliefs from Gandhara, increasingly prized by dealers and collectors, one outstanding Nalanda ninth-century begging Buddha, in perfect condition, and even a few examples of Assamese art, including an eleventh-century dancing-girl, and a rare 'Vishnu with elephant'.

What they all had in common was that, with the possible exception of the Indus Valley seals, which even tourists sometimes come across in India, they had all been museum pieces. Which had prompted Forgeot to make further enquiries, with his Delhi counterpart. The reply had been revealing.

Renewing contact with his past SDECE fieldwork, Forgeot had invented himself a perfectly adequate British cover. He had first toyed with the idea of masquerading as a go-between for a wealthy San Francisco collector who – for tax reasons – did not want to be identified. Too risky: the art world is full of gossipy experts who know every single San Francisco collector, however discreet.

So he had decided to be British: Albert Spurling, claims adjuster, with a London-based office, a firm working for a group of British insurance companies, but this time acting on behalf of the Government of India.

The real Albert, in London, who had been well briefed, and had done this sort of thing for Forgeot before, had responded beautifully to Lazarian's telephone call: just the right mixture of arrogance and suspicion. Yes, we do have a Mr Spurling. He is in Paris, at the moment, actually. Lazarian, you say. Hasn't he contacted you? He was supposed to. No, we haven't dealt with the Indian High Commission in London, or any of the Embassies. The Indian Government felt we should handle this directly, embarrassing to involve diplomats in what might turn out to be a criminal case, I'm sure you understand. It's not something we like to discuss on the phone. However, if you wish to write? Or better still, talk to Mr Spurling. If you feel, that is, that you can help us in any way?

It had been, at first, a mere guess on Forgeot's part. Of course Lazarian Frères were the people to handle Lémeric's booty. They had made a reputation for themselves in the late fifties, disposing of some rather extraordinary items of Indonesian and Khmer art. Also from Lémeric? The dates of his postings coincided.

Forgeot's CID contact in India had confirmed, in precise officialese to put British civil servant jargon to shame, that there had indeed been an investigation into thefts from inventories of Indian museums. In fact it was still going on. Very few of the missing items had been photographed, making positive identification difficult. Nevertheless, a catalogue of missing art was being prepared. In due course it would be sent to Interpol, the FBI, and the American Missing Treasures Bureau in New York. The losses were serious. Some curators were already under arrest. Others had left the country.

Forgeot took a chance and telephoned New Delhi, rousing his Indian friend in the middle of the night.

'Don't say you've recovered our treasures,' he said.

'I have a hunch I know where some of them went,' said Forgeot. 'Look, why don't you put the whole thing on an official basis – without saying I advised it, of course? Put us on the list as well as Interpol and the rest. The middleman may well have been in Paris – and he was probably innocent.

We have a very good guy at the Ministry in charge of stolen art: his predecessor tended to look the other way, but this one's very, very keen to make an impact.'

This was after he had talked to Lazarian Senior, a wizened old man in clothes so immaculate that he appeared to have stepped out of a box lined with cotton-wool. Lazarian had admitted, between cups of China tea, that some at least of the items Mr Spurling referred to had passed through his hands. Where they were now he was unable to say. 'I only provide certificates of authenticity,' he said. 'How could I possibly imagine that the private collection of a French diplomat, whose distinguished forebears had spent so many years in the East, could consist of stolen art?'

The beauty of the situation, in Forgeot's eyes, was that he could simply let events take their course. The Indian Government request for enquiries at the French end would land on the desk of Lucien Menhir, head of the Asian Affairs section at the Quai. If Menhir took his job seriously, he must, sooner or later, implicate Lémeric, and get the stolen art section of the Interior Ministry on to his track. This would mean unearthing records, and looking into the whole diplomatic bag set-up. Would Menhir attempt to protect Rossignol? Forgeot thought not. When something like this occurred, at the Quai, it was every man for himself.

Forgeot got further proof of his rehabilitation: Lémeric invited him to lunch at the Travellers Club, that bastion of bankers and diplomats, the only private house left on the Champs-Elysées, and the only place where rich captains of industry can play backgammon for high stakes until late into the afternoon while their secretaries say they are in conference.

Most of the time had been spent talking about Watergate. Inconceivable in any other country, they had both agreed. Why, under de Gaulle, hardly a week had gone by without some kind of plumbers' job, somewhere. 'Less so now,' Forgeot got Lémeric to admit. 'All three Presidential candidates have had their phones tapped – and I don't think they enjoyed the experience.'

'Not by me,' said Forgeot, and they both laughed.

Lémeric eventually came round to what, in Quai circles, was euphemistically referred to as 'the Chinese Orly affair'.

'My dear fellow,' he said, 'admit that you acted hastily. Whatever possessed you to – to get involved?'

'Oh, that? A short cut. A challenge. A mixture of curiosity and lust. I was never averse to Orientals. You know that.'

'You mean,' said Lémeric, 'you almost compromised your career to add to your collection?'

'Something like that.' Collection was an unfortunate word.

'You're even more of a bastard than I thought you were.' This in a friendly, almost affectionate tone.

'Am I?' said Forgeot. 'Were your motives any more honourable than mine? I mean,' Forgeot happily finished the last of his tinned crab, 'do you really believe in all that crap about French influence in Asia, or that one defector would make any difference to our relations with China? Or were you simply looking at the whole thing from the point of view of your own career?'

Lémeric smiled

'Now who's being cynical?' he said. 'Of course I was thinking of myself. Who cares about the damned girl? But didn't you behave even worse? You fucked her, not I. Literally as well as metaphorically.' That hurt. Forgeot pretended not to have heard.

They talked about Mlle Duval – and this, Forgeot concluded, along with Lémeric's reluctant admission that he had high hopes for promotion if the candidate he favoured won the Presidential election – was the real point of the lunch

'In the interests of Franco-Algerian relations, and to help the new President, whoever he may turn out to be, I'm recommending that we let her go,' Forgeot said. They parted with expressions of mutual esteem. 'For your sake,' said Forgeot, 'I hope your man makes it.' He did.

It was a start Mustn't push one's luck: Menhir had to be kept intact, for the time being. He was useful where he was. Impossible to use one's official connections to get access to the Guillaume-Abecassis file. He was only a small, vile cog, there were others far more guilty than he, but Forgeot had taken a violent dislike to him. Also, he might be dangerous, the next time around.

Theoretically, it was perfectly possible to scan the Guillaume dossier. But there was no way round a rigid Ministry rule, which, in the interests of all concerned, Forgeot had himself helped draft: anyone who did so had to express a valid reason, and records were kept of all who consulted it, with details of their requests. Computerisation had only made the system more fool-proof. Anything that might attract attention had to be avoided.

There were no obvious leads. There was no one, on the right side of the law, he could turn to. And, as far as the wrong side of the law was concerned, the whole French police system was based on the axiom that there was no honour among thieves.

He invented a couple of pretexts for come brief side-trips: a suspiciously zealous Czech consul in Marseilles, who spent far too much time in Fos-sur-Mer, chatting up unsuspecting technicians. But his underworld contacts had vanished. The heat was on: the chemists were scared stiff, the bankers were in Miami, any stranger was automatically assumed to be an undercover narcotics agent in search of the much-publicised and fast-vanishing French connection.

He spent a week sailing. Alone. He was mad to pick this time of the year to sail to Corsica, his colleagues remarked. It would be either rain or mistral, It was as they said, and as he had intended. His Dufour remained at its moorings in Calvi most of the time. Yet it wasn't all time wasted.

There is a small bar in Calvi, close enough to the Foreign Legion barracks for legionnaires to be carried back to their beds in comfort by their less drunken comrades. It wasn't the sort of place tourists went to much, except for lonely middle-aged Swedish women alcoholics in search of legionnaires. It was nowhere near the harbour. There were rooms upstairs, rented by the hour, and the girls were regularly inspected by a Foreign Legion doctor. They weren't communicative, or in the first bloom of youth – or even the second. Forgeot bought what he assumed to be the head barmaid a drink, and asked after the *patron*.

'Henri isn't here tonight.'

'I don't mean Henri. I mean the real *patron*.'

'You a cop?'

'Tell him "*l'intellectuel*" called, and would like a chat. Tell him it's been a long time since Hanoi.'

'Where can he reach you?'

It was Forgeot's turn to be coy.

'Tell him that, if he can see me, I'll be on the waterfront. Tomorrow, six p.m. The Taverne du Port.'

Rossi, a real pro, made it look like a chance meeting.

Abrazos, back-slapping. 'What the hell are you doing here? Christ, you look older. You were practically still a child when we got released.'

Forgeot asked about his leg. Was he okay? Did it hurt?

'Invalid, I am, eighty per cent disability', the brawn belying it all. Behind the girl's back, using a mixture of sign language and lipreading that had so infuriated their North Vietnamese jailers, Forgeot said: the black Dufour at slip 16, row E. Whenever you can. Alone. And Rossi, after insisting on paying for the drinks ('I haven't seen Monsieur in twenty years,' he told the barman, which was not true at all), took his leave, holding his companion's arm. He hadn't introduced her. She was several cuts above the bar inmates, and hadn't said a word, except 'good evening' and 'good night'. Forgeot presumed she was Corsican too.

The Mistral was still blowing hours later, pennants flapping, boats creaking and straining against their moorings, when Rossi came aboard. There is a myth among Corsican underworld figures that Chivas Regal is the only drinkable whisky simply because it's the most expensive on the market. Forgeot had a full bottle when he arrived. It was two-thirds empty when, almost at dawn, Rossi carefully limped ashore.

At least Guillaume and Rossi were not on the same side. Guillaume was in league with the North African returnees, the 'piednoirs', and enjoyed a major advantage: as a member of the Brigade Mondaine, he was supposed to control prostitution. What he did was to collect twice: from the girls he controlled, plus pay-offs from those he did not.

Business was becoming difficult, Rossi had said. Already, before Guillaume had made his presence felt, the girls had become harder to deal with, more demanding, more independent. 'And I'm not a monster, you know.' Guillaume was known to have powerful protectors, probably from his

SAC days. Wasn't he one of yours, once?

And there were nasty rumours about Guillaume: all the Mondaine boys got their freebies, when they fancied a particular girl. Nothing wrong with that, did them good. But Guillaume was a sadist: he liked to scare the girls, do things to them. Otherwise a smart cop. Lucky for Rossi that he had some of his money in hotels, shops, perfectly respectable cafés. Most of them in Corsica. What would I be doing on the continent? Then there was the farm. A vineyard near Saint-Florent. Terrific wine, a shame Parisians stuck to their *traffiqué* Beaujolais instead of drinking this stuff, which was a little heavy, perhaps, but unadulterated. Sure enough, the following day a crate of dark red wine was delivered to the boat. Forgeot drank most of it during a rather bumpy trip back to Saint-Tropez. It was surprisingly good.

Forgeot knew Rossi thought he was still with the SDECE. He had found out on his own, quite some time ago. The '*milieus*'s' information, like the Ministry's, Forgeot thought, was accurate but often out of date. Forgeot hadn't denied it then, and this time Rossi hadn't asked. His pale blue eyes had looked him over, with approval, assuming he was still up to his old tricks.

Towards the end of their talk, Forget had hinted that he might, if an emergency arose, require Rossi's help. Real help. Not to settle the Guillaume business. That would probably be taken care of anyway. But maybe a safe place for a bit, a '*planque*', no questions asked. Would that be possible?

And Rossi had said: 'I'm a patriot, you know. When we were in Indochina together, you were one of the best when times got rough, even though you were so young. When you want. Where you want. I have friends in many places. Just phone these numbers in Calvi and say: Victorine sent me.'

'Who's Victorine?'

Rossi laughed and laughed, slapped his thigh with his mutilated hand, and said: 'There isn't a Victorine. But I'll remember the name. You see, I nearly bought the Victorine Film Studios in Nice last year.'

When Forgeot rang the mumber in Paris that Rossi had given him, the girl called Valentine answered. Forgeot tried to sound like a timid French businessman consumed with sudden afternoon lust. The girl casually asked him how he had obtained her number, and Forgeot gave the name that Rossi had told him to give. She said: 'Very good. Come at four o'clock.'

It was one of those rabbit-warren buildings in the 17th *arrondissement*, mostly small one-room apartments for professional people, that seem to have been designed for call-girls: no concierge, no vis-à-vis, a quiet street, a place to park, and a buzzer on the door to identify callers.

She opened the door in a short, transparent négligé: young, demurely erotic, with a professional smile, but prettier than Forgeot had imagined, with an indefinable appeal, a fake little-girl innocence, but also a hint of humour, that his coming to see her was a big private joke. Rossi had said she took drugs from time to time but there was no trace of it. She stood on tip-toe, kissed him lingeringly on the lips. He tasted listerine, smelt the scrubbed, soapy aura of her, super-clean. She probably showered after each visitor. Her bathroom was damp with heat. She had a good body. Her portable radio was tuned in to France-Musique.

'It's your first time here, isn't it?'

Forgeot said it was.

'Relax. Come over here.'

She spread a sheet over the bed, slipped the nightgown over her head and began undressing him. She stroked him, kissed him, then squatted on her knees and expertly began fellating him. He lifted her up and on to the bed. He turned over, stroked her back, kissed her shoulders, the hollow in her back. There were tiny golden hairs above her rump. And, below, traces of a recent whipping.

Forgeot said: 'What's this? and the girl, frightened and annoyed, turned on her back, pulling him down over her, reaching for him impatiently.

She was very good. Rossi had said so.

Later, still entwined, she smoked a cigarette, fingered the back of his neck and said: 'You're sweet.'

Forgeot noticed the whore's trick of covertly looking at her watch. She probably had another customer soon. He said: 'Someone's been beating you. Do you let him do it for money?'

'It's none of your business.'

'Do you enjoy it? I know some girls who do.'

She shook her head. 'Are you crazy, like some of the others?' The little-girl erotic softness was gone. Suddenly, she looked more like a hard, middle-aged whore. Forgeot dressed quickly. He had the money ready.

'Listen,' he said. 'I really have come from friends. They said a man has been misbehaving. Taking advantage of his rank. Doing things to you. They said I might be able to help.'

'You can help me by leaving me alone.'

He decided to show a card or two.

'It's the Mondaine, isn't it? Stands to reason. They let you operate here. They've probably had you in for a little talk, then they started to come here, have it off one by one, right? And one of them – you may know him under the name of Guillaume or maybe under some other name – has become the pimp that you thought you would avoid by co-operating with them in the first place.'

'What's it to do with you?'

'My dear,' said Forgeot, 'I have far better reasons than you to get rid of this particular little monster.'

'How do I know it's not trap? He probably sent you. I don't want any more trouble.' She was close to tears. She had slipped on her nightgown, and looked scared and small.

Forgeot said: 'There is a number in Corsica you could call, if you want to know I'm on the level. But I don't want you to call from here. Or your apartment. Do it from a post office. I'd prefer you to take me on trust. If you feel you can cope with Guillaume, or whatever he calls himself, so much the better. But remember: people like that always need to escalate the pain.'

'He killed my dog.'

'And it'll go on and on. He whips you, doesn't he, beyond the point where you might reasonably enjoy it?'

She opened a cupboard. Chains, a dog-collar, handcuffs, dildoes, whips. Forgeot made a face, and a noise, signifying mild disapproval. 'There's a certain type of woman,' he went on, 'that's made for someone like Guillaume. But I don't quite see you as *Story of O* material. Let me guess: He doesn't call all that often. He'll not come by for weeks. When he does, it's usually on a Friday – and, if you're not there, you pay for it the next time. He invents reasons to humiliate you, and levies fines – for all sorts of futile reasons. And – forgive me for referring to something so personal – he invariably takes you from behind.'

'How do you know all this?'

'He doesn't want you to be compelled to stop your work. And he knows the marks will mostly have gone by Monday. As to the other thing, he was accused of raping a boy while in the Foreign Legion, but the victim couldn't be found to give evidence: Guillaume probably had him killed. It was in Algeria, during the war, anything was possible then. This was before he became a cop.'

'He says he could have me sent to work in a house in Abidjan. He says he has connections, and that the Interior Minister calls him in to do the really dirty jobs. It's true: he's told me things . . . I read about them later in the papers.'

Forgeot said: 'That part of it is true. But that doesn't mean he's above the law.'

She almost spat: all filth.

Forgeot said: 'I'm going to put a bug in your phone. Unhook the phone and it'll start recording somewhere else. When Guillaume comes to see you, you probably take the phone off the hook anyway, don't you? He can't like being interrupted. He probably gags you, doesn't he? That doesn't matter either: what's essential is that afterwards he's got to ask for money – or you have to mention the word. Say you can't pay him. Ask him to spread what you owe over a longer period. Anything that – on tape – would give a magistrate a *prima facie* case. Remember, they're more interested in money changing hands than in whips. Another thing: don't expect anything to happen immediately. It may take months. But if I were you,' he looked around at the knick-knacks, the giant panda doll, all the sad bric-à-brac of a call-girl's working locale, 'I'd get rid of anything breakable.'

Chapter Six

THE Dulles Memorial Conference Center is thirty-five miles from Washington DC but only a few miles from Langley, Va. a comfortable house in the middle of a large park, with bungalows, a swimming-pool, squash courts, stables, a sauna, a pathetic attempt at an English pub-style club-house, and a gift shop, permanently closed.

Generations of plainclothes police officers and security officials from all over the world had attended courses there, in the bygone years of *pax Americana*. Now, in the year 1975, foreign visitors were few and far between: Watergate had had its repercussions here too. Neither the CIA, nor the State Department, nor the US Embassies abroad were particularly eager to invite even the friendliest foreign guests. At all levels, there was a kind of tacit hibernation. The Watergate experience had been so searing in many ways, so demoralising for the CIA and other agencies, so fatal to their aims and goals, that there seemed no point in instructing others. In any case, all the foreigners who came to the Conference Center asked, sooner or later, why the United States had handed the Communists and their allies such a potent weapon. Rare French visitors, in particular, expressed amazement. Watergate practices were a common and accepted fact of life for them, and they could not understand why a President should be compelled to resign for what they considered to be mere peccadilloes.

The ex-State Department official who ran the Center in 1975 no longer had to cope with status-conscious Latin American police chiefs complaining their rooms were too small or too hot, or African colonels struggling with their laundry lists and their forgotten *lycée* English.

There were environmentalists, now in greater numbers than ever before, and lawyers. The spy and security circuit was no longer the box office attraction it had once been. From a logistical point of view, things were simpler thus. But the environmentalists and antipollution lawyers were also more tight-fisted: bar takings had dropped alarmingly.

The 1975 NATO conference for security and counter-espionage agencies was an occasion to recoup. France was not strictly involved, but Forgeot had obtained permission to attend, as an observer. His reasons were special. He had hoped to be out of the country when the 'Inspection Générale de la Police', the Interior Ministry watch dogs hit Guillaume, catching him, Forgeot hoped, literally with his pants down. There must be nothing to link him with that operation, which had been slow in gathering momentum, or with the other, equally leisurely, investigation into Lémeric's art dealings.

But his most important reason for being at the Center was that the meeting provided the excuse he needed to talk to Adrian Jute, who was bound to show up, as he did every year, going through his routine 'cold war' number which few of the Europeans present now took seriously.

Jute was one of the last of the pre-CIA, veteran OSS hands left. Parachuted into France during the war, he had been old man Dulles' liaison figure in Zurich after a narrow escape: a French double agent had betrayed him to the Germans. He had then, towards the end of the war, surfaced in Mountbatten's Ceylon Headquarters, and boarded an American submarine on the very day the Hiroshima A-bomb was dropped. He went ashore at Vung Tau, or Cap Saint-Jacques as it was still called, a few days before the war ended.

Jute had had even odder adventures in French Indochina than Forgeot himself: in his Georgetown home, tucked away on a grand piano, a Bechstein which Jute actually played, was an inscribed photograph in a silver frame. The donor had scrawled, in French, in a spindly, faded handwriting: 'To my good friend Jute, who helped save my life – September 1945.' There was no signature, but the portrait was, unmistakably, that of a younger, gaunter Ho Chi Minh. Jute never talked about his OSS days. Rumour had it that, among other things, he had extricated Ho Chi Minh from a particularly intricate French plot to murder him. Fanatical anti-Communist though Jute was, he hated the French – some French – even more. The photograph was half-hidden: Roosevelt, Eisenhower, both Dulleses, Morgenthau,

Ridgway, Jean Monnet, the Kennedys had pride of place, along with every CIA director of the last twenty years.

Jute, small, trim, with a neat, pointed beard and old-fashioned 'granny' glasses, still had the jaunty, almost boyish look of the typical Rhodes Scholar of the late 1940s, only the liver spots on the backs of his hands betraying his age. Jute had been a jogger long before the sport had become fashionable. He insisted that Forgeot jog too, even going to the extent of driving him to the nearest shopping centre in Langley to buy shorts and running shoes. He had had quite a hassle with the guards at the Center, because it had meant skipping the inaugural address.

It was not just a craving for companionship on early morning runs that prompted this. He had known Forgeot in unusual circumstances just after the end of World War Two, when Forgeot had been a mere schoolboy. He had even tried to recruit him once, failed and later apologised for doing so. Now, as they thudded along the asphalt two-lane roads around the Center, through forests and along the perfectly-kept lawns of affluent Agency men, he said: 'I don't think the Center is bugged, but you can never tell. These days, I don't even want to know.'

Jute's address to the conference was even gloomier than usual. He knew he was the appointed Cassandra, the in-house pessimist. He insisted that he was in deadly earnest, however, and not hamming it up because it was expected of him.

'I may be almost extinct,' he began, 'one of the last self-confessed, dyed-in-the-wool cold warriors still alive. I have no excuse. We're a dying species.' There was polite laughter.

'We don't really need a conference of this kind,' Jute went on, 'or even that expensive headquarters over in Langley, to make up our minds about the ultimate Soviet goals in Europe. All one needs is access to Soviet papers, magazines and specialized journals. What do they say, gentlemen, behind all the smokescreen they put out about détente? They admit that they are more than ever committed to an avowed goal of hegemony, or, as they prefer to put it, to the pursuit of tactical superiority – by means, of course, of the most ambitious arms build-up the world has ever seen.

'It's instructive, gentlemen, to look at what the Soviet

military leaders are telling their own staffs, and what occasionally gets into print, even in the Soviet Union, as opposed to what their diplomats are telling the world at large. What they admit, to each other, is that they are not only prepared to use chemical and biological, as well as nuclear, weapons in any future conflict, but also – and this, in my view, is more important still – that they are determined to make the first move. And all the while, of course, they are pressing for another step in the SALT talks.

'This determination to be first has the gospel approval of Lenin himself, who once said: we should set all bells a-ringing concerning the necessity for a bold offensive . . . attack and not defence should become the slogan of the masses. This leitmotiv has been repeated by all of the Soviet Union's strategists and military thinkers. Frunze, their leading contemporary military theorist, says: the victor will be the one who finds himself resolved to attack. The side with only defence is inevitably doomed to defeat. Others, like Colonel Sidorenko, Major-General Milovidov, and especially Colonel Kozlov, in his *Problems of Contemporary War*, have all made the same point – that pre-emption is the decisive condition of the attainment of superiority over the enemy. And that, of course, includes nuclear confrontation. How else are we to explain that the whole of the Soviet Navy is geared to a one-shot offensive, with no attention given to resupplies?'

Forgeot had heard some of this before. But this time there had been much creaking of chairs, and little positive response. Jute got bogged down, during question-time, over a semantic and irrelevant discussion on the difference between tactics and strategy. To newcomers, he was a figure from the remote past.

In private conversation with Forgeot afterwards, he revealed a mood even more sombre than the one he had publicly assumed.

They were jogging side by side. Forgeot, exhausted, deliberately put his questions in words of one syllable. 'You – really – think – things – are – that – bad?'

Jute appeared to be able to talk and run without discomfort.

He slowed up just a little. 'Jean,' he said, 'old man, they're worse. Why? Precisely because the Soviet Union's in such a hopeless mess. How long do they have, before their technology becomes so backward, compared to our own, that they'll never, ever, be able to catch up? Two years? Five years? Ten years? I used to think it might be more. Now I know we're on the brink of this realisation.'

'So what happens?'

'Let's stop, and I'll tell you.'

They sat with their backs to a massive oak. Jute mopped his brow with the ultimate jogger's status symbol, the terry-towel wristband. 'Let's face it, the Soviets already have nuclear superiority – both in the punch their missiles pack in relation to their size and in delivery range. But economically, the mess they're in is horrible. The gap between Party members and ordinary Soviet citizens is widening all the time. Even ordinary visitors, including Western Communists, are shocked. At the same time, Soviet expectations are rising. That's an explosive setting, even with a traditionally docile, passive population, which had always learnt to endure the Tsars, new and old.

'So put yourself in the Kremlin's shoes: what do they do about it? While there's still time, that is? They gamble on the belief that, with US leadership in tatters for a long time to come, we won't react. In other words, they can move into Western Europe, the US will let it happen, and when it's all over, there'll be no Western European countries to serve as a mirror-image for their own failures. The Western European régimes will become Finlandised, at best. Some people argue it's happening already. There'll be the usual band of third-force appeasers, and at worst a totalitarian brand of socialism. Big Brother will be there to prevent things getting out of hand. There'll be no European audience to put on a show for, as there was in Buda' in '56 and Prague in '68. And don't think we'll be unable to adapt to the new situation: we'll continue making deals, exporting our technology, making a buck where we can. In fact things would probably be easier for a weak US President if he only had to deal with one power-bloc.'

'Cossacks on the Champs-Elysées,' said Forgeot. 'I thought that notion went out for good in the early fifties – or was it 1815?'

89

'That's what all you Europeans say.'

'But surely the United States won't necessarily let it happen that way? The Kremlin, even if we accept your premise, might be making a costly error. What happens if, after all, the White House decides to press the button, taking out Minsk, or Tomsk, for starters? Do you think the Russians would take kindly to their rulers, after that? And what about our own deterrent? France can press the button too.'

'Don't make me laugh.'

'What you're saying, then, is that the West is doomed, and that there's nothing we can do about it. And if I were smart I'd sell my house and boat in Saint-Tropez and buy a Florida condominium, like so many Lebanese?'

'I didn't say that.' Jute retied his shoelaces. 'Don't put words in my mouth, as the French politicians are always saying. I outlined a state of affairs which many experts, myself included, believe to be realistic. But nothing's fatal in this world. There's any number of ways of ensuring that the other side is prevented from carrying out its ultimate goals. A higher common European defence resolve would be one way. Restoration of conscription, here and everywhere in Europe, would be another. A little muscle-flexing here and there, to prevent the Russians from having it their own way all over the Third World, would help too.'

They rose. Forgeot felt his calf muscles quivering. They must be hardening like cement. Impossible to give up, though, or give any sign of weakness in front of this frail, skinny man.

'And then,' said Jute, 'there are the dirty tricks. The Agency is dead set against them for the time being, but that mood will pass, like all moods. I don't mean dirty tricks of the conventional kind. I mean disinformation, the big con, but on a world scale. Anything that might distract attention from the good V. I. Lenin's ultimate game plan.'

'Like what?'

Jute was already on the move, plodding down the road back to the Center. Forgeot joined him with difficulty.

'Like giving it a lot of thought,' Jute said over his shoulder. Forgeot was now even. Jute looked sideways, a wicked, crazy schoolboy grin on his face. 'And that, my friend, is why I'm so glad you are here.'

Forgeot rebelled on the third day and decided to flunk any more early-morning jogging. 'We can't go on meeting like this,' he groaned after his third run, only half in jest. His feet were blistered. Walking down staircases had become acutely painful. He also found Jute's jogging small talk increasingly irritating: especially when Jute started talking about a California psychiatrist who had cured deeply schizoid paranoiacs by taking them for prolonged and collective jogs, ridding them of their aggression and delirium. Forgeot imagined the scene: a bearded Jute look-alike, surrounded by a wild-eyed squad, probably with a police car not far behind. 'Look,' he said, 'I'm not schizoid but I soon will be if this goes on.' So Jute, unusually conciliatory, had proposed instead a leisurely walk. 'I didn't realise you young people had so little stamina,' he said. 'We could meet at the pub, if you like.'

'I'd prefer the open air,' Forgeot said. 'And so will you, when you hear what I have to say.'

They were walking briskly through a field to get to a shaded copse. 'You asked me to give the matter some thought,' said Forgeot, 'and I have. What you were saying, in your lecture, was that the Soviets have the advantage of numbers, technology and surprise. The inference is that only by drawing them away from the European theatre could we ever hope to restore some kind of parity, since we both agree that the token withdrawals offered through SALT and other such moves are of no practical effect whatever. The best way of keeping them elsewhere is either to engage them elsewhere, or else force a new scale of priorities on Soviet leadership.'

Jute nodded.

'The dream of all cold warriors like you,' Forgeot said, 'has always been to find some way of compelling the Soviets to move a large proportion of their conventional and tactical nuclear weapons to the East – to concentrate on the Chinese border, for instance, much more than they do now.'

Jute grinned. 'Bravo,' he said. 'Someone give the colonel a banana. And how are we expected to do that?'

'One way,' said Forgeot, 'would be to convince them that the Russians are about to launch a pre-emptive strike against them – something much more vast than the Oussouri river goings-on of four years ago. Something that would compel the Chinese to build up *their* forces – and perhaps indulge in a pre-emptive strike of their own.'

'Short of inviting the Chinese general staff to attend specially rehearsed Pentagon briefings,' Jute said, 'how do you propose convincing them? Not that they wouldn't welcome such news, you know that. Our station reports from Hong Kong are pretty illuminating. Whenever any US official goes near a Chinese senior official, he gets the same lecture. Why doesn't Europe treble its NATO forces, have another crack at the European Defence Community, and confront the Russians head-on? To hear the Chinese talk, they'd like to become part of the NATO Alliance. But that doesn't mean they'll act themselves.'

'Unless they have to,' Forgeot said. 'In private talks, most of the top Chinese sound just like you, Adrian Jute, cold warrior extraordinary. Peking's full of Adrian Jutes, spreading gloom and despondency and building A-bomb shelters all over the place.'

'So?'

'So it means,' Forgeot said, 'that their heart is in the right place. That all they need is a little proof. And with your contriving, and my convincing, maybe they would act, after all.'

'What's so special about you?' Jute paused, and kicked at a stone. 'I mean, you're a top-notch operator, I grant you that. But that doesn't mean the Chinese will swallow any old *canard.* Intelligent people, the Chinese. And very, very suspicious.'

'That's why we must prepare our material very, very carefully,' Forgeot said. 'Here's what I have in mind. You put together a really first-class disinformation campaign. Make it look as if, from what all the satellites say, the Soviets are about to take out Chinese nuclear installations, their bomb manufacturing capacity, with satellite pictures, close-ups, the works. Say that I act as your go-between, and get them really interested. What happens? The Chinese start building up *their* forces, for real. Worries the hell out of the

Russians. Makes them think that maybe the Chinese are crazy enough to do something on their own – especially since they've said they wouldn't, and the Soviets always assume everyone is always lying, like them. Makes the Russians envisage real measures of their own. Leads to a real build-up. And almost certainly takes the heat out of any European designs they might otherwise have, or at least postpones them for a long, long time.'

Jute was impressed, but determined not to show it.

'And why would they listen to you?'

Forgeot told him about the Chinese girl, leaving out a great deal, including his own real involvement, his humiliation and Guillaume's role.

'I did it,' he said, 'to win their confidence. I didn't then know what use it would be. As an ace in the hole, I suppose. But it seems to me that having delivered once, they'll be more receptive when I approach them a second time. Provided, of course, the pictures pass the test.'

As he spoke he silently invoked her. May, please forgive me, I'm betraying you a second time, my darling, but in a good cause.

'Another thing,' Forgeot said. 'It's got to look good – and it would be more convincing if the whole scheme appeared to come from you. It'll need teamwork. Maybe more than one person. And whoever works with us will have to be completely committed, as committed as we are. It'll take time, too, to get the stuff together, and make it look real.'

Jute said: 'You're a crazy son of a bitch, you know that? Crazier than I am.'

Forgeot couldn't afford to appear too eager, too pressing.

'It's just a wild idea,' he said. 'You don't have to give it another thought.'

But Jute, he could sense, was tempted.

'It certainly would need a great deal of work,' he said. 'Money too. And someone with the right kind of access. But I think I know just where to lay my hands on him.'

'I'd like to meet him,' Forgeot said.

'So you shall – tomorrow night.'

They drove all the way to Georgetown. Forgeot sensed that Jute didn't want to talk, and respected his mood. They sat at a table in the back room of a restaurant expensively got up to look like a humble family trattoria, complete with dour black-laced mamma at the cash desk, busily checking each order as it passed alongside her from the kitchen. 'Shikken tacciatorio,' the waiters shouted. 'Twelve feefty.' 'Antipasto four dollar.' 'Ice cream odda house, two feefty.' The lady had the narrowest mouth Forgeot had ever seen, a downward bow painted on a harsh disapproving face, in a prim, vivid crimson pencil line. Jotting down figures and playing with a bleeping cash register, she was the personification of matronly Mediterranean sourness and greed. Until suddenly, in the front part of the restaurant, three Monsignors, one of them smoking a huge cigar, got up and left, leaving a handsome tip. Then, briefly, she became radiant, a young, gentle contented girl, bowing to the priests, waving her plump hand in a familiar 'Arriverderci, buona sera.' She was a little puzzled by the cigar, though. And, as soon as the priests had left, her face set again in its former frightening mould.

Jute had been Rome Station Chief in the mid fifties, in the days when such a post was almost as important as that of Italian Prime Minister. He had plotted, made deals, passed on huge sums of counterpart Marshall Aid funds to political parties and newspapers of all political hues, intrigued to get this 'Guardia di Finanza' colonel promoted, that one sent off in semi-disgrace to Calabria, all the while keeping open house in a palatial terraced apartment in the Via Margutta, mingling with trendy Vatican clergy and dour Christian trade unionists. These days, Forgeot thought, he wouldn't last a minute in Rome. Both his own Agency and the Italian Government would have him run out of town for doing one tenth of what he had once got away with. America was an empire no more, and Jute hadn't come to terms with the new America. The restaurant itself may have been a pay-off: Jute, speaking fluent, heavily accented Italian, had been greeted like a *padrone,* waving Forgeot into the back room as if he owned the place. Maybe he did.

When the guest showed up, Forgeot didn't immediately recognise him, and Jute stuck to first names only: 'Jean – Sammy. Sammy – Jean.' Then Forgeot remembered: Oleg Semyakov, one of the Agency's house Russians, something to do with the National Reconnaissance Office. The broad Slavonic features were in sharp contrast with his almost aggressively all-American get-up, iridescent sports shirt, houndstooth leisure pants of the kind worn in Miami at orthodentists' conventions, tasselled loafers. His accent was unmistakably Russian, but not much more marked than Kissinger's Teutonic overtones in moments of stress. Like most Russians, he was incapable of pronouncing the letter V. He shook hands with a confident, firm grip, exuding strength and Old Spice.

Jute was a prodigious eater. Forgeot understood why he ran and ran: simply burning up calories. But how did he keep the fresh, little boy look, the enthusiastic energy of the perennial student? He talked and ate with the same ease with which he talked and jogged. During the evening, he referred, with no apparent emotion, to his blind wife's sudden, recent death at the hands of a still-to-be apprehended hit-and-run-driver.

'Sammy here knows more about satellite interpretation than the rest of the Agency put together,' Jute said after his cryptic introduction. Semyakov had been – was it submarine commander? KGB? Forgeot rather inclined to Air Force. That was it: Assistant Air Attaché somewhere, with lots to sell: after his defection, Soviet passport-holders had left Western capitals in droves.

It was surprising that Jute should put him on public display like this. Forgeot recalled that he had, at first, been a total recluse, living in fear of his life. It was no wonder that, on Jute's instructions, a waiter drew a curtain across the small back room just after Semyakov's arrival, cutting them off from the rest of the diners' gaze.

Jute had said one thing, and one thing only, during their drive to Georgetown. 'I will appear to take the initiative,' he said. 'You will become gradually convinced. It's better so, believe me.' It was a game Forgeot was perfectly willing to play.

'I've known Jean here,' Jute now said, leaving a brown stain on his napkin, 'ever since he was kid. He's the one Frenchman I can trust. Right?'

Forgeot was embarrassed. He tried not to look it. Jute ordered salads all round, his cheeks more flushed than usual after his ingestion of a huge plateful of spaghetti alle vongole. 'Well, gentlemen,' he said in a heavy attempt at parody, 'I suppose you wonder why I've called this meeting. It's to sound our friend Jean out on a little proposition.' Turning to Forgeot: 'How would you like to take part in a bit of play-acting to convince our Chinese friends that we really have their interests at heart, to the extent of sharing some of our secrets with them concerning their Russian neighbours' intentions?'

Forgeot ostentatiously picked his teeth, and paused before replying. 'They don't need any convincing,' he said. 'They're so preoccupied with the so-called hegemonic designs of the Soviet Union that they're even prepared to embark on a policy of friendship with the United States. Haven't you heard? They feel that war with the Societ Union is inevitable. Their one obsessive dream is to get the West on their side before it happens.'

Jute was unperturbed. 'Of course that's what they think, bless their little hearts. But maybe we could feed their apprehensions a little. Encourage their obsessions. Actually provide them with what they're dying to hear, convince them they're in the right?'

Semyakov said nothing. Too busy munching grissinis. A compulsive eater, too, Forgeot decided.

Jute said: 'If we were able to provide them with hard evidence of Soviet war preparations, would you be able to convey them – convincingly?'

Turning to Semyakov, Jute added: 'Forgeot had occasion last year to do them quite a good turn, and maybe they haven't forgotten.'

Semyakov said: 'The idea is attractive. But there's no such thing as gratitude in either politics or intelligence.' Over his Russian accent, there was superimposed an American veneer, as blatant as his clothes style.

'It seems to me,' Forgeot said, playing his role with suitable diffidence, 'that the main thing would be to provide the kind of evidence they would regard as cast-iron. And how would you do that?'

Semyakov said: 'The Chinese have no first-hand access to satellite information of their own. The Cultural Revolution took care of that. They're about twenty years behind us, fifteen years behind the Soviets. All they know they have to find out the old-fashioned way. They have a good intelligence network in some of the Soviet Islamic republics, and among the Tartars and Mongols, but their listening posts are primitive, most primitive.'

Jute said: 'How good would they be at interpreting satellite data?'

'Pretty good. They know what to look for.'

Forgeot said, playing his straight man role: 'What exactly would you be selling?'

Jute, dead serious, a little twitchy, eyes glistening behind his glasses, said softly: 'I'm not selling. I'm buying.'

Even Semyakov looked perturbed.

'I'm buying time. I'm buying the only way of relieving pressure on the West. I'm buying the chance of having the Russians move a significant part of their hardware into the Far Eastern sector. That's what I'm buying, sweetie.'

Forgeot turned to Semyakov. 'Is he always like this?' he asked. The Russian grunted.

Eventually Semyakov spoke. 'What you hope to give the Chinese, I take it, is a complete, graduated picture of Soviet war preparations against China, which would be compelling enough to provide Peking with an excuse to intensify its war preparations, and perhaps even make them try a pre-emptive strike. Am I right?'

Jute nodded.

'The whole series of satellite pictures to be conveyed to the Chinese by our friend here, over a period of time, offering cast-iron evidence of a gradual Soviet build-up.'

Nobody spoke. Semyakov went on. 'And what you propose to ask me, I take it, is: would such a scheme be technically feasible?'

Forgeot said: 'You're both out of your minds.'

'No, no,' Jute said. 'Sammy has got it absolutely right. We're speaking, mind, of a hypothesis.'

Semyakov said, ponderously: 'Technically, it *is* possible. It would take time. Provided there were careful preparations. And someone with intimate knowledge of the workings of the National Reconnaissance Office. Curiously, real satellite pictures of the Sino-Soviet border, even detailed ones, are no problem. They are supposed to be highly classified, but there are thousands lying around.'

'What's needed, then,' said Jute, 'is a way of combining the true picture with the invented stuff. That shouldn't be above the competence of a sophisticated photo lab, provided the person who puts the series together knows what he's doing.'

Semyakov, for the first time, smiled. It was not a reassuring spectacle. 'And that means me?' he asked. 'Well, it's worth a try.'

Forgeot said: 'How do I come in?'

Jute looked at him intently, apparently encouraged that Forgeot had not rejected the proposal outright.

'Put yourself in their shoes,' he said. 'An agency source plonks down some evidence out of the blue. However we try and disguise it, they'll know, simply by following up any available clues, that we're behind it. So they'll see it as a plant, and reject it. Whereas, if the evidence falls into their little hands through a third party, who happens to have access to this kind of stuff, then their reactions are likely to be very different indeed.' He turned to Semyakov. 'Agreed?'

Semyakov grunted again.

'I haven't said I would,' said Forgeot.

'Think about it,' said Jute. 'The risks are mainly ours, not yours. You'll just be the honest broker. I'm the one who's taking the risk – and Sammy here, if he co-operates.'

'Assuming I have established some kind of rapport with the Chinese,' Forgeot said, 'do you see me walking into the Chinese Embassy in Paris waving some computer print-outs? Hiya, fellers, guess what I have for you? You must be out of your mind. And what about my own hierarchy? What would happen to one of your own people, caught playing games like that? We call it treason.'

Nobody spoke. Forgeot added: 'I take it that this place is where you usually come to talk about this and that? If anything ever leaks, it's as much your funeral as mine.'

Jute gave a tough little half-laugh. 'Let me make a small confession,' he said. 'Remember Watergate, the CIA's mafia connections, laundering, etcetera? Well, as you probably know, most of it was true. This is one of the places where we used to meet *gli amici*, when we had to. And still do sometimes. They're very patriotic Italian-Americans, by the way. And there hasn't been a leak out of this room yet. We take precautions, by common accord We sweep the place. They sweep the place. They use a security firm, one of the largest. They happen to own it. You see, they don't fully trust us either. This is neutral territory Secure as one of our own vaults.'

'You haven't answered my question,' Forgeot said 'What if I have second thoughts about the whole thing?' He said this for Semyakov's benefit. It was the kind of thing he might have said had he been approached. It confirmed, in Semyakov's eyes, that it was Jute, and not Forgeot, who was behind the project.

'Jean, Jean, you mustn't even think such negative thoughts. We're a reliable firm still, even if we have been clobbered in the last few months.' Forgeot grinned: 'What you're saying is that the old lady at the cash-desk can still lay on a reliable contract, is that it?'

Jute did his best not to look sheepish

'There's another thing,' Forgeot said. 'I'll have to learn the technical side of what you're going to give them. Interpretation of satellite photography isn't my strong point. And I can't very well go to my Minister and say: please, sir, there's a couple of CIA nuts who want me to peddle stuff to the Chinese, in the interests of détente and world peace, of course, but first I need a few days in Langley to learn it all so I can get it right when I show them the stuff and they start asking questions.'

'I've thought of that,' Jute said. 'In a few months' time we'll be bringing some people in from Europe to talk about information pooling in the Middle East area. We will particularly ask for you by name. It'll make sense, since you already deal with our permanent security attaché in Paris on a regular basis. You still have your appendix, don't you? That's what our records say. Well, some time during your next stay, you're going to wake up in great pain. Stabbing sensation low down on the right side of the groin. Vomiting. Nausea. It'll happen just as we're about to go jogging. I'll call a doctor. One of ours. He'll confirm it's an acute case of appendicitis, and recommend an immediate operation.'

Forgeot made a face.

'Don't worry. You'll be in good hands. There'll just be a

token incision. Just enough to leave a small scar afterwards. You'll be in bed a couple of days, then convalescing for a week. Sammy will occupy a room next to yours.'

He made a Groucho Marx, eyebrows-raised face. 'Communicating doors. We'll have it all rigged up. Sammy will give you a crash course, several hours a day, for all the time you'll be in the clinic. When you return to Paris, you'll be an expert. And you'll be able to tell your girlfriends that American surgeons are the best in the world. They'll agree when they see the size of the scar.'

Forgeot said: 'There's only one thing wrong with your plan.'

Jute looked worried.

'You bastard,' said Forgeot, 'you'll have to do it properly. Think of the explaining I'd have to do, if ever I really needed to have it out.'

Chapter Seven

THERE HAD been a quickening trickle of refugees into Paris for some time. Almost overnight, a 'golden triangle' of Indochinese restaurants, food stores, laundries and supermarkets had sprung up in the 5th *arrondissement*, and now there were more Vietnamese than French in the cafés around the Place Maubert. The trickle had become a stream after the fall of Saigon.

It was a part of Paris Forgeot loved, even before they came: he wished he lived there. Listening to the high-pitched whine of Vietnamese housewives making disparaging comments about the freshness of the coriander or lewd remarks about the durians that were now a feature of the shops, he felt transported back several years, to his tiny flat near Saigon's Central Market, itself a startling neo-colonial replica of the old Odéon Market in the 6th *arrondissement*.

Tranh was one of the new gereration of Vietnamese residents in Paris who had prospered as the Indochina situation became ever more desperate. First to arrive had been the old guard, the followers of ex-Emperor Bao Dai. Then Diem's enemies. Then each successive military upheaval had given the Vietnamese community in Paris an additional stratum.

Tranh had not come as the result of any coup, though. Forgeot had known him for over twenty years, first as an *aspirant* in the French army, then as an officer in the first Vietnamese Parachute unit. Too proud to use his family connections to get a safe staff job, or a diplomatic posting abroad, which would have been easy enough, he had been one of the few Vietnamese field commanders to inflict severe losses on the other side in the early stages of what the old hands now referred to as 'the second Indochina war'.

He had been lucid enough to realize that the combined incompetence, greed and rivalries of the senior generals in charge, to say nothing of the fatalism of his fellow-countrymen, were bound to lead to ultimate disaster, especially after a US pull-out. Always suspicious of American intentions – Tranh was quintessentially French in this respect – he had left Vietnam 'temporarily' after Marshal Ky had emerged as the last of a long string of so-called 'strong men'. He had told Forgeot: 'Strong man, my arse! The little rabbit was just an airport security guard.'

Pulling strings for the first time, he had got the authorities to send him to France for medical treatment. Forgeot well remembered the circumstances of their last Indochina encounter: Tranh had accompanied Forgeot to Hanoi airport, to volunteer for the last desperate sorties over Dien Bien Phu. Forgeot had been accepted, but Tranh, his arm still in a sling from a recent shrapnel wound, had been told to go back to hospital. He had been twenty-two at the time, as lean as a rake. Now he was almost stout: he looked like a muscle-bound Buddha.

Once in Paris, Tranh had scraped together all the money he could get hold of and opened a hole-in-the-wall shop in a mean street on the Left Bank near the Seine, a street then given over almost exclusively to Algerian immigrant slum hotels, cheap couscous restaurants and pushers of every conceivable type of drug. Forgeot had loaned Tranh all the cash he could spare, convinced that he would never see any of it again. It was the least he could do. Almost from the moment he had arrived in Indochina, Tranh had been his best friend, steering him clear of the bad opium dens and brothels, teaching him to distinguish the good stuff from the dross, taking him in hand, making him, for a while, an honorary member of that pathetic, short-lived Vietnamese jet set which had seemed to Forgeot, at the time, unbelievably glamorous.

This was before the Rue Catinat in Saigon had become Tu Do, and begun its sordid transformation into a series of girlie bars and American-style Chinese restaurants, before, as Tranh put it, Vietnam had lost its soul. There were girls aplenty, and on their furloughs Forgeot and Tranh had hunted as a pair. Linh in Dalat had been one of Tranh's many cousins.

After a difficult two years, Tranh had not only made good, he had made a fortune. Somehow, his part-Chinese ancestry and heritage had blossomed into an unsuspected instinct for trade. This, combined with his warrior's risk-taking, had led to a spectacular success. He had parleyed his first shop into a second, then a third. Next he had opened a couple of restaurants, an expensive one near the Champs-Elysées and a cheaper one inside the 'golden triangle'. But his biggest single coup had been, using his army connections, to talk himself into becoming the exclusive agent for a large Thai food-exporting firm, itself owned by one of the Thai generals in power. Finally, he had taken some of his assets, plus a sizeable bank loan, and bought a small farm near Paris: hothouses growing produce previously imported at high cost from tropical areas.

He applied strict army rules to his commercial operation, running his company with a handful of nephews and nieces, 'aunties' and a quiet, ageless lady called Thérèse who was assumed to be wife number two. Wife number one, an exquisite-looking, wayward bitch, a real Saigon princess, had vanished into darkest Colorado with a United States army doctor specializing in plastic surgery.

Forgeot got his loan back within three years. From the start Tranh had urged him to become a full partner, offering him half the business in return for the original loan, which in money terms was now only a fraction of Tranh's monthly cash flow. Forgeot had refused, just as he had refused any interest. He argued that the press might get to hear about it.

Whenever they met, for a while, Tranh renewed his offer. Eventually, he no longer talked about it. But after Forgeot's Washington trip, Tranh, to his astonishment, found that he was now in a slightly different frame of mind.

Tranh was surprised, and also slightly dismayed, by Forgeot's proposal. There was a rage for all things American in France, he had said. Why not open a small, chic, left-bank store, in or near the 'golden triangle', specialising in T-shirts, posters and other American bits of trash that so delighted French teenagers?

'That'll bring in some pocket money,' Tranh had said, 'but it won't make you rich. If you're tired of catching spies why don't you let me give you a couple of restaurants?' But for some reason Forgeot stuck to his original idea. He had contacts in the States, he said, a supplier who could get him everything at rock-bottom prices. A shoe-repair shop near one of Tranh's stores had just become vacant, the old Greek retiring and not finding a successor willing to make do with meagre earnings and long hours. Tranh rented the premises, and 'the three-D poster shop' was born.

It all happened with unaccustomed speed: a team of Tranh's Vietnamese workmen invaded the place, and one day, there it was, all bright lights, piped disco music and futuristic plastic. It puzzled Tranh that Forgeot had insisted on a safe, complicated locks, steel shutters and burglar alarms more suited to Cartier. Tranh put it down to a cop's obsessive concern for security. He had asked Tranh for a suitable person to run the place, and Tranh had suggested a relative, the young widow of a Vietnamese Ranger captain. She was thirty, with two small children, but she looked seventeen. In any other circumstances, Forgeot would have made a pass at her. She was good-looking enough to model the T-shirts herself, and featured in a number of minor French fashion papers. The magic worked: the three-D poster shop was an overnight success.

Tranh had never allowed his wealth to alter his way of life, except for one thing: he had bought, in the now ultra-fashionable Rue du Maître Albert, within a few hundred yards of one of his shops, a huge apartment. It reminded Forgeot of the last of the old West Side condominiums, with high ceilings, vast amounts of wasted space, and a large terrace. Here he lived with at least ten members of his family, and innumerable children. He made one concession to Vietnam: in one corner, there was a small altar. Tranh was a Buddhist, and supported a number of Buddhist charities. But in white singlet and dark blue shorts, cleaning out one of his stores, or handling crates himself in the early morning, he looked like an unusually well-fed, tough coolie. He spoke French with the hint of a Vietnamese accent, and English with a recognizable Southern drawl: his unit's favourite 'military adviser' in the 1963–4 period had come from Georgia. He had been killed, during his third tour, at Ben Tre during Tet 1968.

When the first consignment of posters and T-shirts started arriving, Forgeot had sorted them out himself, arriving late at night, leaving in the early hours. Thérèse had offered to help, and so had his new assistant. But Forgeot had insisted on working alone.

Shortly afterwards, in Tranh's apartment late one night, over brandy, Forgeot had asked another favour.

He explained that his new Minister had a bee in his bonnet about the proliferation of Chinese restaurants in Paris. He was convinced, said Forgeot, that some of them might be fronts for other things: drugs, perhaps, as in Amsterdam, or political activity of some kind. Ridiculous, of course: the Chinese had every reason to stay out of trouble.

Surely Tranh, who knew so much about the local Asian community, might be able to help? Simply by using his contacts to pinpoint those Chinese establishments which might be something more than conventional restaurants. 'You needn't get involved directly,' said Forgeot, 'and between ourselves we know it's a lot of balls. Simply a list to keep my new Minister happy.'

And Tranh had put his people to work. He suspected Forgeot was not telling him the whole truth. Triads, the old secret societies, were beginning to assert themselves in Paris. They were no respecters of ideologies. The pro-Peking owners were paying up just like the pro-Taiwan owners. There had been some embarrassment among the divided Chinese restaurateurs. Some had been in favour of forming a 'united front', others had actually called on the Embassy in the Avenue Georges V, but a minor official had told them there was nothing he could do. It was a matter for the French police, he had said.

Tranh himself had cancelled plans for opening a Vietnamese restaurant in Soho after discovering that the triads were taking a cut on most of the Chinese establishments in Gerrard Street. He had not, as yet, been approached himself: perhaps the gangs suspected he would be a tough customer. And Tranh privately wondered whether Forgeot might not be on the track of the Paris triads, and not wanting to involve him. The problem, he knew, was complicated by the fact the real triad leaders seldom came to France. They had British, Hong Kong, Taiwan or Malaysian passports, commuted between the Netherlands and Britain and used illicit-entry hit men to do the dirty work in Paris, often people with fake identity cards showing them to be French of Vietnamese descent.

Tranh's small list, handed over a few days later, singled out the Fontaine du Matin Calme in the Rue de Bièvre, only a few streets away from Tranh's own little empire. It was on the fringe of the 'golden triangle', a small narrow street, chiefly famous because François Mitterand had bought a house there.

The Fontaine du Matin Calme was a typical Paris Chinese restaurant, all red lacquer and paper lamps, with a huge, bad, vaguely Cantonese menu. Despite its mediocre fare it did good business, for it was cheap, attracting a large day-time student clientèle. It was also close enough to Notre Dame to benefit from an active tourist trade. According to Tranh's information, it was here, incongruously enough, that some Chinese Embassy officials regularly congregated, perhaps only for a quiet meal outside the constraints of the Embassy itself.

Forgeot ran a check on its owner: Tsien Chu-Fai, born Hochan 1917, naturalised French citizen since 1967. He had first arrived in France in 1947, from Hong Kong, and worked as a waiter for seven years. He had applied for French citizenship as soon as it had been legally possible for him to do so. He had no police record. No tax problems, either, which was rare for Chinese restaurateurs. He had sponsored the entry into France of a dozen relatives, all of them now in the restaurant business, in Paris, Calais, Marseilles. This was normal practice.

Forgeot ran further checks on the Calais and Marseilles relatives. They were inconclusive.

The Fontaine du Matin Calme had a side entrance which was not used by the run-of-the-mill customers. Access was through a door on the left of what was, in fact, the entrance to the courtyard next door.

Important visitors, Tranh's report said, met in a back room. One of them, he confirmed, who habitually came and went using a Mercedes with CD plates, was an usually tall Chinese diplomat.

And Forgeot, not for the first time, marvelled at the sense of community, transcending politics, that still existed in China, for Hochan was a medium-sized town in Szechuan, and Feng, Forgeot's records showed, had been born there.

Forgeot had his first meal at the Fontaine du Matin Calme the very day Guillaume was finally arrested. There had been quite a lot of talk about Guillaume, at the Ministry, the day it happened, and a friend, at the Préfecture, had given him a detailed account. The police had burst into Valentine's studio just as Guillaume was getting down to business. Valentine had been spreadeagled on the floor, her wrists tied to a leather collar. It had all happened very quickly. Guillaume, in no time at all, found himself on the bed, face down, handcuffed, and one of the plainclothesmen had hit him on the back of the head with the flat of his hand. Guillaume, dazed, had tried to talk his way out of it, using all the tricks of his trade. 'She likes it, she pays me for it, she craves it, you stupid arseholes,' he shouted. 'Are you going to believe a police officer, or this little whore?' At first the cops had felt some sympathy for him. He would be out on bail in no time, one of them said. But Guillaume was so angry that for once he failed to be clever.

'Where's your friend Forgeot?' he shouted. 'Waiting outside, I suppose. Too scared to do it himself.' And the squad leader gave him a whack on the back of the neck, harder this time, and said: 'Forgeot? I don't think I know anyone of that name.'

Guaillaume's arrest gave Forgeot the breathing-space he needed. The Chinese, he knew, would never seek him out in jail. Meanwhile, he had to allow the restaurant staff to get used to him. He was mildly irritated that Feng hadn't thought it worthwhile to turn the Fontaine du Matin Calme into a Szechuanese restaurant. Bad Cantonese restaurants were two a penny in Paris. Presumably he had not wanted to single it out in any way, to make it too successful or at all fashionable.

Forgeot made no effort to conceal his identity: an official Ministry car with the recognisable DA numberplates occasionally dropped him there, and picked him up afterwards.

When he thought he had achieved some familiar status, he said to the brisk young manager in charge: 'I have a friend you may know. Name of Feng. I'd like to meet him.'

The manager looked blank, and insisted on speaking

French back, though Forgeot had spoken in Chinese.

'No person that name,' he said. 'Must be udder restaurant.'

Forgeot shook his head. 'You tell him,' he said, 'that the one who gave him the girl wants a little talk.'

'No girl. No unnerstann.'

'He will,' said Forgeot. 'Remember, you tell the tall one. Tell him I have more than the girl this time. Much more.'

Forgeot knew the rules. The next time, a few days later, he went back to the Fontaine du Matin Calme he behaved as if nothing had happened, as if he had never been there before. And the time after that, as he had expected, he got his response. He had ordered, but the waiters had kept him waiting. They had not even brought him the green tea that was invariably placed, like water carafes, on each table as the customers sat down. And now the manager, all smiles, said 'your flenn here' and escorted Forgeot to the back door, along a small corridor, past the stinking toilets, and then there was the smell of real Szechuanese cooking, chillies and hot sesame oil. He ushered Forgeot into a small windowless room, equipped with an expensive air conditioner. The flocked purple velvet wallpaper was made even more hideous by blueish neon strip lighting. A round table for three was laid, and, out of nowhere, Feng and a shorter, older man appeared.

They shook hands all round. Waiters began serving an elaborate Szechuan meal, one of the best Forgeot had ever had, outside Hong Kong, Taipeh, and, perhaps, Uncle Tai's in New York in its earliest incarnation.

Conversation was stilted. Forgeot knew better than to make the first move.

'You like?'

'I must ask you to compliment the chef,' Forgeot said. 'He must come from Szechuan.'

'Szechuan food very spicy,' said the older man.

'The owner,' said Forgeot, 'is also, perhaps, from Szechuan?'

'Weather in Szechuan,' said the older man, 'is very warm. Hot place, hot food.'

This could go on for ever.

'A very beautiful part of China, I am told,' said Forgeot, 'but foreigners very rarely are allowed to go there.'

By now they were nearing the end of the meal and, traditionally, two kinds of soup were served, one thick, the other clear. Feng had not spoken. Now he unbuttoned the top of his Mao jacket. 'I was born in Szechuan,' he said in English, with a very faint American accent. 'Same place as the owner of this restaurant. But you know that already. You are Mr Forgeot, from the Rue des Saussaies, also the Oriental Languages School in the Rue de Lille. Also from Saigon, by and by.'

'It's part of your job,' said Forgeot, responding in Chinese, 'to know these things. We are colleagues, in a way. Kan Pe.' They drank the ritual toast, in hot shao hsing wine from the Johnny-Walker-shaped bottle.

'You don't know me, but I know you,' said Forgeot. 'I helped organize the return of the girl last year.'

Feng belched. 'We can't talk here,' he said. 'You have time for a drive? Please excuse me.' He stood up, and said: 'Let's go.' One of the waiters came in. He must have been outside. 'Please don't be offended by what I have to do,' said Feng. 'It is simply we cannot take a chance.' The waiter expertly frisked Forgeot, examining his body and clothing for a concealed microphone. He was very thorough. Forgeot co-operated as best he could, raising his arms, unbuttoning his jacket, even removing his shoes for the waiter to look at.

'No problem,' he said. 'But how do I know you are not carrying one yourself?'

Feng unsmilingly said: 'That is not your business.'

Forgeot said, 'But it is. My conditions are: I will search you both. And no Embassy car.'

Feng and the older Chinese started arguing. They talked in Szechuanese dialect. Forgeot couldn't understand a word.

'Monsieur Guillaume,' said Forgeot, 'may have been more accommodating. But he was only the delivery-boy.'

There was more talk. Feng seemed to be having the last word. 'We have nothing on us,' he said, 'but you are at liberty to see for yourself.' It was Forgeot's turn to search them both. They were telling the truth.

'Now,' he said, 'get rid of your car. We will take a taxi.

Not one of mine, I assure you. In fact, you will pick it yourselves.'

The owner of the battered diesel Peugeot 504 was mildly surprised to be flagged down near the Jardin des Plantes. He had been on his way to try his luck at the Gare d'Austerlitz. The two Chinese and one Frenchman got in, and the Frenchman asked whether he would mind driving them all the way out to Fontainebleau.

'These gentlemen,' he told the driver, 'want to see the Château.' Confidentially, he added: 'Very important customers.'

'It'll cost you.'

'Your price,' said Forgeot, 'will be mine.'

They remained silent most of the way. The driver had a rather smelly dog with him in the front, and smoked a vile pipe. It was not the ideal place for a serious conversation. Feng was constantly looking back, trying to establish whether they were being followed. Forgeot was certain that the Embassy car was behind them. Not that that really mattered.

Halfway through the journey, Forgeot asked the driver not to go directly to the Château, but instead to take them to the rock formations deep in the forest, where rock-climbing enthusiasts went at weekends. The Chinese didn't seem to mind. The driver didn't know the way. Forgeot showed him how to get there.

It was mid-week, and the place was empty. 'It's a pity we're not wearing the right kind of clothes,' said Forgeot, 'it's an excellent way of working off such a splendid meal.'

The two Chinese were now somewhat irritated and apprehensive. Forgeot could see a black Mercedes far, far behind them. 'Let's go for a walk in the forest,' he said. The taxi-driver waited, placidly reading *L'Equipe*. He had received a 500-franc note and was as happy as a clam. 'The only thing is,' he told Forgeot, 'I'd like to be back by eight-thirty. Don't want to miss the film on the telly.'

The path chosen by Forgeot was wide enough for the three of them to keep abreast. He set a fast pace, deliberately. Feng kept up easily. The older Chinese was finding it heavy going.

'You probably wondered,' said Forgeot, 'why I surrendered the girl.'

110

The older Chinese was the first to speak. 'There are imperialists and reactionaries everywhere,' he said sententiously. 'Their aim is always to corrupt, deceive and cruelly suppress the masses.'

Forgeot didn't quite see the relevance of this. Feng looked at his colleague with ill-concealed irritation. 'What he means,' he said, 'is that here was yet another example of counter-revolutionary intervention.'

'At the beginning, perhaps,' said Forgeot. 'But aren't you always saying – for public consumption at least: history is a telling witness? Isn't that the late Chairman Mao's phrase? And the historical record speaks for itself.' He allowed himself one casual question, his heart beating. 'I take it that she will not be tempted again? That the re-education process is taking its course?'

He spoke with what he hoped would be perceived as detached amusement. In his pockets, his fists were clenched. 'The usual course is being followed,' Feng said. 'It will be many months, or years, before the enquiry is completed or she comes up before a court. It is matter of concern not to you, but only to us.'

So she was alive, at least.

The older Chinese piped up. 'She was guilty of a most heinous crime,' he said, 'whether she fell under the influence of the imperialists or not. That is why vigilance, as our Chairman says, is essential at all times.'

Feng looked at Forgeot. His expression was not in the least inscrutable. He sighed. The sigh seemed to mean: I have to put up with this jargon too. Again using Szechuan dialect, he spoke gruffly to his colleague. Forgeot assumed he was saying: cut the parables, cut the Maoist crap, you're not in an Embassy meeting now. Let's get down to business with this man. I'll handle this. Feng was someone the older man would defer to.

'All right, you handed her back.' Feng was speaking conversationally now, no trace of jargon. 'We wondered why. We came to the conclusion you were simply obeying orders, trying to repair the initial counter-revolutionary blunder.'

'That was partly true,' said Forgeot. 'There was a brief debate. Some were in favour of her return. Some wanted to

111

use her as a possible bargaining pawn. Some wanted to sell her to the Americans. The argument that good relations between our countries precluded anything but her return to you prevailed. But that's not why I am here. I am here because, by returning her to you, I wanted to prove my own personal friendly intentions.'

Feng said: 'Monsieur Guillaume has already made that point. *And* been paid for his services. We don't have unlimited funds.'

So Guillaume had milked the Chinese as well. Typical. How many people was he working for?

'I am not asking for money,' said Forgeot. 'I am trying to convey – as best I know – some information that is vital to us all. Information that the French Government is either unwilling to acknowledge, or else, in the interests of détente, wants to ignore.'

They walked in silence. 'May I enquire,' said Forgeot, 'is your friend a military man?'

Feng said: 'Why do you ask?'

'Because – if I may say so – only a military man can fully appreciate the importance of what it is I would like to show you.'

Feng said: 'He is not.'

They were arguing again. But Feng was obviously in complete control. 'I can arrange for another meeting, with the right person, at any time,' he said.

It was Forgeot's turn to call the shots.

'I have to leave the country on a business trip,' he said. 'I should be back in two weeks' time. I suggest we use the restaurant to leave word when it would be convenient to renew our conversation. I will ask to book a table for six, and order a Szchuanese meal on a Monday. The restaurant is closed on Mondays, so the reply will be: can you make it Tuesday? And the person answering will say: Tuesday is no good at lunchtime, but we can manage a Szechuanese meal for two on Tuesday night. If the reply is yes, then we'll meet the following Tuesday, not in the restaurant, but just around the corner, at the top of the street. And I'll take you to a place where your military expert may want to spend some time.'

'What time Tuesday?'

'Late: eleven p.m. You can bring all the anti-bugging devices you want. But please don't come in Embassy cars. Try and look like Vietnamese, if you can.' Conscious of the insult, he added: 'Vietnamese are very inconspicuous, in this area.'

Feng and his companion still looked angry. 'You must understand,' Forgeot said, 'I don't want some arsehole in my own outfit to get involved. He might –' and Feng broke into a slight smile, for the first time since their meeting – 'report to me that some Chinese Embassy officials are wandering around the Latin Quarter, late at night, behaving suspiciously. I'd be forced to take action. We don't want that, do we?'

Chapter Eight

THERE WAS a distant ocean roar, but no trace of an ocean. The glow implied tropical heat, but, strangely, it was almost too cool, almost a sea breeze. He was lying on some dark sandy surface, but it wasn't the usual kind of sand: too dark, not sticky at all, soft and warm like May's own body, which also seemed to be darker than it really was, the same colour as the sand, because either the sun was in the wrong place, or the sky overcast, and they were both in shadow, though there was nothing to create any shade, except that she was leaning over him, her long hair half-hiding her face, and the canopy of her hair was also the canopy of the sky. He could smell the freshness of her and the slightly peppery, nutty-lemony taste of her skin, of her sex. She was as soft as the substance he was stretched out on, and he could feel her arms cradling him, rocking him. They were all alone on this endless expanse of beach, or desert, or maybe inside a glowing tent-like cocoon as huge as the world itself. There was a sense of doom, of dark redness in the air, and May was saying: 'I'm not sick, look! And neither are you,' and turned a cartwheel, away from him.

He reached out, but was hampered by a stab of pain, which didn't wake him, but was sufficiently real to make him conscious of his dream. Then she appeared again, surrounded by a sea of glossy magazines, her legs crossed, her neck arched, and the magazine covers were the exact multiplication of her own image. And he said to himself – still inside the dream, but only just, desperately willing himself to prolong it but knowing with a voyeur's detachment that it might only be a lingering fraction of a second before it all vanished: if only there were a flaw in her, I could remember the flaw, and forget the rest. Then he knew that fate was being kind to him, that he was having a reprieve, or another, separate dream altogether, for she had come to him, and they were speaking Chinese, and giggling, she was tickling his ear with her tongue, and he threshed about, climaxed, and the pain returned, more insistent this time, and suddenly he was drenched, no only in sweat, alone on a high hospital bed not unlike the one in the Hôpital Cochin, and the ocean's roar had become the prosaic hum of an air-conditioner. After the dreadful landing thump and waking from limbo, remembering who he was, it came back to him now that he was in Washington recovering from an appendix operation that had been only too real, and that he now faced the prospect of several days in Semyakov's company, acquiring the knowledge that would make his plan convincing. And he wondered whether the severe impersonal nurse in this CIA dump of a clinic would report that on coming out of his pentothal slumber he had babbled incomprehensibly in Chinese and had had, in broad daylight, what was commonly known as a nocturnal emission.

Afterwards his head cleared, and he was ready for the charts, the lessons, the slide projections in the next room, moving with difficulty, hearing some of the names – the towns called Skovodino, Magdagachi – for the first time. Semyakov incongruously in pyjamas, with a lecturer's cue, patiently pointing out the meanderings of the Oussouri river, and saying: 'Most of this they already know. Therefore it is verifiable. Therefore it establishes your credentials.'

Semyakov was considerate: the first session didn't last more than a couple of hours, and when it was over Forgeot wondered whether Jute, shrewd old fox, might not deliberately have set him up with a strong pentothal injection, simply to check him out. But the dream was, in a way, evidence that he hadn't.

Then, on the second day, came, as Semyakov put it, 'the sticky part'.

'Here we have to practise a little elementary deception,' he said. Enlargements of enlargements of enlargements. Some of the forty-eight Soviet divisions along China's borders, others of one of the five armoured divisions along the Oussouri. 'All above board,' Semyakov was saying. 'With a bit of luck they may have similar pictures, but from much higher. What is different is this: we can get closer. Look.' The magnifications were beautiful: silos, above-ground missile bases, on rails and on huge mobile carriers. 'SS 1-120s,' said Semyakov. 'There are the nuclear warheads, see?' More

115

pictures. Semyakov pointed to smooth oblong stalks. 'SSN-11s. Also used at sea. Note the folded wings.' They looked like fireworks designed by a youthful de Chirico. 'Now this is really something: here is an armoured column. What is different? This and this. How? Because of the kind of protective clothing worn. For heat? For desert? No. This is a decontamination exercise. Watch.'

Different slides, this time: close-ups of Soviet troops, in different battle gear. 'This is what they wear, after the nuclear missiles have been fired. So the radioactive dust, when it blows back, does not harm them. Everything battened down. Like so. Including the tanks.' Back to the enlargements. 'This is important. They are not on the move. They are exercising, *after* they have gone through the motions of firing their nuclear missiles. And it's not an isolated exercise. Everyone is doing it. Here on the banks of the Amour. Here on the Oussouri river. As far away as Irkoutsk, Krasnoyarsk. Here is Novosibirsk. The cumuli formations show it to be the same day. The same satellite pictures. And Irkoutsk is just as far away from the launching sites as Peking. They will draw their own conclusions.'

This was only the beginning. 'T-72 tanks. These they know. But this they haven't seen: different coverings, meaning only one thing.' Semyakov was a patient, relentless teacher, enthralled with his own handiwork. 'Later, there will be more photographs, but first you have to recognise what missiles on the move look like.' He was like a doctor interpreting a complicated X-ray for a batch of students, studying intricate bone fractures for the first time.

Gradually, there were harder equations and sums. What is this? And this? Good boy. No, there you are wrong. A conventional convoy, this time, unarmed missiles, these. Now watch: we put in the warheads, so. It was almost as exhausting as Jute's earlier jogging sessions. Forgeot wanted to fall asleep. When the time came, he willed himself to dream again, but only woke in the middle of the night, mouth furry with tranquillisers, brain dizzy with the vision of hundreds of satellite pictures, not knowing whether he should try to forget the dream, or cling to it, and try to repeat it. He willed himself to dream of May. Instead, a ludicrous Semyakov pranced down the Rue des Saussaies, in his pyjamas, and was arrested by Guillaume.

And gradually, as he became more expert in interpreting the pictures, and the vapour trails, he came to have a healthy respect for Semyakov's work. For the step-by-step accumulation of details in that hospital room converted into a studio was coalescing into a convincing whole. Forgeot knew that he would have been convinced of its authenticity, had he not suggested it in the first place. The overall picture, by stages, was of a Soviet build-up striking at the core of Chinese defence and factory installations. The likely course of events was not simply that the Chinese would be persuaded to strengthen their border defences, causing the Soviets to pull back some of their forces in the West to face a larger, more threatening Chinese Army on their Far Eastern border, thereby taking some pressure off NATO: the inference was that, after studying such evidence, the Chinese would be strongly tempted to strike first. It could mean a nuclear war. Semyakov had made that sequence of events almost inevitable.

All questions about how the pictures had been taken met with Semyakov's blank stare. Even Jute, who visited Forgeot on the third evening after his operation, bringing a rare bottle of claret as a peace offering, wouldn't say what was real, and what was contrived. 'Put it this way,' he said. 'In a sense it's all true. All we did was move some of the players around.' Forgeot insisted that he had to know. 'No way,' said Jute. 'We're not even supposed to speak about any of this.' Tough, pallid and slightly overweight civilians came and went, at the beginning of the day, setting up the adjoining room, removing all gear in the evening. Did they know what was being hatched? None of them would so much as say hullo. But when Jute brought over some visitors from the FBI whom Forgeot had known for years, there was no trace of Semyakov, and the room next door was just another hospital room. Forgeot said he was fine, and that he had contrived the operation so as to avoid those early morning jogging sessions. There was much loud laughter. A great deal of liquor was consumed under the noses of the disapproving nurses. Forgeot's room was the usual expensive clinic tubular monstrosity: paperbacks, magazines, a colour TV portable. No sign of any intellectual activity whatever. No notes, Jute had said. It must all be – he tapped his head – up here.

And after he had mastered it all, and could remember what all the signs meant, so that the greyish-black patterns were no longer blurs but indications of silos, missiles, carriers, train convoys and armoured columns, there was a lengthy session with Semyakov and Jute, again in the next-door room.

Jute said: 'Have you decided where you're going to store all this?' The simplest thing, he added, was for Forgeot to take it all back with him, and keep it until he had made the necessary contact. Forgeot refused. Microfilm was useless. Was he expected to brief the Chinese in their own projection-room? He was in the process of arranging for a secure hiding place. Neither his apartment nor his own office safe would do: there could be spot checks at any time, even at his level.

Forgeot got his way, clinching the argument by pointing out he had arrived at Dulles Airport with simply a carry-on holdall. What was he supposed to do? Pretend to have gone on a huge shopping spree? He decided to tell Jute, when they were next alone, about the three-D poster shop.

For his last three days in the United States, he walked with a stick, a present from Jute, and it was Jute who insisted on driving him to Dulles Airport. On the way, Forgeot told him about his commercial venture. 'Good idea, posters,' Jute said, and Forgeot knew he had overcome at least one hurdle.

They were absurdly early: Forgeot remembered Jute's maniacal anxiety about missing planes. They walked through the huge, under-used airport, and after Forgeot had stocked up on papers and magazines, he said, as they wandered through the waiting hall: 'Sammy – Semyakov, whatever you call him. You're quite sure about him, are you?' and Jute said: 'I'd stake my life.'

'Why?'

Jute avoided a loud whirling twelve-year-old handling his luggage-cart like a Phantom plane. He muttered rude words about American children in general, and shook his fist at the retreating youth. 'Surely,' he said, 'you don't think I would have gone along with your plan if things had been normal at Langley?'

'Normal?'

'Don't be coy with me. You know what the Agency has been going through. Why, if it wasn't for the Brits, continuing to feed us stuff, we might just as well pack up and go home, all of us.'

'How risky,' Forgeot asked, 'is all this for you?'

'Let's just say that freelancing has always been a pretty precarious way of making a living.'

They had come to the end of the hallway, and started walking back.

'We've been extremely careful so far,' Jute said. 'The people involved – the clinic, the guys who set up the displays – they don't know shit. All they were told was that they were taking part in a top security briefing for someone with the highest credentials. Sammy has been working hard, and alone, in a place he's fixed up for himself. Won't even tell *me* where it is. That's how careful he is.'

The face of the former governor from Georgia was on the cover of more than one news magazine.

Jute motioned towards the newsstand with his chin. '*He*'s a problem too,' he said. 'No more dirty tricks. Nothing immoral, like blackmail or bribery. No more of the kind of things we used to do so well. Our new President doesn't realize the other side doesn't abide by any kind of rules.'

'How likely is it,' Forgeot asked, 'that someone might find out about us?'

'In the present state of affairs,' said Jute, 'there's no telling. Some Senator might hear a rumour. Some fucking reporter might start sniffing around. Or the Director himself might hear something, through his own spies. Do-gooders,' he added sourly, 'they cause more trouble than the baddies.' He looked around him with distaste, taking in the cafeterias, the bars, the waiting servicemen, their overweight wives and restless children. 'In any case,' Jute said, after a long pause, 'if something bad happens, it won't necessarily affect you. It'll be Sammy and me for the high jump.'

'Will there be any way of my knowing, other than reading about it in the *International Herald Tribune*?'

'Tell you what I'll do,' said Jute. 'Oldest gimmick in the world. If ever I get the faintest inkling that there's a bad smell – vibes,' he said, turning the word into a sneer, 'I think the younger generation calls it – I'll send you a postcard of the

White House. On it I'll write: wish you were here.'

Forgeot said: 'You must be joking.'

But Jute was dead serious. When the time came to go through to the plane, he gave a jaunty thumbs up, turned and walked away.

Forgeot watched him slip through the airport crowd: a small, neat, nondescript figure, hard as nails. The last of the cold war warriors. The last of the crusaders, and undoubtedly a little mad. Possibly the last of the little band for whom the game existed to be played for its own sake. How would he react, were he told the truth, and forced to admit that he was just a puppet on a string? Badly, of course. To the extent of having me killed? Forgeot thought. Perhaps. But Jute's anger would not just be at the betrayal. It would focus on motive. 'You mean to say you did all this for a *girl*?' He could hear Jute saying – 'A girl you hardly *know*?' Yes, I'm committed to getting her back, Forgeot silently replied, by whatever means I can, regardless of the damage caused to others. I've been in one surrender too many. I have to see this through. Nothing personal, you understand.

Then he was shunted out to the aircraft on board one of those ridiculous mobile waiting-rooms that are the hallmark of Dulles Airport. Settling into his first-class seat and refusing the champagne, still feeling a slight twinge where the stitches had been removed and the queasiness that comes from hospital food, he started to read the latest highly-acclaimed paperback spy thriller, a tale of moles and men, to find out how these things were conducted in real life.

There were flowers on his desk, and jokes about his operation: Forgeot had forgotten how popular he was. There was routine business to attend to, and a quick chat with Leguerrec, who said: 'By the way, Guillaume will be let out on bail any day now.'

Forgeot telephoned the Fontaine du Matin Calme. The code worked perfectly. He wanted to keep Feng alert, though it would be some time before he had anything to show him.

They met on the corner of the Boulevard Saint-Michel as arranged. Feng was not alone this time either. But his companion was a younger man, who said little.

'I haven't anything specific just yet,' Forgeot said, as they walked down the Boulevard towards the Ile Saint-Louis. 'I just wanted to make sure we could reach each other quickly.'

Feng didn't seem put out. 'I have explained our arrangements,' he said, and Forgeot imagined long, complicated coded messages – perhaps hand-carried – eventually reaching the two new Chinese leaders. Since Mao's death, at least the pattern of leadership was clearer.

'There's one puzzling thing,' Feng said. 'At our last meeting, you said that Mr Guillaume was nothing but a messenger. That was not the impression he gave us. He seemed very much in charge.'

'He was the executor,' Forgeot said. 'In cases of this kind, the Government is reluctant to intervene itself.'

'We would still like to talk to Guillaume.'

'By all means,' Forgeot said. 'But he's had his troubles since you saw him last. At the moment, I believe he's in jail, under rather serious charges.'

'He was released today,' Feng said.

Forgeot laughed. 'You see how well up I am in these affairs,' he said. 'I didn't even know. By all means talk to him. I should warn you, however, that he's a pretty unreliable, as well as a rather unsavoury character. He's not someone we're particularly proud of. That, in a way, is why he landed the dirty jobs he did so well.'

As soon as the two Chinese had left, Forgeot rushed to a telephone in the basement of a late-night left-bank café. There was no time to lose. Tranh, and quite possibly Rossi, might have to be brought into the game. He only hoped it was not too late.

Guillaume was in a dark, violent mood. He had spent much more time in preventive detention than he had expected – never a good sign, as far as the trial to come was concerned. His 'piednoir' contacts had been unsympathetic. Even his lawyer had been downright unfriendly. His police colleagues ostracized him. He was apprehensive, but not desperate. If she knew what was good for her, Valentine would never dare testify against him. He also believed that, in the last resort, he might get the charges quashed as a reward for keeping quiet about a whole series of SAC activities which could become embarrassing if he ever talked about them. Returning the Chinese girl was only one of them.

That first night, back in his small bachelor apartment near the Bastille, he took his telephone off the hook. He had always lived alone. It was safer, for a pimp, the French Penal Code being what it was.

He suspected Forgeot of having pulled this particular trick on him, but couldn't rule out the Corsicans. He had been a fool to ask the Chinese for money, but that would never come out. The best course was to lie low, hope the investigation would get bogged down, that the right pressures would be put on that little whore, and that, in the last resort, he might find himself shifted to another, less sensitive, branch within the service. That was what usually happened to suspended police officers who found themselves in trouble. He brooded about the case, and only fell asleep at dawn. When he had been arrested they had taken away his police revolver, but Guillaume had his own personal weapon. This he kept close to his bedside. One never knew.

He didn't wake till mid-morning, and then only because the bell rang.

He reached for his gun.

The voice on the other side of the door was unmistakably Chinese.

'We come from the Chinese Embassy,' it said.

'I don't give a damn,' said Guillaume. 'Bugger off.'

The person on the other side of the door might have been expecting just such a reaction.

'It's from Mr Feng.'

Guillaume said: 'I don't know him. I don't wish to know him. I said: get lost.'

The voice on the landing went on: 'Monsieur Forgeot has been telling Mr Feng that it was he, not you, who was responsible for delivering the girl. It is essential for us to know the truth. Please let us in.'

Guillaume, gun in hand, opened the door.

The two Chinese, in Mao suits, were polite, almost deferential. Guillaume said: 'It's nonsense. Forgeot was the one who . . .'

One of the men levelled a spraygun in his face, and the mace blinded him. The other one grabbed the gun. They sprayed him with unnecessary thoroughness, until they were themselves coughing and sneezing. With quick, precise gestures, they put a black bag over his head, and one of them jerked his arms behind his back. He tried to struggle but one of them expertly broke his middle finger. He roared with pain. He could feel the handcuffs, and was hit over the head repeatedly, not hard enough to make him lose consciousness entirely, just enough to sense the blood, and remained dazed. He felt himself being lifted into a crate of some kind.

On the way down the narrow stairs, they cursed repeatedly at his weight. A grey, unmarked Citroën van was double-parked outside, and traffic was piling up, but this was usual on this particular street at this particular time of day and nobody remembered what kind of van it had been, or its number, when the police started investigating.

At five a.m. the owner of the newspaper kiosk in the Place Maubert opened up her booth next to the Métro, waiting for the 'Nouvelles Messageries de la Presse Parisienne' to drop off its consignment of papers. She was surprised to notice a dark shape in that part of the Place that is used, three times a week, as an open-air fruit and vegetable market.

Had she known anything about modern painting, she would have been struck by the resemblance of the shape to a Francis Bacon painting – one in particular called *The Archbishop*, a screaming figure in such intense pain that it is difficult to look at overlong. The market stall-holders use metal recesses, specially drilled into the pavement surface, to secure the iron bars which provide the necessary scaffolding for their stalls. On the site of the empty market space a slouched, still figure appeared to be crouching. When she came close, the kiosk owner started screaming. She hid inside her booth, shaking and sobbing. She was an elderly woman, and she remained hysterical and incoherent for some hours. She never did open up her booth that day, and later, had to be taken home.

It was the baker in the Place Maubert, minutes after her scream, who gave the alarm. He had heard the scream and left his ovens to investigate. A little later the police arrived. They hadn't far to go. The 5th *arrondissement* police station is just around the corner from the Place Maubert.

123

The police had no trouble lifting Guillaume. He had been impaled on a metal stake and left there, the stake firmly wedged into one of the pavement recesses.

The coroner later determined that he had been fully conscious when the stake had been thrust up his rectum, and had remained so for some time, the stake eventually protruding from his neck. What he – and the police – failed to understand was why, in addition, pencils had been thrust into both his eyes and why his tongue had been torn out. At one stage in the proceedings, his genitalia had been burnt with a blowtorch. It couldn't have been to make him talk, the coroner said, because his tongue had been ripped out, and his vocal chords cut, before whoever was responsible for his death had started on the rest.

Chapter Nine

AT FIRST, in the early months of 1977, there seemed to be no logical pattern whatever to the sudden activities of the Chinese Peoples Liberation Army, as monitored by the National Reconnaissance Office. 'It looked,' said someone at the CIA, 'as if an ant-hill had just been stirred with a stick.'

Not all of it was concentrated on the Soviet and Outer Mongolian borders. It was general, extending as far south as Kwangtung province itself – a frenzy of movement, an increase in railway, airstrip, road and barracks construction. The satellites showed the greatest activity among the 'Second Artillery' units which controlled and operated China's nuclear missile force – some hundred nuclear launchers in all, warheads with ranges of up to 1750 miles. All were being moved from their previous locations , in most cases near the Soviet border. In some cases, not only 'Local Force' units but also civilian population were called in to help build roads and dig holes. Clearly, the order had come down from on high to get some units particularly vulnerable to nuclear attack out of their old positions and into new ones, on a war footing. But some of the conventional 'Main Force' infantry divisions, perhaps thirty out of China's total of 112, were also redeployed, as were China's twelve armoured divisions, all located in the north and north-west. The satellites showed that work had begun on surface mobile launch pads, requiring a considerable road and railway infrastructure. Some of them, said NRO experts, were probably dummies.

Additional reports came not from satellites but from those licensed spies, the long-suffering Peking-based diplomats. In some areas, they learnt, work stopped as all hands were called out to help the army and militia establish the 'Second Artillery' units in new positions, digging silos and hacking rough lanes out of the desert, such work even extending to farmers and factory workers in neighbouring towns. 'Defence comes even before industrial production' was a slogan a Chinese-speaking Dutch businessman spotted while on a trip to Huehot, and it was repeated from one Embassy to another.

In Peking itself a huge new civil defence campaign got under way. Embassy interpreters, translators, drivers as well as household staff of those living in the 'diplomatic ghetto' all absented themselves from work for forty-eight hours at a time, over a period of two weeks, and without any prior warning.

This was not in itself all that unusual. Locally-hired Chinese staff were 'loaned' to the Embassies from a Government-organized pool. Many came from the Public Security Bureau. All were required to brief the Public Security Bureau on the comings and goings of visitors to the Embassies, on the habits, life styles and conversations of the diplomats and the families for whom they worked as butlers, cleaners or cooks. On this occasion, however, they chatted among themselves, at work, and the Chinese-speaking diplomats overheard them comparing experiences. They were talking about the evacuation and shelter exercises they had taken part in, district by district, and about the unusually long time they had spent underground, and how far they had had to walk – at least five miles underground, the Austrian Ambassador's cook had said, emerging in the suburbs, from which, he added ruefully, they had had to walk home.

The existence of a huge complex of anti-nuclear shelters in Peking had never been denied by the Chinese Government: on the contrary, it had always been at pains to draw the attention of diplomats, journalists and even tourists to the existence of this expensive and large network of underground shelters and corridors. 'Dig deeper, stock food, and never practise hegemony' had been the oft-repeated slogans of Chairman Mao in his dotage, and how the inhabitants of Peking had dug! Not always to good avail, for Peking's moats and artificial lakes made any underground work hazardous. The Peking metro (two lines, from east to west) took years to build for this reason, and was nearer the surface than either the Paris or the London underground systems. The shelter complex was an extension of the Peking metro itself, but foreigners were always shown the same portion of it: that part accessible from a trap door in a supermarket in Chien Men Street, in the centre of Peking, which, diplomats suspected, was in any case reserved not for ordinary Chinese, but for selected officials and all the Party's Central Committee and their staffs. The visitors saw wide corridors and dormitories, brightly lit, spotlessly clean, well stocked with food, water and waste disposal units, with emergency power generators. The tunnels were also designed to get the population out of high radiation areas, to the comparative safety of the suburbs.

Such was the secrecy with which business was conducted in China that few people knew whether the elaborate shelter system in Peking was duplicated in other large towns: Shanghai was thought to have a much less advanced network, as was Canton – despite the assumption that it presented a somewhat remote target.

The logic of China's civil defence build-up was obvious: China had no tested ICBM missile powerful enough to reach Moscow. The Soviets had a whole arsenal of weapons to take out Peking. The shelters were a form of deterrent. 'We will bury you,' Khruschev had said of the United States, only part in jest. Mao's reaction had been to bury the Chinese people. Buried, they could remain alive until the worst radiation effects outside had worn off, moving through the tunnels to the less dangerously contaminated areas, thus – in time – overwhelming the aggressor simply by their sheer survival.

At first the diplomats had not taken the shelters too seriously, for, like the factories they visited, they assumed they were show-case 'Potemkin villages' bearing little relevance to the state of preparedness of China as a whole. Comparing notes, diplomats from both East and West had discovered that all had seen a portion of the same shelter, all entering it through the same Chien Men store entrance.

Peking was perhaps the only capital where ideological barriers had completely crumbled simply because the Chinese authorities were so aloof and so uncommunicative that all diplomats accumulated scraps of information where they could. After the shelter exercises, the British talked to the Yugoslavs, the French to the Japanese, the Swiss to almost everybody. The consensus was that, while the network of shelters stretched under only part of the city, all inhabitants had taken part in the exercise, many of them simply squatting in cellars for hours at a time, most of them walking miles through the tunnels to the suburban exits. The exercises had been staggered, and nobody seemed to know why they had been held at such short notice.

The British Ambassador, a bearded, irrepressible extrovert who had survived hardship posts in Kinshasa and Prague, was in favour of making a common representation with his Western colleagues – to ask, head-on, what had triggered off the new concern with civil defence. All Embassies in Peking had been ordered to build air raid shelters of their own capable of housing their own staffs, and all had complied – except for the Soviet Embassy, which refused to open its doors for Chinese inspection. There had been a good deal of grumbling, especially since the sheer cost of building the shelters was regarded as yet another Chinese way of gouging the West, but at least one diplomatic mission – the Canadians – had got some use out of it: their shelter, once completed and approved by the Chinese authorities, was transformed into a disco, and on a Saturday night looked rather like a bargain basement Régine's.

'We could ask them if we can take part in the same air raid practice at the same time,' the British Ambassador told his colleagues. 'Of course they won't *tell* us anything – but it's the way they react that counts, isn't it? Will they tell us to bugger off? Or will they say *why* they've suddenly called the drill?' Most Western Ambassadors were in favour of such a common approach – with the usual exception of the French Ambassador, who prided himself on his privileged relationship with the Chinese Government, and did not bother to conceal his contempt for the British Ambassador.

'It has to be a joint move, André, or they'll simply ignore us,' the British Ambassador had said. But André Terreneuve, the French Ambassador, was non-committal in public, though afterwards, at a meeting of his own staff, he exploded. 'Who does that clown think he is? Does he seriously expect me to take part in such antics? I will not lend the name of France to such childish provocations. The British have nothing to lose. They are not even a second-rate European power.'

The senior Soviet Military Attaché, also an extrovert, a bluff tank specialist called General Bilkov, became even more socially active after the civil defence exercises. He had a fondness for bridge and a tendency to flirt mildly with Western Embassy wives. Bilkov's search for clues was understandable: the Soviet Embassy, despite its size, was handicapped in one crucial respect. it had almost no local Chinese employees. All the lower-grade jobs were staffed by Russians. Unashamedly, Bilkov pursued his guests at dinner parties with questions: was it true that employees from the Bridge of Heaven area had gone to special shelters of their own? Where had Embassy servants emerged from the shelters? As far away from the centre as the West Fragrant Hills? How long had they remained underground? How far had they had to walk?

While Bilkov assiduously courted the Western community in Peking, the CIA pondered the meaning of the latest exercises. Jute, in his Georgetown house, knew that they could have only one meaning – that the scheme he and Forgeot had launched must be working.

He had assumed as much, even before the Chinese troop movements and civil defence exercises had begun. Not that he had taken the risk of communicating directly with Forgeot. There had been no need. For Jute, proof had come earlier, with the arrival, in France, of an unusually large Chinese delegation to the Lyons Trade Fair. At Langley the China section had come to the conclusion, from studying a photograph on the steps of Lyons Town Hall, that one of the Chinese in the group might be Chien Tah, a nuclear affairs specialist at the Chinese Defence Ministry. Regardless of the odd surroundings, his emergence was surprising, for, like so many top members of the Chinese politico-military establishment, he had disappeared during the Cultural Revolution and had even, at one point, been thought dead.

The DST was queried. It was unable to respond with any accuracy. The name of the supposed nuclear expert did not correspond with the name, passport or title, as registered with the Trade Fair organisers. The DST did, however, report that the man who looked like Chien Tah, the nuclear expert, had not spent much time in Lyons, at any rate in public, and had left by car for Geneva with two other officials while the fair was still in progress. They had been greeted at Geneva Airport by a couple of diplomats from the

Chinese Embassy in Paris. One of them had been Feng.

But Jute's own report, written at the request of the Director, 'from the Soviet point of view' after the Chinese defence rehearsals, was unusually bland. On the basis of available evidence, Jute noted, it was premature to assume there had been a sudden rise in tension between China and the Soviet Union. There had been no recent fresh border incidents, no heightening in the war of words in the Soviet press, nothing, in short, to justify any such Chinese behaviour. The inference was that the military activity and the civil defence exercises were simply routine exercises to keep the Chinese 'psychologically mobilised'.

Jerry Brand disagreed. He was one of the new-style CIA analysts, more at home in a university library than in the field. He wrote a contradictory report, outlining the thoroughness of the Chinese military moves, their cost, the fact that precious harvest and production days threatened to be lost because thousands of farmers and factory workers had been compelled to help the military. The industrial stoppages, he said, were comparable in scale to those of the Cultural Revolution period. 'We cannot tell,' he wrote, unsuccessfully trying to break out of his usual academic style, 'why this sudden series of measures has come about, but we must admit that something must have occurred to compel China's political and military leaders to slow down production, delay the harvest and go to such considerable expense in repositioning almost all its operational units.' Brand, thirty years old, with no field experience, conceited but a good judge of character, had been amazed by Jute's report. 'The old boy's round the bend,' he told Diana White, an analyst specialising in third world energy problems. 'He always saw everything in terms of global conflict. Now he refuses to admit the obvious.'

Diana, blue-eyed, dark-blonde, pretty in a conventional, Vassar way, thought Jute was cute, and said so. 'He used to jog a lot around here,' she said, 'but I haven't seen him around Georgetown for the last month.'

Almost unconsciously, Brand stored the information away. He was round-eyed, round-faced, on the tubby side, and disliked the way Jute referred to him as the egg-shaped egghead. A thin mind in a fat body was how a girlfriend had described him. He had total recall, an excellent brain, and Soviet defence planning was his field. He was rumoured to be an heir to a considerable fortune, in something faintly ridiculous, like hair curlers.

Brand brushed away the crumbs from a late breakfast in bed, which he had prepared himself. Women, he always said, were unable to make scrambled eggs properly. Simply lacked the necessary patience.

'Christ, don't tell me you jog too,' Brand said.

'Of course I do. It's the ideal way of picking up desirable men.'

'You find Jute desirable, huh?'

'What the British would call dishy. Jealous?'

'Did he respond?'

'I don't think he's all that interested in women,' said Diana, 'all he's interested in is the cold war.'

'You see, he *is* round the bend. Now, this little bend here . . .' He shifted his considerable weight, lightly touching the curve of her bare hip. A large breakfast always made him feel amorous.

Jute was no longer jogging because he was having problems working on the contents of the next batch of posters to be sent to Forgeot. He was also having problems with Semyakov, who was increasingly nervous.

'Don't worry, it's all going splendidly,' Jute said. They were together in Jute's car. Semyakov grunted.

'Then what the fuck are my compatriots doing? A few months ago, all they could talk about was "solving the Chinese problem". Now they have every reason to react, and they're not moving a muscle.'

'Suppose we try and find out,' said Jute.

The young liaison man from SIS who masqueraded as a British Embassy First Secretary was called, tapped for information, and returned to say that, really, I mean, things have never been quieter, the old boy's sicker than hell, of course, and maybe the generals haven't dared tell him yet, what? It *was* strange, Jute agreed. Soviet satellites were almost as good at monitoring Chinese troop movements. Maybe the Chairman was sicker than was rumoured. Maybe, as good chess-players, they are waiting for China's next move, Jute thought. And maybe they know all about our little game plan, and are laughing all the way to the Narodny Bank.

Diana had a row with Brand, and stopped seeing him. He really was too self-centred, too much of a fat sexist pig, too pleased with himself, too aware of his intellectual gifts, she told her brother on the telephone. Paul White was a reporter on the *Washington Star*.

'Stupid, hon. Who's going to give me any top secret titbits now?'

'That's your funeral,' she said. 'He never did, anyway – and if he had I wouldn't have told you.'

'Come on, sis, you would too.'

'I would not.'

'Well, tell me something now. Something unimportant and totally useless.'

'All right. Jute has stopped his early morning jogging.'

Paul was a Yale and a Columbia School of Journalism graduate who had wanted to be a newspaperman ever since he could read. After two years on the staff of a small New Jersey newspaper, where his investigative talents had been confined to unmasking $500 pay-offs and padded garbage squads, he had been hired by the *Star* to cover Housing, Education and Welfare. He had read every book published about Watergate, and wondered what might have happened, had he already been with the *Star* when Woodward and Bernstein were tracking down 'deep throat'. Such onanistic day-dreams contrasted with his own inconclusive attempts, to date, to become a top-flight investigative Washington reporter. Since being hired, he had only had one scoop: by means of careful scrutiny of HEW accounts, he had accurately determined the cost of the Secretary's newly-refurbished private dining-room and newly-hired personal Greek chef. The story had been a nine-day wonder, picked up by the wire services and front-paged on the *Star*. Its after-effects, however, were not what reporters lusting after Pulitzer prizes reckon on: Paul's sources at HEW had dried up, the Secretary would no longer talk to him, and there was widespread resentment at the fact that a couple of junior aides, wrongly suspected of leaking the information, had been either "let go" or sent to Nebraska. Since then, Paul had had no more scoops. He had asked for a transfer.

Paul had only vaguely heard of Jute, but, with nothing better to do, looked him up, asked questions, read what meagre clips were available from the *Star*'s library. What would 'Woodstein' have done, Paul asked himself – and began a watching brief on Jute, in his own time.

There are skills that even the keenest investigative reporter lacks, skills that are taught neither at Yale nor the Columbia School of Journalism, and require practice, organisation, teamwork. To follow Jute Paul had imagined he need only behave as he had seen people do in movies. He had reckoned neither with Georgetown's narrow streets, its parking problems, on the volume of Washington traffic. Only too late he realized the need for more than one car, teams of trained men, walkie-talkies, radio links.

The first time Paul was still circling the block when Jute left his house. He waited for an hour, double-parked, until moved on by a police patrol. The ignominy was complete. The second time he started too far back, losing him in the early morning traffic, at the first red light. The third time he tailgated him so blatantly that Jute first made sure he was being followed, then memorised the registration number of Paul's Chevrolet and finally accelerated, making a couple of sudden right turns. He was relieved to hear a cacophonous collective motorists' protest, as Paul tried to follow, was surprised by the oncoming rush of traffic as he tried to beat the lights, and snarled up the morning car commuters, immobilizing all concerned in an inextricable jam.

Only partly reassured, Jute drove on fast, parked in a downtown garage, took first one cab, then another, making sure that the Chevrolet had been on its own. A couple of telephone calls confirmed what he had suspected: his pursuer was neither efficient nor official, but a young *Star* reporter.

How long had Paul been watching him? How much did he know? Jute hesitated before mentioning the incident to Semyakov, who turned even more pallid than usual. 'It could be idle curiosity,' said Jute. Semyakov was not convinced.

Semyakov persisted in his reluctance to let Jute know too much about the way the satellite reconnaissance stills were being manufactured. All Jute knew for certain was that Semyakov, as a senior analyst, was able to obtain copies of such photographs, of which the CIA had literally thousands, which he then modified – either in his apartment, or, more likely, in a rented studio, under another name – using his photographer's expertise, his special knowledge and skills. It had not been necessary, or indeed opportune, for Jute to know all the details – though Semyakov had regularly kept him informed of his progress, and had asked for, and received, $20,000 for expenses.

They met more furtively now, communicating through time-honoured foolproof dead letterboxes, not daring to talk openly on the telephone, though they occasionally found themselves at the same conference gathering, and treated each other then with studied casualness, trying to remember what their relationship had been before their plot, in the eyes of their colleagues, and acting accordingly. Jute's attempt to find out more about the motives for Paul White's behaviour got nowhere. Either the *Star* reporter had given up, or he was using more sophisticated methods. Routinely, Jute scanned his street for unusual signs of activity, took intricate detours whenever he travelled by car, and was careful to be on the look-out, at all times, for evidence of surveillance.

Paul White had not given up. Rather, he tried a different line of approach. On his day off, with the pretext that he had been shifted to another assignment, he made an appointment with Brand, at Langley. The CIA will thus, occasionally, license a contact between a reporter and an Agency official, provided the reporter has himself been cleared, is of American nationality, and the Agency operative he seeks to meet is unconnected with covert activities.

The meeting was not a success. Brand knew that his very existence must have come to his notice through Diana, and he was not pleased. Neither was he convinced by Paul's pretext for the meeting – that he was attempting to put together a lengthy piece on US-Soviet relations. It was of course impossible for Brand to talk about the evidence of recent Chinese activity. And Paul, inexperienced and over-eager, mentioned Jute's name too early, and too often. Brand came away convinced that Paul White was in fact attempting to write piece about Jute, and was glad he had refused to be drawn into any controversy beyond mention-ing that Jute was 'probably the most knowledgeable single individual on Soviet affairs' still working for the CIA.

Most of Paul's friends worked, not in Washington, but in New York, and at weekends he habitually stayed, as a guest, in this or that apartment. His New York crowd was of the same age and background: Yalies, Columbia School of Journalism graduates, rapidly rising young thirty-year-olds in teaching, advertising, television, the press. He would drive only when someone came with him, usually a girl friend. Paul was eclectic, easily bored by women, and seldom took the same girl to meet his friends. But on this occasions he had found Julie, a young lawyer working for a firm of prestigious lawyer lobbyists, to his taste, and she was mildly attracted to Paul. She also badly wanted to see an off-Broadway show he had promised to take her to.

Everyone agreed it was one of those ghastly accidents that are liable to happen on any turnpike.

It had occurred about a hundred miles north of Washington, early on Saturday morning. There had been little traffic and police assumed Paul White had simply fallen asleep, and sheered straight into the left-hand side of the turnpike, his car bouncing back, turning over and exploding. The rear tyres were smoother than they should have been, but there was no trace of a long skid. Or else he had been scared by a truck suddenly pulling out ahead of him as he was about to overtake .

At first it had been almost impossible to identify the two bodies, for they were so badly charred that it looked as if the only means of identification would be through their teeth. But, in a small metal sansonite suitcase, they found Paul White's diary.

What puzzled the highway patrol was the suddenness with which the explosion had occurred. Witnesses mentioned a speeding truck, but no truck driver came forward. Nobody had actually seen the accident, though some did recall a beige Chevrolet driving in the wake of a truck, itself travelling at great speed, and repeatedly trying to pass it.

Nobody remembered, either, seeing a white Mustang with two men in it, pausing after the truck had deliberately swerved – it had been waiting for such an opportunity for nearly an hour – forcing the Chevrolet to crash, then precisely and speedily firebombing it, without bothering to

135

stop, and getting off the turnpike minutes later. The contract had been a costly one, and Jute had not known about it till later. Semyakov had taken care of everything.

Brand and Diana came together again after the funeral.

'Did you know your brother came to see me just before he died?' Brand asked. Diana did not.

'What did he want to talk about?'

'He said it was US-Soviet relations, but I felt what he really wanted was a low-down on Jute.'

'I told him that Jute had stopped jogging.'

'Is that all?'

'I swear.'

Among Paul's things, Diana found a scrawled scrap of paper. It read, in Paul's tiny, indecipherable handwriting: Jute not jogging? Another entry was simply Jute's George-town address. There was nothing else. But there was, Diana decided, enough to pick up the telephone and make an appointment with the Agency's Director. The second call was to someone in the FBI.

In his own precise handwriting, Jute – along with many other Agency colleagues – wrote Diana a short but well-turned note of condolence. The *Washington Star's* obituary and the description of the circumstances of the accident took up more columm inches than it had ever devoted to any one of Paul White's own stories during his lifetime.

In Paris, through the indirect communication channel they had decided on, Forgeot received a long, rambling note from Jute, outlining Paul White's interest in him, and the *Star* cutting of the accident. 'He had begun researching a piece about me,' Jute wrote, somewhat inaccurately, 'and in the fashion of today's journalists he thought he was some kind of investigative genius. Has anyone taken an interest in you lately?'

Chapter Ten

THEY HAD all been right – Semyakov, Jute the young man from SIS. The Soviet Chairman had been sick, was in fact seriously, possibly even terminally, ill, and for the last three weeks he had spent no more than a few minutes a day on State business. Exceptionally, to lighten his load still further, his principal aide, Ilyakov, had decided he would not even submit the daily KGB foreign situation report – the digest of world affairs specially written for him.

It was one of the comparatively junior members of the Cabinet, the Vice-Defence Minister Arbatchieff, who suggested that the Chairman be told. When Ilyakov failed to respond, Arbatchieff insisted – at first to no avail. Arbatchieff had requested a session with the Chairman immediately after receiving the first complete report on Chinese troop movements. Now he had to pull rank, wheedle and remind several people on the Chairman's personal staff that he, Arbatchieff, was not unconnected with powerful committees dealing with promotion and overseas appointments, and that his party rank was such as to warrant special treatment, before he was finally authorized to meet the Chairman in person. At first he wasn't even told where the Chairman was 'resting'. Only on the eve of the appointment was he informed that an Air Force plane would take him to Sochi, where the climate, as is well-known, was excellent for what the Chairman's entourage referred to, euphemistically, as a 'passing liver condition'.

The Chairman was wearing a Texas Ranger hat the American President had given him, baggy linen trousers and the ritual striped pyjama top that all good Soviet citizens wear on vacation. His Adidas tennis shoes, specially ordered from the Embassy in Bonn, were unlaced. As a mark of esteem, the Chairman had sent one of his cars – an air-conditioned Citroën DS – to fetch him at the airport. Police had kept the roads clear for two full hours before and after his plane had landed.

Arbatchieff had made the trip alone. His only luggage was a large flat Vuitton portfolio of the kind used by successful architects and top fashion models for their pressbook pictures. It, too, came from the West – a present from the Soviet Military Attaché in Paris, who attentively and persistently cultivated those he considered to be coming men.

The Chairman was in a good mood: exceptionally, his bodily functions had been normal that morning, the ringing in his ears which could afflict him with terrifying suddenness (making him almost totally deaf) had just as inexplicably stopped that morning, and – equally exceptionally – he felt not a trace of morning nausea.

Arbatchieff propped the portfolio on a chair and looked around him on the verandah of the large dacha. About twenty paces away, a couple of grey-uniformed militiamen mounted guard. He looked at the Chairman, interrogatively. The old man understood. 'Everybody out,' he shouted to his nurse, a gaunt Ukrainian who had been with him ever since Stalingrad. The Ukrainian in turn barked out an order. The hand-picked Naval ratings in waiters' uniforms who had brought in platters of cheese, black bread, herring, tea, vodka and minute quantities of caviar (a separate tray for the Chairman consisted solely of a pale liquid that could have been hot lemon juice) hustled out. Arbatchieff noted with satisfaction that he now rated caviar. Last time they had met, there had been none.

He undid the strings of the portfolio. 'Mr Chairman,' he said, 'I am about to show you something –' he paused for good effect – 'which, as the Americans would say, will blow your mind. In our own good Russian parlance, it will make your hair curl. The Chinese seem to be making preparations to drop their miserable nuclear bombs on Russian soil.'

While Arbatchieff was briefing the Soviet Chairman, the new French Interior Minister was fighting a winning battle against the press, but it wasn't making him any happier. The death of Guillaume had led to a spate of stories, all innuendo and between-the-lines references which are the French press's way of circumventing libel laws and avoiding

138

officialdom's wrath. A couple of editors had gone further, hinting that the whole story remained to be told. In one case the Minister brandished the carrot – a discreet reminder, through a mutual friend, that the July 14 Honours List was coming up and that it would be too bad if the Legion of Honour 'for services to French publishing' were to be withheld.

In the case of another editor, the head of a small, shoe-string iconoclastic daily run by a co-operative of leftists, Trotskyites and other nonconformists, all drawing pitiful salaries, the Minister had no carrot: his only stick was the threat of further court cases on obscenity charges which might drive the paper further in debt. They might do the trick. In any case, the Minister doubted the paper's ability to find out anything of value about Guillaume: the necessary orders had gone out to all who might have helped, but Paris was a sieve, malicious gossip the stock-in-trade of every smart Parisian, and the Minister was not even sure of the discretion of his own personal staff.

There was ample material for the kind of scandal that in any other Western country would rock a government but in France only became a brief headline, a nine-days wonder, quickly fading into oblivion. The fact that Guillaume had simultaneously been a police officer and a member of the underworld was regrettable, but could be explained on the grounds that opportunities for penetrating the French 'milieu' were rare, and that people like him fulfilled a necessary if unpalatable role. At least so ran the official line. But even the new Minister was shocked by what the internal inspection team uncovered: evidence that Guillaume had had a hand in everything from organised prostitution to illegal gambling, with maybe a little drug-smuggling on the side. That he had been an occasional – and efficient – odd-job man for the Government only made things worse.

The Préfecture's inspection team itself came under suspicion, for not reporting Guillaume's activities earlier. The head of this small but highly influential and respected squad indignantly denied that any cover-up had been intended. Guillaume, he said, had attracted no special attention as a Mondaine man. It was known, of course, that he had been a SAC member and an occasional 'dirty tricks' freelance operator on the French Government's behalf, but this had only confirmed his professional standing, and the esteem in which he had been held. There was a general, almost panic-stricken denial of any knowledge of his earlier Foreign Legion record.

'But surely you must have known about his sexual habits?' the Minister had asked.

The veteran inspectorate cop, nine months away from a pension, and with nothing to lose, gazed back at the Minister.

'That's just where you're wrong, Minister,' he said. 'The girls never talked. And he didn't boast about them. Not like some people I could name.'

The Minister, across the desk, knew better than to ask for an elaboration of this cryptic remark.

The Interior Minister hoped that a successful investigation into the cause of the murder – and some spectacular arrests – might draw attention away from Guillaume's own un-savoury background, and pressed hard for results, re-gardless of what the findings might unearth. But, apart from the sheer savagery with which Guillaume had been done to death (the Coroner said his was the most messed-up corpse he had ever seen, and he had been in the business for twenty-five years), there was little for the police or the forensic laboratory to uncover: a stain on Guillaume's jacket that was probably soya sauce, but could have been the result of a sloppy eater's mishap, and some minute particles of flesh under Guillaume's nails that could only mean he had clawed and scratched before he died. Police visited every shop, every restaurant, every café in the neighbourhood of the Place Maubert. Predictably, they drew a blank. Nobody had seen anything, or knew anything, no one had been up and about that dawn on the Place Maubert. The underworld, the Vietnamese within a mile radius of where he had been found, all denied any knowledge of the man.

Within the police itself opinions differed: one detective was convinced that Guillaume's death had a Vietnamese connection. Others, especially in the light of the Coroner's report, thought the mafia might be involved. This type of killing, they said, was completely unFrench. In the underworld as they knew it, straightforward liquidation was invariably swift, and by bullet. On rare occasions in the past, suspected police informers had been tortured first, but never like this. The imprint of gratuitous cruelty pointed to a gang with international connections, either the mafia or the triads. Others believed that, somehow, the Guillaume killing went back to OAS days, and was an act of revenge – not by Algerians, but maybe former OAS members.

Forgeot himself was asked for an opinion. He could cast no light on the murder, he wrote, and for all Guillaume's nefarious activities there didn't seem to be any espionage link. The root cause of the whole affair, Forgeot added, could be found in the surprisingly lax way French police had recruited former anti-OAS operatives into the force after the Algerian war.

The Minister summoned Forgeot. 'I believe,' he said, 'that you last met Guillaume in this very office. Don't you feel that what happened then could be linked to his death?'

Forgeot thought for a long time. 'Frankly, I doubt it,' he said, 'Why would the Chinese do anything to draw attention to the case? They probably never knew who was involved, in the first place.'

The Minister was a shrewd, enquiring ex-lawyer. 'But you yourself, Forgeot,' he said, 'how do you feel about it?'

'Guillaume was a bastard,' Forgeot replied, without a moment's hesitation. 'I never liked the son of a bitch, and I always felt it was a mistake to have him in the Mondaine. I can't help feeling sorry for the way he died, though. The question I ask myself is: which of the various rackets he had a finger in provoked his death?'

'Were you gratified when you heard he'd been arrested?' the Minister asked.

'I didn't even know about it' said Forgeot. 'I think I was in Washington at the time, attending some stupid security conference.'

The CIA Director agreed that something strange was up. He had seen Diana White, read the reports on the accident, and had a long session with Brand. They had gone over Jute's report together. The Director agreed it hadn't made sense. It had also been, with hindsight, as the Director himself acknowledged, 'inaccurate as hell'.

141

For at long last the Soviet Union was reacting to the Chinese troop movements. There had been no formal statements, no press comment, no direct clashes, but satellite surveillance showed that Soviet armoured and missile units on and near the Sino-Soviet border were on the alert, and that reinforcements were on their way.

'I can't understand Jute,' said the Director, 'any more than I can understand that poor young man's sudden interest in him.'

To the CIA's Internal Security head the Director was almost apologetic.

'I know your high esteem for Jute,' he said, 'but is it possible he's not quite what he seems?'

The Security Department head had been recruited by Jute and trained by him.

'If you say so, I'll put a watch on him,' he said. 'But I just don't understand it. The odds must be a million to one against. It would be their biggest coup since Philby. Can you see Jute sitting pretty in a dacha somewhere writing his memoirs? I mean, he's already got that boat in Maine.'

'Consider it more as an exercise,' the Director said. 'Say you're picking the least likely candidate on purpose, just to keep the boys on their toes.'

'Do I send out a hold on classified stuff to him?'

The Director laughed. 'You expect Jute not to notice? How many people get those China reports anyway? No, keep everything as it is, or he'll spot it right away. We may want to make it obvious to him later on, but we also want to be able to apologise later – at least I hope we will.'

The Internal Security head rose to leave. The Director had one last point to make. 'Remember to tell your boys that Jute is alive today because, long ago, in the fields, he spotted hundreds of teams like yours in time. That's how he survived in France for so long. Tell them it's a kind of game. That's how we'll sell it to Jute if all goes well, and if, or rather when, he finds out.'

He pressed a button on his desk to summon an aide. 'Shit, we'll all be having a good laugh about this in a few weeks' time.'

In Paris an 'eyes-only' message for the Interior Minister was delivered by a United States Embassy First Secretary who was himself unaware of its true contents.

After considerable reflection, the CIA Internal Security head had decided to inform a highly restricted list of non-American nationals of the opening of an enquiry on Jute. Since Jute had spent crucial war and post-war years in Britain and France, one of the recipients of this information was the French Interior Minister, a new appointee who had never heard of Jute before. But the Minister desperately wished to justify the cost of a highly sophisticated computer system, heavily criticised, he knew, by the Cour des Comptes on the grounds that it was incompatible with the systems of any other country in the world. The computer had been the Minister's baby, in an earlier incarnation as a junior secretary of state, and he was determined to prove its usefulness whenever possible.

Jute's name was run through the computer, and, inevitably, Forgeot's appeared on the screen, along with about twenty other names of officials and politicians who had known him in a CIA capacity. The computer was put to work again on each of these names. It revealed nothing that was not already known: X . . . had been suspiciously pro-American, and suspected of providing Jute with inside reports on Cabinet proceedings in the early sixties. But this had never been proved, and besides, X . . . was now a leading Government Majority political figure. Y . . . had panicked during May 1968, and requested Jute, in a bugged conversation in his apartment, for a plane to flee the country 'should the forces of anarchy prevail'. Jute had promised to help, and the tape of that conversation had been preserved. But it was all water under the bridge. Y . . . had since become an unsuccessful Presidential candidate, and one of the most powerful figures in Parliament. Old cupboard skeletons, buried for good.

Forgeot's record was impeccable on all counts. He had duly reported all his dealings with Jute, not like some DST officials, the Minister noted. But the Minister was a prying, prurient type, an avid reader of gossip columns and a man obsessed by the real and imagined weaknesses of others. He called for Forgeot's dossier, and noted that this was the second time in three months that it had been scrutinised by a

Minister. Why? He read details of Forgeot's sex life with relish and envy. He called for a supplementary report.

A government's reputation in the field of security has little to do with methods or personalities. By and large, these vary only marginally from country to country. What matters, all experts on the business know, is continuity, and the thoroughness with which apparently irrelevant or isolated and even contradictory factual matter is collated and stored.

France has one of the most extensive records systems on its own nationals in the world, at any rate outside the Eastern bloc. But it also has one grave drawback. A great deal of its records, from 1941 to 1944, contain matter of such an explosive nature that there is a marked reluctance on the part of police and intelligence officials to go back that far: they are, quite literally, frightened of what could, and occasionally is, revealed in them, even though, with the passage of time, it is all becoming remote history and has to do with a generation of officials and politicians now, some of them, sixty or even older.

The Minister specifically referred to the war years in his call for a supplementary enquiry. When the Minister read what had been prepared for him, he summoned the man responsible.

'All this stuff on Forgeot's early life,' he said. 'Why isn't it in the main file itself?'

'It's hardly relevant, sir.'

'Let me be the judge of that.'

Crazy old fart, the elderly researcher thought to himself. He held high rank, and like all those engaged in the covert surveillance of his fellow-policemen, he was within a year or two of retirement, a rule designed to prevent unfair reporting by those who might benefit from other people's failings.

What the new file had uncovered, almost by accident, was an episode involving not Forgeot himself but Forgeot's father, a Breton business man who died in 1946.

Young Forgeot had spent the war years first in Ireland, with his Irish mother's family, then at a minor British public school. Forgeot senior had stayed in France, and had been active in the Resistance at a time when this had been both unfashionable and almost suicidal. The price he had paid had been heavy, in terms of members of his cell arrested,

144

tortured and deported. Forgeot's father had also been active in organising escape routes for shot-down RAF and US air crews on the run. This activity had been kept secret even from his Resistance colleagues. Forgeot senior had closed down his construction business in 1941. He had been one of the few in Brittany to do so. Others had made large fortunes, before the war's end, building the 'Atlantic Wall' for the Germans that was supposed to keep the French coast secure from invasion.

Immediately after the war, Forgeot senior had made an attempt to get his business going again. But a rival began spreading rumours that he had been a double agent, secretly in league with the Gestapo. The year 1945 was a chaotic, lawless year in France, with hundreds of old scores being paid off, and in Forgeot's case there were few survivors to come forward and deny these allegations. An inexperienced local prosecutor, who had spent the war years safely in London, and was unfamiliar with the local scene, had acted on these rumours, and Forgeot senior had been arrested, and jailed in Rennes, alongside real collaborators and war profiteers.

The arrest, and the jail spell, had lasted only a few weeks: young Jean Forgeot, home from school, had helped clear his father. Appealed to, the British Air Ministry had provided proof of Forgeot senior's role in smuggling no less than twenty-five RAF aircrew out of the country. Scarcely coincidentally, the 1946 New Year's Honours list included Forgeot as a recipient of the CBE. Young Forgeot had also got the Americans to help. There had been an official *démarche* by the American Ambassador.

But the arrest had destroyed Forgeot senior's life. His marriage had broken up. His business never got off the ground. He started drinking heavily, and in 1946 he committed suicide.

Nor was this the whole story: the business rival who had been instrumental in having Forgeot disgraced and jailed had not lived long either. In 1951, there had been an accident. Travelling along a narrow Brittany road, he had run his Citroën into a tree.

A police report said the car had been tampered with. It also expressed the opinion that the dead man's broken neck in the only slightly damaged car was inexplicable. He should by rights have walked away from the accident with no more than a couple of broken ribs. At the time, of course, there had been other, far more urgent police work to attend to, and in any case the Justice Ministry had been reluctant to enquire too deeply into the case: it knew full well that the whole matter of Forgeot's arrest would emerge, for which Forgeot's posthumous award of half a dozen French and American decorations had been scarcely adequate compensation.

What the Minister now wanted to know was: why had there been no mention of young Jean Forgeot in the police report? Where had he been at the time?

The official conducting the enquiry came back with the answer that it had been impossible to trace Jean Forgeot's whereabouts the month of his father's death.

'What are you trying to do, Minister? Reopen proceedings? According to law, everything's covered by legal prescription.'

The Interior Minister would not be provoked. 'I'm just curious,' he said. 'The noble son avenging his father's death. A classic, almost cliché situation. And it's not even hinted at in the report.'

'Maybe, Minister, the son was out of the country.'

'No, he wasn't. He volunteers for service in Indochina around that time. Indochina in 1951 is a melting pot, a haven for collaborators, criminals, adventurers of all kinds. The pattern is obvious.'

'What do you want me to do, Minister? Ask Forgeot to tell me he had the man killed?'

'Of course not. Simply find out where Jute was in 1951'

It turned out that Jute had been in France most of that year. The Minister was jubilant. More hours were spent on further research. It was then established that Jute, from Switzerland, during the last year of the war, had been on the receiving end of a number of American and British escaping aircrews, furnishing them with fake Swiss and Swedish passports.

'It all adds up,' the Interior Minister told his researcher. 'The Forgeot-Jute connection, going back almost to the man's childhood. Fascinating, isn't it?'

'But largely irrelevant, Minister.'

The Interior Minister prided himself on his insight into hidden psychological motives.

'Not so,' he said. 'It proves that someone who takes the law into his own hands and conceals something as serious and as complicated as murder may well have motivations of another kind as well.'

The researcher shrugged.

'It seems to me, Minister, that it simply proves what we know inside this establishment already – that Forgeot's a smart operator.'

'My dear friend,' the Minister said, 'I couldn't agree more. But don't you see the implications? Suppose Jute was on the receiving end of those aircrews Forgeot's father sent out of the country? It's quite likely that Forgeot would have sought Jute out, got him to act behind the scenes to clear his father's name.'

'The record would show this, surely?'

'Not necessarily. Jute was, and remains, CIA. He wouldn't want to come out and testify openly. Don't you see, if Jute and Forgeot knew each other, as far back as 1945–46, the whole picture is different.' The researcher looked baffled, but concealed his irritation. What he really wanted to do was to bring the heavy ornamental inkstand on the desk in front of him down on the Minister's head.

'What it implies,' the Minister said, 'and you're quite right to stress these are suppositions which may never be borne out by hard proof, is that Forgeot, at an early age, came into contact with a man like Jute, and probably under his influence – and that, if Jute is a security risk, then the odds are that Forgeot is as well.'

'With respect, Minister, these are mere suppositions. They would never stand up in any kind of court, even supposing you wished to bring past events out into the open. Is that what you want?'

'Not necessarily,' the Minister said coldly. 'But if there's even the slightest possibility that their relationship goes back that far, then we may have the answer to all sorts of unresolved security leaks – to the United States as well as to the East. Think of it,' he said, wagging a schoolmasterish finger, 'and don't say I didn't warn you.'

'What do you want me to do?'

147

The Interior Minister put his fingertips together. 'Nothing dramatic,' he said. 'No obvious delving into the past. No making him uncomfortable. If we catch him, we'll catch him off his guard. Simply activate the routine "gamma" procedure.'

He enjoyed displaying his new-found expertise.

'You mean, we begin treating Forgeot as a suspect?'

'Don't try and be clever with me,' the Minister said, and his voice, usually little more than a whisper, became a shout, so that even his secretary behind the double doors could hear it. 'You know perfectly well what I mean. I want immediate action on your part. And don't forget the weekly, "eyes-only" report.'

Chapter Eleven

THERE WAS a bunker immediately below Tien An Men Square that no diplomat, however friendly, had ever been taken to. No Peking citizen, except for the immediate entourage of the Vice-Chairman and the Party's Central Committee, knew of its existence. It had a couple of entrances, one from the basement of the Ministry of Defence, the other from the ground-floor level of the Ministry of Public Security. It was, in fact, the only completely secure underground anti-nuclear bunker in the whole of Peking, radiation-proof, with an expensive air filter system. Here, late one night, not more than a dozen people met in a small low-ceilinged conference room. The air was heavy with cigarette smoke, and the air filter system did a poor job dispersing the fumes. The man standing by a blackboard on which were fastened reams of immense sheets of white paper was the same person who had attended the Lyons Trade Fair. Among the audience was the diminutive Vice-Chairman, Ling, who had made his irrepressible comeback after the death of Mao, and most of the top members of the Chinese Peoples Army command, including several vice-defence ministers.

Chien Tah, a scholarly, bespectacled man in his late fifties, with a shock of white hair, used a Chinese felt pen to scribble in both Chinese characters and in English on the paper, turning each time to do so, but carrying on with his commentary while he wrote, very much the professor he had once been. When each sheet was cluttered, he ripped it off, handing it to an aide, who unceremoniously burnt it, showering the ashes into an old-fashioned spittoon at his feet which looked rather like an oversized chamberpot.

Chien Tah had taken up a full sheet outlining the data on the Soviet moves he had acquired from Forgeot. Now he turned to a second.

'What the Soviet force being put together amounts to, then, is approximately this,' he said. 'About 250 single war-headed missiles within range of almost all our major installations. Why this huge number? Presumably because the Soviets intend to knock out not only our fixed silos and surface launch pads – at least those they've spotted through their own satellite reconnaissance, and despite our extremely fine camouflage work – but also most of our airfields and tactical air strips as well. They want to deny us any retaliatory 'second strike' capability. This is why the whole plan can't simply be dismissed as an exercise. This time, they're playing for real. The last time we had a semblance of confrontation, in 1969, they didn't have more than thirty or forty missiles ready. That was one of the reasons, our dear late Chairman forgive me, why we were able to treat them like paper tigers. We knew they weren't serious. Today, they are. In addition the aerial reconnaissance prints show activity around at least two and possibly three longer range missile sites, the kind the Americans call IRBMs.' He paused and, in a flowing hand, wrote out in English: 'intermediate range ballistic missile'.

'These can easily reach Peking, Shanghai and even Canton. As you know, IRBMs have a range of up to 3500 miles.'

There was silence.

'Let's suppose the Russians strike – as everything shows they will. Let's also suppose the CEP stands at around fifty per cent.'

The Vice-Chairman, like a wizened malicious schoolboy, raised his hand in mock appeal. 'CEP,' he said. 'What's that?' He turned to the rest of the class. 'Unlike Comrade Tah, I am not a graduate of MIT.' There were titters. 'I don't think anyone else in this room is so privileged either. I really must insist that Comrade Tah use language,' he paused, and the roomful knew a joke was coming, 'more in tune with the masses.'

Chien Tah smiled wanly, a tired, donnish smile.

'CEP,' he said. '"Circular error probable". The likely margin of accuracy within which Soviet missiles would land. The Americans say they have a built-in margin of error of up to fifty per cent – except for the new SS-20s in the making, for which the margin is much lower. But these aren't deployed yet – at any rate not in the pictures. I have a private theory: everything goes wrong in the USSR, so why not this too? In which case you have a CEP factor of eighty percent. In which case we're home and dry. They hit one target out of five. Some of them may be dummies we've built to look like the real thing. The rest go into the Sinkiang desert. Unfortunately we can't count on it.'

Ling spoke up again, this time without raising his hand.

'What exactly do we have on our side if this happens tomorrow?'

Chien Tah attacked a third sheet of paper.

'Let's take our first strike potential first,' he said. 'And let's assume we move before they do. We have the capability,' he started drawing yet another rough sketch of the China-USSR frontier, with dots, lines, arrows, 'of taking out some, but by no means all, of their missile sites, but only those within a 500–1750 mile range. We also have a very slight chance of hitting Moscow with one of our own IRBMs – but, I stress, it's a very slim chance indeed. We have fifteen in all, unfortunately untested. Finally, we can also put our TU-16s and F-9s in the air, and hope that at least a few will get through – enough, say, to take out Vladivostok and Khabarovsk – maybe half a dozen towns in all.'

Ling spoke again, without raising his arm this time. He was obviously in command, though he had chosen to sit with the others.

'What about our inter-continental ballistic missile system? What about our submarines? Haven't we been spending huge sums on their development since our beloved Chairman died?'

'Vice-chairman,' said Tah, doodling again in a mixture of English and Chinese characters, 'our attempts to make an ICBM operational, as you may know, have not been entirely satisfactory. The capability exists, mainly on paper, for the greater edification and satisfaction of the Central Committee and foreign observers. In this situation it would be disastrous to put it to the test. We need not go into all the reasons here. The unfortunate consequences of the Cultural Revolution are mainly to blame. There were no scientists graduating between 1965 and 1972, and though we managed to conceal a few of the really brightest students, giving them on-the-job training, many of those who were supposed to train them, myself included, were not – er – available for most of those years. And in those same years,' he pulled a face, 'space and missile technology, especially delivery systems, made a really immense leap forward.'

There was muttered comment from the room.

'Yes,' Tah went on, with a tinge of bitterness in his voice. 'While important developments were occurring elsewhere I was spreading shit on cabbages and getting my face slapped by fifteen-year-olds – like Vice-Chairman Ling. And the result is: we can't afford to fire the ICBM. It could blow up in our face. It could land thousands of miles off-target – maybe in a neutral country. You ask: what about our submarines? There are two. Their delivery systems are out of date. Their missiles have no multiple warheads. The submarine programme is a mess. The crews themselves are dedicated Communists, ready for the supreme sacrifice at all times. But they are very much a last resort, and should be used as such. So our targets are limited, and our force is small. The Trans-Siberian, as many silos and fixed positions of the enemy as we are aware of, and some towns. That's it.'

The Vice-Defence Minister spoke up for the first time.

'And in the event of the Russians striking first, as looks likely?'

'In that case, we might have enough missiles and planes left for about one tenth of the targets I outlined. It depends whether they go the whole hog and take out Peking. The gallant Second Artillery has standing instructions to blast off with everything left on a fire-on-warning basis. But it'll be, to say the least, a confused situation – and, if the Russians have moved some of their firing platforms, we'll be firing at non-existent targets.'

Ling spoke again. 'And how will we know when the Russians attack?'

Chien Tah made a face. 'Again, the situation is not good. Not as good as it looks on paper, anyway. In theory we have a fairly reliable early-warning system. But it was devised in the sixties. We are not fully aware of the Soviet strides made since then, but the Americans firmly believe that most of the conventional early warning systems we have simply wouldn't work, because the Russians know about them and have built-in protection. Why, they practically built our orginal system. They have satellite surveillance – a completely foolproof system, which tells you instantly whether anything goes up.'

'And we have no way of knowing?'

'Before they actually make their strike, there is a certain amount of ground activity which would almost certainly be picked up by the American satellites. Whether they warn us or not is another matter. At best our warning would come through much later, with enough time, maybe, to get our urban population underground, but maybe not enough to get our missiles to fire off their retaliatory strike before the Russians hit us. These matters were not ones that pre-occupied our beloved Chairman overmuch in his later years. He was more interested in moulding men into revolutionary beings. Technology didn't mean a thing to him, especially at the end. It became treasonable to suggest we were lagging behind, or to question the Chairman's theories. Those who exaggerated the power of nuclear weapons were "Khruschev-type reactionaries" and lost their jobs. The camps were full of "defeatists", weren't they, Vice-Chairman?'

There was another pause, and some more subdued conversation in the room. Everyone present knew what Chien Tah was referring to – Vice-Chairman Ling most of all.

'Assuming we strike first,' said Ling. 'What then?'

Chien Tah sounded more than ever like a professor.

'In the event, as you put it, of a nuclear exchange, and assuming we initiate a pre-emptive strike, we would first of all have to go through a series of readiness and launch procedures which might, or might not, be detected by the Soviet satellites. They would certainly come to the attention of the more sophisticated American ones, and the Americans, then, might, or might not, in turn warn the Russians. If we manage to make our preparations un-detected, and if we didn't have to worry about the Russians' retaliatory strike, we would be able to hit, massively, a number of large towns. Some of our aircraft would also undoubtedly get through, and they have a 1750-mile range. But we would, almost certainly, expose ourselves to a Soviet retaliatory strike, though there's a small chance the shock would be so great that it's just possible they might be stunned into calling for negotiations, agreeing to demilitarise and denuclearise the zone north of our borders, that sort of thing. It depends on the extent of the damage done, how surprised and hurt they are, and to what extent they believe that we are able to escalate our attack in a second strike after they have hit us.'

'But' – the Vice-Defence Minister again – 'Ideally, any pre-emptive strike of ours should be confined to the towns? Wouldn't this leave their array of tactical and medium range missiles intact?'

'Not entirely. Our targeting does include some of their known launching sites. The Frenchman's pictures have been most useful in this respect. But obviously we don't have the capacity to take out more than a few of the 250-odd missiles being prepared against us, as shown in the reconnaissance pictures.'

'So, ideally,' Ling spoke up again, 'we should try and get others to knock out the missile sites, while we knock out the towns?'

There was stunned silence. Revelling in the attention, the Vice-Chairman continued, in a conversational, relaxed tone. 'Just suppose,' he said, 'that some other power could be persuaded to co-operate in this way. A preposterous suggestion, you will say. But just suppose that the United States were to assist us, without this ever becoming public knowledge. The onus of destroying civilian lives would fall on us. The Americans could hardly be blamed for that. We would assume full responsibility. But supposing, while we struck at the towns, the Americans struck at the missile sites. Their error factor would be negligible, their accuracy is supposed to be remarkable and the whole operation could be carried out with surgical precision. Then the alternative for the Russians would be either to go all out for a nuclear holocaust, wiping out as many of our cities as possible – or making a deal. My bet is they would make a deal. They know that however much they hope for our total annihilation, China is too vast a country. There are just too many of us. We would survive even a massive series of nuclear attacks. That, as our Chairman saw, is our main, indeed our only, intrinsic strength.'

'But it remains a preposterous suggestion all the same,

Vice-Chairman,' said Chien Tah. 'Surely, the consequences of involving the Americans, in any capacity, would lead to the threat of generalised nuclear war? The Americans are said to be reluctant to risk the destruction of Minneapolis in retaliation for that of Hamburg or Frankfurt, and the Germans are their best allies. I don't see any American President risking the deaths of millions of Americans simply to assist China.'

'Quite right, quite right. The Russians would certainly retaliate against America if it was clear that the Americans, as well as ourselves, were engaged in a joint strike against them. But, Professor, I mean General, we have gone over this a number of times, both when we were on the same farm in the hands of those misguided young people, and when you returned. The core of the issue is not: who strikes? As you put it so brilliantly, it is: who is detected in the act of striking?'

Chien Tah nodded.

Ling said: 'As I also recall, you even used to make the point, when we were in camp together, and allowed to talk quietly between ourselves, that it would be difficult, and perhaps impossible, for us to be absolutely certain where a nuclear strike against us was coming from. The trajectory' – Ling lapsed into English for the single word – 'Vector, I think was the term, was similar for both potential incoming Soviet and American nuclear missiles. It meant, you said, that ideally our second strike capability should be directed simultaneously against the United States and the Soviet Union, since we couldn't immediately know whether the nuclear missiles aimed at us originated from Russia or America, and hence who our real enemy was.'

Chien Tah said, 'But that was in a different world context – when the assumption was that both the United States and the Soviet Union represented an equal threat to us.'

'Precisely. All I propose is that we amend the situation to present-day realities, while conforming to our historic traditions of using one set of barbarians to keep the other set at bay. This means persuading the Americans to position their nuclear submarines near enough to our coast so that, when the time comes, the Soviets won't be able to distinguish ours from theirs. The Americans will destroy the silos and launching pads, we will take out the towns, the Russians will be unable to distinguish the American missiles from the Chinese, and then all that'll be left is for the United States to deny any part in the attack. Of course, there'll be some surprise at the sophistication and accuracy of our nuclear force, with the usual reports in learned journals chiding the intelligence services for under-estimating our technology. And, in one fell swoop, the Soviets will have lost their nuclear superiority, possibly for several generations, most likely for good. There's another consequence: a possible social and political upheaval against their own leaders, who will have led the Russian people into such a disastrous situation.'

A number of people were on their feet. Everyone was speaking at once.

'One at a time,' said Ling. He pointed to Chien Tah. 'You.'

Chien Tah looked worried.

'Theoretically you're correct, Vice-Chairman. Under-sea launchings *are* difficult to detect and could be made to appear to occur roughly on the same vector pattern as our own – though there'll be some unanswered questions about altitudes: the American missiles would undoubtedly have a much higher trajectory. But the main question we all seem to be asking is this: how are you going to convince the Americans to help us?'

Ling pulled out some notes from his loose Mao jacket.

'First,' he said, 'I want to go back to 1969. This was the year our country was most vulnerable to outside attack – and it almost came. At the time, we had no nuclear strike force to speak of, our country was in a complete shambles owing to the Cultural Revolution and its aftermath, our army was spread thin on the ground, administering most of the provinces, and our conventional leadership was in disarray. Hardly coincidentally, this was the year the Russians chose to engineer direct confrontations with our army along the banks of the Oussouri river. We now know – the Americans have told us – that these clashes were originally intended as a preliminary excuse, a pretext, for a preventive strike against us – a strike, I may add, which we were totally unprepared for, with no retaliation capability of any kind. What happened? The Russians – again we know this to be true, because the Americans adı...tted as much to us – made the

156

mistake of sounding the United States out on what an American reaction would be, in the light of such a possible, pre-emptive Soviet strike. And the Americans let the Russians know, in no uncertain terms, that while they would, technically, remain neutral, they would also regard such an act with "marked displeasure" and that the Russians could by no means rely on "American benevolence" in such a situation. In fact, the then American President, through intermediaries, not only conveyed all this information to us, but also told us that, in the event of such a threat developing, he would provide us with some form of material and technical aid. You all remember the international context at the time: the United States was then, in most quarters, China's leading enemy, as well as the world's leading imperialist power. As a result of the 1969 events, the Russian social-fascists assumed this role and our relations with the United States improved, to such an extent that we are being provided, again through intermediaries, with vital information concerning Soviet nuclear war preparations against us. Now we have a very different situation to that of 1969. The United States has actually lost, or is in the process of losing, its superiority in the nuclear field. A combined action, open and admitted by us, covert on their side, provides America with what might, conceivably, be a last chance of checking Soviet nuclear might. We are offering them the possibility of destroying a large part of the Soviet nuclear war arsenal at no cost to them, without being found out. In addition, we can offer the Americans, if they desire, an irresistible package – something that would ensure that the Soviet Union never again becomes a major threat. I'm referring to the positioning, under Chinese supervision, of course, of listening posts all along the Sino-Soviet border, in exchange for our renouncing the construction and use of an ICBM – proving our good faith by giving up for all time the means of striking at the heart of America, a capability, as our friend has admitted, which is more theoretical than real anyway.'

The Vice-Defence Minister asked: 'You think they'll swallow that?'

'Why not? Logically it's the only course of events that makes any sense for them. It solves their major problem, without embroiling them in a nuclear war. The very boldness of the plan, and its simplicity, argue in favour of it. There's an additional reason for saying yes. Whatever happans, the Soviets are going to scream collusion, are going, in some way or another, to blame America for whatever happens. Such a reaction is likely even if the United States stay completely neutral and don't lift a finger to help us. Which is why I say: let's ask ourselves, not, will the Americans take part, but how long have we? Any ideas?'

Chien Tah knew the question was addressed to him.

'The submarines have got to be in place. There has to be split-second co-ordination, so that our strike and theirs coincide. I'd say about three weeks to a month. But, Vice-Chairman, how much do the Americans already know? What reason do you have for believing they'll co-operate?'

'Before I answer that one,' the Vice-Chairman said, 'I have a question for you. From the state of the satellite reconnaissance charts the Frenchman showed you, how soon before the Soviets actually strike?'

'It could be two weeks. It could be a month. It could be a year or more.'

Ling said: 'Then you don't have all that much time, do you?'

Chien Tah looked blank. 'You are going to sound the Americans out,' said Ling. 'A few people in high places still remember the MIT physicist, in his earlier incarnation as Michael Tah. Among them the present American Defence Secretary. I want you to make a quick trip to the United States, any pretext will do, and contact your old college chum. Explain the scheme in strictest confidence. Sound him out on a joint pre-emptive strike plan. Give him all the assurances he needs.'

Chien Tah said: 'I'll do anything the Vice-Chairman orders me to, but he hasn't answered my question. And there's something else I want to raise. Americans talk. Their press is all-powerful. How will any President ever agree to something like that, when, sooner or later, a crew member or someone associated with the scheme will reveal his ship's participation in the operation?'

There was a murmur of assent from the rest of the room.

'On the question of American co-operation,' said Ling,

158

'let me say that your own trip, in a way you may discover, will in itself be crucial. As to your other question: in 1967, during the Seven Days' War, the Israelis "accidentally" knocked out a US missile ship that was cruising too close to their shores. Their radar screen picked it up and the Israelis assumed it was an enemy ship – or so they said. Similarly, it's conceivable that something like that may happen in this case. We may "accidentally" knock out some submarines – on the grounds that our radar picked them out and that we assumed they were Soviet ships. It'll be one of those unfortunate accidents of war, quickly acknowledged, quickly forgotten – and making any charges of collusion unverifiable.'

Chien Tah's visit to the United States was monitored, from the moment he landed in Boston, by at least three different security agencies. But on this trip he seemed this time to court publicity. The *New York Times* was the first to burst into print. 'Chinese alumnus to address MIT,' it said, with a smaller sub-heading reading: 'Chien Tah, widely believed to be responsible for China's nuclear programme, returns to MIT this week to address fellow alumni.' The story referred to him as 'one of China's most distinguished nuclear physicists' who had graduated from MIT in 1949. His visit was described as 'the most important proof so far of the improved relations between our two countries'. His speech, on 'Chinese science – its place in history', was attended by a capacity crowd. Chien Tah also appeared on the 'Today' show, was interviewed by Dick Cavett, and took part in a televised debate with Professors Friedman and Galbraith. A bid by David Frost for a two-hour special was reluctantly turned down because it would have taken too long to prepare. Chien Tah was photographed visiting some beaming relatives in San Francisco. He also spent a day in Washington, where he dined at the home of the Defence Secretary, an MIT contemporary who had been unable to hear him speak in Boston.

It was an informal, family meal at the Defence Secretary's Virginia home. After dinner, the two men talked, alone, in a small sitting-room used occasionally as an office. Chien Tah stayed till two a.m., returned to the Watergate Hotel in the limousine the Defence Secretary had put at his disposal, and left later that morning for Paris and Shanghai. His departure was a five-line story on the AP wire.

But, long before he actually departed, the telephone rang at the White House. The Defence Secretary was one of three people with unrestricted day and night access to the President. The White House Duty Officer did however talk to him first. He knew the Secretary had never called in the middle of the night before. He just wanted to make sure that he wanted the President woken up.

'I sure do, Chuck,' said the Defence Secretary, 'and be sure to make it a secure line. Don't think I'd be doing this if there wasn't a good reason.'

Seconds later, a sleepy President answered the telephone.

'Yes, Jim. What can I do for you?' he said. The voice was somewhat slurred. The President was a sound sleeper.

The Defence Secretary knew the President's aversion for profane language. In his excitement, however, he completely forgot himself.

'Mr President,' he said, 'you may think I'm out of my mind. But I have good reason to believe our Chinese friends have flipped. Mr President, you won't believe this, but they're about to drop every fucking nuke they have on the Russians. What's more, they expect us to join in and help them.'

The President reacted as much to the language as to its content. The rebuke was implicit.

'Come, come, Jim, why should they do such a senseles wicked thing?'

'Mr President, they claim they have proof that the Russians are planning a massive pre-emptive strike of their own – and they want a joint operation to stop them. What' more, they claim we've known about it all along.'

'That's ridiculous.'

'Somehow, they've got hold of our satellite recon-naissance pictures. It's all there, they say.'

'That's even more ridiculous.'

'I know. But, unless we do something fast, they're goir ahead. As soon as they're ready. And the man with his fing on the trigger – he's just left my house – says that, after h US visit, there'll be no way to prove that collusion didn occur. He says the Russians will point to his trip, shortly before the big bang, to prove that we were in it together, so we might as well go along with the scheme anyway, since whatever happens we'll get the blame.'

'Can he be stopped?'

'At the airport, you mean? What good would that do?'

'No. I mean stopped from going ahead.'

'I doubt it, Mr President. Unless . . . Mr President? Are you there?'

'Better come round for an early breakfast at seven, Jim,' the President said. 'We'll talk it over calmly. Decide who to bring in, what to do. Kind of sort things out. In the meantime' – and there was no irony in the President's voice, he sounded, the Defence Secretary noted, almost too calm – 'I'll be on my knees. Trying to get some guidance. There are times, Jim' – and the Defence Secretary belatedly remembered his foul language with dismay – 'when the meaningful answers can only come from Him.'

Chapter Twelve

ALL OVER the United States, the armed forces, the civilian agencies and their millions of employees indulged, at the President's request, in the time-honoured game of closing the door after the quarry had flown: from one day to the next, the security surrounding all America's more sensitive installations was reinforced and overhauled. Hard-faced men appeared at building entrances everywhere, unwilling to say who they were. From their appearance they seemed to be, some of them, members of the FBI. Identities were cross-checked, and all those leaving their places of work liable to full body searches. Even top-ranking CIA personnel were subjected to these indignities. As a result, several high-ranking officials were fired, several dozen investigations were initiated, and three high-ranking officers, two of them Air Force generals, on loan to the National Reconnaissance Office, blamed for the overall laxity prevailing in their installations, found their careers in tatters, and were offered the choice of being transferred to obscure jobs or resigning outright.

The President, as was his habit after a period of reflection which his enemies called shillyshallying ('weighing the pros, the cons, and the votes' as one general put it), had issued perhaps the sternest directive in his capacity as Commander-in-Chief. Because it dealt exclusively with security matters, and was addressed exclusively to the Intelligence Community, the statement was not made public, but sufficient 'leaks' occurred, despite the President's own dire warning, for ripples of unease to spread throughout the Administration, Congress, the press, and Washington's diplomatic community – among all those, in fact, who had not been directly concerned by his order, and therefore had not read it.

Rumours ranged from the discovery of a top Soviet 'mole' in the Cabinet to that of a secret, and successful, Soviet plan to test US defences by firing an unarmed ICBM, equipped with a dummy cone, all the way from Murmansk to the outskirts of Baltimore. Bereft of its nuclear warhead, and containing instead a personal note from the Soviet Chairman to the President, the cone, so the rumour went, had landed in a tract of wooded land between Washington and Baltimore, not many miles from CIA headquarters – and US tracking stations and the elaborate satellite surveillance system, it was said, had failed to spot it until after it had landed, and then only because a Soviet Military Attaché had told a Presidential aide about the shot at a dinner party.

Another rumour which spread throughout Washington was that the President had secretly placed a part of his armed forces on 'second degree' alert, and that a number of units, including the Marines, some special forces and a Parachute Division at Fort Bragg, had been confined to barracks and told to prepare for a quick move.

The various stories and their denials caused the stock market to behave curiously: depressed copper and uranium shares shot up, real estate company prices wavered, airline and tourist industry shares plummeted, and at least one publisher commissioned a free-lance journalist to write a 180-page 'quickie' on 'the great Washington scare'.

Parties combed the woods at all convenient motorway exits between Baltimore and Washington to try to find evidence of the rumoured Soviet crater, and the fact that armed troops, guarding a small secret installation not far from the main CIA headquarters itself, shooed them away, only fed the original rumour. Unusually large crowds also came to Dulles Airport, because it was also thought that part of this large airfield had been declared out of bounds and was being used as an emergency command post. *Newsweek* beat *Time* to a cover story on the scare, to the scarcely surprised satisfaction of its owner, at whose dinner party the much-denied Soviet hint had been dropped.

The hysteria led to various cruel and derisive articles by foreign correspondents in French, English, Italian and German newspapers and magazines. They all compared the present American mood to that prevalent in Europe at the time of the Black Death and in the year 999, when the world was expected to come to an abrupt end. 'The primitive demi-urge of the American consumer, unaware of these myths, reveals the fragility of his mental state and of that of the American socio-political fabric in general,' said *Der Spiegel. Le Monde*'s resident Washington correspondent, in an interminably turgid five-part essay which could have been written from Paris, since it contained no reporting elements whatever from the United States, quoted Camus, Lévi-Strauss, Nietzsche, Freud and Michel Foucault to suggest that the United States population, bored with peace, 'secretly longed for some form of cosmic cataclysm to exorcise an unknown collective demon'.

The prevalence of all such stories led to the following exchange at one of the routine noon-day briefings at the Department of State.

Newsman: Is it true that certain security breaches have recently been uncovered in a number of agencies, in the last few weeks, and what is State's reaction to rumours that an unarmed Soviet ICBM was recently fired into the Maryland area, successfully avoiding US satellite surveillance?

Spokesman: As regards the second part of your question, it is categorically denied that anything of the kind you describe took place. Despite the weekend activities of amateur sleuths in the Washington and Baltimore suburbs (laughter) there is absolutely no truth in this report, whose origins remain a mystery and whose propagation we deplore.

Same newsman: Have security breaches been detected or not? Is it true that the President has issued a directive to certain armed forces and agency members and if so, on what grounds and why has this text not been released?

Spokesman: You'd better ask the President himself – or his Chief of Staff (tired derisive laughter).

Pentagon and agency computers worked overtime, listing all personnel with more than routine access to satellite photo analysis in all its forms. Security specialists discovered, to their alarm, that a far laxer system than they had believed possible prevailed. A number of specialist workers, Semyakov among them, were questioned. Most reported that anyone taking the grave risk of defying routine security measures might well have walked off with batches of vital pictures, but that it would take a trained expert to interpret such pictures correctly. Those questioned said it was quite feasible for such pictures to be rephotographed, touched up and generally faked – though, again, a real expert might not be fooled.

Computers were set in motion to produce lists of people directly connected with the satellite surveillance of the eastern-most Soviet Union, and of the area north of the Chinese border. One security specialist suggested that each name be checked against other computerised data, and, for days, analysts in air-conditioned basements stared dazedly at their screens, punching keys, comparing, rechecking and finally scrawling down their notes on old-fashioned scratchpads.

The comparisons involved every conceivable relevant scrap of information originally fed into the computers on some 7000 people, all of whom had already passed the hurdle of top security clearance. They involved family back-grounds, acquaintances, hobbies, political views, dates of absence from work, possible criminal records and as-sociations. The lists were also checked alongside the names of those currently under surveillance without their knowl-edge. Semyakov's name was among those that came up again and again, but that was only normal, with his past, his interest in photography, and his wide range of acquaintances in the intelligence community. Nevertheless, so frequently did his name emerge that he was one of a small list of twenty-two people earmarked for additional investigation.

The CIA Director had not fed Jute's name into the CIA master computer after his conversation with Diana White and his own aides, so the Semyakov-Jute connection did not immediately spring to light, though Jute figured, quite routinely, among those professionally closest to Semyakov – and this, too, was to have repercussions.

In any case, regardless of the new routines introduced as a result of the President's own directive, the surveillance around Jute had become tighter. Immediately after Paul White's death, Jute had started making weekend trips to Maine, lining up for the Washington-Boston shuttle, transferring to a smaller airline for the thirty-minute flight to Portland where he kept a smelly, battered Volkswagen.

Aboard his boat, a third-hand but immaculate 12-metre Nicholson called *Acteon II* (which he had purchased, along with the VW, from a departing British diplomat), he had begun moving all his confidential personal papers.

He had recently become aware that he was being watched – by people far more sophisticated than the unfortunate Paul White. He suspected that the same people who followed him to Washington National Airport's Boston shuttle line at weekends phoned Boston once he was aboard, and that he was watched, too, as he changed planes. He wasn't fooled, either, by the young holidaying couple he noticed on several occasions at the small Portland airport, with their giggly interest in each other – and in boats. Jute didn't believe anyone would try and break in in his absence. He had had a highly sophisticated anti-burglar device fitted aboard. What surprised him was that he still continued to get all papers on the top internal secret distribution list, still went to the most highly sensitive conferences and working parties, still was involved in the few covert operations being run by the CIA and that the bleeper still regularly summoned him to the telephone for chats with the Director, who was as cordial as before.

Neighbours who lived aboard a sailboat berthed next to Jute's *Acteon* later told the police that much of the time, on his last weekend, Jute had spent listening to tapes of Mozart, Wagner and Boccherini. He had done quite a bit of typing, too, and seemed in a serene, almost jovial, mood, though, as the occupants of the next boat – who knew him only as an occasional visitor – said, 'he always kept aloof from the social life on the marina. He never once invited us aboard – and always found a way of turning down our invitations for a drink, even though he did once lend us a bottle of scotch.'

The events leading up to that last weekend, and to the earlier Presidential directive which was to cause so many ripples around the world, occurred after a secret conference of Intelligence Chiefs at Camp David – a conference that, as far as public records were concerned, never took place. Public life in the United States has become so public after Watergate, and the prerogatives of the press are so great, that it comes as a certain surprise to discover that all the manifold activities of the US President are not necessarily divulged, despite the clinical approach to timetables displayed by the White House press corps and the chronological accounts of his day-to-day activities so lavishly spooned to them by his press aides. Because there is hardly ever a blank space in the President's routine (thanks to the White House press hunger for meaningless detail and the White House press aides' eagerness to satisfy it), it is invariably necessary, when really important matters are at stake, to resort to innocent deception. In this instance every effort was made to pretend that the President was merely spending a relaxed weekend with his family to escape the oppressive Washington summer heat. Those who attended the conference were taken by helicopter from a number of different Air Force bases. They figured under aliases on passenger manifestoes, and the pilots and flight controllers never discovered their true identities.

All had been warned to tell no one, especially not their wives, that they were spending two days in the President's company. They kept out of sight, again on express orders of the Presidential aides, while the ritual family pictures of the President relaxing in Camp David were taken by a small White House photographers' pool. The arrival of the photographers had been timed to occur before that of those attending the meeting, and immediately after the 'photo opportunity' was over the press was made to leave.

It was a formidable gathering: apart from the Defence Secretary, the head of the Satellite Surveillance Processing and Data Bureau, who had first-hand accounts to give, those present included the directors of the CIA, the FBI, the National Security Agency, the National Reconnaissance Office, senior members of the Armed Services Committee, of the Foreign Intelligence Advisory Board, the Pentagon and the Defence Intelligence Agency, along with lesser figures from the inter-agency committee on Intelligence and the co-ordinator of the National Security Decision Memorandum Committee.

The President asked the Defence Secretary 'to start the ball rolling' with his account of his evening with Chien Tah. From there the meeting went on and on, with a short

167

working dinner break, until past midnight. Before it broke up the following noon, all those who had taken part, from the Defence Secretary to the Marine cooks and waiters who had prepared the buffet supper, were required to sign a document pledging their complete secrecy. This unusual step was taken, the President said 'because of the very special nature of the questions under discussion'. One of the decisions made during the meeting was to appoint a small standing committee, operating under the code name of 'Barker' and including representatives of nearly all the agencies or organisations at the Camp David conference. The President had been unwilling to have 'Barker' under the roof of the Executive Mansion – Watergate memories were still too vivid for that – and eventually a secure home was found in an annex of the National Security Council headquarters. 'Barker' came under the direct responsibility of the Defence Secretary, and the head of the DIA. Since Watergate, 'slush funds', even for the most honourable reasons, were impossible to manipulate, and the CIA was reluctant to commit any of its own funds for the purpose, so the funding of 'Barker' became the joint responsibility of the White House, the Department of Defence and the Defence Intelligence Agency. By consensus, it was agreed that the President 'need not be directly concerned' with some of the implementations decided by 'Barker'. As the Defence Secretary said to the CIA Director, 'He's covering his ass. He doesn't want any "Barker" plumbers to plead guilty to obeying Presidential instructions.'

It is doubtful whether the full ramifications of 'Barker' became known to any one individual. Certainly the President himself, by design, was not kept informed of some of the decisions subsequently taken – the reason being that they might have incriminated him. For, as a result of the post-Watergate concern for morality in the US Government, at all levels and in all circumstances, no immunity could be expected for any illegal acts committed on US soil – even for the highest possible motives, including national security. For this reason some 'Barker' decisions had to be concealed, laundered, as it were, until the initiator's trace was lost. Some 'Barker' decisions simply conformed to the security directive issued after the Camp David meeting by the

President. Others were of a very different nature. Since 'Barker' was, for once, a well-kept secret, no reporter has since requested 'Barker' papers under the Freedom of Information Act.

What might happen if this were to occur is an interesting speculation, since some 'Barker' papers still on file prove that on a certain date, and without warning Congress, the President found it necessary to order a preliminary state-of-readiness activation of certain ICBMs, and that a number of the US Navy's nuclear-armed submarines were also put on a 'grey' alert. The papers might show that such a decision was taken for training purposes only. What was unprecedented, if training alone was involved, was the fact that, for the first time, submarine commanders were instructed to ready nuclear arming procedures beyond stage two, for 'certain specific targets to be indicated at a later date'.

Ordinarily, the strain on Semyakov would have been almost unendurable, even without the knowledge of the real purpose of Chien Tah's visit or the boldness of the Chinese proposals. All Semyakov knew was that Jute's plan was running into difficulties, because the Chinese had reacted faster than expected. Now his sole preoccupation was to send as much material as he could to Forgeot, before the risks became too great. He succeeded in doing most of what he had set out to do in time: the latest batch of 'posters' showed the imminent firing readiness of a number of key Soviet silo and surface platform installations. It was, he conceded, a very slick job.

But Semyakov was angry as well as nervous. His anger stemmed from the awareness that his hitherto meticulously successful image and way of life were in jeopardy. 'We Russians play too much chess,' he had once said to Jute. 'We always think several complicated moves ahead. This can be good. But Anglo-Saxon lack of guile, and directness, can make such thinking ineffective. How does a chess-player deal with a Davy Crockett or a Patton?'

Years previously, as a very young man, discussing his future role with Ivan Serov, then the dreaded head of the KGB, he had cynically and somewhat drunkenly advanced the theory that since the Soviet Union offered no rewards comparable to those afforded by the United States in terms of comfort, income, and material incentives, the best that the KGB could ever offer its most promising operatives was not just an American cover, but a lifetime of American service, including the right to remain in the United States long after an individual assignment was over and done with. Serov, surprisingly, had agreed. There were precedents, he pointed out: why, the leading stars and directors of the DDR's prestigious Berlin Theater were – at one stage – rewarded by being allowed to live their lives in West Berlin, commuting to East Berlin only for their rehearsals and performances. Wasn't that a similar incentive?

So Semyakov had become a Serov whizz-kid, his career, from that day onwards, carefully constructed to make him a valuable, credible, cast-iron defector. He had been responsible for the destruction of a number of Soviet spy networks in the United States, for openers. Serov had called this his poker 'ante', and had sacrificed his agents with a chess-player's ruthlessness. Among those betrayed by Semyakov, as proof of his good intentions, were some agents far past their prime, or about to become liabilities. But others had been first-rate. He had had no qualms. In a somewhat emotional farewell party in Kiev, before surfacing in West Berlin, Semyakov had said farewell to his KGB mentors for ever. 'We can't afford many people like you,' said his case officer. 'You are a luxury. Who knows, you might even end up really betraying us.'

What puzzled Semyakov at first was the vague nature of his mission. A few months before his defection, he and Philby were brought together in Moscow. The legendary British double agent had ostensibly retired, and only rarely lectured at KGB seminars. He had lost none of his British charm, stutter or self-deprecation.

'My dear chap,' he told Semyakov, 'I never had a specific brief – ever. I played the part to the hilt. If you ever meet my SIS contemporaries they will tell you, if they're honest, that I was a damn good intelligence operative. I had to be. I amply deserved my OBE. If our masters are willing to pay such a high price for your insertion, you have to justify their faith in you by becoming a top-notch operator yourself. You'll see. It comes naturally, after a time, like a man with two mistresses. He wants them both, doesn't he? He just doesn't want them to meet.'

Philby may have had some part in Semyakov's programming, for, insofar as he was given a brief at all, it was to penetrate, 'to the very hilt', the most conservative, cold-war elements in American society, to assess their importance, and, eventually, to try to manipulate them along exploitable lines. In a somewhat similar precedent, Philby had once ingratiated himself with the Franco establishment during the Spanish Civil War.

Semyakov had accomplished all that, and more. He had served his new masters well. He could look forward to an attractive pension, and he had no intention of jeopardizing his new and agreeable way of life. Was this what his KGB mentors had designed for him from the outset: to provoke a pre-emptive Chinese nuclear strike on the Soviet Union? It was likely. His rare contacts with his case officer (whom he suspected was – ultimately – the Soviet Chairman himself) implied that whoever was in charge in Moscow was delighted to manipulate such an expert craftsman as Jute, delighted, too, at being able to assess at first hand the damage Watergate had done to the United States intelligence-gathering operations as a whole.

But the nuclear confrontation smacked too much of a theorizing chess-player, somewhere in the Kremlin. Semyakov had gone along with Jute's proposals because he had been told to do so. It was clear that there were immense Soviet advantages to be gained: poor Jute. Soviet divisions in Europe would not budge an inch, though there might be token withdrawals to keep him and his like happy. There was a case, too, to be made for a sharp, clean surgical operation on China's nuclear capacity. Semyakov believed this was the ultimate Soviet objective: to provoke a minor Chinese strike, by all possible means, before China's nuclear technology was allowed to become too threatening. No invasion, no onslaught on Peking, though. What the Soviet Union wanted was a course of events culminating in the destruction of all China's plutonium manufacturing capability.

Now, however, Semyakov risked being sacrificed – just as, in his early career as a star defector, he had sacrificed others. Should he be found out, the risk was not only that he would be convicted as a Soviet spy. A far greater risk was prosecution in American courts for taking part in a right-wing conspiracy to embroil two continents in a nuclear war. In its present mood, Semyakov knew, American justice would be tougher on the second count. And there was no one he could turn to, especially not now that the President had called for unprecedented vigilance in the wake of serious security breaches. Semyakov recognised, too, the peculiar KGB tendency towards overkill. Not content with manipulating Jute, the Soviet Union must squeeze the ultimate psychological advantage out of the situation. Hence the spate of rumours. Semyakov knew how easily they could be generated. Keep them on their toes. Keep them guessing. Keep the nerves jangling. Keep the breakdowns coming.

All very well. Terrific on paper, but what happens to me, Semyakov thought? A penitentiary instead of my Maryland farmhouse, a pension forfeited; and, who knows, deportation at the end of it? No thanks. Semyakov had so far channelled his anxiety in such a form as to appear credible to Jute. On his drives to and from Washington, in his air-conditioned Pontiac, he ran the alternatives through his mind, occasionally talking out loud to himself. At best, a Sino-Soviet 'nuclear exchange' would take place, with Soviet objectives fully attained. In that case it was only a matter of time before the full brunt of endless American investigations began, to try to assess how the Soviets had carried off such a coup in the first place.

But the 'nuclear exchange' had not yet occurred, and investigations already *were* in progress, which meant, as his questioning had shown, only one thing: the United States knew that satellite reconnaissance pictures had been faked, to provoke the Chinese into initial action. This being so, it was only a matter of time before Jute, and especially Semyakov, were picked up and questioned again, relentlessly, scores of people combing their past, investigating every minute of the last few years of their lives. I should never have had that reporter eliminated, he brooded. Again, the instructions had been precise: in the last resort, get rid of any interference, if it endangers Jute's plan. All it had required was a bundle of cash. In America, there still were things that only money would buy. How would liberal, peacenik,

172

Vietnam-war-protestor Paul White have reacted, had he been aware who was responsible? And of course White's death, opportunely for *them* (there I go, Semyakov thought – which mistress am I faithful to now?), effectively put paid to any thoughts of confession and genuine defection. The trapped mole. A chess-player at work again, probably. This move blocks off that particular alley. It might almost be worth taking a chance, turning States evidence, throwing oneself on the mercy of the American judicial system. 'Defector defects. Alleges nuclear hoax to serve Russia.' For some time now, Semyakov had been thinking in terms of *Variety* headlines. What was worse? A murder charge and a full confession – or prosecution on charges of a right-wing conspiracy? Personal loyalties or friendship ties had no place any more. Personally, Semyakov liked Jute, but in any event he would be the loser. How would Jute feel if he discovered Semyakov's true role? And Forgeot? How would he react? Was he really just a messenger boy?

The time had come, in any case, to wind up the poster business before anything worse happened. The downtown studio was already almost bare. All that was needed was a formal termination of the short lease, under his assumed name. Semyakov parked on the street, not one mile from the White House, which was a grim succession of junk food restaurants, topless bars, live entertainment in golden lights, 'nude nude girls and they dance' while a hard-core movie ran over the bar, all for the price of a $2 beer, no cover charge, no admission. Semyakov had frequently marvelled at the proximity of the White House to sordid ultra-commercial sex and did so again. Now, he thought, I am being critical of my American mistress. He had justified the strip to foreign visitors, on the grounds of the sanctity of private enterprise and individual freedom, while privately wondering why it was that the United States invariably laid itself open to a spectacle which was beyond caricature. We are so alike, when all's said and done, Semyakov thought, Russians and Americans, same herd instincts, same bureaucratic tendencies, same distrust of individualists – and this, appropriately, was almost his last conscious thought, for a black teenager on expensive skates skidded past him as he emerged from the parking lot, deftly turned, and appeared to lose control. He careened into Semyakov, with a 'hey, man, move yoh fuckin' ass', waving an air pistol in mock threat and was off, round the corner, out of sight and Semyakov was on the ground, a sharp stabbing pain in his right thigh, then an excruciating, nauseating sickness, limbs floundering, passers-by avoiding the drunk in his vomit, Christ, Washington *is* going downhill, that's the second falling-down drunk I've seen today, white, too, he heard one passer-by say. Blacks looked at him curiously, some with sympathy. One of them stole his wallet while ostensibly trying to help him to his feet. A small crowd gathered around the stricken Semyakov, in front of a 14th Street shop whose flashing lights advertised 'adult books, marital aids', model studios and 'the best peep show in town – you must be over 21'.

He was violent and confused when they got him to a crowded emergency ward. The overworked intern diagnosed some form of septicaemia, ordered an immediate saline drip, but the fever rose higher and higher that night, Semyakov was delirious, in English and Russian shrieked he was being killed, and a fat Puerto Rican male nurse rammed a morphine syringe in a vein, saying: cuddidout, cunt. It was only later, during the autopsy, that they discovered 'a circular area of inflammation caused by a central punctured mark about two millimetres wide' and a pellet the size of a pinhead, hollowed out in the middle, below the skin, in the centre of the inflamed spot on his thigh. Then the case was swiftly taken out of the hands of the hospital doctors, and a military ambulance whisked Semyakov's corpse away. The killing was not the first to occur in this fashion, though it was the first in the United States. It was, a DIA scientist reported, a standard Soviet bloc practice to use an airgun to fire the platinum pellet at the target to be eliminated. The poison, ricin, twice as deadly as cholera venom, sent the white blood count up immediately and astronomically, induced acute septicaemia and – almost always – death. Semyakov had had a high blood pressure condition to start with, which made him particularly vulnerable.

The findings were not released to the press. Officially, Semyakov was recorded as having died of acute septicaemia. Unofficially, his employers blamed the Russians – and they were right, but for the wrong reasons. The DIA's report was that at long last the KGB had got even with the most successful, skilled Soviet defector since Penkovsky. The notion that Semyakov had been eliminated because he no longer served a useful purpose, and now represented an intolerable hazard, never crossed the DIA Director's mind.

The Semyakov death illustrated the superiority of certain forms of Soviet 'dirty tricks', CIA probationers were taught. A mock-up of the suspected air pistol was built. Blow-ups of the pellet (ninety per cent platinum, ten per cent iridium) were exhibited. The beauty of ricin, the heavily German-accented lecturer told them, was that, unlike most poisons, it combined quickly with human tissues and could quickly be broken down by the body's natural protein-making cells, making it almost impossible to detect. And ricin was fairly easy to manufacture, certainly easier than the actual pellet, which implied a sophisticated precision-instrument capability, the lecturer added, beaming. 'I haff myzelf zuggesded,' he said, 'zad ve duplicate such a veppon. But our Director tinks such bragdices are un-American. Like reading a genelemen's mail.' A fresh-faced probationer raised his hand.

'Sir, could you repeat the substance ricin is derived from?'

'It is seed of the castor oil plant.'

'Does that mean, sir, that castor oil can be dangerous?'

Looking more than ever like Emil Jannings in *The Blue Angel*, the lecturer chortled. 'Rest assured, young man,' he said. 'Gastor oil is not at risk. Only ze seed. Your Mama,' he said cruelly, 'can continue giving you a spoonful venever your powels act sluggish.'

175

Chapter Thirteen

THE DISTINGUISHED American scientist and his almost
equally tall wife towered above the Chinese welcoming
party – diplomats, protocol members, economists and
Luxingshe representatives. To communicate, they both bent
deferentially, almost from the waist, causing the scientist to
write later, in the account of his travels he invariably had
commissioned to offset the cost of the trip (not for nothing
was he the remote descendant of shrewd, tough Scottish
crofters): 'Our gang of two spent most of its time in China
bent double, in an excruciatingly painful position, listening
to almost equally painful platitudes about the Gang of
Four.'

The trip had been planned for some time. But the
summons to the White House shortly before his departure
was unexpected. The President had been responsible. He
prided himself on his understanding of the Chinese mind,
having read Jerome Chen on Mao and Lipton on 'revolutionary mortality', admiring his wife's taste in books, which
included Han Suyin and a digest of 'Water Margin'. The
original Chien Tah approach to the Defence Secretary had
been unofficial, he had argued. Therefore, to observe full
reciprocity, one had to respond, at least at first, also
unofficially. A list of all prominent Americans due to visit
China had been requested, and the scientist was a natural
choice. The confidant of past Presidents, he had once served
as Ambassador to a large Asian country, with considerable
success.

The scientist was flattered but hardly surprised. Even his
closest friends admitted that modesty was not one of his
outstanding characteristics. He had played no part in the
President's election campaign and had even written
scathingly about him on numerous occasions. And he saw
the White House invitation as a belated Presidential
recognition of his own talents.

In his Presidential briefing, and at the President's request,
the scientist made no notes. The points to be memorised

were few. In a meeting with Vice-Chairman Ling, which was already scheduled 'in principle', and which he was to request as soon as possible, he was to convey the following urgent, verbal message to him from the United States President: recent satellite reconnaissance data showed no trace of a Soviet build-up in preparation for a sudden nuclear strike on China. Such data as had fallen into Chinese hands must be expertly executed fakes. All police and US security agencies were trying to track down their source. The offenders would be severely punished, and the Chinese Government kept informed.

In any case, it was preposterous wishful thinking to imagine that the United States might be a party to an attack on Soviet nuclear installations, anywhere on Soviet territory. In 1969, the United States had taken discreet diplomatic action to discourage the USSR from carrying out such an attack on China. It could not, and would not, 'tilt' towards China now. The US President strongly advised Vice-Chairman Ling to abandon any plans for a nuclear strike on the Soviet Union, which, even if the US remained neutral, as it intended, would have appalling consequences on the rest of the world. There followed an assessment on radiation effects of a Sino-Soviet nuclear exchange, part of a contingency study made at the President's request he had intended to use at a later date to secure the environmentalists' vote. As a staunch conservationist, the scientist approved. Only the North and South Poles, the southernmost tip of Latin America and certain parts of Australia would escape dangerous radiation fall-out as a consequence of even a limited Sino-Soviet nuclear war.

So now, in the shimmering summer heat of Peking, the scientist, in his soft-spoken drawl, was saying over and over again that he had a personal message from the President of the United States which he hoped to deliver as soon as possible to Vice-Chairman Ling.

While the scientist was so engaged in Peking, the enquiry into Semyakov's death was producing leads: the hiring of a studio, under the name of Pilkington, in downtown Washington in a decaying building over a failing bar and grille, screens and cameras and plates in a locked room in Semyakov's home. And more computer usage revealed the strength of the Jute-Semyakov connection, a friendship and relationship going far beyond the needs and knowledge of the Agency.

Later, as always when things go wrong in government, there was considerable disagreement over who was to blame. The 'Barker' committee blamed the DIA and the CIA. The CIA Director disclaimed any prior knowledge of what had been planned.

It was a tape-recording of Jute's voice that somehow turned up – nobody remembered how and where – that set the ball rolling. It was only much later that it was discovered that this was but one of a dozen such tapes Jute had recorded for his blind wife. A small 'Barker' committee listened again and again to Jute's surprisingly expressive actor's voice:

> 'The first-class brains of a senior civil servant
> shiver and shatter and fall
> as the steering column of the comfortable Humber
> batters in the bony wall. . . .'

There was much, much more, including something ending:

> 'But I'm dying now and done for
> what on earth was all the fun for?
> For I'm old and ill and terrified and tight.'

The ravings of a suicidal maniac, one of the committee said at the time. The *Washington Post* obituary referred to his brilliance, his extraordinary performance in the OSS and the early days of the CIA. But it also, perhaps directly inspired by the CIA Director himself, mentioned his 'growing instability', his 'manic-depressive condition' following his wife's 'tragic death', and the fact that, in recent years, he had been shifted to a relatively unimportant 'administrative post'.

It was on a Tuesday that Jute was reported missing, but his body was not found till the following Saturday, floating in shallow water in a Maine creek. His sailboat had been salvaged, abandoned and heading out to sea, drifting in a summer breeze, in the middle of that week. It was almost intact.

Even a few days' immersion in ocean water transforms a corpse almost beyond recognition. But the body, only slightly bloated, was definitely Jute's. There was no mistaking the slight, bony structure. The Coroner reluctantly concluded suicide, though at first the Maine State Police was so perplexed that it had earlier decided to report it as due to 'undetermined' causes. The bullet wound, two inches behind the left ear, had been inflicted by a .38 bullet, but the fish had gobbled up what little evidence of burns there might otherwise have been. The body had had forty-five pounds of divers' weights attached to a scuba outfit Jute had been wearing. It was conceivable, of course, that Jute might have dressed himself in his scuba kit, strapped the weights on to make his death absolutely inevitable, and fired (he was not left-handed) while balanced on the sailboat rail. The revolver, which had in all probability fallen over the side, was not recovered. Nor was there any blood inside the cabin, or on deck, or any signs of a struggle.

The FBI eventually took over the case, but came to similar conclusions, despite further evidence from a marina attendant, who knew Jute and had watched the body carried ashore. Around the neck, he said, there were marks like burns. The coroner had dismissed them as unimportant, mere decaying signs after ocean immersion. But the attendant – and the couple on the boat alongside Jute – were unconvinced. There was no crack investigative reporter, however, to make further enquiries and discover the truth. Jute's death became nothing more than a recurring story in the American press, recapitulating the pros and cons of suicide, speculating on the real nature of Jute's CIA responsibilities (for an internal 'security notice' immediately went out, circulating throughout the Agency, warning that any discussion of the case, in its broadest aspects, or of Jute himself would lead to dismissal and punitive measures) and insisting that all Agency personnel respect the 'white domp' – CIA jargon for the CIA-approved version of Jute's death.

The FBI's takeover did, however, prove that some aspect of counter-intelligence was involved. There were rumours, that remained unconfirmed, that Jute's boat had been full of confidential CIA papers. One *New York Times* story questioned the CIA version that Jute had been 'semi-retired' at the time of his death. It stated that one of the mysteries of the case was in fact that no papers whatever had been recovered, whereas Jute's marina neighbours had heard him typing away on previous weekends, and no typewriter had been found aboard. But even a later story that Jute had been, at the time of his death, closely concerned with a top-secret comparative study of Soviet and Chinese nuclear capabilities, a panel known as 'Team H', on which he had served as co-ordinator, attracted surprisingly little attention.

The *New York Times* urged the FBI to release the tapes proving Jute's suicidal frame of mind. But the official in charge of the case kept the cassettes securely locked up, and gradually there was less and less talk of Jute's disturbed condition in the weeks before his death. As the CIA Director knew, only a dumb cop would fail, in the long run, to identify the poems of John Betjeman – one of Jute's favourite writers and a personal acquaintance from his London years.

It was left to Forgeot to imagine the scene: Jute's sailboat rounding the cape, a diesel-powered cabin cruiser gradually coming closer in a true twentieth-century equivalent of the classic piracy scene, the two boats staying alongside for only a short while, the cabin cruiser peeling off, the sailboat drifting along out of control. How could the police fail to explain that Jute had not even attempted to drop anchor before killing himself? Forgeot knew it had not been suicide. A White House postcard, in Jute's angular handwriting, posted from Portland, saying 'wish you were here' had arrived at his accommodation address near the Place Maubert, the day before the news, on page six, in the *International Herald Tribune*, of the death by drowning, of Adrian Pemberton Jute, a story amended, the following day, to mention suicide and possible 'foul play'. There was another sealed envelope, with a covering letter to Forgeot inside, which arrived the following day. A pencilled note in the handwriting Forgeot knew well said: 'Au cas où . . .' As soon as he spotted the ten-line item in the *IHT*, Forgeot handed it over, unopened, to Feng. He knew its probable contents. And by the time the Professor actually saw the Vice-Chairman it was too late. He had read the letter. He re-read it before meeting the Professor, to remind himself of the endless duplicity of American Imperialists, even in their new guise.

Dear Mr Vice-Chairman (the letter read);
I am taking a very grave risk in communicating with

you, not as directly as I would have liked, but through a third party that can be trusted.

I have little time left, for I feel the entire weight of our own security and counter-intelligence apparatus closing in. It is an apparatus that in former years I myself helped train and put together – and therefore I am well placed to spot certain warning signals. Though my career has been mostly involved in straightforward foreign intelligence-gathering, I served on sufficient committees and inter-agency commissions, to know that – in a form I can suspect, but not guard against – my life is in jeopardy. Despite their occasional clumsiness, these people do not always miss. But you have a rudimentary intelligence service of your own, not entirely destroyed by the Cultural Revolution, and you are doubtless aware of my identity, my functions, my past, in other words, my credentials.

Mr Vice-Chairman, it is highly probable that at this very moment – either through direct diplomatic represen-tations, or else, as is more likely, through private channels of a more discreet, secret nature – pressure is being brought to bear on you to influence you in your dealings with the Soviet Union. Specifically, an approach is being, or will shortly be, made to appraise you of a so-called criminal hoax: the covert propagation of 'doctored' or faked satellite reconnaissance data implying that the Soviet Union is shortly to launch a selective strike on the Chinese Peoples Republic.

I have no idea of the means that will be used to convince you that such data do not correspond to reality. The only foolproof way would be to allow one of your qualified representatives full access to our own most secret installations – and I doubt that such an offer will be made. I myself have never been so honoured. The only other way of verifying the truth would be for you to have access to comparable Soviet data – and I doubt that, in its present, severely run-down form, your own intelligence-gathering facilities have this capability. Had you satellites of your own, the doubt would not arise, and it would not be necessary to provide you with such information in the first place. Unfortunately, the decision not to invest in such technology has been the root cause of China's inferiority –

if I may use the word – to her northern neighbour.

Mr Vice-Chairman, from the distance of tens of thousands of miles I beg you not to be fooled by such hypocritical considerations as may come your way. It is my word against theirs, I know, but I hope and trust that you will not be swayed, or at any rate not be deflected, from any course of action you need to take – even if United States policy appears to you both pusillanimous and unrealistic. The fact is that the most sophisticated data available clearly shows that the USSR, for reasons which can only be guessed at, but which are entirely logical, is planning for the near future a pre-emptive nuclear strike on certain vital Chinese installations.

It is, as you must know, a generally-held theory among those not blinded by the policy of détente that the Soviet Union must, in some form or other, exploit its strategic advantage over the United States at some time before 1985. By that date, the argument goes, the US may be well on the way to recovering some of its lost advantages: in the long run US technology will, beginning in the late eighties, prove more than a match for anything the USSR may then have in the pipe-line. But, until then, the USSR has a clear advantage over us – and is in the fortunate position of being able to use any pretext to initiate a war against us, or to invent one – for unlike the USA it has no need to preoccupy itself, for the time being at least, with the mood of its own people: outside a tiny dissident minority, the passivity of the Soviet people, and its acquiescence in its elderly leadership, are among its natural assets.

There remains the problem of the Chinese Peoples Republic: here, it is unfortunate that your so-called Cultural Revolution resulted in a ten-year technological and manpower gap. Had things been otherwise, it is possible that some form of parity might have been reached which would effectively have dissuaded the Soviet Union from any pre-emptive strike against China. At long last, the huge Chinese potential is geared to action again. But it will take time for you to achieve parity, or even a credible dissuasion force, as you well know.

For this reason, and secure in the knowledge that election year in the United States is upon us once again, the Soviet leadership intends to strike a blow against your country in the immediate future which will be both lasting and humiliating, with the object of ensuring that, when the time comes for the USSR to act against our country, China will have no means to create even the smallest nuclear diversion. It is for this reason that such a Soviet strike is being planned now, and it is my own lasting shame that the United States has decided, in election year, to adopt ostrich-like tactics and deliberately pretend that nothing untoward is occurring.

But, Mr Vice-Chairman, the facts, as conveyed to you already, speak for themselves. The ultimate proof will be my death, very probably made to look like suicide, which will – so the United States authorities obviously hope – put an end to the 'leaks' which have already caused considerable problems in my own camp. And I suggest that the recent death of one of our most high-ranking defectors, Oleg Semyakov, already provides you with proof, if further proof is required, that the Soviet strike preparations are no figment of the imagination.

Semyakov, whose death occurred only last week, in mysterious circumstances, on a Washington street, was one of the most expert of our own satellite reconnaissance analysts. It was he who provided me with the information I was able to relay covertly. He had no axe to grind, and he approached me only after realising the nature of the conspiracy of silence around Soviet war preparations against your country. You will find references to his death in the Western press – but no description of his particular job at the time of his murder. The omission is significant. His status, as a defector, and his expertise in satellite observation, would have made it impossible for the United States Government to admit the nature of his job without at the same time alerting the press as to his real role, and risking the kind of enquiry which would lead to embarrassing revelations.

For all these reasons, Mr Vice-Chairman, do not be misled by reassuring disclaimers. It is not for me to try to give advice to someone with responsibilities such as yours. History will not forgive us if we allow the continued perversion of the truth, and if we persist in burying our heads in the sands. Even if our interpretations of history may differ, we know that one of the cardinal rules of diplomacy is to resist threats of intimidation which – in our modern age – are themselves tantamount to our enemy's victory. Events of recent weeks prove that the 'Finlandisation' of the United States has already occurred. You are, perhaps, the ultimate recourse which will prevent world domination by an unscrupulous totalitarian power whose motives are not the classic ones of self-aggrandisement but much more subtle than that: the Soviet Union, as I suspect you agree, is intent on destroying all systems either more efficient or more conducive to fulfilment and happiness than its own. Its present leaders are haunted by rival models, both to the West, and to the East. In our case it knows full well that the material well-being of our Western system is something that they will never be able to match, except for a tiny, privileged governing élite, and that, sooner or later, the contrast between our system and theirs is going to raise questions among the masses, for which its own leadership has no reply, and nothing to offer but the use of brute repressive force. And to the East it knows there exists a larger, more industrious and intelligent nation, kept in a shackled state through certain misguided policies of the recent past, but nevertheless about to prove its resilience, its adaptability and its technological skills. For this reason, Mr Vice-Chairman, your actions will have a decisive impact on world history. That they involve huge sacrifices is certain. But it may be said, as was said of the ancient Greeks, that civilization was once saved by a small band of courageous men. I hope and pray that this will be so.

Yours sincerely,
Adrian Jute.

The Vice-Chairman rose to his full four feet eleven inches, put the original letter, its Chinese translation and a number of press clippings back in a folder, and pressed a button on his desk. 'Tell the American scientist and his wife,' he informed an aide, 'that I am ready to see them.' He added, to himself: but if he thinks I'm going to change my mind, he needs to have his head examined.

*

The city emptied, ritually, immediately after the ritual 14 July, Bastille Day celebrations. The Place de la Concorde was no longer an angry car-drivers' ant-hill, but became a huge, sleepy parking lot for air-conditioned buses, with German, Dutch, Danish and Belgian number-plates predominating. French was no longer spoken on the Champs-Elysées, and café terrace waiters and predatory taxi-drivers robbed the tourists with imaginative, good-humoured cunning. Police in their blue shirt-sleeves were helpful when bra-less American girls approached them with simple requests, but resolutely refused to speak anything but French, even when the miniature flags on their shirt-sleeves identified them as linguists: in any disputes involving foreign visitors they invariably sided with their fellow countrymen.

With Parliament on vacation, the Government functioning with a small quorum of rotating ministers, most of the influential Cabinet members away on official junkets and the trade unions quietly preparing their October offensive, French editors were once again desperate for news. They fastened on any 'crime passionnel', however insignificant, with alacrity. Every wife-murderer became a Landru, every bank robbery another fabled Nice 'Société-Generale' saga. The cyclists' 'Tour de France' was a welcome, reliable standby, and the performance of the French rugby team in New Zealand afforded some relief, as did the alarming, but equally ritual and recurring, series of car crashes involving prominent French personalities – a process of elimination and renewal of the French élite as efficient as nature's past methods involving war, duelling, pox and the plague. An average number of German women tourists were raped and the large North African immigrant population in the South invariably blamed, even when, as frequently happened, the culprits turned out to be blond legionnaires or fresh-faced Naval ratings.

It was, in short, the usual summer doldrum period, happily saved by the Lémeric-Dutoit *affaire*. It was not just the summer news hiatus that made it a publishers' bonanza: it always pleased the French to discover that their rulers were as corrupt and as greedy as their own cynical instincts assumed.

In the case of '*L'affaire Lémeric*', the scandal was

compounded by its tragic *dénouement*. Had it not been for an ambitious, publicity-conscious police officer, it is possible that innocent lives might have been saved. But the news that a senior diplomat had been involved in a stolen art ring afforded such endless possibilities that, for once, something in the nature of investigative journalism occurred in France. There were colour pictures of missing Oriental masterpieces, and celebrated black and white pictures of a haggard, tearful Lazarian outside his Boulevard Haussmann gallery. The investigating magistrate was a young man of the new school, not averse to publicity either. One paper called him 'the Saint-Just of the art world'. Two French weeklies sent their best reporters to India.

At first the name of Aymeric de Lémeric-Dutoit was not even mentioned. He was the 'Mr X', 'the high functionary who acted as a go-between'. Then – a calculated indiscretion by Lucien Menhir, this, anxious that no stigma should be attached to his own name, for he too had served in Asia – the confirmation of Lémeric's 'temporary suspension' gave the story a new lease of life. A Sikh police commissioner, a former Indian Army colonel with exquisite manners and a self-deprecatory stammer which charmed the French press, arrived with a bulging briefcase for conferences at the Interior Ministry and the missing art treasures bureau nearby. He refused to give interviews, praised Interpol's tentacular communications system, and never once spoke with Forgeot, though he knew him well, and had indeed been tipped off by him in the first place.

There were news pictures, too, of a confident, disdainful Lémeric-Dutoit outside the magistrate's office, brushing off reporters and photographers, side by side with photographs of famous recent art acquisitions in museums throughout the United States. A convicted 'fence' described in one national magazine how Switzerland played a key 'laundering' role in stolen art. There were pictures of the façade of Lémeric's Rue de Varenne apartment, and an Opposition daily cruelly recalled that he had recently been in line for a key Presidential appointment.

Then, only forty-eight hours later, the controversy on the rights and limitations of reporting ethics once more became a major topic after Lémeric had been photographed one last time, open-mouthed and drooling, having shot his wife and

186

three small children. His gun had jammed, and he tried to gas himself, but neighbours gave the alert and the entire Paris fire brigade got into the act, their pillar-box-red machines bristling with revolving lights within a few yards of the Prime Minister's office. The general feeling was that Lémeric would never stand trial. As frequently happened with scandals of such magnitude, even those with impeccable records who had been close to him suffered some guilt by association, and Menhir was almost immediately transferred to a French Embassy in a small, land-locked African state, with the title of minister-counsellor and few prospects of advancement.

In an effort to restore the reputation of the French Foreign Ministry, Government spokesmen referred to the Lémeric-Dutoit affair as 'an unfortunate aberration', an 'inexplicable and absurd isolated case'. Privately, however, the President ordered a full-scale internal investigation, and the rules governing the use of the Foreign Ministry's 'diplomatic bag' were drastically overhauled.

Forgeot's own connections with Lémeric were tenuous enough to be overlooked. There was a problem, however: after being charged, but not arrested, for disposing of stolen goods, Lazarian senior promised the French Government investigation team full co-operation in return for a 'private understanding' over back taxes involving the Lémeric transactions. And Lazarian senior confessed that he had been ill at ease, and had almost fled the country, after a visit some six weeks previously from a certain Albert Spurling, a claims adjuster from London. Try as he might, Bergerol, the French cop in charge of the stolen art section, failed to trace any such figure in the London art or insurance world. Lazarian had noted the London phone number, and Bergerol, to his surprise, discovered that it corresponded to a highly confidential London secret service number. Normally, such calls could be only traced through official logs, and this required making an approach to London. There were two alternative channels – through the British Embassy in Paris, or through the liaison office which Forgeot ran. Bergerol was not only bright: he had an exceptionally suspicious, tortuous mind. He knew, vaguely, that Lémeric and Forgeot had been more than casual acquaintances. He sensed there was an aura of mutual protection, of unconscious collusion almost, among high officials who had graduated from the same *grande école* the same year. He also vaguely remembered that Forgeot had once rubbed shoulders with the infamous Guillaume, in his earlier, SDECE incarnation, that Forgeot was on exceptionally good terms, too, with other secret services in far-flung places, including India. He tried to pin the Indian visitor down. In casual conversation, he mentioned Forgeot's name, and that of Spurling. There was no response. But, when he went a step further, and invited Forgeot to meet the Indian Commissioner, for all three to have lunch together, Forgeot unexpectedly declined, and Bergerol discovered later that Forgeot's excuse had been a spurious one. He had made a note to look into Forgeot's own telephone bill for the past few weeks. Direct dialling made it all much more hazardous, and there was no certainty that there would be any proof.

But for all these reasons Bergerol decided to approach the British Embassy directly rather than call on Forgeot for assistance. And Forgeot knew. And worried. When he was not brooding over May, which he found himself doing more rather than less with the passage of time, wondering whether she was alive, and, if alive, hating him for his callous betrayal of her, he began brooding over Lazarian, wondering whether there was any likelihood of Lazarian recognising him. And finally, stopping at a phone booth late at night, after the ritual exercise of covering his tracks, he dialled a Calvi number, recognised Rossi's growl, and, without introducing himself in any way, said softly, 'Victorine sent me.' Suddenly awake and alert, Rossi barked: 'Get out of here.' There was a rustle of bedsheets. 'No, not you,' Rossi said, 'I was talking to a girl. Nice kid, but not your type. Big tits. Big ears too.' Forgeot started to say something about not wanting to disturb him in the middle of the night. 'You're not disturbing me,' Rossi said. 'I suppose you called to say you want to buy the car after all?'

Forgeot said he'd like to talk about it.

'Tomorrow,' said Rossi. 'You still play that stupid English game – squash? At the Club Lauriston? I thought as much. You'll get a message. Try and play tomorrow lunchtime. Ciao.'

Forgeot hung up. There was a cascade of unused one-franc coins. He pocketed them slowly.

Chapter Fourteen

THE TAXI-DRIVER was not a real taxi-driver at all, but the taxi-driver's temporarily unemployed brother-in-law. The real taxi-driver had gone to the races at Maisons-Laffitte, at somewhat short notice, after a flaming row with his wife. It had started over lunch, and the pretext – the abnormal shedding of the hairs of the taxi-driver's admittedly exceptionally shaggy, moulting dog, allegedly fouling Madame's wine-red, nylon, neo-horsehair sofa – was as futile and unexpected as most family rows usually are.

The taxi-driver had retorted, reasonably at first, over his stringy *boeuf aux carottes*, that the sofa was in the front room and used only when there were visitors. He added, warming to his subject, that there weren't many of those any more, because of his wife's foul disposition and obsessive pre-occupation with spotlessly clean tiled floors. She would be better off washing more often between her legs than swabbing down the tiles continually, nagging bitch that she was, he said, adding the Frenchman's final insult – 'you can't even cook a decent meal.' Then the taxi-driver's wife started screaming at him, and they were off to another of those hideous, sudden flare-ups that the neighbours were constantly complaining about, ending as often as not with sounds of broken crockery, scuffles and thuds, and an uneasy status-quo period of armed neutrality lasting sometimes for weeks.

A raw slice of working-class life, the unemployed brother-in-law pondered, as mysterious and as worthy of study as the fertility rites of the Ivory Coast Baoulé tribe – about which he was something of an expert, having recently obtained a degree in social anthropology, not so far conducive to sustained gainful employment, and written a thesis on the subject (though he himself had never travelled further than Marbella). He mused, as he drove his brother-in-law to the races. He frequently saw himself in print in his mind's eye. This time it was: *Saturday lunchtime rites in Levallois – a study in aggression* by Fernand Lespinasse.

He was reading a review of it in *Le Monde* ('this subtle, enchanting, yet disquieting monograph, worthy of Professor Lévi-Strauss at his best') when his day-dreaming was suddenly interrupted

'Try and pick up some fares this afternoon, stay away from the *flics*, and don't get lost,' the real taxi-driver said. 'And if you're not back here by five-thirty, you can find another place to stay.' Truly, the brother-in-law thought, my sister and this vinous ape, they deserve each other.

There were no fares on the way back into town, of course. Everyone was going to the races. The mean son of a bitch didn't want me to stay because he was afraid I'd borrow money from him to play the horses and he couldn't very well refuse, the budding author thought. There was a monograph waiting to be done on the social attitudes of horse-race handicappers. He had a title for that, too. *The Happy Losers.* By Fernand Lespinasse. Rounding the skyscraper complex of the Rond-Point de la Défense, he nearly ran down his fare, who yelped, making foreign noises.

'Where to?'

'Yambassadiyah di Grandye Britannia.'

The monographer was in no mood to be trifled with.

'I said, where to?'

The middle-aged man had clambered inside the Peugeot 504 as though pursued by an army of wolves. He repeated what he had just said, but more slowly, reading from a crumpled piece of paper. It dawned on the brother-in-law that he wanted to be taken to the British Embassy. 'Doesn't even know the address, shit, it's not true, another fucking tourist,' the taxi-driver-for-a-day muttered to himself, reaching for the taxi-driver's bible, and discovering that the British Embassy was on the Faubourg Saint-Honoré, a one-way street. The tourist at the back didn't know Paris from a hole in the ground, obviously, so the thing to do was to go all the way down the Champs-Elysées, round the Place de la Concorde, try and approach the Faubourg Saint-Honoré from the wrong end, say 'damn, it's become a one-way street again' as his brother-in-law had taught him, and then edge round towards it, missing it the first few times, and clocking up maybe an extra twenty-five, thirty francs in the process. Which he did.

Except that, when he did stop outside the Embassy, the huge doors were closed. His fare got out, nervously, rang a bell, and the brother-in-law, a Cassandra delighting in other people's disasters, said unkindly: 'There's no one there on a Saturday afternoon, for sure.' But the door opened a crack and a huge Englishman conferred briefly with the fare, eventually letting him slip through, then closing the door in the taxi-driver's face, so that the budding anthropologist had to ring and ring, and the huge man eventually opened the door again, handed him twenty francs and said redundantly: 'Nah hop it an fuck orf'; and, when he rang the bell again, the door remained obstinately closed. A policeman, sidling up to the cab out of nowhere, muttered something about not loitering in front of an Embassy, or did he want to be taken in, and the brother-in-law took the hint and drove off in a cloud of diesel fumes, cursing. It was that kind of a day.

Inside the Embassy, there was a good deal of coming and going, telephoning and well-bred whispering. The Consul-General, as usual, was nowhere to be found, and the functionary referred to as 'Knacker of the Yard' had gone to the country. Thank God there was a car with non-diplomatic plates available, and Albert came over on the late afternoon plane, carrying two passports, his own and a spare, a beautiful job, the Vice-Consul could cope, the photograph and the seal turned out perfectly. Albert kissed her on both cheeks. 'In nineteen forty-three they'd have given you a medal for that kind of work,' he said. The Vice-Consul said: 'I wasn't born in nineteen forty-three, *duckie*.' Albert wasn't fazed by her tough, *gamine* poise. 'Ze Resistance,' he said, assuming his Maurice Chevalier accent. 'Ze false peppers. Lysanders at ze Pré Catelan. Our last night togezzer before ze Gestapo she come.'

The Vice-Consul sighed. 'You'd better help me find this geezer a bed,' she said. 'As far as last night is concerned, you'll be keeping an eye on him.' 'Jesus' said Albert, 'Why did he have to pick on us? And why here?'

But the Russian understood. He spoke English, slowly but fluently. 'After what happened to the Chinese girl,' he said, 'I would not go anywhere near *them*' – pointing in the vague direction of the French Interior Ministry. Albert, remembering his own part in it all, said 'too effing true' and wondered whether he should not, nevertheless, and as a friendly gesture, tip Forgeot off. He decided against it, for the time being.

The Vice-Consul busied herself with sheets and pillow-cases. Albert struggled with a folding camp bed. 'Do you speak any Russian?' she asked him, 'Only a few words.' She said: 'What the hell do they teach you at the hospital, then?'

'I'm learning Chinese,' Albert said. And the Vice-Consul, her evening ruined, said 'a fat lot of good that is tonight', but relented and brought them both a bottle of whisky and some ice. She was there again next morning at seven a.m. The two men were already dressed. 'Stick him in the boot,' Albert whispered, 'and tell him he can come out when we're inside the parking-lot.' The Vice-Consul giggled. 'I don't know the Russian for boot,' she said. So they gestured. The visitor, with great dignity, and a sudden, charming smile, climbed in of his own accord, deftly kissing the Vice-Consul's hand as he did so. 'Astarogena,' said Albert, using one of his few Russian words. 'You can come out when I knock, like this, compree?' tapping the car with his knuckles. He entered the Champs-Elysées parking-lot, found an empty alley. Thank God it was summer, and the whole place almost deserted.

It was plain sailing after that all the way, the customs people at Calais and at Dover never noticed a thing. George Murray, Company Director, the passport had said.

Albert drove him straight to the country house near Lydd they used only for real emergencies. In the end they got on fine. The Russian's English improved gradually with practice. Hurry, hurry, he said, no time to lose, and plied Albert with long-stemmed Russian cigarettes, but only after they had cleared the Dover Customs. He wasn't as dumb as he looked.

The Russian had once, as a young man, been sent to Manchester as part of a Soviet trade delegation. He had been successfully contacted then, and been played back a few times, never for anything really important. Now he explained to the small group assembled in the safe house that he had been brought over to Paris to look over the computers being exhibited at the Paris Trade Fair near the Défense. The idea had been to pick up as much technical material as possible in the shape of brochures and hand-outs and maybe make contact with some unscrupulous French manufacturer to work on the side for a trading company which was a 'front' for a Soviet Defence Ministry subsidiary. They were especially interested in flat TV console screens, perhaps for tanks. That was all he knew about his Paris mission, he said.

The real questioning began. The Russian made no bones about being a KGB member. Well, not a member, exactly, more a kind of affiliate, like almost all Russians involved in computer work. But he did have the kind of skills that would serve him in good stead in industry in the West, no? Provided, of course, that his English improved.

And he had an exclusive piece of information. It was only gossip unfortunately. The rumour was that the Soviet defector, Semyakov, who had been killed in Washington, had not been a defector at all, but a deliberate 'plant' whose death had come as a surprise to them all.

Maitland, in charge of the questioning, was suitably casual. What had been the purpose of Semyakov's Washington role all along then? Disinformation, the Russian said, puffing on one of his cigarettes. Making the Americans believe things were so when they were really otherwise. Including the nuclear field? The Russian nodded, eagerly. There were all sorts of rumours, he said, that the Soviet Union was deliberately trying to provoke the Chinese into making an initial nuclear strike so that they could really clobber them. *And* show up the Chinese as barbarians, and maybe cow the United States into the bargain.

'How did you hear these rumours?' Maitland asked, again casually. The Russian went into a long, involved explanation. It wasn't any one person, he said. It had started with the Deputy Defence Minister flying down to the Crimea to talk to the Chairman. He had been very worried about Chinese military preparations, foreshadowing a possible nuclear strike. The Chairman had reassured him and the Deputy Defence Minister had returned to Moscow a chastened and fairly angry man. It turned out that the Chairman knew all about the Chinese preparations, that they had been deliberately fomented, as it were, and that, somehow, Semyakov was involved in that part of it. Semyakov was a trusted member of the American politico-military establishment of the United States, the Russian said primly, and had been a skilled manipulator.

'Which is why he was killed?' Maitland asked.

The Russian said he didn't know.

'And what part did Jute have in all this?'

The Russian looked blank. The name was not familiar to him. Maitland explained that an Adrian Jute had also mysteriously died though the Americans were claiming he was a suicide. Jute and Semyakov had worked together in the past. The Russian shook his head. He had never heard the name.

Then how, Maitland asked, had he heard about the rest?

Vice-Defence Minister Arbatchieff, he said, is my cousin. He was the one who went to see the Chairman.

The interrogators glanced at each other. Maitland asked the Russian whether he was prepared to take a lie detector test. Of course, the Russian said. Did they not believe, then, that he was the Minister's cousin? Maitland quietened him down. Of course, he said. It was just a way of testing his responses. There was so much that was hearsay, interesting hearsay, admittedly, he added deprecatingly, but it was facts that were needed, not gossip, however fascinating. While they were on that track, however, what more gossip did he have to offer? The Russian thought a while. After his cousin had come back to Moscow he had made certain enquiries. He had, while slightly drunk, talked about the Chinese provocation that the KGB was trying to do its best to initiate, using the unsuspecting Americans as a conduit. And there was a Frenchman mixed up in it too.

'In what capacity?' Maitland said quickly.

The Russian shrugged. 'I don't know. Just that there is a Frenchman. Working for Semyakov.' Whose side was the Frenchman on? 'What his political views are, I don't know,' the Russian said. 'All my cousin said was that, objectively, he was serving Soviet interests.' The word 'objectively', he added, as the roomful of people present knew, had a very special significance in Communist parlance. 'It could mean that he is unaware of the real nature of the service he is performing. It could mean he is simply a leftist dupe.'

The meeting adjourned in the middle of the night. It had been intended simply as a sampler of the kind of debriefing that was in order. 'It's all gossip, gossip, gossip,' Maitland told his own committee after the Russian had been taken to his bedroom. There followed a rambling, whisky-laden debate. Albert deliberately kept silent, while the others argued the pros and cons of keeping him in Britain, or of 'trading him off to the Yanks', as Maitland put it, 'simply to get him out of our hair'.

The consensus was to put him on the first plane out. Hackenback should be informed, someone said. Maybe they can make something out of all this. 'It would take us months,' said Maitland. 'Why should we do their dirty work for them?' Hackenback arrived the next morning. Everyone was puzzled by the CIA station chief's sense of urgency – but then the US President had given strict instructions that no one, not even the Brits, be told about the 'Barker' committee. It had been assumed that the Russian would be escorted out on the same passport, by commercial flight, maybe with a couple of Hackenback's men. It was with some surprise that Maitland discovered that Hackenback intended moving the Russian to Washington by chopper to the nearest US base and then by US Air Force plane – with Hackenback himself holding the Russian's hand. Hackenback even had a code-word out for the operation. For such a meat and potatoes operator, it didn't lack flair. 'I'm calling it,' Hackenback told a bemused Maitland, in Albert's earshot, 'Operation "Cousin Cousine".'

Albert asked Maitland how much should be passed on to the French about the defector. 'We'll have to tell them something, I suppose,' Maitland said. 'After all, the Russians must be wondering what happened to the guy. Forgeot's probably getting hell from all sides as it is.' Could Forgeot be told about the notional Frenchman co-operating with Semyakov? Albert asked. 'I suppose so' was the grudging answer. 'But what favours have the frogs done us lately?' Albert could have replied, at length. Instead, he kept silent.

The news that a 'low-level functionary of a State Purchasing Commission had been kidnapped' in Paris appeared first on the Tass, and then on the Reuter's wire. The functionary, whose name was not given, was, said Tass, 'believed to be suffering from a nervous breakdown' and had been 'spirited away against his will'. An hour later, the French news agency put out a bulletin, noting the Tass report and stating that no demand for political asylum by any Soviet visitor had been made in the past twenty-four hours. Forgeot covering himself, the Embassy said.

Operation 'Cousin Cousine' dovetailed into operation 'Barker' in a way which surprised even Hackenback. The news about Semyakov enraged the President. In the privacy of his office, he exploded. 'Until yesterday,' he told the CIA Director, 'this guy Semi-jackoff was the biggest thing since sliced bread. Now it turns out he was working against us all along. Ah can't understand you guys,' the President went on. 'What ah you all tryin' to do to me? Make sure that on top of everything else, we lose more points at the polls on an espionage issue?'

'It isn't just the polls, Mr President,' the CIA Director said, thinking: if the Russians really knew the score, they'd do everything they possibly could to keep him in office for a second term. 'What's now at stake is the very security of the nation.'

The President stared coldly back. The CIA Director said, 'You probably haven't had time to read the memorandum about the implications of the Semyakov turnaround. What it quite possibly means, Mr President, is that Jute may have been right after all – could be, they'd use the pretext of a Chinese nuclear strike, however small, to clobber us as well. They've got the capability.'

That night, the President put certain units on 'grey' alert. He went through the whole routine, with the Joint Chiefs of Staff, of recapitulating procedures in the event of a satellite warning of impending nuclear attack. The most sobering aspect of the situation, he realised, was that he had between four and seventeen minutes to decide what to do between the moment a Soviet ICBM was tracked, and its moment of impact. At no time in his life, he realised with horror, had he ever taken a decision, however minor, in such a short space of time. And that, too, was something the KGB had foreseen. Demoralisation as an essential part of destabilisation.

The middle-level British diplomat was kept sitting for almost an hour in the ornate waiting-room of the French Interior Ministry, just two days after the Russian had been spirited out of the country. His appointment was with Forgeot, and he had been carefully briefed to make the British handling of the case plausible. As with almost all Embassy affairs, endless discussion had preceded action. The Head of Chancery wondered whether the Ambassador himself should not be called in. But H.E. said no: it would be an unfortunate precedent if the Ambassador had to deal with every routine police matter. But it wasn't something that 'Knacker of the Yard' could be entrusted with, the Minister-Counsellor said. *Much* too uncouth. So in the end it was the First Secretary who was chosen, and given a complicated, contradictory and typically Foreign Office brief.

He was to say that they had acted as they had because it was a weekend, that the man had specifically requested a safe passage to Britain, and that the whole matter had been routinely handled.

He was to deny that they had used underhand techniques: unless specifically asked, he was not to volunteer information about the man's travel documents. There were some things best left unsaid. If pressed, he was to admit that, for the sake of expeditiousness, they had issued him with a temporary passport. The First Secretary had been cautioned against ruffling French feelings. At the same time, the Ambassador said, he should have no hesitation in referring to 'certain precedents' to justify the British course of action. 'Certain *unfortunate* precedents?' the First Secretary had asked. 'No, just precedents. Don't overdo it.'

He doubted whether Forgeot would press the point. 'Good man, Forgeot,' the Ambassador said. 'His mother was the daughter of a drunken Irish peer.' The conversation had gone off at a tangent, and at one point the Ambassador's personal secretary had surprised the librarian by asking for, and carrying off, a copy of Debrett's. They were looking up Forgeot's Irish descent.

It was unlike Forgeot to keep a British diplomat waiting. The First Secretary gave some visible signs of impatience. Eventually the black-coated *huissier*, looking positively regal, like a Hollywood butler, half-bowed, half-gestured the First Secretary to precede him. But they did not take the steps and the corridor leading to Forgeot's office. Instead, the First Secretary found himself in the Minister's antechamber, effusively greeted by the Minister's chief aide, the Directeur de Cabinet, asked to sit down, offered a cigarette, coffee, and the ritual small talk.

Jean Forgeot was out of town, the Directeur de Cabinet eventually said. An urgent mission. You know what life is like, with responsibilities like that. Sorry he hadn't had time to warn his friends and colleagues. The First Secretary explained that he was simply calling to give some details about the Russian Trade Mission defector. He gave a brief account of what had happened, and how it had been decided to take him to London, where he had requested asylum, because he had friends there. The First Secretary was surprised to detect indifference, almost relief, in the Directeur de Cabinet's manner. Oh, that, he said, think nothing of it: our Russian friends simply can't believe that we don't know what happened to him, they'll be relieved to know he's in safe hands. They both laughed. Things were going much better than expected.

By the way, the Directeur de Cabinet said, the Interior Minister would appreciate it if the British Ambassador could find time for a small, intimate luncheon with the Minister personally. Whenever was convenient. There were certain matters he wanted to discuss. No, nothing really important, but it would be useful to have an exchange of views on certain security matters. The Minister would appreciate it if the news of such a lunch was kept private. Would Wednesday be convenient? The First Secretary said he would ask, but he was almost certain that the Ambassador would revise his programme to make himself available. Would Forgeot be there, he asked? No, Monsieur Forgeot would not be back in time. In any case, he was probably due for another posting soon.

The First Secretary wondered whether he should refer to the remarks made by the Russian concerning a Frenchman operating with the dead Soviet defector, Semyakov.

Rehearsing the probable course the conversation would take beforehand, with two other Embassy people, he had been told not to raise the topic but wait for the French to do so. Had Forgeot been there, he might have disobeyed these instructions, if only to find out whether the Minister's lunch was connected with the Soviet walk-in. What the hell! Let the Ambassador deal with that problem when it arose.

He left the Ministry on foot, the uniformed police saluting him, the First Secretary acknowledging their salute with a flourish of his furled umbrella. He went straight to the office of the Deputy Chief of Mission.

'How did it go?'

'Extremely well. They couldn't care less.'

'They? Who else did you see, apart from Forgeot?'

'I didn't see Forgeot. I saw the Directeur de Cabinet. Forgeot,' the First Secretary said, 'isn't there – not for the time being. Perhaps not any more. It's my guess,' he added, 'that Forgeot may be in trouble. They talked about him in an odd sort of way. Could be he was finally caught screwing the girlfriend of someone really important. I got the feeling they were on the brink of asking us if we knew something about him that they didn't. And finally they didn't have the nerve.'

The First Secretary was only slightly off the mark. To the consternation of the Interior Minister, and the French President, when he was told, Forgeot had disappeared.

Chapter Fifteen

THE TELEPHONE call to Rossi had been spur-of-the-moment insurance against disaster. Forgeot hadn't expected trouble so soon. Without Forgeot's knowledge, Tranh had been keeping a watching brief on him: Forgeot had come to recognise an occasional Vietnamese face in odd places, but had not wanted to challenge Tranh, or even thank him. Tranh had his own reasons for doing things, and was stubborn in a Chinese way. That was the reason he had taken care of Guillaume in such an appallingly barbarous fashion. Tranh acted as he thought fit, in all circumstances.

From the day of the telephone call, Forgeot had not slept in his apartment: always under assumed names, in small, unpretentious out-of-the-way hotels. His guise was that of a sales representative and he had samples to prove it. Coming back to his apartment block garage-door entrance early one morning, two days later, he was suddenly aware of a scurrying Oriental form beside his car, the young Vietnamese silently but urgently gesticulating, his left hand shaken from side to side violently, index finger raised. A warning in any language.

Out of the corner of his eye, Forgeot tried to detect danger signals. There was no police car that he could see, but that meant nothing. As he accelerated down the street, weaving in and out of traffic to lose a possible 'tail', he assumed they were upstairs in his apartment, and maybe waiting for him inside the garage.

He parked. To return to his office would be a brazen but futile gesture. Assuming they knew even part of the story, they could get him on a variety of charges. Cold-bloodedly, he ran through the list of possibilities. The Guillaume murder. The Lazarian connection. His masquerading as a British insurance adjuster. The Jute-Semyakov connection. That was not all. Maybe the Chinese had gone to the French Government and asked for some form of corroboration? On the other hand, not showing up at his office on the Rue des

Saussaies was tantamount to a confession, to whatever crime had been detected. There was no real choice. From now on, Forgeot thought, I go underground. I am an agent in a foreign country, on the run. It's happened before. It's all in a good cause. Remember, they came for her too, without any warning. And you didn't budge.

He realized, with some satisfaction, that though he had only vaguely envisaged this eventuality, his preparations were adequate. The problem was not knowing which of the many facets of the case interesting the authorities involved him. This precluded holing up in his Vietnamese sanctuary near the Place Maubert, at least for the time being. The risk was too great. He might, however, still benefit from Vietnamese eyes and ears. And it was a good thing Tranh understood and spoke Chinese. Forgeot doubted that any telephone tap on Tranh's shops or restaurants would yield a quick response from his pursuers, if he delivered an oblique message in Chinese. Tranh and his assistants were on the phone most of the day, mostly in Vietnamese. The tappers might not even tell the difference, especially if Forgeot were to speak with a Vietnamese nasal twang.

And Rossi, as an exchange after the Club Lauriston squash game confirmed, had agreed to help until his plans and options became clearer. One final batch of posters was on the way, Forgeot knew – and it was this that would in all probability send the Chinese over the top. In the meantime, he had lots to do, some of it elsewhere, and most of all he had to survive. The immediate problem was one of identity.

Forgeot was an expert on the subject. In books, he had read with mild amusement how those on the run invariably stumbled on skilled forgers or specialised middlemen. Truth was more complicated. Of course, there *were* men in shady bars and cafés and student haunts who would, once certain they were not dealing with the stool-pigeons, come up with faked or stolen identity or work papers, driving licences and even passports. In most cases these were not worth the paper they were printed on, though they might fool an unfortunate Senegalese or Algerian on the run. Some of the papers that had crossed Forgeot's desk wouldn't have taken in a traffic cop on his first day on the beat, but the purchasers couldn't know that, the racket was a thriving one, but only for the sellers, not the buyers.

Stolen passports were a little more reliable, but most countries a fleeing man might find desirable these days had computerised security data, and high on the list of stored information – retrievable instantly at the touch of a button – were the numbers of stolen or missing passports around the world, however skilfully the seals and photographs had been doctored. Numbers were difficult to forge, and numbers were what counted.

Forgeot knew he would be unable to pass as an Arab, and this in a way was unfortunate for the Arabs operated on a different plane altogether. They pooled their resources, and were constantly shuffling packs of passports – Iraqi, Algerian, Syrian, Lebanese, whatever. One agent would borrow a passport from such a pool, and it would be a perfectly legitimate document, straight from the Government issuing authority concerned. Such regular interchanges of identities were what drove the various Western counter-espionage services crazy. But for that kind of swap you not only had to look the part. You also had to be a member of a recognised group in good standing.

There were other sources of supply: though most Latin American countries had tightened up their rules, some at the request of Forgeot's own government, using data he himself had prepared, it was still possible, here and there in Europe, to lay one's hands on a genuine Venezuelan or Uruguayan passport – admittedly at a huge price. But Forgeot knew, also from past experience, that the supplier of the passport would not be above tipping off the authorities if he thought it would be in his interest to do so, after the sale, and after he had covered his tracks.

The only really fool-proof methods were quite different. There were some frontiers where a white face, a clean shirt and a respectable-looking car would get you across the border without any papers at all. The Franco-Belgian border was a good example, except when the heat was on. The Franco-Luxembourg border, just east of Longwy, was even better. It helped, here, to have local number-plates, for thousands of Lorrainers regularly crossed the border to shop for cheaper liquor and petrol on the Luxembourg side, and the cops and customs officers on both sides of the frontier tended to look the other way.

Which meant, as Forgeot had good cause to know, that neither Belgium nor Luxembourg was neglected by the underworld, 'burnt' agents or others on the run. From Luxembourg, itself a financial haven as efficient as and a good deal more discreet than Switzerland, it was possible to fly direct to Canada and the United States. The Belgian police had, to say the least, an indifferent record in tracking down illegals, and the frontier between Belgium and the Netherlands was even more open than the one between France and Belgium.

There was, of course, a different track altogether for the more fortunate and that was the dual nationality gimmick. The Israelis used this device in countless ways in their own permanent, underground secret war: a British citizen with dual nationality might retain and renew his British passport for the whole of his life, but at the same time actually be a Moshad agent and Israeli citizen under a completely different name. And operational agents had considerable access to identity papers and passports of all kinds. During his SDECE days, Forgeot had had three or four different identities at the same time, passport, identity cards, driving licences, the works.

The British were equally extravagant in their use of passports, but they had tighter security. A British agent, operationally using a passport which was in a different name and occupation, only obtained access to that passport by turning in his own, real one to his own headquarters for the duration of his trip. It was all done in a most gentlemanly way, Albert had told him once. 'Wouldn't like a cat burglar to find half a dozen passports under different names in your shirt drawer, what?' Albert had said, affecting an exaggeratedly upper-class intonation. The sordid possibility that the agent in question might conceivably walk off with two passports, or sell one, was never mentioned.

The French, Forgeot knew from his own experience, were far more careless. Forgeot himself retained, from his SDECE period, a set of documents, including a driving licence and valid passport, in the name of Jean Lepiller. He had another, even more coveted possession: unknown even to the DST, he had a perfectly valid Irish passport, under his mother's maiden name of O'Malley. This he had renewed, with an open-end US visa, throughout the years, and nobody had been any the wiser. Even Albert didn't know about it. But for the time being Forgeot needed not Albert but Rossi, not on the phone this time, but in flesh and blood. Leaving his car outside a bar near the Soviet Embassy in Paris (a nice touch this, he thought) he took a taxi to Orly, and a plane to Ajaccio, calling Rossi not from the airport – all airport phones were suspect – but from a callbox in town.

The young man who picked him up in a modest Renault 5 looked like a smart croupier or hotel management trainee. He chatted about the weather in response to Forgeot's small-talk, not volunteering any himself. They drove for hours over the centre of the island, to the outskirts of Calvi, along the two-lane winding road that is both a delight and death-trap, and turning off suddenly, still in the hills, on to a dirt road and into a private estate which was so concealed by trees and walls that no one could have guessed that a long, low, two-storey house had been built there. Forgeot sensed there were roaming guard dogs on the premises and some sophisticated devices at the gate.

A gaunt elderly lady showed him to his room. Swimming trunks had been laid out on the bed. There was a bottle of Chivas, ice and soda water on a tray. He swam in the pool outside. Forgeot was not alone in the house, he soon saw. Valentine was practising sharp dives off the diving board. She blew him a kiss.

Rossi's car, another Renault 5, didn't arrive till eight, and the three of them – Rossi, Forgeot, Valentine – sat down to a simple but memorable meal at nine: some home-made pâté and Corsican ham, slices of pink *gigot*, Corsican cheeses and what must have been home-made raspberry sorbet. The wines were from Rossi's vineyards. They talked as if Forgeot was on a brief vacation, visiting an old friend. Valentine was at ease, joking, pouring them a brandy afterwards. She wore a white dress so décolleté at the back that the top of the cleft of her small round cheeks was just visible. Her tan likewise was total: obviously, since Guillaume's death, she must have spent a considerable amount of time acquiring it in the vicinity of Rossi's swimming-pool, topless. But after the brandy, and without a word, Valentine kissed Rossi on the cheek and said good-night. More formally, with the ghost of a wink, she shook hands with Forgeot, but Forgeot grabbed her, held her and said: 'I'm really glad to see you're okay.'

'Thanks to him.' She pointed at Rossi with her chin, slowly stroked the back of Forgeot's neck, kissed him, saying: '*A tout à l'heure, peut-être.*'

'A good kid,' Rossi said, after the door had closed. 'She'll stay here awhile, while the heat's on. Then she'll take over a beautician's shop in town I have ready for her.'

'That's very generous of you,' said Forgeot.

'Not at all,' said Rossi. 'Whoever was responsible for her little troubles was also involved in the Guillaume business, and I can't ever thank the person enough who put a stop to that. I felt almost sorry for the son of a bitch, though, when I learnt what they had done to him. Whatever was the unnecessary violence for?'

Forgeot said: 'You sound like my own Minister. I told him several weeks back that I knew nothing about it, that I was out of town when it happened.'

'I'm aware of that,' said Rossi, 'and I don't want to know any more than I have to.' He poured himself a glass of Corsican mineral water. 'But if it's in connection with the Guillaume affair that you're here, you know I'll do everything . . .'

Forgeot broke in: 'Listen. I'm on the run. I don't know why they're after me: it could be one of several reasons – maybe the Guillaume business. Maybe something else. Maybe you'll even read in the papers that I'm wanted on some treason charge. That's baloney. It may look like that, but I assure you it's not. I don't want to talk about it.'

Rossi said, softly: 'What do you want me to do? Just tell me what you'd like.'

Forgeot said: 'I have two perfectly clean identities, and could get out of the country with no trouble at all. But I'm expecting a drop – it's not drugs – and have to remain in Paris for that. And there are people, maybe, who don't want me to stay alive for that. I ought to have a gun, but that's always tricky, when you're on the run and liable to cross frontiers in a hurry. Besides, they're probably in my apartment right now, which is where the gun is. They're probably watching my boat too, my haunts if they think I have any, and I'm not even sure that the people looking for me are my own countrymen. They could be Americans, possibly even Russians, as well. And you know the way we work. In my particular branch, we're not given to lengthy enquiries, public juries, open trials. At a pinch, if I cause too much embarrassment, they'll just snuff me out. And, for various reasons, I don't want to go just yet. I'm in the middle of a rather fascinating poker game.'

Rossi didn't answer for a minute or two. Then he burst out laughing. 'I have just the thing for you,' he said. 'I don't know how long it can last, but it's brilliant. Not only will you be armed, legally, but you'll be wearing your gun in the middle of the Champs-Elysées and still be invisible.'

He gestured to Forgeot not to reply. 'No, I haven't gone off my rocker. I have shares in a company' – he shrugged deprecatingly – 'yes, I know, it's true, we gamblers have a thirst for respectability; it's a very reliable company indeed, affiliated with a big British one, what you might call a multi-national, really. Securor. We guard banks, we handle huge quantities of cash. Our men wear rather dreadful uniforms, almost like cops, except for the insignia on the peaked caps. You must have seen them. We're very, very careful indeed about who we hire.

'You'll return to Paris tomorrow. You'll see the personnel head. I'll warn him by the time you arrive. I won't tell him any more than I have to. He'll fix you up. Perhaps not for very long, because there are proceedings for permanent hiring which may be too complicated in your case. Let's just say you'll be a holiday replacement for someone, under an assumed name. We'll give you a quiet assignment – not too much in the public eye. And you'll be armed at all times, at any rate while you're on assignment. I can't guarantee the uniform will fit all that well, but if you looked too smart, you'd be drawing attention to yourself. And if you need a further spell of gainful employment, you could always come back here. Or operate for a bit in another town.'

'That shouldn't be necessary.'

'And if you need another kind of disguise, if you need to look like an attractive young couple, you could always borrow Valentine. She thinks the world of you.'

'She's sweet.'

'She's tough, too. Didn't tell the police a thing.' He winked. 'I'll leave you. There'll be a car tomorrow morning to take you to Bastia. Do you think they'll be watching you at Orly?'

'That's a risk I have to take,' said Forgeot. 'There just isn't sufficient time to do it any other way.'

He undressed, brushed his teeth, poured himself a light scotch, read *Corse-Matin*, which was full of forest fires and fatal traffic accidents. There was a quiet knock on the door.

Valentine's voice said: 'Can I come in?'

She was in her white dress still, but not for long. She slipped into bed with him. 'If you're tired,' she said, 'I'll leave you. If you want me, I'll stay. He's been a prince, your friend.'

'I know. He is.'

'You're quite a prince yourself.' She started caressing him, going down on him, her fingers, her mouth softness itself. Her hair was silky on his stomach. He didn't respond at first. She stopped. She turned her head, looking up at him. 'Do you like me, just a little bit? I know you didn't really want to do anything, last time. It was just a pretext, wasn't it? You were really after Guillaume, all the while.'

Forgeot didn't reply, simply stroking her hair, holding her firmly but gently by the back of the neck, to keep her from starting again.

'Come on,' he said, 'you know very well I was aroused. You'd rouse a corpse.'

She giggled. 'I know. I'm pretty good. My friends tell me I have an unusual rotary motion, and other qualities.' She slipped his hand from her, determined to succeed. When he tried half-heartedly to pull away, she moved over him masterfully, determined to continue. I've become a monk, Forgeot thought, I haven't had any and I no longer want any. Not with her. Then he gave in to the blank void, the pleasure, the release, and when it was over he pulled her up and said: 'You didn't have to do that, you know.'

'I like it.'

Forgeot patted her, affectionately. 'It's true,' she said. 'I almost always like it. But I love it with some people. All except the Guillaume types. And even Guillaume . . .' She

207

whispered in his ear. 'I sometimes enjoyed what he did to me.'

Forgeot didn't want to discuss Valentine's sex life, but it seemed only polite to do so. 'You miss it all, then,' he said lamely. Valentine said: 'Yes, I miss some of it. I'm a *pute* at heart, a natural. If it hadn't been for that shit I would have gone on for another five, ten years. I loved it, having several different men in one day. Many women do. Most of them fantasise about being in brothels – or in harems. Didn't you know?'

'And now you're all alone. Is that what you mean?'

Valentine nodded. 'I've got no one. You perhaps?' She gave a mock histrionic sniffle, part of which might have been real. 'You don't really give a damn about me, do you? And Rossi's the superior kind of hood who's far too grand to fuck his own girls. He keeps them for his friends.'

'He has a lot on his mind at the moment.'

'I know.'

Forgeot decided to trust her – up to a point.

'If you wanted to,' he said, 'you could help me a lot.'

'I owe you a great deal. Just ask.'

'I may need a safe place, a hide-out, for a few days, in Paris. Any ideas? It doesn't have to be in the Avenue Foch.'

Valentine said: 'Is the Pigalle any good?'

Forgeot didn't reply. She went on: 'There's this friend, Françoise. For some reason she calls herself Janine. She operates in the Rue Blanche. She doesn't have a "Jules", she's entirely on her own, for some reason the Mondaine have never bothered her. The other girls like her. She has a studio which she only uses for tricks. You could use it from one a.m. to four in the afternoon. She only works from four to one. Here, I'll write her a note.'

She got out of bed, found some paper and wrote, in an upright, sturdy but somewhat childish scrawl: 'This will introduce a friend who helped me out in a big way recently. He wants to use your place while you're not there. He is on the level and won't bother you. Please help him if you can. I'm lying low for a while because I got into a bit of trouble. Love Valentine.'

'You must know her very well indeed,' Forgeot said.

'She's my little sister. I tried to talk her out of it, but my example was contagious. She didn't do as well, though, so she went on the street. She's okay – for the time being. I don't think she's a stool-pigeon – yet.'

'How do I recognise her?'

'She's just off the Place Blanche, on the corner of the Rue Fontaine. Occasionally, she'll stop in at a place called the Lord Jim. She looks exactly like me, but with a blonde wig. She usually wears white jeans, see-through tops and dark glasses, even at night. She started off as a stripper, but found there was more money doing what she's doing now. She knows all the staff of the clubs in the area, and they know her.'

'Thanks.'

They remained in each other's arms, comfortably. 'If you want me to leave, just say so,' Valentine whispered. 'But I'm good to sleep with. Really sleep, I mean. I bring nice dreams. Everybody says so. Little Miss Nembutal, that's me.'

It was true. He woke from a heavy sleep, refreshed, almost tingling. Valentine was no longer there, and he was sorry. He would have made love to her with pleasure this early morning, without foreboding, comparisons or angst of any kind.

Before leaving by car for Bastia airport, Rossi looked him over, critically, insisting that he alter his appearance slightly, fussing over him, fiddling with a comb to change his parting, lending him a pair of sunglasses, finally letting him go, with the same young man at the wheel.

'Remember,' said Rossi, 'we can hide you on the island for a long, long time if we have to. At a pinch, for the rest of your life.' And Forgeot hadn't thanked him, not knowing what to say, but had slapped him on the back and said: 'Whatever you do, don't come to my funeral and get spotted by the cops. And don't believe everything you read in the papers.'

At Orly he slipped quickly, luggageless, through the crowd, avoiding the arrivals hall. It was surprising, if you knew the layout, how many ways there were of leaving an airport. He ended up standing in a queue with everyone else at the taxi rank, hiding behind a group of garrulous French Canadians. He told the driver to take him to Montparnasse, and there did some complicated twists and turns inside the station after paying off the driver. It's getting monotonous,

Forgeot thought, like SDECE training all over again. I'm too old for this sort of thing. The headlines of *France-Soir* loomed at him: top counter-espionage personality missing. He bought a copy. There was no photograph, thank goodness, and the story didn't say very much, but it meant that he was in even greater trouble than he had imagined.

There is a pattern about luncheon parties in any French Ministry which puts British and American government hospitality to shame. Those who gathered in the main reception room of the Interior Ministry in the Place Beauvau, the day Forgeot returned from Corsica, were suitably impressed. They stood around, or lounged on priceless Louis XVI furniture, sipping champagne and other drinks provided by the Interior Minister's own personal confidential secretary, a formidable, somewhat withered lady in smart black. The Minister's own aide for security matters, a taciturn young ex-army officer, also helped out. There were no waiters around. 'Nothing in front of the servants' was the Minister's old-fashioned rule.

The British Ambassador had finally been asked to come alone. After shaking hands with the Minister, he said 'Good God', spotting Maitland in a corner, talking earnestly to, of all people, the head of the CIA. The American Ambassador was not present. There would be a god-awful row about that later, but the Minister knew what he was doing. He had tapes of the Ambassador's numerous telephone conversations with a large number of American correspondents in Paris. The Ambassador still had a promising political career ahead of him, and made sure he got into the papers back home at every available opportunity. The Minister, who in any case distrusted the ability of any political appointee to keep a secret, had vetoed his presence. He couldn't stand people who leaked to the press for the sake of their careers, he told his aide – conveniently forgetting that he did so himself at the slightest opportunity.

For the CIA head to have flown over was most unusual. Even more unusual was the fact that the British Ambassador hadn't been told in advance, just as he had been unaware of Maitland's arrival. 'Just over for the day,' Maitland said to him, in a quiet aside. 'Terribly short notice. Nothing I could do, old boy' – not sorry at all, and quite unabashed.

The French Interior Minister, small, dapper, in dark suit and too-loud tie, should have enjoyed playing host but was obviously nervous, his laugh too loud, his movements febrile. The lady in black now staggered round the room carrying a tray of scotch, fruit juice, bloody marys. In deference to the CIA Director, she had made some dry martinis. At her insistence, the CIA Director took one, tasted it and winced.

They were ushered into a small, circular high-ceilinged room overlooking a small garden. (Ministry buildings in Paris have hidden gardens in the most unlikely places.) They sat around a circular table that would have put the combined resources of Tiffanys and Harrods to shame. The cutlery was gold, and there were four crystal glasses of different sizes in front of each seat placing. The British Ambassador sat on the Minister's right, the CIA Director facing the Minister. By common, unspoken consent everyone talked trivia while the white-coated waiters were in the room, though they too were policemen. The conversation was mostly in French, the CIA Director occasionally bursting into English, and the British Ambassador producing the right word for him. There were no interpreters. Nobody took notes. The Minister's aide did not say a word for the greater part of the meal. He did not eat much, either: he was obviously memorising the whole thing.

It was after the feather-light quenelles de brochet Nantua and before the rôti de boeuf en croûte that the Minister got down to business. Raising his voice to command attention, he said: 'Your Excellency, gentlemen, I wish to thank you for coming at short notice, especially' – he gave a little bow across the table – 'those who came such a long way.

'I want to inform you of a very grave incident that has just taken place, affecting my own Ministry, and the country as a whole: one of our most senior officials, connected with counter-espionage affairs, has disappeared. We have no reason to believe he has either defected or is preparing to do so. We are keeping a close watch on airports and frontiers, as well as on the airlines of Eastern bloc countries, and I can assure you that to our knowledge he has not left French soil – yet.

'Our British and American friends' – he nodded now in Maitland's direction – 'have linked him with a Soviet-inspired operation of considerable magnitude. As we understand it, their plan is to induce the Chinese Peoples Republic's leaders into believing that they are in danger of imminent Soviet nuclear attack.

'The aim, apparently, is to get the Chinese to indulge in a pre-emptive nuclear strike – a decision which would then enable the Soviets to go in and retaliate massively, wiping out the Chinese nuclear capacity in the process. The implications, of course, are incalculable: not only would there be a complete shift in the balance of power, but once a conflict of this kind starts God knows where it might end. The dangers are so numerous it would take too long to run through them: the radiation hazard would in itself be catastrophic not only for the belligerents but for ourselves, especially at a time when we are all attempting to develop our nuclear power resources.' There was the sound of cutlery being laid down. Nobody was eating now.

'Our President is being kept fully informed,' the Minister went on. 'He is determining the best, most proper and fruitful diplomatic course of action. He has ordered me to find the missing man – Forgeot – at all costs. Forgeot is believed to have provided the Chinese with data on which they are expected to act. One aim of today's lunch,' he smiled bleakly, his own plate untouched, 'which I hope you find enjoyable, is to help us to find Forgeot at all costs.'

The CIA Director, to Maitland's intense annoyance, had lit a cigarette. He said: 'Is that the only purpose you had in mind, Minister? Or shall we also talk about Soviet intentions in their broader aspects? I could, maybe, spread a little light there.'

'The purpose of this meeting,' said the Minister quietly, 'is to look at all aspects of the situation. We don't have very much time. Any ideas would be greatly appreciated. Sir?'

The CIA Director spoke slowly, as though from a brief.

'The game plan,' he said, 'is highly ingenious. It involved two prominent intelligence personalities, on our side, now dead, in whom we had total trust. One was a vintage Soviet defector, a man of high standing who had repeatedly proven his worth to us, a former Air Force officer who had become a senior satellite reconnaissance expert for Soviet territory. Between them, they appear to have doctored satellite reconnaissance data in various ways, using old material, recon pictures from earlier flights over training areas, etcetera, to show Soviet preparations for an imminent all-out nuclear strike on China.

'Naturally enough, the Chinese responded by intense mobilization procedures, moving their firing sites around, and – more important, though I trust nothing will ever get outside this room – by appeals to us to take part in a combined pre-emptive strike on the USSR. Which appeal, I need hardly add, our President instantly rejected.'

The Minister was pale, and swallowed the Volnay '73 without even tasting it.

Maitland spoke for the first time. 'It was another Soviet defector, more or less by chance, who confirmed the nature of the plot,' he said. 'We handed him over to Bill here whose boys were able to confirm he was telling the truth.'

The British Ambassador thought: damned fool. The last thing he wanted was any reference to the whereabouts of the defection. He was relieved when the conversation took another turn.

The Minister was saying: 'We are making an announcement today about Forgeot's disappearance. Some of you doubtless know him. The possibility of his being a double agent is of course horrendous, so we are giving out the bare minimum. We are not even mentioning his name. One of the reasons for this lunch – incidentally my President is aware that it is taking place, and approved the idea when I submitted it to him – is to make absolutely certain that no reports of a possible imminent nuclear war between China and the USSR occur in the media.'

Maitland was whispering into the British Ambassador's ear: 'And that's why your counterpart isn't here, old boy.' Everyone must have heard.

'In today's present economic context,' the Minister said, 'such news would be catastrophic, to say nothing of the impact of nuclear protesters, ecologists, all the protestors our democracy engenders and protects.'

The CIA Director smiled a wintry smile. '*Our* President,' he said, 'is so aware of the need for secrecy that all those with

213

any knowledge of the case have been made to sign a special secrecy oath. We don't have D notices, unfortunately, so we would be at the mercy of the first indiscretion. It's conceivable that, if cornered, Forgeot might unburden himself to the press simply to draw attention away from his own actions. Have you thought of that?'

It was the British Ambassador, surprisingly, who asked the most undiplomatic question of all. 'If we do find Forgeot for you,' he said, 'what do you want us to do with him? If he resists arrest, is he to be killed? Do you simply want to eliminate an awkward customer, or find out the ramifications of the whole story?'

Maitland remembered: the Ambassador had once been a World War Two Royal Marines commando. Madagascar in 1942, was it? Probably killed a few frogs in his time already.

The Minister seemed ready for that one, almost relieved such a question had been asked.

'Considering we may have a third world war on our hands,' he said. 'I think we all agree our topmost priority is to prevent it. What happens to Forgeot is of secondary importance. Of course we'd like his full story, but what we want most of all is to put a stop to his activities. We think we know who some of his Chinese contacts have been. Needlesss to say we're watching them round the clock – the Embassy, phones, everything. We also have some Vietnamese-born staff nosing around some of the haunts he used, over on the left bank.'

The British Ambassador was mercilessly, crudely persistent.

'So you don't really mind if he's bumped off?'

'Obviously, we should prefer this not to happen,' the Minister said patiently. 'But if it does happen, rest assured, there'll be no diplomatic outcry. We'd prefer it to happen before he hands over what we believe is still in his possession rather than after.'

The CIA Director cut in. 'We believe he has the last satellite reconnaissance data still with him, showing the final stages of Soviet missile activation in widely separated areas.'

Everyone was silent. Maitland was discreetly trying to fan the cigarette smoke away from himself. 'Surely,' he said quietly, 'the simplest thing would be to tell the Chinese what you've found out, and get them to realise that it's all a plot.'

The CIA Director smiled. 'Our President tried doing just that. And was rebuffed. It didn't work. The Chinese really believe this stuff. They think it's in our interest to stand idly by, and that we must obviously be against them since we refused to act with them. They say they have independent proof of their own.'

There was cross-table conversation for the first time. Mineral water was liberally poured.

Maitland said: 'Isn't there the danger that, if Forgeot is eliminated, the Chinese will regard it as further proof that he's been telling the truth all along?'

The Minister said: 'There is that possibility, I suppose. More especially if we eliminate him after he has made his last delivery. If before, they might have doubts about the whole thing.'

The aide spoke for the first time. He was expressionless, efficient, bloodless. 'Minister, there's some evidence that, if we don't do it, the other side will.'

Irritated, the Minister lapsed into French. 'What are you talking about?' He said querulously. 'Why didn't you tell me earlier?'

'The facts only came to light a few minutes ago,' the aide said. 'What happened is that Forgeot's department – excuse me, the DST – has just told us that some killer squads might be on the way.' In an aside to the CIA Director, he added: 'Once here the KGB prefers to keep its hands clean. The suspects in this case are Czech. We put a trace on them, and, thanks to *your* computer, we think we know who they are, and what they're here for. The same pair has operated before, in West Berlin, under a West German cover. They gave fake addresses on their foreign entry registration cards, of course. Probably holed up in their Embassy near the Trocadéro. We're watching it. It's playing hell with our summer holiday schedule.'

'Are you saying,' the Minister asked his own aide, 'that the Soviets want Forgeot out of the way too?'

'They probably killed Semyakov when he was of no further use to them,' the aide replied. 'That is, if our American friends are telling the truth when they say they didn't do it.'

The CIA Director said briskly: 'Believe me, it wasn't us.'

He thought to himself: what the hell do I say if they ask about Jute? But nobody did, though Maitland winked.

There was another pause while the waiters changed plates.

The cheeses remained untouched, but the Minister helped himself to a small slice of an elaborate bombe glacée. The British Ambassador followed suit. With the waiters once more out of the way, the Ambassador said, addressing himself to the CIA Director, more than to the table at large: 'I'm sorry to bring this up again, but I still don't understand: why don't you make a clear breast of things? Invite the Chinese over to your space centre or your lab or whatever it is. Show them the real works. Leave nothing out. Ask the experts in for a pow-wow, American and Chinese both. Keep showing them what's really going on, what's really on the bloody satellites, until they have to admit they're wrong.'

'That's another thing I want to talk about,' the CIA Director said, lighting another cigarette. 'It's too late. We can't do that any more.'

'Why the hell not?'

The whole table was poised now, expectantly.

'Because it wouldn't accomplish anything. That's the worst part of it. The Russians are gradually activating their missile sites for real. Have been for the last few weeks, just the way those buffoons faked it earlier this year. In other words, if we showed them the satellite data now, it would only convince our Chinese friends that they were right all along.'

The Minister rose. 'Coffee is next door, gentlemen,' he said, adding, 'we seem to be in something of a quandary, wouldn't you say?' There was a scraping of chairs. Above the noise of people leaving the table, Maitland heard the CIA Director say: 'Too fucking right.' The Ambassador said, also under his breath, to Maitland: 'Up shit creek.' And Maitland, responding in the archaic ritual of World War Two slang, replied: 'Without a fucking paddle.'

Chapter Sixteen

FORGEOT STOOD on the pavement of the Faubourg Saint-Honoré. In his right hand, ostentatiously drawn, was a loaded Smith and Wesson .38. He looked suitably bored. Nobody even looked his way. He anticipated, and repressed, a hysterical urge to laugh. Two other Securor men, also with pistols drawn, were carrying money-bags into the armoured van. A couple of uniformed policemen walked by, and nodded amicably. Rossi had been right: Forgeot's shabby grey uniform and peaked cap made him an invisible man.

The Franco-Arab bank whose cash they were retrieving was on the same side of the street as the British Embassy, and Forgeot almost willed someone he knew there to appear, and walk past, simply as a conclusive test. No one did. The Securor squad leader motioned to Forgeot to get aboard, and they left. It was their third call.

He had not expected to go on public display, at any rate not so soon. Rossi had said he would almost certainly get an indoor job, perhaps as a night watchman. Forgeot had reported to Securor headquarters just as the Interior Minister was finishing playing host to his British and American guests. The Rossi phone call had worked wonders. A laconic, somewhat harassed and overworked personnel officer had apologised for kitting him out and sending him out on the street so soon. 'We are a bit short-handed just now,' he said, 'and Monsieur Rossi mentioned you are exceptionally qualified for all kinds of useful work.' It would have looked bad to turn anything down. So now, in mid-afternoon, at bank closing time, they were making the rounds of a number of their regular customers.

Forgeot had assumed his 'spare' identity, and given his name as Lepiller. The personnel officer, who obviously stood in awe of Rossi, had requested neither references nor other details. All he required were Social Security details. Forgeot had invented a thirteen-digit number on the spot.

The cover wouldn't last long, of course, but it wasn't

meant to. And the game would be up immediately if the Ministry decided to publish his photograph. Forgeot recalled that they must have one, but naming him would bring out the Dien Bien Phu past, with all the attendant unwelcome publicity. So the chances were that his name wouldn't be released, not for the time being. But even the infinitely malleable French press, by a process of elimination, was bound to stumble on his identity sooner or later.

It was the standard tourist trip around Paris. There were banks everywhere these days, near the Etoile, the Opéra, even the Luxembourg Gardens. The armoured van took Forgeot across the Seine again, to a couple of small banks in the 17th, and finally home on the Left Bank, behind the Invalides, to the parent Securor organisation, itself a fortress with vaults, offices, a communications room, a small armoury. Forgeot turned in his gun but remained in uniform, leaving his civilian clothes in the locker he had been assigned.

He was free, but wanted to know more about the layout of the place. After consulting the work roster for the following day, and discovering his duties would be the same, he wandered down empty corridors, and was near the main exit when the alarm went off. It was a series of short, high-pitched noises, of the kind made by the New York police cars on emergency calls. Forgeot nodded pleasantly to the guard at the door. 'Someone playing at it again,' he said. 'They told me they'd have a rest tonight.' The guard replied: 'They're always fooling around.' Forgeot walked briskly away from the building, checking a compulsion to look over his shoulder. Instinctively, he knew he was on the run again.

The alert had come from an elderly uniformed supervisor, himself an ex-cop, who supplemented his income by acting as an in-house informer for the Renseignements Généraux. He had called his police contact. The supervisor routinely had all new Securor employees checked out on the Ministry computer, in case they were criminals enrolling in the organisation to do a job.

'Lepiller, you say,' the young inspector at the other end had said. 'What does he look like?'

The supervisor was versed in the absurd jargon of his former calling.

'Morphology? Big, on the thin side. Clean-shaven. No distinguishing marks. Tough. Anywhere between thirty-five and forty-five. Maybe even more. A well-educated voice he keeps trying to conceal. Probably down on his luck, and has taken a job which he regards as somewhat beneath him.'

'Anything further?'

The supervisor said no.

The next question surprised him.

'Does he look anything like Forgeot?'

'How the hell do I know what Monsieur Forgeot looks like?' the supervisor said. 'I never had anything to do with the DST. And I never met him when I was in the service. What's Forgeot got to do with it? Is he interested in this new guy?'

'It's Forgeot we're looking for. He's on the run. He's in bad, bad trouble, and if any of this gets out, you'll be in trouble too. Hold the new man on some pretext or other, if he's still in the building. Don't let him get away. We're coming round.'

Forgeot was down a side street, some distance away, when the Securor staff began searching his locker. He was suddenly aware of his appalling vulnerability. A faceless Securor guard in uniform wandering round Paris was a safe, anonymous figure, and so far it had been a great disguise. But a Securor guard hunted by the entire French police was something else. If they had found him out – and Forgeot believed they had – they would immediately tap the phones of all those connected with Securor. That meant pin-pointing Rossi. So there was one valuable escape route cut off for a start.

A couple of métro stations later, again in Montparnasse, which Forgeot was rapidly beginning to look on as a second home, he found it safe to use a phone. He closeted himself inside the booth. He knew by heart all the numbers where Tranh was likely to be.

He reached him at the third attempt. Forgeot spoke conversationally, quietly, in what he hoped was Vietnamese-accented Chinese, hoping that any eavesdropper would assume he was Vietnamese, hoping, too, that his disguise would not be successful enough to fool or baffle Tranh. But Tranh recognised him right away.

The background noise was that of a busy food shop, with cash registers going and lots of noise. Forgeot found himself saying: 'I am having difficulties with my supplies. Exceptionally stuck for cash. I will not be able to pay you this week. In fact I may have to borrow.' Tranh grunted.

'I'm also having problems with my waiters' clothing.'

Tranh's voice was jovial, brisk, the entrepreneur helping out a reliable business associate. 'You were expecting them today? We help you out. Easy. How about your van? Is it still out of order? If so, we lend you one. Where you want?'

On the Rue de la Boëtie is a garage with a notoriously surly staff, who mind their own business, only interested in their regular customers and in manning their petrol station. Forgeot knew the place, because he had once, unsuccessfully, and in Tranh's company, tried to have a puncture mended there. Its advantage was that it had two separate entrances, which might be useful if Tranh were being followed. The only snag was that the Rue du Colisée entrance closed at 8 p.m.

Assuming that any telephone tapper would imagine he was a Chinese restaurateur, of whom there were several in the Rue de la Boëtie, Forgeot said: 'You know my restaurant near the garage – where we had that puncture? Park there. But it must be by seven-thirty. My first customers arrive early. Americans.'

Tranh said: 'Can do, can do. Your waiter, big man. Same like you?' And Forgeot knew that Tranh had remembered the place and understood what he required. Tranh was saying: 'Don't worry. Your customers will be okay. I will deliver in person, like last time.' Forgeot marvelled once more at Tranh. Some people had the nerve to assert that the Vietnamese were unreliable: only when they were indifferent or actually hostile.

He emerged from the Champs-Elysées métro station, idled away some minutes in the crowded corner Prisunic, bought a plastic shoulder-bag, a razor, toothbrush and some handkerchieves, assumed a feigned interest in a range of men's toiletries, watching his surroundings all the while, then crossed into the maze of arcade shops towards the Etoile. Here were mirrors and reflecting surfaces everywhere, which was an advantage – like having eyes in the back of your head.

Then it was nearly 7.30 and Forgeot strode briskly down the ramp of the garage, knowing that Tranh would turn in, positioning himself.

If Tranh were being followed, he would, with luck, manoeuvre himself into a traffic lane where it would be impossible for a tracker to tail him to the garage directly. Sure enough, out of the corner of his eye, Forgeot saw a small Renault 12 utility van nosing along in heavy traffic, with Tranh at the wheel just ahead of a little old lady who by no stretch of the imagination could have been a covert member of the Sûreté. And behind her, blocking the whole street, was a bus.

Moments later, Forgeot was on his way to Montmartre alone, in the Renault, the richer by about $15,000 in dollars, francs and a few gold coins, a good lightweight suit, a cashmere pullover belonging to Tranh, and a fairly innocuous-looking but lethal pocket knife. Tranh had had a handgun for him, but Forgeot had made him take it back.

Forgeot had also asked Tranh to retrieve anything that might recently have been mailed to the three-D poster shop from the USA. 'If it's in some kind of a cardboard scroll,' Forgeot had told him, 'hang on to it for a couple of days. Guard it with your life. If I don't show up to collect it, I'll find someone to get a message to you, telling you what to do with it.'

There had been a quick briefing from Tranh before he had slipped away, on foot. The Maubert-Mutualité area, he said, was hot. To be avoided at all costs, for the time being. Crawling with *flics* of every sort. Uniformed, plain-clothes, even Vietnamese-speaking. That had been some joke. A French Sûreté inspector of Vietnamese origin who was a third cousin several times removed had told him all he knew, which wasn't much. 'They themselves haven't been told the full story,' Tranh had said. 'But everyone is out looking for you. Your own people are furious, for some reason. Everyone seems to want you out of the way. They've been told, Americans, British, Germans: watch out for Forgeot.' He lapsed into the broad, southern Georgia tone of his long-dead military adviser, grinning: 'You plenty bad news, just now. Number ten!' Just like the old days, he implied. But don't worry. Your real family is standing by you.

Forgeot parked near the Place Clichy. Suddenly, he was exhausted. He bought a cinema ticket, slept through a spaghetti Western, slipped out, moved the car, looked for another cinema, found only a hard-core porn joint, bought a ticket, slept through a dismal film. He changed his clothes in the toilet. Outside, he stuffed his Securor uniform in a dustbin.

It must have been nearly midnight when he walked up to the Place Blanche and round the corner, down the Rue Fontaine, as far as the Nouvelle Eve and back again, past the Lord Jim. Outside, there was a small blonde who looked slightly like Valentine, hovering in a doorway near a cheap hotel. He decided to be bold. 'Good evening, Janine,' he said, behaving like a regular customer. The reply nonplussed him. A deep baritone voice said: 'My name's Billy, but you can call me Janine if you want.' Forgeot gave her a closer look, said 'excuse me' pleasantly, and walked away. It was almost impossible to tell the girls from the boys these days. Or else he was still tired.

He found her eventually, inside the Lord Jim, drinking a *menthe à l'eau*. The bar was full of heavy, raddled, blousy older women, the air heavy with scent and talcum powder. As Valentine had described her, she wore a see-through blouse, white jeans and dark glasses. Forgeot sat on a stool next to her, bought her a glass of champagne which was probably stale Vouvray and ordered himself a scotch.

She was brittle, mechanically interested, a little too obviously venal for Forgeot's taste. The other women present ignored them. Forgeot knew the score. Invite the most dreadful-looking hags to drink at the bar's expense, and business will automatically go to the one good-looking hooker present. But that was an experienced pimp's trick, which made Janine potentially dangerous. I have no choice, Forgeot thought. But she was in no hurry to leave. 'Buy me another glass, *chéri*?' she said. The owner, a villainous-looking man of immense girth, was ready with the champagne before she even spoke. Another bad sign. A clip joint meant police protection, which in turn meant informers. She hummed a Sylvie Vartan melody, gave him an affectionate pat. And Forgeot behaved like a man with limited time at his disposal, visibly impatient for sex and expected home by a nagging wife. 'Let's go,' he said, leaving far too much money on the counter.

They walked arm in arm down the Rue Fontaine, and round a corner. She said: 'You're not very talkative.'

'I'm the strong, silent type.'

She laughed. They were now inside a modern apartment block only recently built but already shop-soiled, with peeling paint, with hand-prints on the dirty white walls and a smell of cat's piss.

She unlocked a door, using two keys. Inside, she kissed him on the mouth. 'I'll do anything you want, you stay as long as you like, and you give me five hundred francs, okay?'

'Fine.'

She started to undress, taking off her blouse. 'What I really want,' he said and saw a flicker of fear on her face, 'is to stay till tomorrow afternoon.'

'You crazy or something?' She had picked up a shoe, and was holding it by the toe, stiletto heel at the ready.

'I don't like this sort of thing at all,' she said, 'but not at all.'

'Valentine sent me.'

He produced the letter. She relaxed, dropping the shoe. 'My damn sister,' she said, 'I hardly know her. She only gets in touch when she needs me. Who are you, anyway?'

'I'm someone who's prepared to pay to use your apartment till tomorrow afternoon.'

'It'll still be five hundred francs, dearie.'

'You run an expensive hotel.'

'But discreet.'

She was moving briskly around the studio apartment, changing out of her bar-girl clothes, showing herself naked without the slightest shyness. She kept her black plastic bag within reach at all times, though. 'You can pay?' She eyed him greedily.

Forgeot produced a note. She looked at it carefully.

'It's fine,' he said. 'I printed it myself.'

He stretched out on the huge low bed. 'Look, I'm tired as well. Can I put my feet up?'

'Sure,' she said. Then: 'My sister knows the strangest people.' She stood over him. He yawned back at her. 'Don't

223

answer the phone,' she said, 'and don't stay any later than four. It's surprising how many middle-aged men like to fuck in the afternoon. Night.' She was gone.

Forgeot waited a few minutes. He was refreshed, alert. Something about the bar, the girl, was not quite right. If she were to tip off the police, how long would it take? Twenty minutes? He rose, picked up his shoulder-bag, and, leaving the door slightly ajar, slipped out on to the landing, down the stairs, and out into the street. He walked back to where his car was parked. He moved it again. Now there was room to park almost opposite Janine's apartment, but he halted on the corner of the Rue Fontaine, where he could see without being seen. If they didn't come soon they wouldn't be coming at all, and he could go up again and sleep soundly. Drugs and espionage: two instances where the police were not bound to wait till dawn to make an arrest.

He didn't have to wait long for the good old Brigade Criminelle, in an assortment of small-size, anonymous saloons. Dozens of them, all armed. He knew most of them by name. Without waiting, he drove away, up the Boulevard de Clichy, towards Pigalle, trying to remember where the roadblocks were likely to be. There goes my last chance of laying my hands on the stuff in Paris, he thought. He spent the rest of the night in the van.

While Forgeot was preparing to go into hiding the people in the command post inside the Interior Ministry set up to co-ordinate all information leading to his whereabouts were being subjected to some harsh, unjustified abuse by the Minister's security aide, himself abused and reviled by the Minister in the privacy of the latter's office. The Minister's private persona was very different from his public one. Partly to get away from the Minister, the aide insisted on spending the rest of the night by Bergerol's side.

The Minister had shunted Bergerol from the stolen art section to head the task force looking for Forgeot, on the ground that he was not only the brightest cop in the Ministry, after Forgeot, of course, but also the first to have spotted the anomalies in Forgeot's conduct. Bergerol had been unable to refuse, especially when the Minister had hinted that, if he succeeded, Forgeot's job would become his for the asking. But when the aide became too persistent, echoing the Minister's own recriminations, Bergerol threatened to walk out on them all and to return to his office on the Rue d'Aguesseau. 'I didn't ask for the job,' he said, 'and there's plenty of work waiting to be done in my own department.'

Frustrated by Bergerol, the Minister tried to take it out on the Mondaine. He called its head, angrily demanding why the prostitute, Janine, hadn't been arrested and brought in for questioning. 'Minister,' the cop said wearily, 'we don't have that many informers to start with. If we bring them in for questioning every time they do us a favour we soon won't have any left at all.'

Not for the first time, the Minister regretted taking the Interior portfolio. At the time it had seemed far more attractive than Foreign Trade. He would know better next time.

'Cops,' he thought. 'They're all alike. Dumb or corrupt.' The suspicion that some of the Interior Ministry staff might themselves be shielding Forgeot crossed his mind. After all, during the May 1968 'events', even the telephone operators had walked out – and most of the cops as well. You couldn't trust anybody these days.

The Minister was himself under the gun: the President wanted results, quickly, to show the British and the Americans that the French police network was as efficient as their combined secret services. Which prompted the Interior Minister to request a meeting with the President. It was granted, 'provided', an aide said, 'you can keep it to under ten minutes'.

We're nothing but office-boys, the Interior Minister thought with venom. These Presidential aides think they run the country.

The Interior Minister came straight to the point. 'Monsieur le Président,' he said, 'do I have your consent to co-operate with the other side, just this one time?'

'What do you mean?'

The Minister explained about the Czechs. 'It would simplify matters,' he said, 'if, in the last resort, we were not ourselves involved in the final stages of the hunt. Then the whole story could be perceived as just another episode in a twilight, secret service war. We would be spared all sorts of embarrassing explanations.'

'You mean you want me to authorise you to tip off the Soviets so the Czechs can be in on the kill?'

'It doesn't have to be done as directly as that, Monsieur le Président,' the Minister said. 'We can always convey such information through third parties.'

The President pretended not to have heard. He's very good at skirting difficult decisions, the Minister thought, but to hell with subtleties this time. He made the mistake of saying: 'It would be nice to have a yes or no answer.'

The President smiled. Stupid little sod, he said to himself, if he thinks he's going to get away with that sort of threat, he's even dumber than I thought. I picked him because I thought he was loyal. If he's going to play around, he's out in the next reshuffle.

The benign smile belied such thoughts. The next question was so unexpected it took the Minister completely unawares, and he simply remained open-mouthed, mute. 'I repeat,' the President said, with a dangerous streak of impatience, 'have you read Shakespeare's *Antony and Cleopatra* lately?'

The Minister had never been much of a Shakespeare fan. Feydeau was more his idea of an evening at the theatre.

'I confess, Monsieur le Président . . .'

'If you had, you would know what I am referring to. Look it up, my dear fellow.'

'But, Monsieur le Président, that hardly answers . . .'

'Shakespeare makes the point,' the President said with scarcely concealed contempt, 'that public servants aren't supposed to ask such questions. Right or wrong, moral or immoral, they're expected to take that kind of decision of their own accord, without questioning their masters.' Caesar rose. The meeting was over. 'Read the play, and act accordingly.'

Back in his office, all hell broke loose. The Minister's secretary made a phone call to the Paris branch of W. H. Smith's. She in turn screamed at the uncomprehending duty motorcyclist, who couldn't understand the reason for her vile temper, and was duly dispatched, with twenty-two francs of the French taxpayer's money, to buy a British schools edition of *Antony and Cleopatra*.

The Interior Minister – after cancelling his afternoon appointments – eventually found what he was looking for, having brooded over the play for hours.

So I am Menas, he thought, and the President thinks himself as Lord of all the world. Curious. He had finally reached the part where Pompey says:

'Ah, this thou shouldst have done,
And not have spoke on't! In me tis villainy;
In thee't had been good service.'

What the hell does the bastard mean? the Minister asked himself. We never did get down to specifics. 'Being done unknown, I should have found it afterwards well done, but must condemn it now.' To hell with him. Am I to talk to the Russians or not? In a rage, he brought his small fist down on the rosewood desk-top. Nothing happened. He slammed a drawer shut with destructive intensity. This time expensive splinters flew.

The lady in black in the outer office was used to such tantrums. Raising her eyes to heaven, she made a note to call the usual repairman, a sixty-year-old craftsman at the Mobilier National who had mended the Minister's desk before. It wasn't the first time that the Minister had wrecked priceless state-owned furniture. The taxpayer paid in the end. Spoilt brat, she said to herself. She had always had a soft spot for Forgeot, anyway.

Chapter Seventeen

FOR a country with strong centralised traditions of Government, the French Police presents a number of anomalies. The Interior Ministry controls all police departments throughout France, but in Paris the Préfecture is a separate entity, and the Prefect of Police has fairly wide powers of his own. Police rivalry in France, though, is not just confined to the Préfecture versus the Interior Ministry: the sheer size, and overlapping, of different sections and sub-divisions in both the Interior Ministry and the Paris Préfecture itself result in a fairly constant duplication of activity.

No régime has ever managed to solve this problem, which so infuriated General de Gaulle. Evidence of conflict only comes to light accidentally, when something silly happens, like two rival police squads staking each other out and ambushing each other, each side under the impression the others are gangsters. The pursuit of suspects frequently mobilises several rival sets of plain-clothes men, unaware of the parallel activities of colleagues in other branches of the service.

To keep such untoward incidents to a minimum, a liaison group is supposed to operate full-time, but the need for secrecy and undercover work, and the individual ambitions of department heads, all contribute to its limited effectiveness.

In the Forgeot affair however, all senior police officials knew that their jobs were at stake if they failed to co-operate. The longer he remained at large, the more pressure the Interior Minister would put on them. They pooled their information about him meticulously. Even the SDECE was briefed, and volunteered its services.

The job of watching Forgeot's Saint-Tropez home went to a Marseilles squad, whose leader spent much time on the phone grumbling about the inadequacy of local daily allowances in France's most expensive summer resort. He was met with scant sympathy and an order to cut down on hotel rooms. Since two of them were supposed to be on duty at all times, he was told, one hotel room was quite enough. They could always sleep in the car.

The fact that Forgeot was an insider made the task of Interior Ministry and Préfecture officials easier in some respects and more complicated in others. As an experienced cop, Forgeot, they knew, was well versed in all their tricks. This meant he was unlikely to try to disguise himself to cross a frontier at an airport or frontier checkpoint. He was aware that every frontier police squad would have a picture of him. He was also unlikely to leave any personal trace, such as handwriting on a hotel registration card, knowing that the Ministry computer could scan such cards at great speed, picking out any that resembled Forgeot's telltale scrawl, even if he tried to disguise it. Forgeot was also aware of the bounty system, which he himself had used countless times. He knew that a 5000-franc reward for information leading to his arrest had been earmarked from the Interior Minister's own slush fund, a reward extending to neighbouring Italian, Belgian, and Luxembourg police.

Just about the only frontier area imperfectly under control was the Franco-Spanish mountain border, a traditional escape route for Jews, Resistance members and Allied aircrews during the Second World War, an equally successful escape route for wanted criminals and terrorists since. Gendarmerie squads in the area were warned, and put on special alert. In Madrid, a French Embassy Attaché dealing exclusively with security matters called on a senior officer of the Spanish Guardia Civil and assured him that, if any Spanish official or informer came up with anything on Forgeot in Spain, he too would get the reward.

In his improvised headquarters on the Rue des Saussaies, not far from Forgeot's old office, Bergerol began using the same techniques that had made him such a successful retriever of stolen art. He thought of Forgeot impersonally, as a valuable picture to be found at all costs. It was a characteristic of high-priced stolen art that it was always on the move, transported from one place to the next by fences. In the same way, he was convinced, Forgeot must be on the move himself. But, unlike a painting, Forgeot needed to eat, sleep, visit laundries, even get his hair cut.

His enquiries began with Securor, and it took him a mere ten minutes to discover, from the scared personnel officer, that Forgeot had been recommended by Rossi. Here was a formidable figure for Bergerol to confront. Rossi, Bergerol knew, had connections, political clout and an informers' network of his own, maybe even a few people from the police on his payroll. He was on intimate terms with a number of Cabinet Ministers, past and present. The Gaullists regarded him as one of them. He had helped them in their election campaigns, providing not only funds but also bodyguards, bouncers and bill-stickers. Rossi was the quintessential adventurer who had battened on the Fifth Republic and found the Gaullists the most accommodating partners in the French political spectrum, the party most able to look the other way when certain laws were flouted.

But politicians were fair-weather friends, especially where suspected criminals were concerned. And Rossi, for all his respectable façade, *was* vulnerable, despite his war record, his decorations, his fortune and his contacts. Bergerol studied the long Rossi dossier from the Ministry archives. The more he read the more he was convinced that Rossi could be made to co-operate. There was plenty that Rossi wouldn't want to lose.

And plenty he would rather not have revealed. Pencilled into the dossier on the blue paper margins were notes on some of the suspected Rossi activities that had never been proved: the hijacking of a gold consignment at Orly Airport in the late fifties, the masterminding of a number of heroin deals in Canada and the United States in the early sixties. Rossi had never been charged. He was not even listed on the *Fichier du banditisme*, the roster of major criminal suspects kept up to date in the Préfecture. Almost all the evidence against him was rumour and innuendo, underworld gossip emanating from Paris and Marseilles. But underworld gossip was not always unreliable, especially when spread by established criminal bosses who feared competition from a brilliant outsider.

Bergerol was used to dealing with white-collar criminals, and his telephone call to Rossi was a model of tact and subtle pressure. Would Monsieur Rossi be coming to Paris in the foreseeable future? If so, Bergerol would be most anxious to have a quiet chat. No, not about stolen art. 'I see you know who I am,' he said. 'Congratulations. Very few people do.' What he wanted to discuss was a mutual acquaintance.

Rossi had said: 'I don't think I can be of any assistance to you there.'

'My dear Monsieur Rossi, I think you can. We believe one of your ex-employees, one of your *temporary* ex-employees, is a very good friend. We are even more concerned about him than you are. If you're too busy, I could always fly to Corsica to see you. Any excuse to get to your beautiful island, even for the day.'

Rossi said he would be coming to Paris in the next day or so. He added: 'Is there a magistrate on the case? What are the charges?' And Bergerol said: 'It's a security matter. We're still determining the precise charges. But they won't be minor ones.'

They met, not in Bergerol's office, but in the basement bar of the Pont Royal Hotel, a favourite hang-out of French publishers and art dealers. Rossi had brought a bodyguard with him, who remained upstairs.

They eyed each other warily. Rossi made the first move. 'No sense beating about the bush. You want to know where Forgeot is, I take it.'

Bergerol nodded.

'So would I,' Rossi said.

'Really? He has something you want to recover?'

'I just want to make sure he's all right.'

Bergerol decided to take the initiative.

'Why did you give him that job?'

'Because he asked me.'

'Did he say why he required it?'

'He simply said he needed temporary employment.'

'You realise he registered under a false name and social security number?'

'I was unaware of that.'

'You personnel officer says you referred to a Monsieur Lepiller, not to a Monsieur Forgeot.'

'I had no idea that Forgeot was running around using different names.'

'The Ministry of Labour inspectors,' said Bergerol, 'could take a dim view of this.'

Silence. Bergerol tried another line of questioning.

'What is your relationship to Forgeot?'

'We were at Dien Bien Phu together, and later in a camp. He saved my life, I think. I may have saved his, later.'

'That creates rather a bond, doesn't it?'

More silence.

'Do you know what Forgeot does for a living?'

'I had the impression he was connected with the SDECE.'

'You never asked him?'

'No.'

'What *did* you talk about?'

'Indochina. Women. Wine growing. Sailing. The way arseholes are taking over the country.'

'Would you say that Mr Forgeot was a man of strong political views?'

'He's a patriot. So am I.'

'I don't doubt it.'

'Did Forgeot mention his – er – current difficulties?'

'No.'

'Does the name Jute mean anything to you? Did you ever hear Forgeot refer to such a person?'

'Never.'

'Sure?'

'Quite sure.'

Rossi drank down the rest of his Chivas. The bespectacled Bergerol sipped primly at his Kir.

'Monsieur Rossi,' he said, 'I could have done things differently. I could have asked a magistrate to take down your evidence. I could have had you summoned officially – and arranged for the press to be there, so that everyone would know about it.'

Rossi sat still. He knew what was coming.

'I prefer to be more discreet. But finding Forgeot has become a top government priority, even if it means twisting the laws a bit.'

Bergerol opened a folder he had kept under his chair.

'I have a good deal of information here,' he said. 'Lists of your various holdings, interests, businesses. Very interesting.' He started enumerating them. The Securor bodyguard company. One of the most efficient in Europe, and the most lucrative. Bars in Toulon and Bastia. Three restaurants in Calvi, and a bar there near the Foreign Legion barracks. Interests in a London casino syndicate. A quarter share in the largest privately operated gambling club in Paris. A disco in San Francisco. Hotels in Lyons, Grenoble, Mégève and Montreal.

'As you know,' Bergerol said, 'my usual beat is stolen art. I use a technique with indelicate art dealers whom it would be difficult to prosecute and it almost invariably works. I stick the tax people on them. In your case, it would be pretty easy. Some of your bars are used for prostitution purposes. We could close them.

'Some of your hotel acquisitions were made in dubious circumstances. We could look into conditions of sale. We could start leaking unfavourable reports about you to the British Gaming Board. There has been a report that your Paris club has infringed currency laws by taking foreigners' checks without clearing them with any banking authority. I know every casino does this, but it's technically an offence. You know how averse gamblers are to any hint of trouble. We might even re-open a number of other investigations. Some go back a long, long time. There's no time lapse for drug offences any more, is there?'

Rossi's huge hands were curled into fists. He said: 'You want me to lead you to Forgeot? I won't do that. Even if I knew where he was, which I don't, I would tell you to get stuffed. Nobody does this to me.'

'You have friends in high places, I know. They may not help you this time.'

'I see no further point to this conversation.'

'Monsieur Rossi,' said Bergerol, 'I'm not asking you to betray Forgeot.'

'You're not? Then what *are* you after?'

'Just this,' said Bergerol. 'Simply leave the word you can no longer help him or protect him. Say that the pressure on you is too great, the risks too high, and that from now on he's on his own.'

They were inseparable that month: Olga, the elderly tramp known as Vlassov and the youngish ex-hippie they called Rotgut, because he drank anything, having once, he claimed, been a fire-eating busker.

233

Olga was an ageless mountain of rancid fat, smelling of urine and stale sweat. She claimed, when drunk, that she had once been a general's mistress. The Ukrainian-born tramp called Vlassov, because he was always boasting about his exploits in the Vlassov army alongside the Germans on the Russian Front, constantly needled her by proclaiming it must have been a German general. This was invariably followed by Olga trying to clip him one. Olga the Ogre, Rotgut called her. She broke a wine-bottle over Vlassov's head, once. For Olga was not only a patriot. In her wine-soaked make-believe world, she was convinced she had been, in her youth, a beautiful young Resistance heroine. She had medals and papers to prove it, she said. Many tramps entertain such fantasies. Nobody believed her. Olga, Vlassov and Rotgut hung out near the Place Maubert, a favourite location for veteran, scavenging winos.

Rotgut was not only much younger. He was also more articulate. He claimed to have several university degrees. He stayed with Olga and Vlassov because for a tramp even bad company is better than none. Rotgut stole. Olga and Vlassov begged. From time to time, they would all get rounded up for vagrancy, but the very stench Olga exuded gave her a kind of immunity. The others had stopped being bothered by it after a time.

One day they were joined by a tall man wearing a soiled hospital attendant's coat, which wasn't white any longer. He and Rotgut rapidly developed a kind of bond. The tall man bought lots of cheap wine, and listened to all three of them patiently and interestedly. He neither approved nor disapproved, and what he said occasionally made Rotgut laugh, though the others couldn't understand it. He was not even particularly shocked when he caught Rotgut going through his pockets, while they were all taking a nap on the warm métro air-vent near the Place Maubert. When Vlassov openly masturbated, which he occasionally did, and when Olga relieved herself over the air-vent, he simply looked the other way.

Rotgut should by rights have resented a fourth person intruding in their cosy little world. But he was flattered by the tall man's attention. It wasn't clear whether Olga approved or not of the tall man's company. She was

234

comatose much of the time. Like the three of them, the tall man was anxious to avoid the attentions of the police.

Rotgut suspected he was an escaped convict, though he didn't use prison jargon. He listened to Rotgut's life story, and confessions, with some amusement. Rotgut brightened when the tall man said that he was the only true philosopher he had ever met.

There were moments when Vlassov was fighting drunk and violent, and broke into tuneless Ukrainian song. The tall man always managed to calm him down. Friendships among tramps are ephemeral but immediate. Within three days it was as if they had always been a foursome.

Rotgut was aware that the tall man had deliberately sought them out. He also realized that he was being conned into doing something alien to his nature. It was after the Saturday market at Maubert-Mutualité, a good time for scrounging spoiled fruit and vegetables. The tall man asked Rotgut to cross the Place, to one of the Vietnamese stores, and deliver a written note. He spun a complicated tale about not being able to go himself, because he owed money there, and had been caught stealing in the shop. The owner had it in for him, he said, but there was someone in the shop he knew who liked him, and would give him money.

Rotgut grumbled that he was not used to working, that he had become a tramp for that very reason, but he finally shuffled away, coming back a little later with a message which baffled him. It was in Chinese. He was also more impressed than ever with the tall man, because a burly Vietnamese had pressed 200 francs into his hand.

The tall man read the message, and tore it up into small pieces. It was the only time, Rotgut felt, that he looked dejected or demoralized. Later, the tall man used Rotgut on other errands, on one occasion even getting him to take the Métro and deliver two letters across the Seine, on the Right Bank, including one to what looked like an Embassy on the Avenue Georges V. On a further occasion he even talked Rotgut into making a couple of phone calls for him. The messages had been cryptic, in some kind of code. For his services, Rotgut got a couple of bottles of cheap calvados.

The tall man left a little later, without warning. One morning they woke up and he was gone. They never saw him again. Olga got hit by a taxi shortly afterwards, and was taken to the Hôtel-Dieu hospital, where she died. Their little world broke up. Soon afterwards, Rotgut decided it was time to lead a slightly more active life. He went back to selling stolen ties and transistor radios out of an umbrella at street corners. Eventually he was arrested again. The police knew he wasn't dangerous, and allowed him to wander around the precinct. He looked at the 'wanted' notices on the wall. The tall man's picture was among them.

Forgeot cleaned himself up as best he could, threw away his foul coat, bought some clean shirts and underwear, and was careful to spend a long time in the 5th *arrondissement* municipal baths, liberally dousing himself with DDT after his shower. No matter how many times he washed, he would always remember Olga's smell, and Vlassov's. He needed to get rid of any trace of those four days. He was on his way to the richest, and possibly the stupidest, man he knew.

So good natured was Delmare that he had never realised that Forgeot's interest in him had been determined by his lust for Delmare's young wife. And that, when his wife had left him, running off with a ski instructor, Forgeot had dropped him too.

What had it been about Laure Delmare, Forgeot wondered, that had made him behave so badly? She had flattered him, told him how good he was as a lover. Only later, exchanging mildly obscene reminiscences with a polo-playing cad at the Racing, did Forgeot discover that Laure had said that to all the boys. She had been just another hard French bitch, beneath the little-girl helplessness and vulnerability and endless analyst's sessions. But what a lively, imaginative, unrestrained little thing in bed! It had been an exclusively physical affair for Forgeot. The ski instructor had disappeared, and Forgeot had no idea what had happened to Laure. Should he pretend to know? Or should he assume that Delmare didn't want to talk about it?

Delmare had seemed, on the telephone, delighted, if somewhat surprised, to hear from him. Some people simply exist to be used – and Delmare was one of them. Old friend, Forgeot thought, I'm going to cuckold you once more.

'Come down for the weekend,' Delmare had said. And Forgeot had replied: 'I need to talk to you – alone.' He hoped he had sounded sufficiently conspiratorial. Delmare had said: 'There won't be anyone else, except Monique,' whoever she was.

Delmare had suggested sending his car to Deauville station to pick Forgeot up. But Forgeot preferred to hitch-hike. The less he was seen by Delmare's people the better. He knew, when he arrived at the Delmare mansion, which was almost the size of a Normandy château, that he was the object of considerable gossip, at any rate in the servants' hall. Most guests to a Delmare weekend arrived with one suitcase at least. All Forgeot had was a shoulder-bag, and he was distinctly on the shabby side.

Nevertheless, he was treated like a guest of honour, and given the best bedroom suite, all toile de Jouy and gold-plated bath fittings. He slept till evening, in a too-soft bed.

Monique turned out to be smart, middle-aged, and several social cuts below Delmare, perhaps his former secretary. Forgeot found it difficult to indulge in small talk. Four days on the métro air-vent had taught him to concentrate on essentials.

After dinner, Monique left them together. Forgeot lost no time.

'How closely,' he asked Delmare, 'have you been following the news?'

Delmare probably expected to be quizzed about the latest happenings in the Chamber of Deputies. Instead Forgeot said: 'Did you read about a senior police official on the run, with the security services after him? It was a headline in *France-Soir* a few days ago. I am the person the story referred to.'

Delmare said: 'Good God.' Then, as an after-thought: 'Whatever made you do it?'

'Do what?'

'Whatever it was that turned you into a fugitive.'

'You don't understand,' Forgeot said. 'The whole thing was deliberately planned, but the scheme went overboard, got out of hand.'

'A hoax?'

'Sort of. I volunteered to be set up. There was someone we needed to tempt. We've been working on him for years. I had to appear credible in order to get him to make a pass at me. A form of coat-trailing. The trouble is our side overplayed its hand. Made the story too dramatic. A handful of people in Government know the real truth, but they can't help, at any rate for the time being.'

Forgeot explained they were in a quandary. It was too late to cancel the operation. There was no way of calling off the police hunt without alerting the very people they wanted to deceive, and putting a number of undercover counter-espionage operatives at risk.

'We don't usually go to outsiders for help,' Forgeot said, 'but in this case I decided to make an exception.'

Delmare said he didn't see how he could help.

'You certainly can,' Forgeot said. 'You have a boat, not far from here. You have a private jet. All I need is a means of leaving the country discreetly.'

'Where do you have to go?' Delmare asked, still dubious. When Forgeot told him, he brightened. 'I have some racehorses going in that direction,' he said. 'You can be one of the lads.'

'Lads?'

Delmare explained that, for insurance purposes, there had to be one lad for every four racehorse yearlings transported by air. 'You can't believe what it costs,' Delmare said. 'A charted 747 specially fitted out as a stable. I'm selling some racehorses to the Chinese and the Australians. Insurance premiums are out of this world. The pilot must be exceptionally good, too. The slightest jolt on landing and the horses risk breaking their legs. So they drag the wheels to make sure of a soft landing. They charge extra for wear and tear on the tyres, too.'

The following day, in some of Delmare's borrowed clothing, Forgeot was leading a horse up a ramp into the belly of a Luxembourg-registered Boeing 747, in a secluded corner of Le Bourget field. There were lots of formalities for the horses, none whatever for the lads. He used his last spare passport, in the name of John O'Malley, Irish citizen, and tried to duck, but without too much success, when a French TV team, alerted by Delmare's PR adviser, filmed the horses' departure, for a thirty-second local news clip on the regional newscast of the French Third TV channel.

Seen from the cockpit of a plane, Hong Kong is a mass of gold and silver lights in the middle of nowhere. Landing at Kai Tak airport is like touching down from a sea approach into the middle of a brightly lit fairground. Forgeot had slept during most of the trip, but watched the landing from the cockpit, at the invitation of the Icelandic captain. It was a perfect landing, butter-smooth. The captain said something to the engineer, in Icelandic, which sounded like Chinese spoken with a Swedish lilt. 'He says,' the engineer translated, 'that he's worth every penny your rich friend is paying him.'

A crumpled *Bangkok Post* by the captain's side – brought aboard at a crew change in Bangkok – spoke of increasing world tension, gold, silver and copper price madness, and of a further boom in uranium shares. How did they know? There was also a short, garbled piece from France about a manhunt involving a senior police official, who had disappeared.

A small committee at the cargo end of the airport was on hand to greet the plane, and a single uniformed policeman kept TV cameramen and photographers at bay. The other three lads, who had assumed, not entirely erroneously, that Forgeot was one of Delmare's smart free-loading friends, remained behind with the horses. Forgeot didn't even produce his green Irish passport. Emerging from the cargo area, he walked the long way round to the passenger terminal exterior, without being stopped. He hailed an air-conditioned taxi.

In a really well-run hotel nothing is ever lost, or goes astray. 'Mr O'Malley? We were expecting you. But you never did cable us the day you'd be arriving.' The desk clerk, smart as a barrister in court, held out the pen for him to register. 'We have something for you.' It could have been architect's plans, or a set of large posters, inside two strong cardboard tubes, covered with French stamps, taped at both ends. Forgeot put them not in a strong box – there were none big enough – but in the large hotel safe.

Despite the fatigue of the long trip, he needed exercise. Forgeot's last trip to Hong Kong went back over a decade,

239

to his earlier SDECE incarnation. Now he felt like a long-term convict returning to his small suburban villa to find it sandwiched between two enormous skyscrapers. He no longer recognised the place. The traffic was murder: like trying to walk along the Pittsburgh-New York turnpike.

He took a taxi to Wanchai. The taxi-driver tried the old familiar trick of charging him ten times the fare (whoever designed Hong Kong taxi-meters has made the decimal point invisible) and shamelessly grinned when Forgeot cursed him in fluent Cantonese. He got out before Lockhart Road, and on impulse stopped at an all-night tailors to get himself measured for a white linen suit, to be delivered at the Mandarin hotel in twenty-four hours.

He ordered a beer in a Lockhart Road nightclub. The R and R GIs had long since been replaced by sailors of all nationalities, but the bar-girls remained, getting older by the year. Now the lights blinked 'topless' and technically this was correct, for they had simply trimmed their evening gowns to expose untypically large, ageing Chinese breasts. The effect was the reverse of erotic.

Only one girl he saw had a trim, pert figure, and she was heavily tattooed. Inevitably, Forgeot bought her a drink. It was her stock-in-trade, her conversation piece. He asked her why. 'Because I like,' she said laconically, pouring herself a brandy. She had an eagle on her left upper arm, a rose on her right, and 'love' tattooed on both wrists. 'Anything more that's not visible?' Forgeot asked. She turned, displaying another large undefinable bird (an eagle? a turkey?) on her smooth left shoulderblade. 'A budderfry on my bottom, and a snake coming out of my cherry.' She had the tired, vacant, slightly drunken smile of the drug addict. 'Which you wanna see – my snake or my cherry?'

'Tomorrow, honey, tomorrow.'

Escaping the harsh air-conditioning, he left and bought himself a bowl of noodles from a street stall. He ate standing up. Nobody took any notice of him.

He walked back to the Mandarin, gradually adjusting to the crowds, the all-night neon glow of small bargain shops, the bars. It was dawn. He eventually fell into a deep and troubled sleep, in his large room overlooking the harbour, while the Star ferries kept up their orderly, patient shuttle, and the ceremonial junks waited for their weekend taipans or Hilton tourist parties.

He dreamt, sequentially, of horses and planes and airports. In his dream, his heart came almost to a standstill as his passport was scrutinised by a keen Chinese eye. Then, still in the dream, he fingered an old coloured pencil he had treasured as a child and kept for years, dented by the toothmarks of a drooling, lolloping, infuriating golden retriever he had once nursed through a major operation. And, in the dream, a masked Chinese villain of traditional Peking Opera, but wearing a Hong Kong's policeman's uniform, suddenly brought down a hammer on the dog's head and smashed its skull. Death to the dogs-head traitors! – a favourite slogan during the Cultural Revolution. He woke with a start as the dream became unendurable.

The sound of the telephone ringing had been part of the dream, and it was ringing still when he woke, sweating and unsure of his whereabouts. He lifted the receiver. The line went dead.

He called the operator. No, he had not been cut off. 'The party must have hung up, sir.'

From room service, he asked for orange juice, coffee and the loan of a typewriter.

Outside, it started to rain. Hordes of elderly American tourists came and went, some in transparent plastic macs, hailing each other with dreadful morning cheerfulness, describing the prices of things they didn't need and intended buying.

The waiting game had begun. He wondered how long it would be before Feng's people made a pass at him.

Chapter Eighteen

II WAS beautifully done, Forgeot had to concede that. A touch on the shoulder in the hotel lobby, a look of surprised, delighted recognition on the part of an immaculately dressed, elderly Chinese who accosted him.

'It can't be! You naughty boy! Right here in the Mandarin, and you never even bothered to call!'

Bubbling with excitement, lightly pressuring his arm, he led Forgeot to the bar.

'All those promises you made at Cannes, and you never even phoned your old friend,' he said. He oozed goodwill and prosperity. There were gold signet rings on the fingers of both hands, and a gold chain circling a thin wrist. The watch was the plumpest gold Rolex, and there was a hint of gold, too, in the teeth. The face was lined, cynical and wise, with a streak of toughness, the blur of mild smallpox scars on both cheeks. He spoke English perfectly, and Forgeot, from his size, assumed he was a Northerner, or, at least, a Shanghaian.

'Tell me, old friend,' he asked Forgeot, 'how are your plans going?'

Forgeot remained silent.

'Are you still thinking of co-productions on the mainland? A splendid idea, I said at the time. You remember, we talked at the Festival. I always said: if there's one person who can negotiate with the Chinese, you can.'

He ordered a martini.

'Scotch for you, as usual? Or would you prefer a Pimm's? I don't think you'll find them up to the standards of the Carlton.'

Forgeot nodded. 'Scotch will be fine.'

'By the way.' The card appeared out of nowhere, like a magician's ace of spades. 'Just in case you've forgotten.'

Forgeot read: Lee Fu-Seng, and underneath 'Golden Bird Productions', followed by a New Territories address that meant nothing to him.

'That was a superb meal you gave me in Saint Paul de Vence,' the Chinaman said, and Forgeot thought: this is too much. He's really mistaken me for a producer he met at Cannes.

'You must see my studios,' the Chinaman was saying. 'I insist. I said so in France, remember? We really must work together some day.'

Forgeot saw this as an imperceptible signal that, after all, there had been no error, and that here was the contact he had been waiting for. The message that Rotgut had delivered at the Chinese Embassy must have found its way to Feng after all. Was this Feng's man in Hong Kong? Forgeot acted as if he was.

'Maybe we already have,' he said.

His host chuckled. The bar was crowded with tourists, bankers, florid Britishers, dapper Japanese businessmen and their short-legged, shapeless wives in unsuitably warm cashmere.

'Maybe,' he said quietly, a little less effusive now, adding, for only Forgeot to hear, 'this is a very public place – and I am a very public person.'

Then, back in his first incarnation as the proud host, welcoming a friend from Europe, he said: 'I simply must show you our latest. It's mainly for the local market, but I might try and sell it in Cannes next year.' And Forgeot, rising to the bait, said: 'I have something interesting for you too. But I don't think the time is quite ripe.'

His Chinese host didn't appear to have heard. He was talking to the barman, a wizened old veteran of pre-revolutionary Shanghai. They seemed on intimate terms.

Again, Forgeot recognised it was expertly done. The Chinaman was establishing Forgeot's credentials. In Chinese, he was telling the barman: 'A producer from Europe. Haven't seen him since the Cannes Film Festival last year.' At the same time, he was making it easy for Forgeot to assume his correct persona.

Lee glanced at his watch. 'I insist we have lunch. I simply won't take no for an answer. You can't be *that* busy. Afterwards, I'll take you to my studios.'

Lee kept up his Cannes film festival patter, and Forgeot found himself responding. He recalled scraps of conversation from Paris dinner parties attended long ago, and said, mainly for the barman's benefit: 'Our trouble is that we try and make too many films, and not enough people go and see them.'

'Europeans are always complaining,' said Lee. 'You get help from your Government. Nobody here does. The only force in Hong Kong is the market force.'

'All producers are gamblers,' Forgeot said. 'Only three films out of ten make any kind of money, but everyone's always looking for the jackpot that never comes.'

Lee Fu-Seng laughed, and insisted on ordering another round.

'You go bust all the time, but have you seen the way you live?' Like all exceptionally rich men, he regarded himself as a special case. 'I've never met a poor producer yet. Bankrupt producers, yes, all the time. You just change the name of your companies, and start up all over again. We do the same.'

When the time came to leave, no money changed hands, no chits were signed. For special customers like Lee, the trusted barman obviously kept his own records.

Lee bundled Forgeot into a pale-beige, chauffeur-driven Rolls. The restaurant, near Causeway Bay, looked drab and undistinguished from the outside. There were partitioned booths on the upper floor, and much loud Chinese conversation, sounds of toasts being drunk and the clinking of glasses.

Sea-slugs, jellyfish and thousand-year eggs appeared on the table almost as they sat down. There followed the learned, bantering dialogue between customer and Chinese head waiter without which no really good meal can be ordered in a first-class Chinese restaurant. Lee was of the old school, a stickler for detail. Was Wuh still number one chef? The day he leaves, I leave, he said. Had the 'drunken shrimp' really been smothered alive in sherry? Sometimes, he told Forgeot, they try and cut corners, but not with me. I can always tell. Forgeot hoped he would keep the meal simple, and wondered when he would come to the point.

The studio was thirty air-conditioned minutes' drive from the tunnel linking Hong Kong to Kowloon, along a narrow traffic-clogged road. Mr Lee, suddenly looking his age, which must be over sixty, Forgeot thought, scrutinising him closely, lapsed into silence and then into a quiet sleep.

So near the border with China, there was no let-up in the frenzied Hong Kong building boom. Factory sites encroached on what little farmland was left. Billboards everywhere vaunted the qualities of expensive Japanese TV sets, Toyotas and locally-made soya bean brews. At lunch Mr Lee had remarked that, in Hong Kong, the definition of pervert was an individual who preferred the company of women to the making of money. Forgeot had heard this one before, but laughed politely just the same.

In his youth, Mr Lee must have seen movies about the great vanished Hollywood studios of the thirties, for the entrance to the 'Golden Bird Productions' lot closely resembled the old MGM entrance, complete with portico, burly guards and mobile hinged gates, through which the Rolls swung. Mr Lee, awake now, pointed out the details: cutting rooms here, lab there, main office here, and the three indoor studios, inside what looked like, and indeed was, an ancient aircraft hangar. 'I bought it cheap,' said Mr Lee, 'when they modernised the airport.'

Next to the door they entered was an illuminated sign, in English and Chinese, saying 'no entry' but that didn't bother Mr Lee. He gestured to Forgeot to keep quiet, ushered him in and followed. They stood at the back, unnoticed.

The set was Peking-Moorish, of the kind used in an infinite number of costume dramas that remain overwhelmingly popular wherever Chinese is spoken. The lights were dazzling, and it was difficult, at first, to distinguish the cast from the crew. Taking advantage of a short break, the actors had discarded their brocaded, jewelled clothes. Then an assistant director barked the order, 'All quiet on the set please,' and they moved into position. Make-up men and stagehands milled over the papier-mâché décor, which centred on a huge, low Chinese bed, on which the 'Emperor' climbed, and reclined, now fully clothed in his extravagant attire. Cameras slid on their wheeled platforms, panned to an archway, and a procession of uniformed courtiers appeared, carrying a heavy rolled-up carpet shoulder-high. There were gongs and cries and cacophonous Chinese music.

With flourishes, under the Emperor's attentive, concupiscent gaze, they set down their burden, unrolling the carpet, and as it unrolled, the girl inside was revealed, practically naked, in an almost transparent shift, wrists and ankles tied, her face a mask of exaggerated fear, and Forgeot almost cried out, because the girl was May.

Someone yelled 'cut' and Forgeot knew Mr Lee was looking at him intently. The 'Emperor' was getting up off the bed, and saying something to the girl, who was laughing, and calling on the make-up man to wipe her face. 'It's bloody hot inside the carpet,' she said, in Chinese, and Forgeot knew he was giving himself away, but edged closer to the set. It couldn't be. And as the girl, still laughing, was wound back into the carpet for a retake, her voice increasingly muffled in mock-protest, he realized that, though she looked astonishingly like May, the voice was different, more high-pitched, with a Cantonese lilt. He watched the next take, riveted, and Mr Lee, smirking, said: 'Pretty good, no?' There was no telling whether he was referring to the beautiful Chinese actress, the set, the film, or the studio in general. Forgeot nodded, fully in control now, alert, realising here was some form of elaborate test, even managing to stifle a simulated yawn.

Afterwards, still in her transparent concubine's shift, the girl joined them, as did the Emperor, a young man of huge, wrestler's build, and Forgeot noted the girl's astonishing likeness to May. Mr Lee introduced Forgeot as a distinguished producer from Europe. 'This is Tanya,' he said. The girl, poised and used to visitors on the set, shook hands, asked Forgeot whether this was his first time in Hong Kong, and wasn't it dreadfully hot under the lights?

Filming resumed, and Forgeot said he had to go. Mr Lee insisted that his Rolls take him back to Hong Kong island. 'By the way,' he said 'I am having a little dinner party this evening, at my house in Stanley. Some of the cast, and a few friends. You will come, of course? I will send my car for you.' Except for this ambiguous cautionary remark in the bar he hadn't once said anything that would have clearly indicated that he was the man Forgeot was looking for. But Forgeot knew that Mr Lee, successful film producer and millionaire, Shanghai émigré and probably triad boss, must be the intermediary chosen by Peking to intercept and possibly trap him, and that the resemblance between the actress and May might not be coincidental. At least it could mean that she was still alive.

As Forgeot had expected, Tanya was at the dinner-party, adorable in a deceptively simple silk T-shirt and baggy Saint-Laurent trousers. They sat side by side at the huge round table, and she made it clear that she found the French producer with the Irish name most desirable. Later, when the other guests, Chinese and European, sat making conversation in a huge cluttered living-room, Tanya took Forgeot to a terrace on the upper floor to show him the view, and the flickering lights of the scattered Chinese fishing fleet below. She seemed familiar with the layout of the house. She reached out for him and they kissed. Forgeot smelt a clinging musky perfume.

She said: 'I have to be up early. That damned bedroom scene isn't finished yet.'

'Tough life, being a *tsip*.' Forgeot used the Chinese word for concubine.

'You realise it's based on fact.'

'I know,' Forgeot said. 'Some of the Ming Dynasty Emperors were so scared of assassination that they had their night-time companions stripped and delivered stark naked to the Imperial bed-chamber wound up in a carpet, to make sure they weren't carrying poison – or a knife.' He stroked her arm lightly. 'Are you carrying poison for me?'

She gave a shy, actress's smile.

'No, and you don't need a carpet either. My car's outside.'

They slipped away unnoticed. She drove her Mini with reckless brio, taking the sharp bends in the road from Stanley like a rally driver. With each bend, they were thrown together. To steady them both, and because he knew it was expected of him, Forgeot stretched his right arm out and held her firmly.

Taking a horrendous risk, she once let go of the wheel completely, grasped his head in both her hands and kissed him full on the mouth, grabbing the wheel again just in time to avoid an oncoming garbage truck, whose driver leaned out and shouted something mildly obscene as they swerved past him.'

She parked outside the Mandarin, ignoring the 'no parking' sign. Upstairs, she made straight for the bathroom, and he heard the shower being turned on, then silence. He slipped into bed. When she came to him, her face scrubbed of make-up, her long black hair swept back, wearing only an enormous hotel bathrobe, Forgeot, with the pain that never ceased to surprise him whenever he thought of May, recalled their first meeting, in the Hôpital Cochin, and something inside him died. Had Mr Lee known about that too? There was a truly extraordinary physical resemblance, and Forgeot, on guard and tense though he was, felt himself harden and explode.

Was it because he was on the lookout for any tell-tale signs of deception, or was it simply that, as an actress, she found it necessary to play an assigned role to the hilt? Every time she cried out with pleasure, Forgeot thought he heard a carefully rehearsed sound. As he laboured over her, he thought: I too am just a competent fucking machine. Because of his detachment, because he could think only of May, he failed to climax, though he kept on with the act, spun it out interminably, in fact, and all the while the girl under him writhed and groaned, unaware that his prolonged performance was the result not of passion but of the lack of it.

There could be no faking her last, loud climax, and as she clung to him he felt her racing rabbit's heartbeat. Shyly, she whispered: 'Do I remind you of someone you once knew?'

Forgeot laughed. 'What gave you that idea?'

'The way you made love to me. It's hardly ever that good the first time.'

'Are you sure,' Forgeot said, 'that it wasn't something that Mr Lee said.'

She shook her head. 'He simply said to be nice to you, and be sure and ask you for the stuff you put in the hotel safe.'

'And if I don't hand anything over?'

'Mr Lee,' she said, 'is a very rough man. He has gangster friends. He also is very close to the Communists. He usually gets what he wants.'

'I don't doubt it, my little one,' Forgeot said. 'But he's going to have to deal with me directly.'

She didn't reply. That's your business, her silence implied.

'Tell me,' Forgeot said casually, lightly stroking her back, 'are you sure he said nothing about a look-alike?'

'He said,' she giggled, 'that if you couldn't make love to me, something was seriously wrong, and that you must be' – she paused, trying to recall the exact words – 'a poor security risk.'

She nuzzled up to him, slowly caressing his chest, sliding down first to his belly, then lower. He was reminded of a devious, calculating kitten. Despite himself, he felt his unspent desire return.

Later, she said: 'If he asks me, I'll tell him you were sensational.'

But when she left, some hours later, she had a sad, almost pitying look. Her eyes said: you may not know it, but you're doomed.

Forgeot didn't have to wait long. There was a knock on the door. 'Who is it?' he asked.

'Your suit.' At least he would look the part, if Lee called.

Forgeot half-opened the door, and there, carrying a cardboard box, was a young Chinese. As he entered, two other men, who had been concealed behind the door, rushed in. They were ominously silent. One of them wore an open-necked white shirt and baggy blue trousers. The other man, despite the heat, wore a turtle-neck sweater and a jacket.

They must have followed me from the moment I landed, Forgeot thought.

One of the men moved towards the telephone.

Forgeot said, in Chinese: 'Gentlemen, I'm surprised at you. Bursting in on a guest like that, and in the Mandarin. You'll give the place a bad name.'

Turtleneck produced a knife and stood guarding the door. The other man grabbed him from behind. The young Chinese who had delivered the suit hit Forgeot a horrible blow in the solar plexus. Forgeot realised he had used a knuckle-duster.

The pain made him react recklessly. He calculated the distance a kick would travel to be effective, and decided against it. Instead, he deliberately started going slack and groaned exaggeratedly. The man holding him was well-trained. Though Forgeot felt himself beginning to fall, he failed to relax his grip. It simply wouldn't do to allow oneself to be bludgeoned into having the safe opened. Despite Turtleneck's knife, he realised the most dangerous member of the trio was the knuckle-duster man. He continued to buckle against his captor, and his own bulk began to tell. Then, as he fell, simulating a dead faint, and bringing the man behind him down too, he collided with the man with the knuckle-duster and made him lose his balance.

Scrambling free, Forgeot aimed the hardest kick he had ever given at knuckle-duster's ear, and heard him roar. He kicked at the man with the knife, hit a kneecap and was out of the door in a flash, shouting: 'Help! I'm being robbed.' He could hear the frightened cries of a couple of Cantonese maids down the corridor. The three men bolted, Knuckle-duster holding his hand over his ear, moaning.

He could probably have grabbed one of them, but sounder instincts prevailed. He wanted no enquiry which would reveal his identity. To an apologetic assistant manager, he explained that it was unlikely they would return, and that it would be simply too boring to have to call in the police. All it was, he said, was a threesome of drug addicts trying to pick up some easy money. This sort of thing sometimes happened, even in the world's best-run hotel. Nothing had been stolen. A waiter arrived with a peace offering: a bottle of champagne. Round one to me, Forgeot thought.

The telephone rang. It was Mr Lee, not at all contrite, but not angry either. He sounded pained. 'Why didn't you give the girl what she asked for?' he said. 'It would have made this unpleasantness unnecessary.'

'I'm not going to hand anything over to someone I don't know,' Forgeot said. 'And that includes you. You may not know what is involved, but I do. The stakes are too high.'

Mr Lee said he was coming round to see him.

'I'll meet you downstairs,' Forgeot said. 'But no tricks. I'm not impressed by how many Rolls Royces you own, how many little whores you have on your payroll, or how many films you make a year. If you want something, you'll have to answer a few questions. I can play pretty rough, too.'

*

'Young man, you are asking me questions for which there are simply no answers.'

Lee, in a corner of the deserted Captain's Bar, smoked a long thin Havana cigar and shrugged in mock-despair. Forgeot almost believed him.

'I am a well-known producer. I also have a few other investments: a shirt factory, a movie magazine. And I happen to have close relations with our friends in Macao and Peking. They don't care how much money I make. That I am a successful capitalist is in my favour. It gives me the proper credentials in this capitalist town. But that doesn't mean to say I carry any weight with them. I, too, deal with intermediaries.'

'But the intermediaries,' Forgeot said, 'also do you favours from time to time.'

'Once,' Lee said, 'it wasn't considered smart to get too close to them. Now, with everyone falling over himself to do deals with Peking, those of us who were a little more far-sighted than the rest are in a marginally better position. My films get distributed in China. Peking pretends it doesn't know that I also make films for the Taiwan market. The Bank of China makes loans all the time to people of my kind of standing. Are you telling me I should deal only with Jardines, or the Honk Kong and Shanghai Bank?'

'But your friends don't just make loans. They also exact a price?'

'Of course,' Mr Lee beamed. 'That is the Chinese way.'

'And they asked you to be sure and put me in touch with the girl called Tanya, because it was important to see what my reactions would be?'

'That,' said Lee, 'was strictly my own hospitable initiative. They had nothing to do with it. In fact, they would have disapproved.'

'Tell me,' said Forgeot, 'who is "they"?'

'I can't answer that. Let's just say they're respectable, hard-working people: Bank of China clerks, New China News Agency men, Luxingshe personnel, doing their patriotic duty. What does the cover matter?'

'I want you to convey the message to them, whoever they are,' Forgeot said. 'Tell them I want to talk to the Vice-Chairman.'

251

Lee looked around him, uneasy they might be overheard.

'You're being completely unreasonable,' he said. 'We have been too nice to you already. All we want is access to what you put in the safe. In an emergency, we could always get hold of it without your permission.'

'You would have to rob the hotel first.'

'That we would not do.'

'Or you'd have to kill me.'

'Exactly,' Mr Lee said, as though he were discussing the possibility of rain later on. 'All we have to do is stage an accident, and hire some good lawyers. The hotel wouldn't want to keep the effects of a dead man.'

'You really would kill, wouldn't you?' Forgeot said. 'They must be pretty anxious for it. What'll they do if you don't produce? Take away your girls? Your Rolls? Burn down your film studio?'

Mr Lee shook his head, sadly. 'You don't understand,' he said. 'China is a vast and secretive bureaucracy. I am told only what I need to know. What little I have been told, in your case, implies there is an element of urgency. I gather your previous dealings with them were cordial. Now they will wonder why you're holding out on them. They won't like that. Perhaps you can tell me. Is it money? Within limits, that could be arranged.'

'I've already told you what I want: a session with the Vice-Chairman, either here or in China.'

'Ridiculous.'

'Then everything stays here.'

'Young man,' Mr Lee said, not unkindly, 'you are throwing your life away.'

'I don't think so. They don't want me killed, not for the time being, anyway. They might even want to protect me from those who do. It's only a matter of time before a lot of people discover my whereabouts, and then I'll have to go into hiding all over again. Better here in Hong Kong than Europe: at least the KGB can't operate here quite as openly.'

Mr Lee sighed. 'I'm only an intermediary,' he said, 'dealing with intermediaries. But I'll propose a meeting, if only you'll hand over what you agreed to give them, here and now.'

It was a graceful way out for Forgeot, and the means of buying time he had been hoping for.

'What are my chances?'

'Come on, you know better than to ask that kind of question. I'll tell them you're a persistent young man who won't take no for an answer.'

'Not so young any more.'

Rising, Forgeot moved to the cashier's desk in the lobby, with Lee close behind.

'I want to withdraw something from the safe,' he said. 'Some old film posters for Mr Lee, here, to add to the famous producer's collection.'

He wondered what their reaction would be when they discovered that that was precisely what the scrolls contained, and nothing more.

Chapter Nineteen

EVERY MORNING, for the next three days, Forgeot woke up expecting trouble. When they found out what he had fobbed them off with, they would get angry, and dangerous. That was necessary, that was part of the plan. But they might lose control, stun him, drug him, perhaps even bring him down with a bullet. It would, he knew, be very different from the abortive raid on his room by Mr Lee's blundering, incompetent thugs. There was no sure way of remaining alive long enough to get even, and the hotel was by no means secure. He got the telephone operator to intercept all calls, and relay them later. He told the concierge that he wanted to be warned as soon as any visitor made enquiries about him. The only message was from Tanya, asking him to call her. He disregarded it.

It was no worse, in some ways, than the boredom of his bygone days as a junior SDECE operative, waiting interminably in a hotel room for a sub-agent to contact him, waiting for a phone that never rang.

There was safety, of a sort, in the streets. On his way to the new Post Office, he was careful to stay in the thick of the crowd, deliberately choosing groups of women shoppers, or tourists. In Hong Kong, this wasn't difficult: simply walking the streets at any hour was like being in the vortex of a métro rush hour.

On the third morning, he wondered whether they had given up. Perhaps they were no longer interested in what he had to provide. Perhaps they had found out the truth. If so, they would certainly seek revenge. He might as well court disaster. So, with his written work out of the way, and safely in the mail, he boarded the crowded ferry, and watched with delight the smart shop assistants and office workers reading the astrological forecasts in their Hong Kong papers and magazines. Despite the garish headlines, he noticed they always turned to the fortune-teller's page first.

He behaved like a tourist, treating himself to a trip to the

Tiger Balm Gardens, with its shrill hordes of children, and to the covered Central Market, where, years ago, he had used a certain stall as both meeting-place and letter-box. The small, bald man in singlet and dark blue shorts who sold fattened ducks to restaurants was still there, Forgeot noted. The man had been both reliable and incurious, and had insisted on presenting Forgeot with a huge duck on what had proved to be his last Hong Kong assignment. Disposing of the duck had been a major problem: Forgeot had finally left it with the French Consul-General.

Walking back to the Mandarin, he was moving against the tide: most people were going the other way, towards the Queen's Road stores and the market, with the sullen determination not to be deflected from their path which is a feature of people living in a town bursting at the seams. But two men, one on either side of him, and moving in the same direction, gradually converged on Forgeot until they practically touched. There was nothing threatening in their behaviour. The older of the two men, with the face of a retired boxer, said, between the waves of oncoming pedestrians: 'Do not go back to your hotel.'

He spoke in Chinese, with and indefinable accent. Fukien? Swatow? The other man, on Forgeot's right, smaller, younger, echoed: 'They know who you are. They are looking for you, all over.'

Forgeot kept moving but slackened his pace. He found himself asking the same question he had asked Mr Lee. 'Who is "they"?' This time, there was a reply.

'Security,' the man on the right said. 'Not the Hong Kong police, though they might be brought in later. Some foreigners have arrived. They want to put you on a plane and take you back to Paris with them.'

I bet they do, Forgeot thought. In a way, it was surprising it had taken them so long to locate him. He entered a crowded cake shop just off Queen's Central. There was, he knew, a tea-room at the back. The two men followed him. They sat at a small circular table. All round them were teenage Chinese schoolgirls, in demure school uniforms: dark skirts and white shirts. They chattered excitedly about classes and boyfriends.

'Are you from Mr Lee?' Forgeot asked, and the smaller

man now switched from Chinese, and said, in excellent English: 'Mr Lee is in slight trouble. He is being criticised for his behaviour.' The stilted language seemed to identify the speaker as a Party functionary, perhaps from the Bank of China, perhaps from the New China News Agency. The eyes and ears of the motherland, they called themselves. But the burly man with the scarred face was no bank clerk, nor was he likely NCNA material.

'What did he do wrong?'

The smaller man sipped his hot tea noisily. 'He was not sufficiently alert. You played a trick on him, and he did not realise it.'

'You were a long time finding out.'

Not so long really. It was possible for British Intelligence to sample only a small, random selection of phone calls from Hong Kong to the mainland, but in any case the Party would never discuss anything important on an open line. The NCNA, the Bank of China and a few other commercial companies had direct lines to China, but these were constantly monitored. Chinese attempts to install scramblers in Hong Kong had, regularly, been foiled. That had been one of Forgeot's minor liaison duties with the British, the Americans, the Germans and the Japanese: the security industry was too dependent on lucrative contracts with the Western agencies to risk a boycott as a result of a couple of minor, unauthorised sales to Eastern Bloc countries or Chinese intermediaries. Even so, it was only a matter of time before the Chinese started making their own. This left encoding and decoding, a lengthy and not entirely secure procedure. That meant that someone had gone all the way to Peking, and returned. Three days was not too long for such a trip.

'You are in trouble too, Mister,' the scarred man said, with a grin showing some white metal teeth. 'No place to stay any more, huh?'

Uninvited, two Hong Kong schoolgirls squeezed themselves into a tiny space at their already overcrowded table, to the two men's visible annoyance. But there is no such thing as privacy in a Hong Kong tearoom.

'The hotel situation in Hong Kong,' said Forgeot, 'is really ghastly at this time of year.'

256

The younger man rose. 'You stay here,' he said.

Forgeot wondered what the ex-boxer did for a living. His weather-beaten face suggested he might spend some time at sea. There were so many ways the activities of the Party in Hong Kong impinged on those of ordinary citizens. At the top of the scale there were people like Mr Lee, with his Rolls, his millionaire's house overlooking the sea, making mildly left-wing film spectaculars about the bad old pre-revolutionary days. Then there were the property tycoons, acquiring, step by step, and with profits from other lucrative enterprises already owned by China, the funds that were used to feed the building boom, the new smoked-glass skyscrapers that would generate still more profits, before everything one day reverted to China. There were the managers, accountants and staffs of supermarkets, multiple stores and arts and crafts shops that were proliferating all over Hong Kong and Kowloon, selling Chinese-made goods available only for export. And beyond these legitimate activities there were others: informers inside the Hong Kong Government and Police services, informers in the lawcourts, the City Centre, the Consulates, the hotels, the prison, the hospitals and airline compaines. There were also the middlemen, drug addicts, underworld criminals, all dependent to some extent on Chinese goodwill for their continued existence. My boxer friend, Forgeot thought, is probably one of these.

The scarred man could be running refugees out of China into Hong Kong, with the Communist authorities' knowledge – charging $3000 a head and handing over half to the Party as a kickback, occasionally handing back the refugees as well, or simply drowning them. He might be one of those triad members in league with ships' captains engaged in smuggling the Vietnamese boat people into Hong Kong, exacting huge fees for bogus temporary residence permits. He might even be part of the triad group which in effect controlled the small but burgeoning prostitution ring in Canton itself. This would not prevent him from giving the Party a helping hand, if and when required, if only to avoid possible later trouble. The Chinese, like the French, had a matter-of-fact approach to crime: without informers, they felt lost.

Forgeot eyed the ex-boxer covertly. He might not be any of these things, but simply an honest smuggler, taking vegetables or herbal medicine by junk from China to Hong Kong, returning with TV sets, transistor radios and watches for the black market. Chinese ingenuity was such that many small farmers in Kwangtung province managed to divert part of their produce to middlemen, over and above the quotas they were obliged to hand over to the State at fixed prices. Some even accumulated bank accounts in Hong Kong as a result, and remitted money back to themselves. One could live quite well in China with one $100 postal order every two months.

Forgeot lifted his tea-glass, toasting his companion silently. The ex-boxer afforded him another glimpse of his appalling teeth.

There was no sense in asking him any questions. Forgeot knew there would be no replies. These were no garrulous Hong Kong fat-cats proud of their wordly success. They were professionals. The younger man, returning, Forgeot suspected, from a phone booth, said: 'Wait', and ordered sticky cakes all round. Forgeot tried to pay, but was too slow. The ex-boxer ate most of them. The schoolgirls, unasked and giggling at their boldness, ate the rest. The younger man scowled.

It was raining again, and more people crowded into the teashop to escape the downpour. The younger man looked at his watch, rose. Forgeot was about to follow him, but the boxer grabbed at his jacket and said: 'You sit.'

A few minutes later, Forgeot caught sight of the younger man, very wet now, gesturing to them from the doorway. Without a word, the ex-boxer and Forgeot left the table. Outside, along Queen's Road Central, a traffic jam of formidable proportions had built up, as always when it starts raining in Hong Kong. Gesturing again, the younger man led them out into the street, to a far from new Mercedes, with battered sides, smoked glass windows, and a driver who chewed gum and said 'hao' as he turned up the volume on the car radio so that speech became impossible.

They stopped in front of a narrow, dingy, green-painted hallway on Lower Lascar Row. An elderly watchman was listening to the same radio commercials, also at full blast. He nodded to them as they walked past him, along a corridor, past an illuminated sign that said, in English and Chinese characters, 'The Arthur Rubinstein Beauty Centre'.

They took an old-fashioned freight lift to the seventh floor, and led Forgeot along another dark, airless corridor. There were doors with inscriptions on them but it was too dark to read them. The younger man unlocked a door at the far end. Inside, an air-conditioner which had been left on made a noise like a distant blast furnace, itself dimmed by what seemed to be a dozen noisy mahjong games going on above, below and on either side of the room they were in.

There was a camp bed, a cheap glass-topped table, three badly slashed black plastic armchairs, losing their stuffing, and the inevitable gaudy 'New Life Enterprises' calendar on the wall.

'What on earth,' Forgeot asked, 'is the Arthur Rubinstein Beauty Centre? For musicians only?'

The younger man snapped: 'It used to be called Helena Rubinstein. But there was a court case. The old lady objected. We changed it. The new name works just as well. Nobody knows the difference around here.'

He was irritated that Forgeot should have asked, even more annoyed when he laughed.

'You will stay here,' he said. To the ex-boxer, he said: 'Ring the bell if you need help.' There was a large buzzer on the table. He addressed Forgeot again. 'You have caused a lot of trouble,' he said. 'The hotel manager is quite distressed. He is complaining there are plainclothes-men all over the lobby. He says this sort of thing has never happened before.'

Forgeot sat on one of the armchairs and propped his legs up on the table. He wondered how best to while away the time with the gorilla. He decided to see whether he was an orthodox Communist or not. 'A game of mahjong?' he said sweetly.

Few tourists leave Hong Kong without at least one trip to Aberdeen, the second largest open-air market in the Colony, and the original, authentic boat people's capital. Nowadays the tourists come mainly to be photographed against a background of sampans, and to be ferried out to the ex-ocean liners converted into expensive floating restaurants.

They assume that the sampans are simply decorative floating taxis, but they are wrong.

Sampans house whole families, who prefer the inconvenience and the damp of a small boat to the impersonal high-rise cheap housing units the Colony authorities have built for them. Some of the sampan-dwellers hold down regular jobs. Some are illegal immigrants from China. There are sampans that are floating brothels, gambling dens and minuscule opium parlours – sometimes all three at once. Try as they might, the Hong Kong police has never established more than a tenuous hold on the floating Aberdeen population, and Forgeot guessed, from the moment they came for him that night, that this was where he was heading. It meant his plan was working after all.

He could smell the Aberdeen smells, and remembered a useless, long-stored scrap of information: there were no seagulls in Aberdeen, because its inhabitants threw nothing away that could be eaten or sold.

'Quick, quick,' the younger man was saying, and Forgeot was hustled out of the car, down some waterfront steps and into a sampan. The tough, stout, elderly lady in black grunted. 'Hullo, skipper,' Forgeot said to her in Chinese, but she didn't reply. She knew where to go, but Forgeot was not able to watch: his ex-boxer guardian, a highly competent mahjong player, it turned out, pushed him inside the tiny confined sampan bunk area, where a couple of small Chinese children also sat, looking at him curiously.

It was dark now, and there were put-putting sounds of motorboats, cries of families greeting each other, shouts from the shore of touts with tourists groups requiring transportation to the floating restaurants, and some hawking and spitting – presumably from the boat lady herself. Then a bout of silent paddling, and a bump as it came alongside a much bigger boat. Once more, Forgeot was hustled out on deck and up a rope ladder, hauled aboard a large decrepit-looking junk.

It was at least twelve metres long, and nearly half as broad. There were cooking utensils out in the open, and some washing hung out to dry, but the crew was all-male, and avoided his gaze. He was pushed down a ladder, into the boat's very bowels, shown a tiny sleeping area, given a dirty

260

brown quilt, and told to lie there and be quiet.

There was an argument going on above his head: he recognised the voices of his two captors, and a Cantonese voice, presumably the captain. The captain wanted to leave in the middle of the night. The other two were urging him to leave immediately. Forgeot thought he overheard the word 'dangerous', and something about 'a friendly boat for another hour'. Presumably a harbour patrol boat paid to look the other way. Then there were sounds of the two men leaving the junk, gruff farewells and the sound of the departing sampan. They never even said goodbye, Forgeot thought.

Below the waterline, the junk was surprisingly large. He sniffed, to try to determine past cargo. But he could smell nothing but diesel oil, and noticed a huge German-made diesel engine which must give the junk an unusual turn of speed. It was newer inside than it appeared to be from the outside. Forgeot suspected it was a smugglers' junk, made in Taiwan, to order. With the flapping laundry, it must look from the outside like an ordinary family junk.

It was cooler now, and pitch-dark. Forgeot looked at his watch: it would take, maybe, four hours to reach Canton. Less if they used the engine at full speed. No sense worrying, he thought. Cradling his head in his arms, he kicked off his shoes and immediately fell asleep, rocked by the junk's slow pitch.

But, when he awoke, it was daylight, the junk was still at sea and pitching far more, the engine running at half-speed. Forgeot climbed on deck, stretched and asked the helmsman: 'Where are we heading for?'

The man didn't reply. Two of the crew unceremoniously turned him round, half-guiding him, half-pushing him below. From the sun, Forgeot could tell they were headed east. They must have passed Canton some while back.

He wanted to ask his captors: whose side are you on? With a rising sense of panic he did his best to quell, he realised that he had assumed, all along, that the two men who had taken him aboard were acting on orders from Peking. But they had never, themselves, confirmed this. What if they were not?

It was just possible they were from Taiwan. In the recent past, a common hatred of China had brought fiercely anti-Communist Taiwan and the Soviet Union closer together, not to the extent of establishing any formal links, but sufficiently for the intelligence services of both countries to have met on neutral ground. What if the Soviets were behind his kidnapping? The Russians might want to establish what he knew. But it was far more likely they simply wanted him dead, like Semyakov. If the KGB were after me, Forgeot thought, I'd already be at the bottom of the sea. And if they were heading for Taiwan, they must soon veer south. In his stockinged feet, Forgeot crept up the ladder, and saw, on the port side, the dim outline of the coast. China, he thought with relief. We are hugging the coast. They must simply have decided that Canton was too public a place.

The Swatow Peoples Local Force Militia is unlike any of the other Chinese coastal defence units: the close proximity of Taiwan means that the local population is kept constantly aware of the possibilities of a Chinese Nationalist invasion, bombardment or infiltration of agents or spies. Whereas, in other parts of Southern China, such indoctrination has become meaningless, the Swatow people are deliberately kept on a war footing; they are constantly reminded of the time when Chinese Nationalist gunners, from the fortified island outposts of Quemmoy and Matsu, used to indulge in sporadic artillery fire, the shells falling short of the coast but keeping them in a constant state of alert. The sound of war had been more symbolic than real, like the Chinese crackers used in Peking Opera to give an added dimension to stylised war dances. The Nationalists had been more successful with their symbolic gestures than with their real-life attempts at destabilisation: all their agents had been ignominiously rounded up within days, sometimes hours, of their landing.

It was all distant history now, but the emergency, and the war-mongering propensities of Taiwan, were constantly invoked still, in films, operas, ballets and newspaper articles. The local Swatow militia was better armed, and better trained, than many regular units. All possible landing sites, creeks and beaches along this rugged coast, with cliffs oddly reminiscent of Dover, were regularly patrolled.

So it was somewhat humiliating for the local Swatow militia commander, near a small beach known pretentiously as Sweetwater Bay, to be told one morning that his forces were to withdraw from the area: for a twenty-four-hour period, the duty of patrolling that part of the coast would be taken over by a half-battalion of regular Public Security forces.

The local militia commander, who had been responsible for the arrests of several Taiwan agents, and was something of a local hero, knew better than to argue, or ask questions. All he needed to be told was that this was in connection with 'a special, high-level political task' – a phrase which implied, almost always, that a critical decision was being taken by top authorities in Peking. He was not even allowed to relay this information to his own men. He was simply told to ensure that no one – neither militia, nor fishing crews, nor local villagers – was anywhere in the vicinity of Sweetwater Bay for a given twenty-four hours.

The militia commander, though smart enough to ask no questions, was also sufficiently experienced to take certain precautions, just in case there were later enquiries from other, higher quarters: the Lin Piao business had shown that no one was above suspicion, and that anyone, however exalted, might turn out to be a traitor.

So, after issuing the necessary orders, he summoned a local fisherman who happened to be his wife's cousin, a man he knew he could trust, whom he paid to keep him informed of the state of mind of other fishing families in the village, of their degree of political reliability and enthusiasm. He asked him, exceptionally, to run a small risk, all in the higher interests of the motherland: he was to stay behind during those twenty-four hours, hole up in a safe place from where he could observe the beach at Sweetwater Bay, and report back on what he saw. This was an unusual, delicate 'political task' for which he would, in the long run, be rewarded, as long as he kept his mouth shut.

The fisherman himself had been a militia NCO. He hid in a clump of bushes on a low cliff overlooking the beach, with a water-bottle, some cold sticky rice and a couple of raw onions. He duly reported what he saw. At dusk, a large junk, of the kind that occasionally, but not frequently, ventured along this part of the coast, hove to, flashing first a red then a green light. A series of torchlight blips came from the beach itself, where a knot of uniformed men had gathered. Then a dinghy put out to sea, and came alongside the junk. A tall man in white, almost certainly a foreign devil, climbed down the rope ladder and into the dinghy, and was rowed ashore.

There were about fifty Public Security men on the beach, and more guarding its access. The fisherman hadn't dared take too close a look. But he heard the sound of a vehicle, and presumed it was taking the tall man away. The junk swung out to sea, made a wide arc and vanished in a westerly direction. The Public Security troops assembled and marched away.

The man, he noticed, walked up the beach with long, eager strides. He seemed not at all aware of his plight. He expected to shake hands. But before he scrambled back into the safety of his hole, the fisherman noted that his outstretched hand had been ignored and that the man in white had been roughly handled, and handcuffed, before being taken away. The Public Security troops had had their guns trained on him from the moment he waded ashore.

Forgeot, blindfolded, relied on a succession of smells to guide him: the cigarette smoke and sweat of the soldiers squeezed on either side of him in the jeep, the smell of the interior of a military plane, an old C-47, probably, though he would never know for certain, and the distinctive smell of Peking, a blend of diesel fumes, dust and coal-smoke.

It was only when he was past the first of several gates that they took the blindfold off. It was necessary for him to see where he was going because there were many steps and twisting turns. He nearly fell anyway, his eyes adjusting only gradually to the half-light. Not once had he been told where he was headed, but he knew he was in Peking, because of the cold, the length of time he had remained in the air, and because one of the guards, forgetting that he understood Chinese, had mentioned to the Swatow Public Security escort that they were headed for Prison Number Two. Forgeot knew what that meant: a small pentagon-shaped jail within a jail, the place foreign prisoners were kept, as well as some of the 'Gang of Four'. It was, he knew, some three miles north of Peking.

The thing to do was to count one's blessings. They hadn't beaten him up: that meant they wanted to keep him presentable. They had used a military plane: it proved they were in a hurry. They had taken him to Peking, which was where the Vice-Chairman was. They hadn't so far tried to make him confess, nor embark on a detailed handwritten report of his own crimes, nor had they interrogated him, or indulged in any hysterical 'struggle' sessions: that meant they intended to negotiate.

If only it wasn't so appallingly cold. If they thought they could wear him down through prolonged solitary confinement, they were in for a surprise: he had prepared himself, mentally, for just such an eventuality. In any case, he marvelled that they were prepared to wait this long. They had so little time. In any other country, he thought, they'd be firing off questions the moment I hit the beach.

The prison food was good, distinctly better than the staple fare of the Fontaine du Matin Calme in Paris where he had first met Feng. The warders who brought him his meals never spoke. They simply ladled out the soup, counted the steamed bread rolls, and set down the smaller bowls of pork and vegetables. To keep warm, and in shape, he did press-ups, and what Canadian Air Force exercises he remembered. The guards stared at him curiously through the small metal grille. They had taken away his tie, his belt, his shoes, his papers, passport and watch. His white suit was no longer white, and looked very much the worse for wear. But it was all he had. There were no such things as prison uniforms in China: those serving time had to rely on clothes supplies from their families.

It was another four days before anything happened. He had begun to adjust to the prison routine, and learnt to recognise familiar noises. Outside the cell, nobody spoke much, and he believed he might be the only prisoner in that particular block. It must be a maximum security area, but by Chinese standards it was luxurious. His bed was a platform of three wooden boards, but they were raised off the floor, and on his second night he was given two thin quilts. There was a bucket smelling of creosote. He got a basin of cold water to wash in every morning, and a barber came every second day and shaved him with a blunt cut-throat razor. This was the most painful moment of his confinement. He wondered whether to talk to the barber, or complain to his guards, but decided against it.

He was never told not to stretch out on his bed during the day, and he would lie there for hours, pleasantly lulled by his three square meals a day, doing his best to keep alert. He ran through all the events that had occurred since his first meeting with May. He relived all the time they had spent together. When he could no longer do that, he tried to recall, from memory, the various satellite reconnaissance details Semyakov had taught him, in that Washington hospital room. He added and subtracted, tried to recall scraps of poetry, memorised lists of names, phone numbers, street layouts in familiar cities. He even attemted to draw up, in his mind's eye, a list of all the women he had ever made love to, with their names, circumstances of their first meeting and other details. He found himself going through such routines increasingly frequently.

On the fifth day, when he was finally taken out of his cell, the men who came for him were not the regular prison guards, but men he had never seen before: Public Security troops, these, probably from the unit guarding the prison perimeter. One soldier said: 'Quick – outside. Move,' and thrust him into the corridor. Forgeot moved ahead of the soldiers. He knew they would tell him where to go, and they did, shouting 'left', 'straight on' and 'keep your eyes down'. But they didn't lay hands on him, and their commands, though brutal, were ritually impersonal. They must have ordered prisoners about like this hundreds of times before.

The office he found himself in was in another wing of the prison, and Forgeot suspected, from its size, that it might be the hastily vacated prison governor's office. Forgeot faced two officials in the centre of an L made by a desk and a trestle table. He sat on an uncomfortably small, low and narrow wooden chair.

'Name? Age? Profession?' They wrote everything down laboriously.

'You say your name is Forgeot,' one of them said. 'This,' he held up a green passport, 'is in the name of O'Malley.' He read the word in English, haltingly. 'Why do you lie?'

Forgeot explained that he had two passports, quite legally, and that the green one was in his mother's name. He had used it, he added, to leave France.

'Why?'

'Because I wanted to leave discreetly. I was in trouble with the authorities there.'

'So you entered Chinese territory illegally, without passing through passport control, wilfully deceiving the authorities?'

In their eyes, of course, Hong Kong was Chinese territory.

'If you feel strongly about it,' Forgeot said, 'you could always send me back to Hong Kong.'

The senior of the two interrogators, a broad-faced civilian with the slightly stupid, ponderous bureaucrat's manner, suddenly raised his voice and pounded the table. 'Don't answer back, don't be insolent. you are the lowest of the low. you are a traitor, a faker, and a blackmailer. We could execute you tomorrow, and nobody in the world would lift a finger to help you.'

The second man, fitter-looking, perhaps an army officer, said: 'He is right. We could have you shot.' He spoke softly, almost pleasantly. Forgeot thought: even in China, they have the good guys and the bad guys routine. I suppose they take turns at assuming their roles, just as we do. He said: 'What you say is technically correct. In my country nobody would lift a finger. In America or Russia neither. In fact it would suit them fine. The only person who would not be pleased is the Vice-Chairman.'

'He is questioning our word,' the soft-spoken man said, more in sorrow than anger. 'He is still insolent. He is answering back again.' And the other one responded: 'He is scum. He has no face. He is the lowest of the low. He thinks our motherland welcomes swine like him.' Turning to Forgeot, he said: 'You will not comment on what we think or say. Our Government is omniscient and just. It will be all the worse for you if you do not believe us, and if you try and spread your kind of filth here.'

Forgeot recalled his own lectures to SDECE trainees, drawing on his own painful experiences after his capture at Dien Bien Phu. The first moments are the worst, he used to

267

tell his audience. They try and scare you, break you in the first few encounters, so that later on you are pathetically grateful for any sign of humanity. He kept saying to himself: the reason they have brought me here is that they need me more malleable, to establish who is boss.

The first interrogator said: 'How will you feel, when we close your file, and you alone will know that you are still alive, stuck in jail for the rest of your life?'

Forgeot was silent.

He banged the table with his fist. 'Answer!'

'You told me,' Forgeot said, 'not to comment on the decisions of the State.' The soft-spoken man was next. 'You came here as a spy,' he said, 'and to stir up trouble. Tell us about it.'

'I will confess everything,' Forgeot said, 'but only to the Vice-Chairman.'

The officer said, still in a conversational tone of voice: 'You will do whatever we think fit. A criminal, a liar, a degenerate will not waste the Vice-Chairman's time. You have tried to fool us. But we will be fooled no longer.'

It was a possible hint that they might, perhaps, be aware of some of the circumstances of his flight from Hong Kong. Perhaps the officer knew, and the civilian didn't. Perhaps they were just doing their routine act, performed for all illegal arrivals. Or perhaps there was a faction, in the Public Security Ministry, that badly wanted to keep Forgeot from seeing the Vice-Chairman, because it didn't want its own shortcomings to be revealed. Where is Feng? Forgeot asked himself. In Paris still? On his way? Or in a cell next door?

'I have the interests of China very much at heart,' Forgeot said. 'It is because of this that I got into trouble in my own country, and that a lot of people, including the Soviets, are after my blood. You are loyal servants of the State, but you do not know everything. There are some secrets of a military nature that only a few people are aware of. Those who want to keep me from seeing the Vice-Chairman may bear a heavy responsibility before history, later on.'

'What are these famous secrets?'

'The Vice-Chairman knows,' Forgeot said. 'I will talk only to him.'

'You will do as we say.'

'You are power-holders,' Forgeot said. 'You can keep me here until I rot. But meanwhile matters of crucial importance remain unresolved. Of course you can lock me up, kill me, bury me. You can keep me busy writing my confession for the next five years, and I will confess to sabotage, to all the crimes of an imperialist, counter-revolutionary criminal. But in the meantime irreparable moves may be made. Sooner or later, those responsible will be ferreted out. The State, as you said, is omniscient.'

Taking advantage of their silence, Forgeot said: 'There is so little time. There may be war. And, if there is, it will be over in a matter of days, hours perhaps. That's the way with wars these days, in the nuclear age. And all because I didn't see the Vice-Chairman in time.'

The plump civilian turned to the officer. 'He is a lunatic,' he said. 'Or else he is pretending to be criminally insane. He is making his case worse by the minute. Do you hear?' Again the sharp, parade-ground bark. But the officer seemed slightly shaken. Maybe, Forgeot thought, he knows a little more than the civilian does.

'And what,' he asked, 'is it that is so important that you can only tell the Vice-Chairman?'

'The very nature of what I have to convey,' Forgeot said, 'is for . . .'

'The Vice-Chairman.' The civilian had decided to throw a tantrum again. 'You think he has time for criminals, for lunatics like you?'

'When it comes to the vital interests of the State,' Forgeot said, 'I think he has time for anyone. If he knows I'm here, I believe he may even ask why I was not brought to him earlier.' Don't antagonise them, show neither fear nor resentment, and above all don't be patronising, Forgeot said to himself. But inculcate a vague sense of unease. Make them go to a higher echelon, even if they themselves have no direct access to the Vice-Chairman.

The two men were talking to each other, so softly Forgeot could not hear what they were saying. Then, without looking in his direction, they both left the room. The guards came and collected him. This time they were more brutal: one of them slammed him against the wall. Another prodded him in the small of the back with his rifle. They pushed him out into the corridor, and Forgeot knew he was being led back to his cell.

Three uniformed men crowded in behind him. The one in authority said: 'Take your clothes off.'

Forgeot gave them his white suit.

'The other things too.'

He took his shirt off, then his socks, and stood in his drawers.

'I said everything.'

He stripped naked, and wrapped himself in one of the quilts.

'Squat.'

He remained on his haunches, wrapped in the quilt, using the other as a cloak. He felt distinctly cold.

The uniformed men left, and after a few minutes, disregarding their order, he stood, then went to bed.

There was no food that afternoon, nor the following day, nor was there any water to wash in. His bucket remained unemptied. They are furious, Forgeot thought, and the subordinates are reflecting this anger in the only way they know.

It's not advisable to loiter along a street in Peking called Nai Tze Fu, especially not outside the old ducal palace with peeling crimson pillars that was the home, between the two world wars, of the Apostolic Delegate. A mocking Chinese pastiche of a Regency building, with pillars painted red, it stands a few hundred yards north of the covered market, and cyclists stream by from dawn to dusk. Nobody glances up at the building itself. There is nothing, in any case, to see. All windows are shuttered, even during the daytime, and there are always a few plain-clothes men hanging about, ready to move people on, though they rarely have to intervene. From time to time the main doors swing open, and a man on a bicycle or in a car leaves the place.

This is the Chinese Lubianka, the Headquarters of the Second Department of the Ministry of Public Security: only those directly connected with this dreaded branch of Government, including informers from the Party, the police stations, labour unions, educational establishments and hotels, or those in serious trouble, ever cross its portals.

So no one was curious enough to peep inside the Poboda which entered the main gate at six a.m. one morning, even though it had to cut a swathe through hundreds of Chinese cycling to work, and was escorted, front and rear, by jeeploads of Public Security troops. The inhabitants of Peking have acquired, over the years, a remarkable immunity from curiosity and an instinct to avert their gaze from any sights they might later be expected to report back to their street or building-block committees.

For Forgeot it was the break he was beginning to dread might not occur. Even in his most euphoric moments, he had not expected it to come so soon after his earlier interrogation. He had almost resigned himself, twenty-four hours previously, to a long-drawn-out period in solitary confinement, and to writing confessions which might, he knew, take months or even years. He suspected the army officer was the one responsible for the change in his circumstances.

The first intimation of this change came in the middle of the night, when a guard woke him, bringing soup, steamed bread and roast pork – the dinner that had been denied him the day before. It wasn't everyone's idea of breakfast, but tasted marvellous.

Then the sleepy, surly barber – almost certainly a prisoner himself – arrived, and, miracle of miracles, had used a freshly-honed razor for the first time. Another prison guard brought him a basin of lukewarm water, and Forgeot washed his feet. They're either preparing me for the kill, he thought, or they're about to treat me as a human being. He knew his status had changed considerably when a prison trusty brought him his white suit, shirt, underwear, socks and tie, all pressed and laundered. His shoes had been dried out and polished.

The waiting-room inside the Ministry where Forgeot now sat was a curious mixture of pre-revolutionary kitsch and austere utilitarianism. Some of the chairs were of the straight-backed kitchen variety, but there were also relics of the ducal, or possibly papal, past: tapestried, gilt Louis XV reproduction armchairs, the tapestry designs frayed to a mere blur, a mirror over the mantelpiece that would not have been out of place at Versailles. There were small canisters of green tea on a round table, along with some stacked white mugs and wicker thermos flasks full of hot water.

The guards and prison escort who had delivered Forgeot had left with the jeeps, and the doors of the waiting-room had been locked behind him, but that could well have been standard Ministry practice. On another table were old back numbers of *China Reconstructs* and the *Peking Peoples Daily*. Forgeot avidly read both. In a corner, oblivious of the rest of the company, a serious-looking, bespectacled Chinese sat reading what looked like an official report in a bound folder. Forgeot recognised him: he was the interpreter who habitually accompanied Chinese leaders abroad, a graduate of the Geneva Interpreters School and a protégé of the late Chou En Lai.

Of the other three men in the room, two were obviously Ministry guards, from the supine, bored look that all subordinate officials acquire when they are in undemanding sinecures for a long time. They neither read nor talked. The third man was a civilian, in his late fifties, with a shock of white hair.

Forgeot had to caution himself inwardly against too much unjustified optimism, but it was difficult to repress a sense of elation, the same kind of elation he had experienced a few days previously when he had boarded the junk in Hong Kong. And the elation returned when, an hour or so later, in mid-morning (at least he thought it must be mid-morning, for they had returned neither his passport, wallet or watch) Forgeot was led out into the courtyard and made to wait once more, along with the interpreter and the white-haired man. For a large black limousine drew up, of the kind known in China as 'Red Flag', a copy of the Soviet Zis which is itself a faithful reproduction of the Cadillac of the early fifties. The Vice-Chairman, Forgeot said to himself, has actually sent his own car for me.

Chapter Twenty

'SO WHAT have you got to tell me?'

The Vice-Chairman was like all the cartoons of him Forgeot had ever seen, down to the baggy white socks bulging gracelessly at his ankles over his tiny black shoes. One eye looked fixedly at him. It was, perhaps, sightless, or else the Vice-Chairman had recently had a stroke. The other eye, alert, bird-like, was always on the move.

Tough as a walnut, small as a wizened child, he sat in an armchair that was similar to all the others in the room, yet imperceptibly lower, so that his feet rested comfortably on the ground. To the right, there was an old-fashioned Chinese spittoon, as big as a soup tureen, ludicrously shaped like a chamber-pot. Forgeot rested his head against his own armchair, conscious of the grey lace doily protecting the yellow cotton slipover cover from Chinese hair-oil or, more likely, hair-dye.

It must be the hair-dye to turn them that colour, Forgeot thought. Even the most aged Chinese leaders clung to the fiction of youth. The Vice-Chairman's hair was an unconvincing shade of grey. White hair and other stigmata of age were only for those with no public image to preserve. We are timeless, the disguise implied. Don't try to outsmart us, for we will outlive you all. Our wisdom has suspended the ravages of age. We alone are immortal because we alone are good.

The interpreter repeated, in flawless French: 'The Vice-Chairman says: what have you got to tell him?' He looked nervous, leant forward and fiddled with notebook and pencil.

The white-haired man was the only other person present. The air was thick with stale cigarette smoke. There was tea on a table before them, but it remained untouched.

The room was nondescript, almost shabby. There were stacks of files on plain wooden shelves. It was so quiet they could have been inside a secluded monastery. Within the Forbidden City there was no traffic, no hubbub of voices, none of the usual city sounds. It was like being in limbo, and it was easy to understand, sitting there, why China itself had been in limbo for so long.

'Mr Vice-Chairman,' Forgeot began, speaking slowly in Chinese (as he did so the interpreter, visibly disappointed, snapped his notebook shut), 'I have a lot to tell. But may I know, before I start, who the other comrade is?'

'Tell him.'

Forgeot noted with delight the incongruously high, almost squeaky voice, the voice of an aged Szechuanese child. With such a voice as an initial handicap, he must indeed have been and extraordinarily brave warrior in his heyday. Forgeot thought: I am in the presence of the only person who ever stood up to contradict Mao to his face – and lived.

The white-haired man spoke English with a marked American accent. 'My name is of no importance,' he said. 'I am one of the Vice-Chairman's advisers on defence matters. In earlier times, just before the Liberation, I was at MIT. I got to know the American Defence Secretary when he was a student there. We have remained on speaking terms, intermittently, since.'

Forgeot, for the first time in his life, and despite the endless rehearsals he had silently conducted in his cell, was overcome with stage fright. He was saved by the Vice-Chairman, who raised a tiny arm, silently gesturing the interpreter to leave the room. When he had closed the door behind him, without a word, the Vice-Chairman said: 'The less there are to hear you the better. You are more fluent in Chinese than I have been led to believe.'

Forgeot started talking. He began almost at the beginning, not with May but with Jute. He gave a brief account of Jute's obsessive but lucid concern with the growing US-USSR power imbalance. The danger, Forgeot said, and it was one the Vice-Chairman himself had voiced many times in his conversations with foreign statesmen, was that sooner or later the whole of Western Europe, and indeed the United States itself, might gradually, imperceptibly, become Finlandised. Not that the Western Intelligence community believed in the Soviets using Western Communist parties as a Fifth Column any more. They didn't need to. The CIA, after Watergate, had been a shattered, useless tool, Forgeot said,

274

and the CIA's plight had, to some extent, been duplicated elsewhere. An increasing number of Western intelligence officials had a growing sense of doom.

And Western intelligence organisations, whether engaged in espionage or security, had always taken a poor view of the politicians they had to deal with, Forgeot said, and this lack of esteem had reached dangerous levels in the last few years. Even the hawks, when they acquired political office, almost invariably became doves. For what mattered to Western politicians was a healthy GNP, growth, full employment, prosperity, and, above all, re-election. Increased defence expenditure was the negation of all these things, except for the boost it gave the armaments industries, and the surest way to oblivion at the next elections. This was a built-in weakness of the Western democratic system, Forgeot said. Some believed it to be fatal.

And it had led a small group of intelligence specialists to seek another, more devious way out. Since the imbalance between the Soviet Union and the West was bound to continue, something had to be attempted in another direction altogether. It involved deceit, and leaving out the politicians altogether.

'We devised a plan,' Forgeot said, 'to make you believe that the Soviet Union was beginning to concentrate its forces dangerously along the Chinese border, and was gearing itself for a full-scale nuclear attack on China. The reasoning was that you would alter your own Order of Battle, and respond in such a way as to cause the Soviets to shift some of their hardware away from the European Theatre.'

Forgeot told of his appendicitis operation in Washington, of the briefings from Semyakov, and of his meetings with Feng. 'It was then,' he said, 'that things started getting out of hand. First of all, you approached the Americans to suggest a possible joint nuclear strike. You were, of course, rebuffed, but in doing so, you revealed our plan to them, unwittingly, and made the Americans curious. They began tracking down those responsible. More important, the very man chosen, because of his expertise, to brief me and fabricate the evidence, turned out to be a Soviet "mole" of long standing, who kept the Soviets fully informed at all times of the plan's progress.'

Forgeot said he was convinced the Americans had had Jute killed, to avert the scandal that would have ensued had he been charged, just as the Soviets had likewise executed Semyakov when they realised he might reveal the extent of his responsibility to the US authorities. 'For Semyakov,' said Forgeot, 'seems to have feared the moralistic mood of the American courts more than the wrath of his real Soviet masters.

'I am no one's emissary,' Forgeot went on. 'I planted the seeds of the idea in Jute's mind. Now, before the irreparable happens, I want you to know the truth. Call off your plans for pre-emptive strike, Mr Vice-Chairman, and you will witness the slow dismantling of the Soviet force concentrations, the gradual deactivation of their missile sites. This time around, the dice are loaded against you.'

'Where is the proof?'

The voice was not angry. It was not even surprised. Maybe he has been hoping all along to hear this, Forgeot thought.

'If I may, Mr Vice-Chairman, I hope to convey it very soon.'

The Vice-Chairman lit a cigarette. 'And what guarantee do we have that any stand-down on our part won't be interpreted as a sign of weakness on a par with the West's, and that the Soviet Union won't exploit it in the same way?'

Forgeot said: 'I don't think they'll strike first. Even in 1969, Nixon assured China of some support if the Soviets moved first at the time of the Oussouri incidents. You are in a far better position now. China has rejoined the world. Your relations with the USA are almost cordial, and there is far more at stake on their side. Believe me, the Soviets always know just how far they can go.'

'Why should I believe any of this?'

'Because it's true.'

Forgeot poured himself some tea. It was cold. The Vice-Chairman suddenly looked older, but his voice now had a resonance which it had lacked earlier.

'I am an old man in a hurry,' he said. 'You know my age? I am over seventy. What storms haven't I braved, what worlds haven't I faced? The year you were born, I was eating stray dogs to keep alive during the Long March. At a time when

276

most men can look forward to an honourable autumn twilight, I was twice disgraced, twice thrown down and almost killed. I returned to a position of responsibility to find our country backward in all fields, our scientists hopelessly isolated and out of date, our people cretinised by slogans, unable to reason rationally. What are we now that we need to preserve at all costs? Sometimes, I say to myself: nuclear war would be an acceptable way out. It would at least transform the survivors. Look at what it did to the Japanese!

'That is why, old man in a hurry that I am, I would accept any sacrifice, any postponement of my plans, to prevent us from becoming a helpless giant again, rich in nothing but people. I will of course not be around to see what will become of us eventually. Who knows, except your God, what kind of system we ourselves will have in twenty years' time?'

The Vice-Chairman was about to say something more, and decided against it. He smiled, for the first time. It was a smile of ineffable, radiant sweetness, and Forgeot was conscious for the first time of his charm, as potent a weapon as his courage and inner strength.

'We entertain so many delusions about each other,' the Vice-Chairman finally said. 'If only I could be certain that the rest of the world would not sit back and enjoy the spectacle of the two major Communist powers at each other's throats. When I say Communist, I do so only to simplify. Everyone knows the Soviets are no more Communists than I' – he paused for the right analogy – 'am six feet tall.'

'There is another worrying matter,' he said. 'The games you yourself have been playing with us.' Forgeot looked hurt. 'Yes, you. Games in Paris, when you suddenly disappeared. Games in Hong Kong, when you played tricks on us. You took in poor Feng, who thought he could trust you. I circled his name recently for promotion. I will have to recall him. Only a war can save him now.'

He stood up. 'I want the proof,' he said, 'and I want it soon.' And Forgeot, realising the interview was over, strode to a table, took a piece of paper and wrote something down. 'Mr Vice-Chairman,' he said, 'all you have to do is to get someone in Paris to call this number, issue a tourist visa to the person named by the caller, and allow me to meet the plane here.'

They had prepared a room for him in the Ministry. It was a gilded prison, and reminded Forgeot of his days as duty officer in his own Interior Ministry, confined for twenty-four hours every month to an ornate apartment on the top floor, with white-jacketed servants bringing him over-elaborate meals. Except that at the Ministry he could invite guests, whereas here he couldn't leave his room.

Two days later, he was taken to the airport, and watched passengers disembark from the Air France Boeing 747. He recognised none of them, but a middle-aged French lady, his Tranh contact without a doubt, picked him out, and delightedly waved. 'What an unexpected holiday,' she said. Mr Tranh had insisted on flying her first class. 'Such an extravagance. But what fun. I'll be here for a week. I've always wanted to see the Ming Tombs, and the Great Wall. By the way, he asked me to give you this.'

Now they were back in the Vice-Chairman's office. The white-haired man was present, and the interpreter too. This time his services would undoubtedly be required. From the activity outside the Vice-Chairman's office, Forgeot got the impression that another meeting had been called, and that it would begin as soon as his own briefing had ended.

As the tape-recorder was switched on, Forgeot recalled the evening in the small, chic, Mafia-owned Georgetown restaurant. He could almost smell the simmering clams and the olive oil. Above the restaurant hubbub, the tape began with their own informal conversation, restaurant small-talk a discussion of the merits of spaghetti alle vongole at this particular time of year. Then the voice. 'I've known Jean here ever since he was a kid. He's the one Frenchman I can trust.' Forgeot remembered how apprehensive he had been that Jute might notice something while they were both in the car, might actually frisk him. But he hadn't. He trusted me all right, Forgeot thought. He trusted me too much.

And, as the tape continued, the interpreter began his simultaneous translation, English into Chinese. Occasionally, to catch up, or when there was a particularly tricky sentence to translate, he switched the machine off and

278

wound it back to listen to again. They played the entire tape several times, so that the clink of cutlery, the sound of wine being poured and the waiters' loud routine were repeated again and again. They even picked up the sound of the lady cashier saying 'arrivederci, buona sera' to the departing American priests. One day, Forgeot thought, I must go back to that restaurant and tell the lady that Vice-Chairman Ling listened to her in his office in Peking, and as a result decided not to go to war.

Forgeot heard himself saying: 'Whoever goes to Washington might like to take the tape with him. The CIA will gladly identify the voices. The waiters are probably the same. It's a family-owned restaurant.' Maybe the white-haired man would go. He might also confer with the National Reconnaissance Office people, verifying their records day by day, month by month during that period, comparing them with what they already had. The Vice-Chairman might want to go himself. That part of his trip would not be on any agenda.

The Vice-Chairman said nothing, and Forgeot knew he was already preparing himself for his next meeting. He is going to tell them, Forgeot thought, and he may want me on hand to answer some additional questions. He will keep me out of the picture if he can. This time he was taken to a small windowless room, and more tea was brought.

As he expected, the Vice-Chairman summoned him again several hours later. It was now past midnight, but he seemed in no way exhausted. He was in jovial mood. Tapping his burly little frame, he said: 'I am hungry. Are you hungry too? Let us eat.' A plain screen was whisked away, revealing a small round table set for two places. A succession of Szechuanese dishes, each hotter than the last, was brought.

Now was the time for Forgeot to name his price, having played almost all his cards. He did not do so immediately. The Vice-Chairman had a good appetite, and Forgeot decided to let the man eat first. Raising his glass of mao tai, he silently gestured to Forgeot to do the same.

'To peace?' Forgeot asked. 'No,' the Vice-Chairman said. 'That would not be a good toast, since war is inevitable in the long run.'

279

'Then to war as late as possible,' Forgeot said, and they both drank.

A few minutes later, the Vice-Chairman said: 'What is it you really want out of all this? Promotion? A small footnote in history?' and Forgeot took the plunge, and said: 'A girl.'

The Vice-Chairman looked first puzzled, then dismayed, then annoyed, and Forgeot knew what was passing through his mind. He thought Forgeot had made a joke in poor taste, and requested the services of a woman. The late President Soekarno had done just that, on a visit to Peking, and the Vice-Chairman had had to deal with him at the time. So Forgeot added quickly: 'I don't mean any girl. I mean one particular person. Her name would probably not mean anything to you. She defected, back in 1974, but only for a very short space of time. My Government handed her back. I pledged myself to secure her release.' He heard himself adding, lamely: 'She means a great deal to me.'

Where the British splutter, the Americans bray and the Germans roar, the Chinese laugh. It's a reflex action, signifying not mirth but angry embarrassment. The Vice-Chairman revealed the extent of his shocked surprise. He let out a wild, high-pitched guffaw.

'You did *what*?' he said shrilly. 'You mean to say that all this was over a girl?' His one good eye peered at Forgeot balefully now, and he swallowed some mao tai, without proposing a toast this time. 'You're not serious.' Then he caught sight of the expression on Forgeot's face, and realised he was. In a more calm tone of voice, he said: 'Tell me about it. Tell me everything this time.'

Forgeot found it surprisingly easy to talk to this fiery, gnome-like, wise old man. He began, not with his first encounter with May, but well before that. He told of his childhood, his father's role in the French Resistance, and how his spell in jail after the war had broken his heart and shortened his life.

He described his role in the Indochina war, the undercover activities as well as the straight-forward soldiering he had done, culminating with his drop over Dien Bien Phu. He told of his early civilian years after captivity, his enrolment in the Ecole Nationale d'Administration where he had been something of an anomaly – and a celebrity – because of his

280

Dien Bien Phu past, and his studies at the School of Oriental Languages, more hobby than work. He told of his decision to become the first ENA graduate to enter the SDECE, and of de Gaulle moving him to his counter-espionage post.

He described at length his past conflicts with his own hierarchical superiors, and his growing resentment at their own lack of moral courage. He explained how, in countless cases involving the exposure of Algerian, Cuban, Czech or Soviet networks, his own political masters had deliberately decided not to prosecute in order to avoid any hint of tension or scandal, to avoid 'rocking the boat'. He added that, in some cases, some proven French traitors and informers for foreign networks had been allowed to resign, and live out the rest of their lives, some of them, in honourable retirement, because cover-ups had been regarded as politically more acceptable alternatives to the scandal which might have ensued – and adversely affected the reputation of certain politicians in office. Forgeot contrasted this leniency with the harshness of the measures taken against some of those who had challenged French official policies in other fields, and how he himself had had to manipulate his own secret funds to pay meagre gratuities to loyal Algerians, Moroccans and Vietnamese who had been abandoned to their fate after their usefulness had ended.

He explained how May had crystallised all these tensions and resentments. 'Not only was I attracted to her to the extent that I wanted to share the rest of my life with her,' Forgeot said, 'I saw her as a test case. I said to myself: this time there will be no political considerations to get in the way. I intended to give up my career and start a new life altogether. So that, from the day she was kidnapped, I was not only determined to get her back. I was determined to get even.'

And he told of getting even with Lémeric and with Guillaume, for what they had done. The dishes grew cold as he spoke, but the Vice-Chairman had stopped eating some while back.

'Mr Vice-Chairman,' said Forgeot, 'you said earlier that you had braved all storms, faced all worlds. You were referring not only to your campaigns, but also to what happened later. You were a hero of the Long March, an

281

army commander, the architect of change and victory. Suddenly, you became a non-person. You were made to wear a dunce's cap, paraded in front of jeering young people, made to wait on them in a community dining-hall, and to spread their nightsoil on the cabbage allotments you tended by day. Your brother committed suicide, partly because he could not bear what they were doing to you during the Cultural Revolution. Your daughter was beaten up by a mob inside the campus of a university and is a cripple to this day.

'Let me ask you a question: were you not filled, at the time, with a comparable sense of outrage? Didn't you swear that one day you would pay off old scores, and haven't you kept this promise? Wasn't the determination to get even the only thing that kept you going?'

The Vice-Chairman did not answer directly. 'I never allowed my own private feelings to come into play,' he said. 'What I did was not out of revenge, but to put the motherland back on a straight course. But then,' he added with a slight smile, 'I am of a different generation.' Ever a practical man, he added: 'What makes you think she's still alive?'

Forgeot said she had been a healthy young woman, and there was no reason to believe her dead.

'And you expect us to find her, and return her? What if we fail to locate her?'

'Mr Vice-Chairman,' said Forgeot, 'may I be allowed to tell you a story, something a colleague, a French diplomat, once told me? Once upon a time, not all that long ago, when our Embassy opened in Peking in 1964, one of our staff applied for the services of a butler-cook. As you know, all Chinese employees of foreign embassies there are recruited through a special Bureau under the control of the Foreign Ministry and the Ministry of Public Security. It so happens that this particular diplomat had been born in Shanghai, where his father, in turn, had been French Consul-General. The only applicant was an elderly man, who said to my diplomat friend: "You don't remember me, do you?" "No," said the French diplomat, "I've never seen you before." "Oh yes, you have," the elderly man replied, "when you were a baby in Shanghai, I dandled you on my knee, and took you for walks. I was your father's houseboy." So you

282

see, Mr Vice-Chairman, if your people can go all that way back into the past and retrieve such a man, for a particular purpose, some forty years later, surely they can find a young woman who has been in jail or in a labour camp for the last five years.'

'And what happens,' the Vice-Chairman asked, 'if we decide not to return her? You must be aware of the enormity of her crime, in our eyes, regardless of the prevailing circumstances?'

'With stakes so high,' said Forgeot, 'what does a single individual matter to you?'

'You are wrong,' the Vice-Chairman said, 'every individual matters. That she should recognise her crimes is of the utmost importance. Five years is a very short time. Besides,' he added, 'you have conceded your advantages already. There is nothing now to compel her return except our own goodwill – which might not be forthcoming.'

'That is not entirely true,' Forgeot said. 'I have given you the fullest possible account of what has happened. I have omitted only a few odds and ends. One is that I am a hunted, desperate man. The other is that I have told my story to others. In Hong Kong, before I was taken by junk to China, I had time to write everything down. I sent it all to a Swiss lawyer in Geneva. I have used him before, in other circumstances. He is discreet and reliable, and also extremely independent-minded, and responsive to his clients' wishes.

'He has instructions, by a certain date, if he has heard nothing further from me, to release this full account of mine to a number of leading newspapers in Washington, New York, London, Paris and Frankfurt. He also has copies of the tape you have heard, which will also be released. It will be a nine days' wonder, of course: almost everything is, these days. But it would be highly embarrassing to a number of people, and lead to enquiries I am sure you would prefer to avoid. The Governments affected by such a release will be embarrassed because of their different roles, but they will also blame you for not releasing the girl, which would have enabled the matter to remain hushed up. It will cause editorialists all over the Western world to wonder whether the liberalisation of China is not, after all, a myth. It will lead to awkward questions in France, and in leading American political circles, which might affect your foreign relations adversely. In a word, it will cause China to lose face.'

The Vice-Chairman was expressionless. Forgeot smiled. 'There are few people in the world I hold in higher esteem than Vice-Chairman Ling,' he said, 'but from now on we are hostages, she, you and I. Were anything to happen to her, or to me, there is no way the lawyer can be stopped.'

'Five years is a short time to repent, but it can also be a long time in other ways,' the Vice-Chairman said quietly. 'You are familiar with the very thorough rehabilitation programme she has been submitted to since she returned? You would call it brainwashing. We call it the cleansing of the mind. Are you sure you want her back?'

'That,' said Forgeot, 'is the question I was hoping you would ask me. The answer is that I have thought of little else for the last five years. Yes, it is a risk I am prepared to take.'

'And if she happens to be dead?'

'Then my instructions to the lawyer would stand,' Forgeot said. 'It would be inadequate revenge, but it would be telling enough.' The Vice-Chairman's expression hadn't changed, but Forgeot could see that he wanted to convey an agreement obliquely, without appearing to strike a formal bargain.

'And what,' said Ling, 'if I had decided after all to have you eliminated in Hong Kong? Or ignored your warnings, and failed to act on them?'

'As long as I remained alive,' said Forgeot, 'I was determined to try and reach you. I gambled on your need to know, your life-long curiosity. And if I had died, a nuclear war with the Soviet Union would have been the ultimate way of getting even.'

They returned his passport in the name of O'Malley, his watch and his money. They escorted him to the airport once more, and he boarded a plane for Geneva. There, he knew, he would be as safe as anywhere, as long as he kept a low profile, and a look-out for Guillaume's successors. He hoped that, eventually, his real role would be understood by his own masters. But he could hardly be taken back into the fold for putting a stop to a crisis he had himself created.

Daily, he called a certain number in Berne. Not long after his arrival he was given a date, a flight number, and an arrival time. He expressed some surprise. 'You don't suppose,' the voice at the other end said, 'we will pay more than we have to? This is the first stop out of China.' And Forgeot left the callbox, and made arrangements, once more, to fly half-way round the world.

The air had that indefinable smell of swamp and vestigial marshlands, of rotting fish and spices. In the hotel lobby, he could have been anywhere East of Suez. There were local businessmen in dark suits and shiny white ties, enormous jewelled cufflinks flashing from their wrists as they gestured with their plump hands. There were fancy-dress sheikhs from across the Gulf in Hollywood Arab garb, and beaky society ladies, their nails lacquered black, in demure yet suggestive national dress: tight jodhpur trousers, form-hugging tunics and transparent muslin scarves trailing the ground. They chattered like parakeets.

Aircrews came and went, swaggering in anticipation of a flight, or exhausted from the boredom of long hours cooped up in small, smelly cockpits. A plump French blonde, in the uniform of a little-known Middle Eastern airline, said to her companion: 'No! I won't. Not tonight. I don't give a damn about their fucking money any more.'

The bar was dry, offering only lemon juice and sticky fizzes. Forgeot fled to the rooftop dining-room, unable to read or sleep. Here a band played the tunes of the past: 'I could have danced all night' and a medley of Beatles tunes to a Pakistani lilt. A male crooner came on and whispered hoarsely: 'I got so much saddis-fackshunn outa you.' He held his microphone close to his face, lovingly, like an electric razor.

Forgeot ate to anaesthetise himself. Later he slept briefly, fitfully, waking from a nightmare too elusive to recall. He dressed in the middle of the night, shaking with fever, his stomach fluttering – a nervous child embarking on its first day at school. Outside was a dull yellow neon-lit smog.

Downstairs a line of guests was checking out, and the black-coated hotel managers, their collars so immaculately starched that they glowed, endlessly punched old-fashioned calculating machines. Karachi is a place where all travellers arrive and depart at dawn.

In a taxi, along the main airport road, the suburbs flashed by, the houses a garish succession of styles, getting seedier as the city receded. The driver attempted conversation, was rebuffed and lapsed into sullen silence until the airport loomed.

'Wait here,' Forgeot said.

Turbaned porters, exhibiting brass insignia with engraved numbers, crowded round him briefly, jostling each other and losing interest when they saw he had no luggage. A chattering crowd waited patiently outside the passenger exit in the hot, humid night. Armed guards were on duty. Forgeot caught the eye of an airline employee, and alone was allowed inside the building, masquerading as a privileged French official for the last time.

The dimly-lit customs arrivals area was a microcosm of minor Third World dramas and injustices. One section was littered with lost luggage from innumerable earlier flights, shapeless bundles, battered tin trunks, an occasional brand-new suitcase. The names on the labels were Pakistani, the addresses from all over the Gulf.

A planeload from Bahrain was slowly edging its way towards the Customs officials: Pakistani labourers returning home, bearing the unmistakable signs of their newly-acquired wealth. They were bowed under the weight of their new electric fans, blenders, mixers, air conditioners and TV sets. The Pakistani customs officials had the blasé air of inquisitors who know the questions are rigged. Their behaviour was arbitrarily, frivolously partial, probably the consequence of bribes already disbursed or to come. A tall man with several crates of electric goods swept past them unchecked, but a veiled woman with several small children was made to unwrap and expose every bundle.

Most of the returning travellers were Pathans, and they eyed the customs officials with fierce, mute hatred. Forgeot would for ever remember this wait, their faces and cries, the humid night, the labels on the lost luggage in the dark, doomsday transit hall.

The PIA plane from Shanghai was announced. It took a long time for its passengers to appear. They were a mixed

286

bag: European businessmen in transit with bulging briefcases, a group of elderly Scandinavian tourists, sussurating with shock at their sudden proximity to Third World poverty. At another airport, in another world, he had watched her arrive once.

He saw her first in profile, without recognising her: a shuffling little Japanese lady in black, he thought at first, travelling alone. He did a double take. She was smaller than he remembered, shrunken, ageless. Her gait was no longer jaunty. Bastards, he thought, and looked some more, his heart leaping, before she was able to see him, and hoping it was not she.

But it was. Holding a white travel document, she spent minutes being questioned by a police official before the paper was stamped and folded. She looked up and saw him. As she came closer, he saw that her face was drawn, her skin coarsened, and that one of her teeth was missing. Only her eyes were exactly as he remembered them.

They did not touch at first. Too late he twisted his features into a sickeningly reassuring mask. He saw her tears, too, then the rictus of a smile. Suddenly, shyly, she reached up, touching the back of his neck, covering her mouth with one hand, saying something he couldn't grasp. He put his arms around her, and held skin and bone. There was a small scar on the side of her head, the remains of an angry boil on her wrist.

'Are you sure you wanted this?' she said. 'I very nearly said no, but they insisted. I am not the same. They have changed me. They have turned me inside out.'

Protectively, he hugged her, saying 'there, there', oblivious of the grinning Pathans elbowing each other, mouthing coarse jokes and leering at the unusual spectacle of a tall white man in a white suit with tears running down his face, clasping a small sobbing Chinese woman.

Her body was shaking, and, looking straight ahead, beyond her, he thought: this is the moment I have been waiting for, scheming for all these years. For this stranger I gambled my life away. He desperately wanted to be somewhere else, alone, uninvolved, whole. You got what you wanted when you no longer desired it. He had plotted, bluffed, play-acted, used up his nine lives and had people killed, and all the while, he had preserved, in his mind's eye, an image of someone who no longer existed, and perhaps never had, except in his imagination.

May was saying, over and over again, in Chinese: please help me, you've got to help me now, I can't go back any more, you should never have tried to find me, and, somehow, he found trite, reassuring, lying words of love, hope, consolation and even laughter, trying to get her to see the absurdity of it all, wondering as he spoke how long the numbness would endure and whether he and this stranger would ever salvage what remained of their shattered lives.

'I'm an outcast too,' he whispered, 'we're in the same boat, you and I,' with a sudden vision of the timeless void ahead, the almost unbearable intimacy in store for them from now on.

Gently, he led her to the waiting car.